ALINA MARTYN

Secretly Born

First edition

This book was professionally typeset on Reedsy.
Find out more at reedsy.com

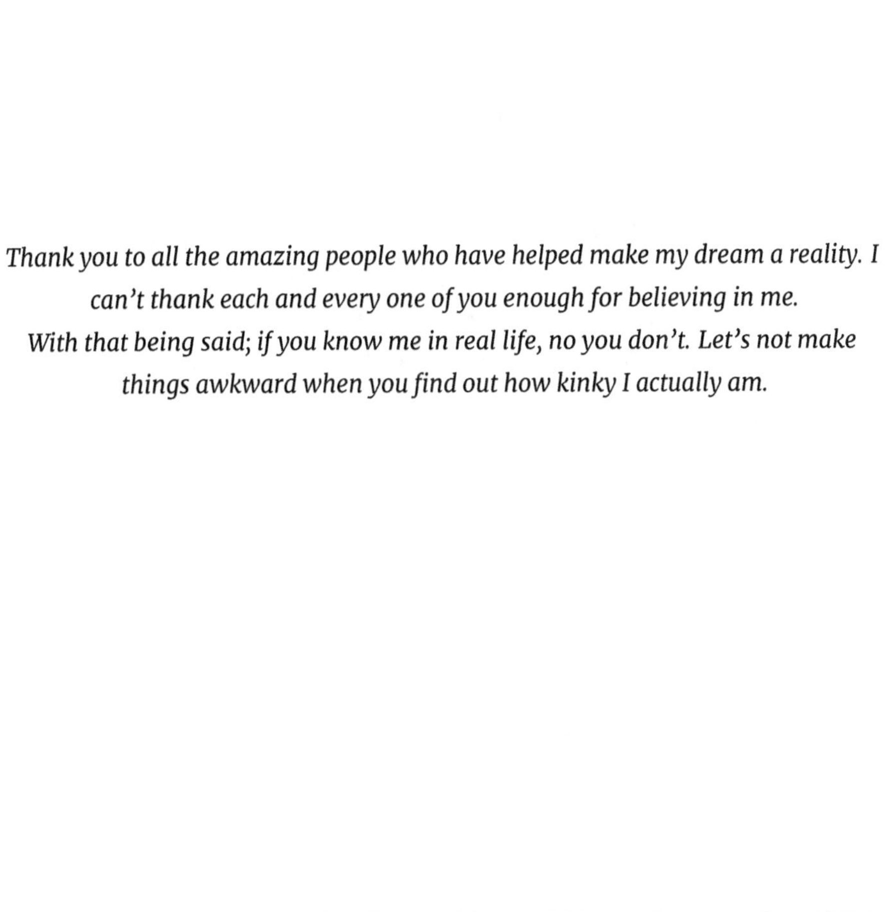

Thank you to all the amazing people who have helped make my dream a reality. I can't thank each and every one of you enough for believing in me.
With that being said; if you know me in real life, no you don't. Let's not make things awkward when you find out how kinky I actually am.

Contents

Before

"Audrena, you don't have to do this." A man said in a hushed tone. He had light brown hair, speckled with grey and a beard to match, covered in a tattered, matted blue cloak and had his arm wrapped about her shoulders as they stayed hidden in the dark alleyway, trying to shield the bundle in their arms from the rain pouring down on them.

"Anders, you know we have to." She said, her green eyes lined with silver, with tears refusing to fall. Her red hair was curling with the rain, her own tan, dirty cloak turning darker with each passing moment.

The couple huddled close, staring at the entrance of the church that their personal advisor and well-known warrior, Tomais had properly vetted. He had traveled to the Terraus realm and returned with promising information about where to leave a newborn, where they would get immediate care and be cared for. From where they stood, hidden in the alley, they could see the front of the Navitus Church of the Brave; strong, Gothic, and dark. The sole pointed arch rose high above, topped with a haunting and hollow cross.

There was not a speck of light coming from any of the windows, but there was one lone lantern that buzzed with its old bulb that hung right over the entrance. Two large, ornate wooden doors with brass knockers in the middle of each door greeted the couple.

With great reluctance, Audrena walked up the worn stone steps, leaving the safety of the arms of her love. Tomais said, had *promised*, that the humans within this building would care for their baby, would make sure that she grew up in a family, a *non-magical* family, until her time to come home finally came.

They had to keep her safe, even at their own expense.

"Audrena, I...We..." Anders grabbed around her bicep, pulling her back to him harshly.

"Anders, we've been over this. This is her best chance to make it to adulthood."

"I don't think you've thought this through! We can't come back to Terraus again. We are taking a great risk by coming here this time. We won't be able to come back here now, no matter how much we want to." He raked his fingers through his hair, his waves curling even more and darkening with the rain. Audrena stared into his eyes, taking in the clench of his jaw.

"I don't want to lose her. She's our daughter." He said, his deep voice breaking with emotion.

Audrena softened. This was tearing her up inside to have to do this. This little, soft, sweet baby that laid snug in her arms, clutching her rough, peasant dress she wore under her cloak. They had wrapped her, their Audra, in a soft pink blanket and written her name on the inside. So no matter where, no matter what, her name would be Audra.

Audrena couldn't stop the tear that ran down her cheek at the thought of letting this precious child out of her arms, out of their lives, until she could find them again.

"We have to. It's her best chance at life, Anders. You know this. If she stays with us..."

"I know." He cringed, screwing his eyes shut at the imagined horror that would become a reality if the little girl stayed with them in their realm. Oh, how they would hunt her. At least here, she could be anonymous, practically invisible until she had to go through the change.

"Then this is what we have to do. Not for us, for her. For her." Audrena said with a passion, her fire burning brightly in her eyes.

"What if she doesn't come back? What if–"

"It's called hope, my love. Hope that she will come back to us. Hope that she will make it to her 20th birthday. Hope that the change doesn't harm her or bring unwanted terrors. This is the best thing for all of us, for Vesperitus, but for her especially."

Audrena pulled her darling daughter up to her face and took a moment to memorize each of her soft features, how she twitched and moved in her arms, how she smelled. It took all of Audrena's strength to give her one last kiss on her small forehead and handed her off to her father.

Anders took hold of his newborn daughter, and mumbled softly, small promises and words of love. He had tears flowing down his cheeks, in sheer agony at what they had to do.

"Goodbye, my sweet girl. May this life be good to you." He whispered to her. It broke his heart that she wouldn't know how loved she was. How she would grow up not knowing who her true parents were, her legacy.

Audrena sobbed heavily, the despair of what was about to happen threatening to overtake her. They needed to do this and leave as soon as possible. The longer they stayed in Terraus, the more attention they would attract. The goblins would sniff them out and try to destroy them, lamias would come to drink their blood, Wincts would stop at nothing to get their blood and bones to try to replicate their powers.

Anders handed the baby bundle to Audrena one last time and knocked on the door.

"No going back now, darling."

She nodded at his words and kissed her daughter one last time.

"Hello, can I help you?" A kind looking older woman said through the opened crack of the heavy wooden door. It was open enough that Audrena and Anders could feel the warmth radiating from inside and her face, but not much else. The lone lamp overhead illuminated the nun's face, emphasized by her covering. They saw just how honest and open her eyes were. The different shades of brown swirling through. She could be no older than 60-years-old, and her tone of voice, soft and light, made Audrena more comfortable.

"Hello, we have come to ask you to care for our daughter." Anders said with care and sorrow. "We cannot and she deserves so much more than we can give her right now. Please."

"Please." Audrena whispered, never tearing her eyes away from Audra.

"Of course, my dears. Does she have a name?" The kind nun asked as she opened the door more to be able to step out and take the child.

"Audra. Her name is Audra." Audrena said, softly. "Please, please make sure she is cared for."

The nun looked at the couple, able to see their heartbreak at having to do this, having to abandon their child. But she could also see the love and devotion they had for the small babe in their arms.

"I will. She is one of God's children. I will watch over her as best I can." The nun kindly reached out to hold the baby and Audrena froze.

She shut her eyes and the nun lifted her darling daughter out of her arms, tears and sobs breaking through.

"Come, darling. She's safe now." Anders said, wrapping his arm around Audrenas shoulders, pushing a lock of dark red hair behind her ear.

Together, the couple hunched together, leaning on each other for support and strength as they started walking down the stone steps back out into the rain.

"Wait!" Audrena called out, turning quickly back to the woman who held her daughter. The two figures, the nun and the baby, illuminated dimly under the lone lantern. "Keep her safe. She is...so important."

The nun smiled softly at Audrena, standing at the bottom of the church steps, soaking wet with rain and tears, and called out, "I will."

Chapter One

Audra Jackson stood at the hostess stand waving off the last family as they walked out of the small, hole-in-the-wall diner with their toddler daughter wobbling on her chubby little legs. The father had opened the door, causing the bell overhead to chime, as the mother grabbed the toddler's hand to steer her towards the exit.

"God, that baby was cute." Audra heard from behind her. Her co-worker, Kalia, came up to stand next to her with a knowing smirk on her face. Kalia ran a hand over her teal mermaid-length braids that complemented her brown skin so nicely. Audra often found herself envious of her friend's complexion and glow. Kalia's skin was always dewy and fresh, adorned with makeup that, no matter how brightly colored her outfit was, always matched her clothes. Today her eyelids were a bright metallic gold, her eyes lined thickly with a charcoal black line. The makeup caused the browns in her eyes to shine like sunlight.

"Right? She was *so* cute. Just babbling up a storm the whole time they were eating." Audra said with a smile. She rubbed her eyes, trying to clear out the dotting in her vision. Her head was starting to ache, and the ache must have been starting to bother her eyes.

Kalia laughed and walked away with a flick of her braids over her shoulder.

Audra rubbed her temples, hoping that a migraine would not start forming.

But Audra loved kids, always had. She liked being the one that they felt that they could look up to, the one that they could lean on, rely on.

She had grown up in an orphanage in the heart of New York City after being left at the Navitus Church almost 20 years ago. After they moved her to the orphanage when she was a few months old, she waited. Waited and waited to be adopted, and cared for by people that wanted her. But while she waited, she cared for those younger than her. She would do her best to attend to their needs, keep them safe, and provide some kind of sisterly love. Even if it was for a little while until her foster parents had her moved. Again.

As she ran a hand through her mid-length chestnut brown hair, she let her natural waves fall back into place and detangled the curls wrapped in her large golden hoop earrings.

"Only a few more months and I can actually be a teacher and be done with these long shifts." Audra said, seeing a couple walk in the door, picked up two menus and folded silverware from within the stand and put on a blinding smile.

"Welcome to Moe's, two of you today?"

* * *

"That dinner rush was something else." Kalia said as she stood up from wiping down her last booth.

They were two of three waitresses working today, and Georgina had left halfway through her shift because she wasn't feeling well. Even though Audra was also feeling under the weather, she was all for it. More tables meant more tips. It also meant more people complaining, more running to and from, and more of a headache by the end of the night.

"Made bank though, didn't we?" Audra said as she walked over to one of her tables, started stacking all the trash and things left together and quickly pocketed the few dollars left for her.

"Yes, thank god." Kalia said with a sigh.

Both girls were struggling to save and pay their way through life in New York City. Kalia was trying to work overtime in order to afford rent on the newer, more expensive apartment she moved into and Audra was just trying to make it through the day. Any money she made went right back into her education, into her dream of having a stable, consistent income doing something she loved, rather than scraping by.

"What are you going to do with your two days off?" Kalia called out from across the room. They were the only two left in the front; the cooks cleaning the kitchen, they both were told to clean up the front.

"Sleep for as long as I can. Between school, the diner, and the library, I haven't had a day off in the last two weeks."

"You work way too hard." Kalia muttered as she threw the dishes that she had gathered into the tub full of dishes that they needed to take back to the dishwasher.

"I work so that I can afford my rent, tuition and still eat." Audra said, her tone mocking but with a twinge of truth. She knew she just had to keep her head down, stick to her grind, and one day it would all be worth it; the long hours, the lack of a social life, the rare moment to breathe.

Kalia smirked and stepped back behind the diner bar to wipe down the faded cream linoleum top. Audra loved working at the diner. It was a throwback to the 80s, silver chrome, bright plastic booth and barstool cushions and a jukebox in the corner. Moe's was a rare spot within the hustle and bustle of New York City. It refused to change. It stayed true to what worked, and the food was good enough that people talked.

"Okay, ladies." Their shift manager called out as he stepped to the front room from being back in his office for most of the shift. "Time to tab out and lock up."

Both Kalia and Audra walked over to the register, pulling their receipts and tips from their black apron pockets. Their shift manager, Freddie, was a scrawny, middle-aged man who definitely felt drunk on power every time he worked with them. He always seemed to order them about, never accepted their side of the story and sided with the customers who tried to feel them up or act incredibly rude. Kalia rolled her eyes and stepped up to the register, putting in all her tips, all her receipts and waiting for Freddie to pay her the credit card tips he owed her.

"Must have been a good night, Kal." He said with a smirk, his too-long mustache hanging weirdly over his top lip. "Here you go, $85.94." He took money from the register and counted it out in her hand. "But don't forget you owe $25 even for your meal and tip to the cook."

"Wait, what?" Audra stepped up. "Our meals were comped today. We both worked over 5 hours. And we don't split tips. Never have."

"You do today." Freddie's smirk dropped, his eyes pointed to her with a hard gaze.

"Freddie, that is not fair." Kalia cut in.

"If you want the rest of your tips, you'll give me the $25. Both of you."

"That's not how this works. We've never split tips. Did Maureen approve this?" Audra demanded. Something felt off to her. Freddie wasn't always truthful.

"Of course, she did. Now, are you going to give me the cut or are you going to not get any of your card tips?"

"That's bullshit and you know it. That money is ours. You can't withhold it."

Freddie leaned in close to Audra, close enough to make her feel uncomfortable and so she could smell the dollar store aftershave he doused himself with.

"Try me." He muttered.

Audra stood there, staring at him with fire in her eyes. Most of their tips were from card receipts, and if he didn't sign off on them, they couldn't get their cut. But she wasn't going to let him walk over the two of them simply because he felt like it.

"Fine, take it. But you can be damned sure that I am calling Maureen about this later. It is her restaurant after all." Audra poked his chest. She knew Maureen, or to those she liked, Moe, always had her employee's best interests at heart. For the past three years that Audra had worked for her, Moe was always trying to maximize the amount of money that Audra left with. This cut didn't make sense.

Freddie's eyes briefly flashed with pure panic, and then he slid back into his dismissive, arrogant norm.

"Audra, you made $98.75. But your tip out and meal is $45. So here you go." He said with an evil smirk. They both knew that he increased her amount because she had challenged him.

"Now, come on Freddie..." Kalia said, trying to step up and help her.

"Want to make it $55?"

Audra clenched her teeth and put her hand out, "Fine, give me the $54 so I can get the fuck out of here."

Freddie smiled in victory as he handed over the money and shut the register drawer.

"I'm leaving." Audra folded the bills over her thumb and shoved the cash into her back pocket of her jeans. She untied the black apron and roughly pushed it into the bottom drawer of the hostess stand. Pulling out her wallet and phone from the drawer, she walked towards the front door where they kept the coat rack and grabbed her threadbare jacket. Then she walked out the front door without a look back.

Let Freddie deal with the rest of the cleanup. Kalia was done with her side already, so she could walk out whenever she wanted.

Audra took a deep breath of crisp Autumn air and counted backwards from five.

Five...Four...Three...Two...One. Deep breath. In...out...

She took her phone out and powered it on, then turned towards the direction of her apartment and started the journey through the New York night.

Chapter Two

Audra was tired. More than tired. She was exhausted. The walk back to her apartment was dragging on. It seemed like it was a never-ending trip.

After back-to-back evening shifts at the diner, a morning shift at the library on campus, night classes at the local college. She had not had a day off from work or school in the last two weeks. All she wanted was to crash on her bed and sleep for as long as possible.

Eric, Luc; her two neighbors who had become her best friends in the three years they had lived next to each other, and even Kalia was always very vocal about how much they worried Audra was running herself into the ground, but what exactly could she do? She had to make rent somehow. She refused to drop her course load, wanting to graduate on time and finally get into the workforce. Audra was sick of working part-time jobs, barely making ends meet. She wanted a career. A steady job, a steady paycheck.

As she walked through the streets of Manhattan, she clutched her phone and wallet tighter to her person, shrinking into her oversized coat as much as possible. She had her keys stuck between her knuckles in the off chance someone tried to mug her, just in case. It wasn't necessarily late at night, but Audra had seen too much bad shit to not be cautious.

The crowds had died down, the after-work rush was gone. There were teens walking in clusters, sharing sugary drinks and cigarettes they'd stolen from their parents. The odd messenger, running to his next delivery destination, trying to make it before his deadline. Groupings of people, tough on their luck, huddled together for warmth. New York was cold in the fall, even worse in the winter. Snow was falling in clumps, not sticking before it melted onto the surface.

Audra flipped the collar of her worn, large pea coat up, trying to keep as much warmth in as possible. Her next paycheck had to go to a new coat. She had fixed the holes in this one too many times for it to truly retain any warmth anymore.

She put her head down and continued her long, slow, cold journey to her apartment, a matchbox sized studio with just enough room for her twin bed on the floor and a small kitchenette. The building itself wasn't great, always dirty, and dark, but it was home. She could afford it, and she was relatively safe.

Audra took great pride in being independent. She took care of herself when no one else would. It didn't matter that she would only be turning 20 years old tomorrow; she was old enough to never have to go into another foster house again and that was all she cared about. The climb up the steps to her apartment felt like she was climbing Everest. She was so worn out that she had to stop every five or six stairs to catch her breath and gather the courage to start again.

But she made it. She saw her battered, chipped door and pulled her keys out.

Her little room was overflowing with trinkets, odds and ends that she had collected over the years. Things that had been gifted to her or things she had forged for. A small bouquet of wildflowers rested on the one ledge by the window that she found outside the library that she had worked at for one day. They had long since wilted and died, but she had dried them to remember to see the beauty even in the hard times. A few different pictures were hung up that one of the little girls from her foster home given her, with scotch tape. A string of lights she had found in the dumpster and was able to fix up like new.

Audra took off her black boots and set them next to the door as soon as she entered her home, not wanting to track dirt through. She had barely taken off her coat and shut the door when she heard a fist knocking loudly on her door.

"Audra, you home?" Came muffled through the wooden door.

"Just a second Eric, I just got home." She called back. Eric Taylor, her neighbor from across the hall who lived with a friend of his named Luc. The boys had been supportive and her very good friends since she moved in, always offering to help with anything and bringing her food whenever one of them cooked too much, which was pretty frequently.

"Hurry up, it's cold out here." He said sharply and she couldn't help but roll her eyes that the big burly man was upset because he was cold. Eric was at least 6'3" on a bad day and looked like a Greek God. He had blonde curly hair that framed his face like a halo and his smile...his smile was like the sun. So bright and full of life. His golden-brown eyes and naturally tanned skin completed his God-like look.

Girls couldn't help but notice and he was pretty good with the ladies if the revolving door to their apartment meant anything.

"What's up, you big baby?" Audra said with a hand on her hip as she opened the door wide to let him in.

"That's not very nice. Especially when I come bearing gifts." He said with a small smile, holding up a big Tupperware container which looked to be full of cookies and a smaller one that more than likely contained a nutritious meal that Luc had obviously prepared for her.

"Cookies and a home cooked meal? Oh my God, you guys are the best." Audra said as she reached out to grab the top container and ripped the lid open.

Eric was always the one to bring her junk. He liked desserts and preferred comfort food to the healthy stuff, unlike Luc. Luc was the one to bring over proper meals, things with actual nutritional value.

"I know it. How was work?" Eric said as he sat with a plop on her bed, his hands going back to prop his upper body up.

"Same old, same old. A dinner rush of people and then the occasional drunk who needed hangover food. Then my asshole of a manager tried to take half my tips. How was your day?" She asked, stuffing a chocolate chip cookie into her mouth, and trying not to be obvious about checking out Eric in his tight fitted maroon tee. How the boy ate what he did and in the insane amounts as he did and still looked so muscular, fit, and delicious was a complete mystery to Audra. And a source of envy.

"The joys of working from home. Luc and I have been on the phone and communicating with clients all day. There was an issue with the latest edition of the game, so we've been hearing about it non-stop." Eric said with a huff as he ran his fingers through his curls. They both worked for a video game development company and freelance designed certain characters, the backgrounds, and other things that Audra, honestly, didn't understand about. They got so interested and heated in discussions about work that Audra couldn't follow when they got into those debates. "Luc went out for a run. I said I would stay here and make sure you got home, okay."

Audra rolled her eyes. After a few months of the three of them hanging out, the boys had gotten very protective over her, and designated her their kid sister, almost.

After a night of heavy drinking, she had opened up and explained her upbringing: the way her parents had given her up close to her birth. She had lived there, in the Navitus Church, with Sister Leah, the one nun that kept in contact with her as she grew, until she was a few weeks old. But the state came for her after she turned two months and then she had to be put in foster care or orphanages. Since the guys learned about her difficult upbringing, they had pretty much stepped up to be her protectors, her confidantes, and self-appointed guardians.

"You guys don't have to watch out for me. I can handle myself." Audra said, her mouth full of chocolate chip goodness. Damn, could that Greek God bake.

"I know you can, but it makes us both feel better." Eric said as he reached up and stretched, lifting his arms over his head, showcasing his toned triceps before laying down on her bed.

"Overgrown oaf." Audra mumbled. She had been on her own for a long time now. She knew how to take care of herself. Her third or fourth foster house was a very hands off, eat or be eaten kind of house. Audra had to learn quickly how to protect what space, toy, or morsel of food was hers before it got stolen from her.

"Anyway...I just wanted to give you those and check in on you before your enviable hibernation." Eric said with a smirk as he stood up. His tall frame caused her to have to look up slightly to meet his eyes, a welcome surprise seeing as Audra is taller than most people.

"Thank you, I'm fine. Just more tired than ever and I'm worried that I'm coming down with something."

Eric whipped his head to face her, a startled, worried look on his face.

"What do you feel like?"

"Oh, it's probably just a cold or some bug from running on empty these past two weeks. I've been so incredibly busy that I don't think I have been sleeping as much as I should or eating enough."

"Audra, what do you feel like?" Eric came next to her and grabbed her upper arms. He had an intensity that she wasn't used to seeing from him. She would be lying if she said that it didn't scare her. His tone was harsh and demanding. It was a way that he never really was with her.

"Relax, big guy. I just feel like I need to sleep, like my bones are empty and I need to lie down. My head is starting to hurt as well, although that could just be my overuse of caffeine these past few days. It was incredibly difficult to get home after work. Like my muscles didn't work." She touched one of his shoulders, squeezing gently to hopefully calm him down a bit.

"Anything else?" Eric stared into her eyes, leaving no room for her to brush off how she was feeling–he would see it, the lie, in her green eyes. His heavy hands never left her arms, keeping her locked into place, barely a foot in front of him.

"My eyes..." Audra said in defeat.

"What about your eyes?"

"They ache." She brought her hand up to rub her eyes. "At work I was seeing double and sometimes my vision would dot. I just think it's due to lack of sleep."

As soon as the words were out of her mouth, Eric nodded and pulled away. She could feel the lack of warmth that always seemed to radiate from Eric.

"I promise, I am fine." She reached up and cupped his chin. A soft, loving smile crossed her face. "You don't need to be so worried."

Audra stared into his eyes. Had his eyes gotten brighter? More golden? No. No, eye color doesn't change like that. She's just overtired, overworked and now her body is demanding rest. She shook her head slightly to try to clear her vision.

"Right, right. You're probably just getting sick. That's going around, you know. The weather is changing and all that." He said, pulling her hands from his face.

No, his eyes were definitely brighter, she thought.

"Have your eyes always been more gold than brown? I could've sworn they were darker." Audra mussed.

Eric immediately dropped her hands as if she burned him, started blinking rapidly and backing up towards the door.

"You know, I think I have something in my eyes. I'm going to head home." He reached his hands out behind him, fumbling for the doorknob while keeping his eyes shut tightly.

"Wait, Eric, let me help you," Audra reached for him but he pushed back further. "If you can't see, let me walk you across the hall. Or I have saline solution here to rinse your eyes."

"No, no, it's fine. I just need to get home. Luc will be home soon. I'll send him over to check on you. Get some sleep."

"Eric," Audra started to argue but was cut off.

"Back off!" Eric snapped as he closed her own door in her face.

That was weird. Very weird. Audra thought as she started stripping out of her work uniform, getting ready for a nice long shower and then to sleep for as long as she could.

Chapter Three

Opening her eyes, she knew she was in a dream. No longer was Audra in her apartment, but an open field filled with vibrant green grass, lined with pine trees and shrubs. She felt safe. She felt at peace. Looking down, she noticed the hands she was controlling were young, very young, childlike. She was playing in the dirt, with a wooden statue of a horse next to her pike of soil. Audra knew she was trying to build a fort, somewhere for her horse to live but the soil kept crumbling.

Feeling frustrated, she huffed, and the child hands lifted two handfuls of dirt in the air, unworried about making her light pink dress dirty. Closing her eyes and forcing her wish into the dirt.

'You will be built.' A childlike voice whispered. When her eyes opened, the soil had transformed into a structure. A small house, complete with an open door and a roof.

Audra felt an immense amount of pride and put her wooden horse into the barn she'd made.

'I wonder what else I can do.' The child's voice rang through her mind as if she had said it.

The hands went out over the loose soil and started to slowly move. The child whom Audra was watching through was focused. She wanted to see the soil move and change.

'Darling girl, what have you gotten into now?' Audra looked through the eyes of the viewer to see a tall, regal woman with fire-red hair dressed in a soft blue silk dress, with red gems covering the trim, walking over to where she stood. She looked like a Princess, a Princess with fire in her eyes.

The woman bent over to pick her up.

'Mama! I'm making the dirt dance! Look!' Came from Audra's mouth unwittingly, and her attention turned to the ground where soil was vibrating, pulsing as if being transmitted through radio waves. Audra could see her hand (or the hand of whomever she was looking through) slowly twist and glide through the air, making the soil change forms, a shooting star, a volcano, a horse running.

Laughter rang out through the space, young and childish, full of joy and mirth.

'Very good, darling! You're learning so well.' The red-haired woman said as she snuggled into the child she held.

'Mama, do yours!'

'Very well, just this once.' The woman smiled and brought her hand up in front of her, palm up.

A small spark began to form in the center of her palm. The spark grew to a flame that shifted and moved into a rose, holding that form for a moment, and blooming into a lily. The flames sparked out like sparklers and Audra couldn't look away.

A child's hand went reaching for it and the woman transferred the fire flower into its hand.

'Mama's magic won't hurt you, but others will. So don't go running off trying to hold the campfire, yes?'

Audra looked into her eyes. She could see the bright gold shimmering through. A light with magic.

'Yes, Mama.' The child responded, and they both watched the lily burn out, the sparks never once getting hot or harming her hand.

'One day, you'll be able to do that. One day you'll be able to do so much more.' The woman whispered into the child's ear.

'I can't wait to be strong like you, Mama!' the child cried and wrapped her arms around her mother's neck.

'My dear, you will be so much stronger.'

The dream, a wish of another life, faded to black. Shadows curling in around the edges like the room was starting to be filled with smoke. The darkness wasn't scary; it comforted her. She felt calmness overload her senses, forcing her to relax.

"It's been a while since we have spoken. I was starting to worry."

"I didn't mean to worry you" Audra replies to the deep, honeyed voice floating through the darkness. In some part of her consciousness, she realized she should be scared, but she wasn't.

"You're going to be great, sweetheart. I can't wait to see you again."

"Me neither. I wish we could be with each other now."

"I know, sweetheart. Soon." The voice promised, and the shadows released her back into the dreamless state.

Audra sat up quickly.

It seemed so real. So visceral. Who was that woman? Could it be her birth mother? Who was the deep voice? What did it mean that he was going to see her soon? What did he mean to see her again? What did the woman mean that she would be able to do so much more?

Leaning over, Audra looked at her phone as the bright light shone in the darkness, causing her to squint to see the time. 4:45 in the morning. The whole world around her seemed to be quiet, having gone to bed hours before. She couldn't even remember falling asleep. Shadows covered her apartment as the filtered light came in from her open windows.

Running her hands through her waves, she could feel the tangles, signaling that she hadn't even brushed her wet hair before she fell.

God, she felt even worse now, even more exhausted than she had gotten a few hours of sleep than before. Her whole body felt like it was breaking apart and trying to restitch itself together. Audra felt the ache set deep in her bones, turning hot and everything felt as if it was catching fire.

It was only getting worse. She tried to shift in her bed, but it felt as if any movement made the fire in her veins worsen. It had started in her chest, and she had taken some antacids, thinking it was just heartburn from all the cookies she devoured earlier, but now...it was like someone had interjected lighter fluid directly into her bloodstream and somewhere a match had been lit. Liquid fire roared through her veins.

What is happening to me?

Audra bit her lip to keep from screaming, but even she could tell that at some point she would have to get help to go to a hospital. But she couldn't move.

Before she could cry out in pain, pounding sounded on her front door. So strong, so violent. The whole door shook.

"Let me in, let me in." The pounding continued. An unknown person was hissing to her through her door.

"Who are you?" She cried out, unable to move from the pain.

"No, no, no, no, who are you?" The voice said, a manic tone bleeding through. "I can smell you, Fae. I need in, I need in!" Its voice was chilling, causing a zing of panic to shoot through her.

Her doorknob was jiggling. The person trying to break in was becoming more desperate. Audra could hear them rambling and clawing at the door. She tried to wiggle her fingers, but the more she moved, the more the fire burned, the more her bones were breaking.

"I'll get you, I will. I'll have the power. I'll have all the power." The voice cried out and Audra started to cry in fear as well as pain.

She pushed through the pain and got her hand free of whatever paralysis it was under. Each movement felt like torture, but she had to get some kind of weapon. She had to get ready to fight. That door and lock weren't high tech. They were barely strong enough for her to feel safe normally, and with how much this psycho was fighting it, he was bound to get in.

Just as she heard the person kick the doorknob, she ripped her arm free, crying out in pain as she freed it from the pain. Moving her arm to an almost painfully awkward angle, she groped around the small, battered table she kept next to her bag for anything that could be used as a weapon; a pen, butter knife, hell, she'd even take one of her textbooks to this guy's head if needed.

Another kick sounded. The wooden door rattled on its hinges.

Her fingers grasped something thin and sturdy, a mechanical pencil. It would have to do. One more hit and the door was gone.

But the kick never came. In fact, what sounded like people fighting was happening. She could see multiple feet through the crack under the door, the hallway light shining brightly.

Grunts and groans, curses and obscene references were thrown around as Audra screamed through the pain of freeing herself from the paralysis torture.

She couldn't quite sit up when she heard no more fighting. Two pairs of feet were back-lit, just ominously, standing in front of her door. She clutched her pencil and gingerly stood on both feet, ready to defend herself.

"Audra?" Luc called softly. Audra felt an astounding amount of relief at seeing him standing there. His tall, broad frame took up most of the doorway.

"Luc? Eric?" She cried out in relief. She moved herself to a sitting position and with a cry she stood up, walking as quickly to the door as she could and threw herself into their arms, the pain bleeding through the adrenaline.

"Who was that?"

"I don't know, just a creature after her. We'll figure it out later. We need to leave. Now." Eric said, passing her to Luc so he could survey the rest of her apartment. "We have to get her out of here. It won't be much longer before others come." He said to Luc.

"What?" Audra said, voice wobbly with tears.

"Go get her a bag packed. I'll grab ours." Eric told Luc, then went back to their apartment.

"Come on." Luc pulled her into his side, wrapping her as tightly as he could, and led her into her apartment. Luc was just as muscular as Eric, but Luc had much broader shoulders and was just barely taller than Eric, which made him seem like a bodybuilder. Luc had more of a swimmer's body, lean but chorded with muscle.

When he turned the lights on, he immediately grabbed her backpack next to the door and shoved in all the things she would need for classes, notebooks, pens, her textbooks. Then he yanked open her tiny closet and pulled out a small duffel bag and started throwing clothes in there. Any and all of them.

Audra just stared as he worked. What was happening?

"Luc, what are you doing?"

"Aud, we have to get you to safety. Anything in particular you want, grab it. We leave as soon as Eric's back." He said, as he opened her plastic, cheap set of drawers and he threw in socks, underwear and a few pj shirts.

"Where are we going? Who was that?"

"A bad person. We need to get you safe first and then I will answer your questions, I promise."

"Luc, what was that thing?" Audra asked, tears still wet on her cheeks.

Luc slowed down for a moment, his shoulders tensed, and then resumed tearing through her home, stuffing things into the duffel bag.

"Luc. What was it?" She asked, more force behind her words.

"Audra, please." He whispered; shoulders so high from being tense she almost felt bad.

"No, tell me now. Who was outside my door? Why did Eric say it was a creature? What did they mean, 'I smelled good' and why am I in so much pain?" Tears threatened to leave her eyes again, but she had to be strong.

Luc took a deep breath, shoving her phone charger and phone into the duffel and zipping it shut. He ran a hand over his dark, trimmed beard and looked at her in the eyes.

"I think it was a Winct. A Winct is a dangerous creature, able to shift their scent and blend in with their surroundings. They believe that if they ingest the blood of a Fae, especially a High Royal, they will absorb their powers. So, they go around, searching for them; magical people who were born with elemental powers." He explained in a rush.

"Let's go, I've got the car's waiting. I did a sweep. We should be okay for the next few minutes. Still, hurry." Eric pushed his head in and disappeared.

"Come on, Aud. I promise I'll keep you safe. We both will." Luc said. He put her duffel bag down and slipped his oversized red hoodie off his body, and quickly dressed her in it.

"Perfect. Grab your keys and backpack." He ordered, and she obeyed blindly. So much had happened that Audra felt completely overwhelmed and close to a breakdown, not to mention still aching and in pain from whatever sickness she was suffering through.

Luc slung the duffel onto his back and wrapped his free arm around Audra, tucking her into his side.

"Don't look." He whispered and led her through the hallway.

She screwed her eyes shut, burying her head into his chest, and trusted the boys to lead her in the right direction.

This night...What was going on?

She turned and peeked through her eyelashes.

A guy, no older than 25 years old, lay on the floor outside her apartment, neck at an unnatural angle and his mouth open. His eyes were open and unseeing, looking straight at her. But his mouth...his teeth...

He had fangs.

* * *

"Luc..." Audra said, breathlessly, eyes locked on the thing that had been trying to break into her apartment.

"I said not to look. I promise, I'll explain everything, but we need to get out of here. Now." His tone left no room for arguments and Audra was getting more and more panicked.

What was happening? What was that Winct thing Luc talked about? What sickness do I have? Why do I feel like I am on fire?

They got outside and Luc handed Audra to Eric to get her put in the car. Seamlessly transferring her so that Luc could drive, and Eric could help Audra. Audra wanted to pout at being taken from Luc when he smelled so good, and he was so warm. It made sense that Luc wanted to drive; he was the best driver out of all of them. So, she turned and latched onto Eric.

Audra gripped Eric's white shirt, breathing in his familiar scent.

There was something more now. He always smelled good; a bit of spice and his laundry detergent, but now his scent was deeper. Like she was able to take in more notes. Like a fresh sea breeze and sunlight.

Audra took a deep breath, pressing his white shirt as close to her face as she could.

"Luc! Hurry!" Eric's deep voice boomed over her head. She could feel the rumble in his chest. Looking out the side window, Audra could see three other people chasing after the car. They had gotten close enough to scratch the door before Luc peeled off the curb with a screech of the tires.

Audra couldn't seem to make sense of what was happening. She still felt like everything was on fire, but she was able to move at least this time.

They finally made it out of the building, the world still covered in the darkness of night with only one point of light. The full moon shone brightly and boldly in the sky above, threatening to overpower the hazy city light glow.

"The change is starting. It's only getting worse. We need to get to the safe house." Eric said, his voice sounded strained.

"She's never smelled like this before." Luc said stiffly. Audra wondered what that meant. Did she normally smell better?

"I know, and it's only gotten stronger since we left her apartment. Soon, everyone will be able to scent her."

Naively, she had thought that the worst of it was over when she broke out of that internal paralysis. But the liquid fire she felt running through her veins was only growing. The pain seemed like it was going to burst every blood vessel she had. The pressure in her body was excruciating; her head was throbbing, and her heart was beating much too fast.

She let out a cry; the pain was too much.

Maybe letting out a scream would make some of this pressure go away, and out ripped such a guttural scream from her lips. It surprised her that she was even capable of making such a sound. Her body arched and thrashed within the confines of the black cloth interior of seats, her body seemingly no longer under her own control.

Audra crashed forward into the driver's seat, her head pushing into the back of the seat. The pressure provided some relief from the headache, but not enough at all. She thrashed her arms and legs, trying to get the fire to go out. Vaguely aware of each sharp hit to her limbs, she couldn't stop.

"Audra, stop! Stop!" Eric yelled, climbing in the back with her. His large body scrunching awkwardly in sideways, he reached out for her and quickly gripped her body to him. She vaguely felt him wrapping his arms around her waist and heaving her onto his lap to try to reduce her thrashing.

"Luc, please!" Audra felt the car speed up. She didn't know where they were going, or if she should just be blindly following what they said but she didn't have much of a choice. She couldn't concentrate, couldn't sit still, couldn't do anything that wasn't trying to survive the flames.

"Audra, we're almost there. Just hang on." Luc tried to calm her from the front seat, only looking back to put his hand on her forearm. The only bit of her skin he could reach while still speeding through the streets, but the touch didn't quite do the trick like it had before. She was still burning.

"Eric..." Luc said, voice tight with stress.

"I know!"

Eric grasped both of Audra's wrists and twisted her body so that her back was flush with his chest and wrapped his legs around hers. She tried her best to wrestle free, but his grip left no room for any kind of movement on her part.

Audra could feel his heart beating against her back. He held onto her so tightly. His head tucked into her neck, and he breathed in deeply.

"Breathe, Audra. Breathe and be calm. Be still." Eric's voice was rough.

The fire in her veins was still there, but she tried to pull in more air to gain control of herself.

"Deep breaths." He ordered, and she tried. She took a few shaky, deep breaths before she was able to feel her heart rate lower.

"That's it." Eric's deep voice soothed in her ear. The car was zooming through the streets so fast that Audra wasn't able to actually see where they were to know where they were headed. Even if she could, somehow, she doubted that she would have been able to figure it out with as much pain and torment as she was going through.

"What's happening to me?" Audra whispered softly, hoping that he had answers to make this pain go away.

"You're changing. Everything looks sharper, right? Smells are more pronounced?"

Audra just nodded.

"You're becoming one of us."

"What are you?" She whispered.

"I'll explain after. You need to rest while you can. It will get worse, but we'll be here for you through it." Eric said softly, just loud enough for her to hear. "Luc?" He said, slightly louder.

"Two minutes."

"Hurry."

"What do you think I've been doing?" Luc snapped. Audra looked to the rearview mirror and saw that Luc was staring right back at her. Concern etched into his features; his blue eyes filled with worry. Audra tried to smile but was sure that it came out as more of a grimace. She wanted to tell him she was okay when another spark of pain started.

Audra felt that calm wave burn away, the fire turning more liquid and cold.

"It's changing...Guys, it's changing."

"What do you mean?" Luc asked, his fingers gripping the steering wheel tighter.

"The pain," she said as she grit her teeth together. A shiver violently ripped through her." The pain isn't fire anymore. It's turning cold, too cold."

"What did she just say?" Luc called from the driver's seat. "How is that possible?"

"She's High Royalty. They knew this could happen."

"It's too cold. Oh my god, I thought the fire was painful!" Audra bit down on her lip to keep from screaming and she was sure she drew blood.

"Audra, hold on. Hold on. We are pulling in now." Luc said from the driver's seat.

"It hurts so much." She whimpered, trying to squirm and move. The fire in her veins had turned to ice, causing every part of her body to lock up with the cold. Somehow it felt like it was rushing through her, wave after wave of ice.

And all she could do was brace herself for the next wave.

"I know it hurts and I'm sorry." Eric said sadly, his arms wrapping around her tighter.

The car slammed to a stop, and Luc jumped out. He slammed his door shut with so much force, Audra could feel the car shake.

Another wave of ice flowed from the crown of her head, all the way through her head, down her neck and spine, flowing out all the way to her fingertips and toes. She felt each muscle lock up and was unable to move at all.

"Give her to me." Luc ordered when he yanked open the backdoor.

Audra could feel them jostling her, her limbs being positioned and moved.

"You got her?" Eric asked, bags slung over each shoulder and in each of his hands.

"Yeah," Luc grunted out.

Audra could only imagine what she looked like at that moment. A girl with locked out arms and legs, trembling and in the arms of a large man holding her like a manikin in the middle of the night.

Eric ran past them, and Luc turned to follow. When he did Audra was able to see where they were.

It truly looked like they were in the middle of nowhere special; an open field with pine trees and oak trees lining the property. They seemed to be just enough outside of the city that Audra could see the haze of all the lights in the distance, the soft glow forming a dome in the night sky.

Audra stretched her neck as much as she could in her paralyzed state to look around. There was forest behind them, a thick line of pine trees forming a barrier with an open field shining in the night sky. It looked like a painting, like a dream.

Luc carried her towards an old farmhouse; a two story, wooden home painted white and weathered with age. Not one light in the farmhouse was on, only adding to its haunted look. Audra couldn't wait to see it in the daylight if she made it to daylight.

God, that's morbid, she thought as another wave of ice rolled through her. She let a soft whimper escape her clenched jaw.

The guys looked down at her, seeing the tears rolling down her cheeks and into her ears, and Audra could see a pained expression cross their faces.

"I know, I'm so sorry." Luc whispered.

As they made their way up the steps, Audra could hear the floorboards creak with each step the men took. They stopped right before the front door, not entering. She darted her eyes to Eric and saw that his eyes were glowing, that same bright gold that she had seen before. He was staring at the front door in silent concentration. She looked over to Luc. His eyes were glowing a rich, bright blue, and he was staring at the door with that same concentrated look as Eric.

"What is happening?" She stuttered through her clenched teeth.

With no answer, she looked towards the door and was able to see a shimmer. A shimmer of gold and blue twisting and rippling right in front of the weathered door. The shimmer became brighter, more opaque-like she should have been able to touch it if she could have moved. But right in the middle of the door, she could see a hole forming in the shimmer. Like a stone being thrown into a pond. It got bigger and slowly continued to grow.

Audra continued to stare, unable to look away, until the hole in the shimmer stopped. It was the perfect size for the door.

Eric reached forward and twisted the doorknob, stepping into the farmhouse and started flickering lights on, brightening up the space.

"It's okay, it's safe here. We made sure of it." Eric told her.

"Let's get her into the warded room." Luc said, as Eric dropped the bags at the foot of the stairs. He turned to the side and opened the sliding French doors right off the side.

Luc flipped the switch on the wall with her still in his arms, and the whole room lit up. Audra remained locked within her ice prison, but she could see now. Someone had obviously decorated the room in the farmhouse aesthetic, floral wallpaper, and beige carpets. An older, well-loved light red couch in the middle of the room and small side tables on either side, both topped with a bronze lamp. The walls had built in bookshelves, filled to the top with books and decoration.

Luc walked over to the couch and set her down gently.

"Just rest. We will be right here. I promise." He said, his voice comforting and soft, soothing in the way that she needed.

She let her eyelids shut and her exhaustion took her down into the world of shadows.

* * *

The darkness was soothing, calm, refreshing. There wasn't any pain, any yelling or tension. Just peace.

She was pulled from the dark abyss. One pale hand gripped her bicep roughly, but with desperation in the touch.

"Audra, there you are, sweetheart."

It was the voice from her dream earlier. The deep, masculine tone that sent shivers down her spine with want.

"Please, who are you?" Audra called out into the darkness.

The hand on her shoulder squeezed gently and slid down to hold her waist, thick fingers spread to hold more of her at once.

"Someone who cares for you and who has been watching out for you your whole life."

"Then show yourself."

"Not yet. You need to stay on the course you're on for now. I'll find you when it's time. I promise."

"Please...don't leave me." Her chest constricted at the thought of being all alone in the dark. Just because she wasn't afraid didn't mean she wanted to be alone.

"You're never alone in the shadows." The hand on her waist squeezed tightly, pulling her closer to the invisible man and then let her free fall backward.

Audra woke up.

Chapter Four

Audra woke up after what felt like mere minutes, but her body felt better. Like it had a small reprieve from the pain it was determined to keep going through.

Her dream visitors, whom she still had no clue as to who they were, if this man who called her 'sweetheart' and spoke of care for her was real. Or if the woman had any kind of relation to her. Why was the vision so visceral? Maybe she was going crazy. Luckily, the ice was gone, the fire was gone, but in their place was a floating feeling. It wasn't torturous like the other two. But off-putting.

She felt like she had no body, like there was no way for her to ground herself back to Earth. Her eyes popped open, and she saw that she was floating.

"Guys!" she screamed. The two of them weren't in the room with her and she still had no idea what was happening, but now she was floating above the battered couch they had laid her on. She heard running footsteps, the sound of the biker boots the guys wore hitting the wooden floor, and saw Eric run in. Panic and fear clear on both their faces.

"Audra?" Eric stopped when he saw her floating through the air, at least three feet from the couch.

"I can't feel my body. I have no control over it." She said, even she could hear the fear in her voice.

"It's okay." He said, hands up in front of him. It was meant to be a calming gesture, but it just incited more fear in her.

"It's okay." He repeated.

"How is this okay?!" she snapped at him. "Nothing about this is okay."

"I know it's disorienting, but you're safe. See, you're not going any higher or zipping around the room. Are you hurting?" Luc cut in; his face also contorted in panic. Audra watched Luc set his coffee mug down and stand next to her head.

"No, it's just...odd. I feel numb, like there is nothing for me to feel." She said, struggling to put into words the weightlessness she felt.

"Can you feel me?" Luc asked, reaching to take her floating hand.

As soon as he touched her fingers, she dropped back to the couch, landing with a thud and a puff of air as her breath was knocked from her lungs.

"Audra, you, okay?" Eric asked, coming to where she had landed to help her readjust on the couch to a more comfortable position, pushing Luc out of the way slightly.

"Yes, I'm okay. Just got the wind knocked out of me." She said with a chuckle.

"Can you move?"

Audra felt like feeling had returned to her when Luc touched her. She could feel his warm fingers threading through hers. She could feel the dip of the cushions of the couch beneath her, her leggings that covered her legs, and, unfortunately, the aches and pains of being sick. Her headache was back, her eyes ached even worse now.

But she could sit up.

"Good, that's good. Slowly." Eric helped guide her into a fully seated position and sat next to her. She released a deep breath that she hadn't known she was holding and let some of her weight rest on him.

"What is happening?" She whispered.

"It's a long story, Aud." Luc said with a sigh.

She holds up her arms weakly to gesture around the room, "I have time."

Eric chuckled and nodded, running a hand through his hair.

"I don't know where to begin." He admitted.

Audra turned her body slowly. Each movement felt like moving through molasses, like she was fighting against a heavy wind wall that affected no one else but her. Her hips and legs angled towards Eric.

When she finally got her lower half angled towards him, she took a big breath.

A gasp of air to brace herself for the next half.

"Audra, you don't have to move if it hurts you. I could move to see you better."

You tell me that now. She thought with an eye roll but continued to fight the invisible wall.

Her chest moved, and her arms pushed. It was kind of amazing to her how much this force was pushing but would not hurt her. She didn't feel crushed or trapped, just struggled to move. There was no loud air current or draft moving anything, just the hum of air holding her.

She heaved and groaned, but after persevering, she was able to move her upper body towards Eric. Luc reached over and braced her back for her, so when she got into a comfortable position, she was able to let her weight rest on him.

"I'm ready." Audra said. The rest and relief she felt was so nice. Like she had worked out in the sun all day, got completely sweaty and then jumped into a cool lagoon. Where Eric was always warm and his skin always felt like he was running a fever; Luc was cool, like the first dip in the water after a day working in the hot sun.

Eric took a deep breath and let it out slowly.

"It's...I... Okay, let me start at the beginning." He stuttered.

"Sounds like a good place to start." Luc snorted.

"Smartass." He said to their friend, with a smirk to which she smiled at their banter.

"Your parents."

"The ones that left me at the church?" She asked, leadingly.

"Yes. They didn't want to leave you. They had to."

"How would you know that?"

"Please, Audra." He snapped, as if he was already aggravated at her. She wanted to scoff at him, at his attitude about *her* life. So, she just rolled her eyes at him, watching him pinch the bridge of his nose in annoyance.

"Fine, but you better hurry up. I can only hold my silence for so long."

"I know your birth parents. *We* know your birth parents. I've actually known your family since I was born. Both of us have. Your parents are King and Queen of Vesperitus, our realm. You are High Royalty like your parents and their parents, and so on. You come from a long line of High Royals; they have crazy strong power over an element. Air, fire, water, or earth. Everyone in our realm has some kind of power, some kind of ability, but the High Royals always have exceptional control over an element. No one else in our realm can control elements in their pure form."

"Okay, wait time out." Audra said harshly. "You are saying my parents are royalty? That I'm royalty? And not only that, but I'm from somewhere else? Another 'realm'? Funny guys, really. What movie is that from?"

"I know. It's a lot. But I'm telling you the truth. There's more, though, wait." He ran his hand over his face, as if this talk was stressing him out. Which Audra was sure that it was.

"In our realm, there are opposites to light magic, we call them the Dark Fae. The Dark Fae have powers just like ours, are able to control and manipulate most of the elements. They are a radical group that has grown throughout the centuries to try to overthrow the High Royals by any means necessary. The High Royals - your family - and their court have tried their best to control them, bring peace. They roam through the lands, taking and wreaking havoc everywhere. People are murdered, innocent civilians if they choose to oppose the Dark Fae. But more importantly, they kidnap and torture powerful Fae who have exceptional power in order to build their army." Eric closed his eyes.

"The most coveted of powers, of abilities, is called a Total Elemental. They possess all four elemental powers and have complete control over them. People who have this extremely rare gift are powerful. More powerful than anyone."

"I thought only these High Royals have 'pure' elemental power." Audra said, putting air quotes up when she said pure.

"They have the raw elemental power and are much stronger than the average Fae. That is why it is legend that the first High Royal was a Total Elemental. That the original, all powerful being was your ancestor." Eric said, eyes locked on hers to portray the seriousness of his words.

Audra was still unable to truly move, the wall of air still trying to force her into place. But she was stunned. In this one conversation, there had been so many things shared about her family, about herself that she didn't even think was real, let alone happening to her.

"A Total Elemental hasn't been born in generations, hundreds of years. Back in the day, technology wasn't as good, our medical services weren't as advanced as they are now. But now, we are able to determine supernatural ability through a simple blood test. In fact, the Royals decreed that each baby born would be tested and their ability put on record."

"Then what is your power?" Audra asked, too curious to let him show her at his own pace.

"I'm able to produce and manipulate light." Eric said with a confident, easy smile. The fluorescent lights in the room grew brighter and then dimmed quickly.

Audra looked around. It had happened so quickly she wasn't sure that she had really seen the lights change or if she had just blinked.

"Did you do that?"

He nodded and held up his hand, palm facing upwards.

"If there is light, real or man-made, I can bend it to my will." The lights started to brighten slightly. "I can also create it."

In the center of his palm, a small orb appeared, like a speck of glitter stuck to his hand. It flickered and grew larger.

Audra's jaw dropped. In his hand was a baseball sized miniature sun, pure light dancing and flickering like it wanted to cast out any shadows in the room. She looked up at Eric and noticed his eyes were brighter, the golden overtaking any brown in his iris'.

"Your eyes..." she murmured. "They looked like that at my apartment before you ran out."

Eric flicked his wrist, and the light vanished. His eyes faded back into their beautiful golden-brown color that she was so comforted by.

"That happens when you use your magic. The user's eyes will glow a certain color correlated with their ability. Most fire users' eyes turn red or orange, water users' eyes turn blue or teal, and so on. But it's really interesting to see the people with abilities that aren't so close to the pure element. I knew a person and their ability was being able to make the flowers bloom, not grow or anything, just bloom. And their eyes would glow purple." Eric tells her with an easy smile.

Audra couldn't help but feel almost sorry for all she didn't know about Eric. Then she was hit with a fierce anger. She had completely opened up to them; told them her fears, her past, her pain. And they had kept things from her, had lied to her face.

"Was anything you told me before this whole thing true? Either of you?" She asked.

"What do you mean?" Luc asked, sounding as if he was genuinely confused by her question.

"All the things you told me back when we would hang out...was any of it true? Are your parents really living out in Florida? Obviously not. Do you both actually work for a computer game company? Did you guys go to college at the University of California? All of the things that we talked about, all I thought I knew about you two. Is any of it true?" As her rant continued, her anger grew. Everything was fake if what they were saying about this other realm was true.

"Audra...just wait a minute."

"No! Eric, tell me the truth!" She yelled. The wall of wind was gone, and she was in full control over her body once again. She stood up from the couch and put her hands on her hips. The anger she felt filled every part of her, from her head to her toes. Her close friends, her best friends, had been keeping things from her. Important things. Things about *her*.

The ground beneath them began to vibrate slightly.

"Audra..." Luc started, standing up with his palms out in front of him, the gesture was meant to be calming and one that allowed her to know what he was going to do, where he was going to go out and touch her. But at that moment, it just caused her rage to explode more.

"Do I even know you?"

The vibrations in the ground picked up more. The books on the shelves started to rumble, the lamps were jostling slightly on the tables.

"Yes. Yes, you do. You know me, you know us." Eric said, gesturing at Luc who was staring at her so intensely, she was surprised that he hadn't grabbed her and held her close yet. Luc tended to do that when he could tell she was overwhelmed. It was so Luc; it made her heart ache that he wasn't doing it now.

"So, some of our background information isn't true, but at our core, you know us. We've never lied about who we are as people, who we really are deep down." Luc grabbed her hand and placed it on his chest, right over his heart.

"You know me. Just as I know you." Luc said, wrapping both of his arms around her waist to ground her. She could feel his strong body against her, his deep breaths bringing her back to herself.

The shaking under their feet continued while she wrestled with her thoughts, but slowly, the tremors stopped.

They were right; she knew them. But she couldn't help a deep fear that the two men she had come to depend on would pack up and leave her had caused her to try to leave them first back when they first started becoming a little family and it reared its ugly head now.

Audra looked Luc dead in the eye, baby blue meeting green. He looked so nervous, so scared.

"Don't you two ever lie to me again." She sneered.

A huge smile broke out across Eric's face; straight white teeth shining brightly, his face much more relaxed than before and Audra could feel Luc's shoulders slump as the tension left them.

"First things first," Luc said as he and Eric pulled away, giving Audra her personal space back. Eric's posture changed; more formal and stricter. His chest puffed out and his shoulders squared.

"My name really is Eric, but my last name isn't Taylor. It's Tayorkoven. My full name is Eric Callan Tayorkoven, I am the Crown's First General, and I volunteered to come and bring you home."

"My name is Lucien Keirem Antonov. I am the First Lieutenant to the Crown, and I also volunteered to bring you home."

Both men then dropped to their right knees, arms crossed in an 'x' over their chests, and they bowed to her.

Chapter Five

Audra stood, mouth fallen open, staring at the two oversized men down on their knees, bowing to her.

"You volunteered to bring me to this other realm? I'm supposed to go back?" Audra asked. They both stood and Eric gestured for Audra to sit back down on the couch. He then turned his body away from her and let his body fall against the couch. Luc took up residence in the armchair right across from the couch.

His elbows were bent as he leant over his knees, his long sleeve t-shirt bunched up on his forearms. That man was a treat for the eyes. Audra always thought Luc and Eric were attractive, but she was sure that they didn't see her that way.

"You are. We are supposed to bring you back so you can return balance to the kingdom. It was a mission that many warriors asked for. It's a great honor." Eric said.

An honor. To come and retrieve me from my home so that I can go off to some unknown land and do what? Be royalty. Yeah, no. The news had surprised and terrified Audra all at once. Luc stayed silent, letting Eric do all the explaining.

After a few moments of awkward silence, she got back to asking questions.

"So, Luc, what is your power?"

"Water. I can manipulate, conjure, animate and communicate through water." He said, waving his fingers in an elegant gesture and a baseball size orb of water appeared above his palm. His blue eyes shone with an aqua light, giving them the appearance of an ocean. They were truly beautiful. "It's not a pure element like one of a High Royal, but over the years and through lots of practice, I've been able to grow stronger."

"Wow…"

He formed a ball with the water again, then slowly had it flow back to the water cup on the table that he had pulled it from.

"You're saying that I have some kind of power like you guys?" Audra asked, nervous that suddenly there was a dormant part of her that had just been waiting to pop through.

Both Eric and Luc nodded.

"And my…parents…are King and Queen?"

"Your mother, Queen Audrena, is the reigning monarch in Vesperitus. She is from the Helios bloodline and therefore, she is the one with the more dominant power. Your father, Anders Heliander, is the Queen's Consort. However, she decreed decades ago that he is to be addressed as King. He comes from a powerful bloodline as well. They run strongly with the affinity for light." Eric told her as if he was reciting facts from a history book.

Audra Leah Heliander. Audra thought as she tried out her true name in her mind. *It could have been worse.*

"I know none of this. None of the history. Hell, I didn't even know the place existed until a few hours ago." She put her head in her hands. "If I go…"

"Yes?" Eric prompted.

"If I go, you realize I'll be going to a completely new place. And we aren't just talking a new city, or country. We are talking a new world and that is… I need to think about it. But if I go, I'll need you and Luc to teach me all about the customs and everything. I don't want to accidentally offend someone."

"So, you are thinking you'll go?" He asked, a careful, cautious excitement playing in his eyes. Luc watched her carefully as she thought through what she wanted to say. He folded his hands in front of him as he leaned his elbows on his knees.

"I didn't say that. I'm so close to graduation. To getting the life I worked so hard for." She mused. "I'm going to need time to make a proper decision. But more importantly, I need to know, why do they need me now? Why leave me only to bring me back years later?"

"You're the princess. You were only supposed to be in this realm until you turned 19 years old. That is typically when powers in our realm manifest and show themselves. But because you have been in Terraus your whole life, Luc and I theorized that your powers might have taken longer simply because you are in a realm that is inherently magicless."

"Woah, hold up. A princess? Me? The orphan who barely makes enough money to eat most days? You've got the wrong girl." Audra stood up quickly, turning away from both of them to walk out of the room when a vibration, deep heavy shaking, started under her feet.

"I don't think we do." Luc said, strong and sure. "Think about this evening, Audra. The fire in your veins, the ice water in your muscles. You're changing. You had said that you were feeling sick for the past two weeks, fatigue, weakness, extra hunger, and thirst. All of those are symptoms of the change in our world."

Audra whipped around to face him, her anger and annoyance getting the best of her.

"Those are also symptoms of getting sick! Of a cold! Of working too hard!" The vibrations were getting stronger. She was sure that the whole house was shaking now but for some reason, Audra wasn't scared.

"The burning? The cold? Fighting against some invisible force to simply turn? What about the Winct coming after you? What are those symptoms of? Because in our world, those are symptoms of the change, a process you go through when you are finally getting your power and receiving your affinity! Don't start running away from this because you're scared. You know there's truth in what I'm telling you." Eric shot back.

The shaking intensified; the lamps fell off the end tables, a painting of an open field fell from the wall, the glass breaking. Audra could hear the French doors rattling, but she couldn't care. She was trapped in a staring contest, a show of wills with Eric. He had stood up from his relaxed position and had his fists balled by his hips.

Audra realized somewhere in the far recesses of her mind that she was probably coming at Eric like this because she was scared and he was coming at her, raising his voice. She wasn't one to back down from a fight, especially when provoked.

"You son of a —" Audra started, her anger once again making its presence known.

"Guys, calm down. We are going to need to get to safety if this shaking gets any stronger." Luc said.

"He's not wrong." Audra said through her clenched teeth, still staring up at Eric, refusing to be the first to break.

"She's causing it." Eric said, his gold eyes burning brightly, and his head tilted slightly as if he was studying her.

"What? I am not."

"We live in New York, princess. There aren't a lot of earthquakes here. Plus, it only happens when you get pissed off."

"Stop pissing her off, then! The entire house is shaking." Luc interjected.

"I'm not doing this." Audra was frustrated, sure. They were dropping bombs of information every which way and giving her ridiculous stories about things that only happen in fairy tales.

"Audra, just breathe." Luc told her. She stood there, still angry. Her eyes were defiant, wanting to fight him, but knowing that she should calm.

She took a deep breath and felt herself relaxing, a small bit of tension leaving her shoulders. She took another breath, allowing the motion to relieve the strain in her muscles.

"There you go." Eric whispered.

"Holy hell. She really was doing it. They didn't lie." Audra can hear Luc say with an awed tone of voice.

"I told you." Eric murmured to his comrade, but his eyes never left Audras. A look crossed his face; one of awe, much like one would look at a performer on a stage, but also something more sinister.

Audra continued to breathe and calm down. That's when she realized that the shaking had stopped.

It...It can't be...I didn't mean...what is happening to me? Audra felt her eyes line with tears, the truth of what they were trying to tell her facing her now. She had gotten mad, and the ground shook uncontrollably; she calmed and so did the shaking.

Audra stepped back, her even, calm breathing spiking, each breath turned to a pant. A gasp. An attempt to calm back down from the panic rising within her.

If what they are saying about the powers is true...then it must all be true. She turned from Eric, from Luc, and felt the panic spike higher. Her breaths were coming in shorter, shorter pants.

"Audra..." Luc said, slowly walking up to her, to keep her from running like a wild animal. The guys seemed nervous, scared of what she might do.

She was scared of what she might do.

"Audra," Eric started to walk towards her, but her hands shot out in front of her to stop him.

She didn't want anyone to touch her. She didn't want anyone to talk anymore.

She was so tired. Still so tired and exhausted about everything. Her body felt as if it might drop.

There was absolutely no energy left in her.

"Are you okay?" Luc asked, stepping closer to her. A look of alarm on his face. "Eric, she doesn't look so good."

"Audra," Eric stepped closer to her as well. Her back was now pressing up into one of the bookshelves that lined the wall. She grabbed out, grasping for something to help her stay upright.

There was no air. She couldn't get a breath in. The world was spinning, and she couldn't keep up.

"Help me." She whispered, her eyes locked onto Luc and his panicked expression as she lost the fight against the darkness.

Chapter Six

Audra could feel herself slowly coming back to her body. She could feel the soft, lumpy couch cushions, she could hear two deep voices whispering back and forth. Her world was still dark, unable to open her eyes just yet. The darkness had a hold on her, she couldn't shake it. Her conscience started to go over all the information that she had just learned; her family - she actually had a family, her powers, her birthright.

"I know finding out about your true family was hard. I'm so sorry that it had to be this way." *The smooth, calming voice from her dreams brought her back to the darkness.*

"Did you know too?" She asked the void.

"Yes, sweetheart. I'm sorry. It wasn't my place. You must be feeling better with the Change. Your energy is easier for me to latch onto." He said.

"When are you going to show yourself?"

"Soon, sweetheart. Very soon."

The anonymous voice frustrated Audra, whispering sweet nothings into her ear and trying to help her. She forced herself to wake up, not wanting to be in the comfort of the darkness any longer.

She tried moving, turning to her side. One of the boys must have caught her and laid her down.

"Audra?" A panicked whisper she heard over her.

"You, okay?" Another.

"I'm okay." She said, her voice groggy and hoarse.

Her eyes felt heavy. The effort to lift her eyelids seemed like moving a boulder uphill. But she did it.

Light filtered in, fractured rays filled her vision, but she was able to see her two guys staring at her with deep worry lines that furrowed their foreheads.

"How long was I out?" Audra asked as she sat up gingerly. Her head felt like there were elephants stomping inside her skull.

"20 minutes or so. But how are you feeling?" Eric asked. He was much closer to her, kneeling on the floor close to where her head was resting.

"Not great." She said honestly, as she brought both hands up to her head to cradle the pain.

"She must have overdone it. Her magic is trying to force her body to change. She needs to rest, you know that, Eric." Luc snapped at Eric. Like it was Eric's fault, she overdid it. It probably was. She was getting so annoyed and frustrated with him that her powers were out of control. Eric turned to face Luc, his clean-shaven jaw clenching in annoyance.

"Watch your tone, Lieutenant." Eric grumbled. Luc lifted his hand and pushed down the dark brown hair at the nape of his neck and shook his head.

My powers, that's weird to think. Not as weird as thinking that the world I've always known as the only world, is one of many. And that I'm from another realm.

"What else can I look forward to during this 'change' that you guys keep speaking of?" Audra asked with added sass to her tone. She wasn't about to just let these two off without some of her attitude.

"Everybody has a different time. It is kind of like a cold; there are the same overall symptoms, but everyone experiences it differently. Some things affect you more than they would others, and vice versa." Luc said from the side, his arms crossed over his chest like a bodyguard. Looming over her, silently protecting her.

"What was yours like then?" Audra put her hand to her eyes. The lights were a bit bright in there for her comfort. The headache she had was throbbing and the bright lights were not helping.

Suddenly, the lights dimmed to an acceptable level. They were soft and warm rather than the bright, white, and fluorescent that they were. Audra looked over at Eric and saw that he was already staring at her.

"That's you, isn't it?"

He smiled and dimmed them a bit more; the lights stopped making her head hurt. She could open her eyes fully without fear of the headache hurting even more. Letting out a sigh of relief, she gave Eric a small smile of thanks.

"What do I do now?"

"Now, you rest." Eric said, "You rest. Let your body adjust to its new form and then we can get to work."

"New form? To work?" Audra said, with a confused look on her face.

"This change, these powers. They change you at your core. You will look different. Leaner, stronger, sharper. It will be tougher to get hurt or sick, but you aren't infallible. Injuries can still happen. But most importantly, your life cycle will be much longer." Luc said from the side, his tone all business. With his tousled hair and trimmed beard, he looked every part the dangerous protector that he was.

"How will I look different?" Audra asked, wrapping her hand around a strand of her long brown hair in worry. "And how much longer will my life cycle be?"

The boys - men - looked at each other with Audra could only assume was apprehension. They both turned to her.

"Normal humans live to be 95, maybe 100-years-old. We live to be upwards of 950, but closer to 1,000-years old." Luc said with such ease, completely nonchalant, as if he hadn't just caused Audra to lose all the breath in her lungs and had to rest against the back of the couch in shock.

"A thousand years..." she whispered, and her eyes were stuck in front of her, blinking and unseeing. She sat astounded and terrified at what this meant.

She would be able to see so many things, she could see everything. She had the time to do everything she had ever wanted; travel, work, read, write, draw! Everything seemed open to her.

She had never truly grasped how short life was, how quickly it passed her by. That was until she was told she had a seemingly endless supply.

"Wow." The word slipped, unmeaningly, through her lips and she started to laugh. The laughter bubbled up and out. She started to feel like a crazy person. Her laughter was turning hysterical.

Eric turned to Luc and shot him a look of panic, but even that couldn't quite stop her laughter, only bringing her back to her senses a bit.

"Sorry," she said, pulling herself together, and she reached over to give Eric a reassuring squeeze on the shoulder. "I just realized how crazy this all is. How long my new life will be. How short my old one was." She ran a hand through her brown waves, pulling and tugging at the knots that had occurred.

"There are going to be a lot of new things, a lot of new, crazy things. But we are here for you. I am here for you." Eric said, his words sounding more like a vow to her. "Plus, you'll need help learning your new powers. And who better to show you than us?" Eric said with a smirk, and he gave her hand a squeeze.

"Do you guys know what powers I do have or...?" She trailed off.

The two men looked at each other with almost a nervous expression crossing their faces. Audra looked between the two as they seemed to argue with each other with their eyes yet again.

"What? What is it?" Audra asked sternly.

Luc looked pointedly at Eric, and Eric let his head drop.

"Do you guys not know or something?"

"We know." Luc said sharply. "We know what your powers are. We also know that your change will take a little longer and be a little more aggressive than others in our realm."

Audra's mouth dropped open slightly as she took in what he said.

"Why? What is going to happen to me?" She asked, voice soft and timid. The lack of answers was starting to not only piss her off but also scare her. They wouldn't stop talking earlier and now they wouldn't start.

"Luc?" Her voice wobbled a little.

His eyes met hers quickly, the blue of his eyes seemed to swirl with concern. Concern for her.

"Do you remember when we talked earlier about total elementals?"

She nodded, nervous and her eyes widened slightly.

"But that's a rare thing, right? You said it yourself that there hasn't been one in centuries."

Eric shook his head.

"That's true." He said quickly.

"What are you saying, Eric?"

"I'm saying, Audra, that you are a total elemental. You have the primary power of your ancestors, all four pure elements: air, water, fire, and earth, with troves of strength. The first Total Elemental our realm has seen in decades, centuries even."

"Centuries?" Audra said.

"Yes, centuries. The last one was your ancestor, the Queen Maeve, and the Dark Fae, attacked and *murdered* her and the King consort, Callum, because of her power. They wanted it for themselves. They wanted to bring her to their leader, have him gain her power and then overthrow our monarchy." Eric explained.

Audra's head seemed to explode with this new information.

"This is too much, too soon." Luc muttered, taking a deep breath, and crossing the room to plop down into the worn wooden chair in the corner. Audra expected Eric to continue telling her things - things about her family, about her power, about what dangers lie ahead of her - but he must have agreed with Luc, and he stopped talking.

"You need to rest. Your change will be harder on you as it is, but the more you fight it, the longer and more intense it will be." Luc stood up, walked across the room, and grabbed the crocheted, woolen throw blanket that was adorning the back of the couch and urged Audra to lay down.

"Wait, what else am I to expect through this change? You guys have only said it is like being sick." She asked with urgency, but let herself be wrapped in the scratchy, but warm, cloth.

"Headaches mainly, growing pain type aches, fever and chills, but really, you are going to feel exhausted, overly exhausted. My family said that when I went through it. It was like I was in a fugue state, fading in and out of consciousness. All I remember though, is that I slept through most of mine. I was so tired and hurting so much. But I only have one power and not the strength you have, princess." Eric said as he bent down close to her face. He had a smile on his face that lit up his features. His eyes sparkled as he pushed a lock of hair from Audra's face.

Audra gasped quietly. Eric hadn't ever shown her affection in that. He was more likely to give her a fist bump than to hug her unless necessary. She looked to Luc and saw his eyes shimmering with fury, his eyes were trained on where Eric's fingers had touched her. But he remained silent.

"We will take care of you, I promise. Just rest." Eric whispered as he ran his fingers through her hair, lightly massaging her scalp while she felt the exhaustion settle in her bones.

"We're not done talking about this." She said with her eyes fluttering shut, too heavy to open again.

"I know. We can answer all your questions when you wake up."

"You better." She said as she let the fatigue pull her into the welcoming darkness, Luc's blue eyes meeting hers over Eric's shoulder before she fell asleep.

Chapter Seven

Audra woke up some time later, still on the couch. She must have slept so deeply that she didn't move at all because her hips and shoulder hurt from laying on her side for so long. The old couch was comfortable at first glance, but after a while, the springs and thin cushions were not ideal.

That, and the pain searing through her body, was unnerving. Her mind was foggy, like a grimy film was covering her thoughts and processes. She could feel that she was sweating, the sweat leaving wet marks on the material of the cushion. Audra tried to sit up, but as soon as she put any weight on her arm to push up, she couldn't do it. Her muscles were so fatigued she couldn't even lift herself. And that really, really bothered her.

"Oh, good. You're up. How are you feeling?" Eric's voice came from behind her, but she was unable to move her neck to look at where he was sitting without a sharp, debilitating pain that shot from her shoulders to the base of her skull. A small cry left her lips at the sudden pain.

"Don't move, I'm coming." He said with a sigh. It could have been the pain she was feeling, but he seemed to be irritated with his words, having a groan to them.

Audra waited, relaxing once more into the cushion as much as she could. She was so cold, so tired. As she pulled the wool blanket up around her ears, she heard objects clattering down behind her and Eric's murmured curses.

Audra would have laughed if she had the energy.

"Hi, Princess." He said with an easy smile as he crouched down to get on her level. His golden curls fell over his forehead, the ends tickled his eyes.

Eric's hand came up to rest on her forehead and he tsked softly.

"You're burning up."

She rolled her eyes.

"I'll be fine. You said this was part of the process." She whispered, her voice sounding hoarse and her throat dry as sandpaper.

"Here, let me help you sit up." His strong arm slid underneath her upper body and gently lifted her into a sitting position in a move so smooth that it seemed like she weighed nothing.

She didn't care, everything hurt, she wanted to go back to sleep but Audra didn't want to be alone. Eric was so warm as he sat down close next to her. She felt safe and like she would survive this, no matter how shitty she felt in the moment.

"I have water for you. Do you think you can sit up to drink it?" He asked.

Audra was so thirsty, but she did not want to move, so she nodded limply.

"Come on, you have to stay hydrated." He shuffled around so he didn't move Audra too much but was able to grab an obscenely large glass from the side table.

She tried to lift her hands out to take it from him, but he lifted the rim to her lips to let her drink.

The cool water felt heavenly.

Eric didn't let up until she had drained the whole cup. On the last swallow, her head fell back to rest yet again on the back of the couch. Eric held onto the empty cup, and she could see it refill on its own.

"What…" she said puzzled and Eric lifted the cup back to her lips, encouraging her to keep drinking.

"Luc enchanted this glass to refill when emptied." He explained.

Audra nodded and rested her head again.

"How do you feel?"

"I'm so tired, but I hurt too. Can I sleep more?"

Audra heard the chuckle and felt one of his hands come to smooth her hair over her back.

"Of course. Do you want me to show you to your bed?"

"I have a bed?"

"Of course, the Princess has a bed. I would have taken you up to it already, but I didn't want to disturb you."

"I want to go lay down in bed." She told him, trying to put as much strength as she can behind her voice.

Eric wasted no time as he stood, holding his arm out for her to take.

"Where is Luc?" Audra asked, looking weakly around the room. It was odd, but she needed to know where he was. It was an overwhelming need that she hadn't had before all of this.

"We decided to do shifts to guard you. So, he's sleeping now for the next few hours and then we will switch. We didn't want to leave you alone in case you woke up."

Eric's footsteps sound out, the wood creaking under their weight as he led them up the stairs.

"You're going to be okay." He said to her. It was hard for her to step up the stairs, but Eric slowed his pace and helped her. Audra wrapped a hand firmly around the handrail and tried to pull herself up.

It didn't make sense to her. Eric had always been rough and tough. A 'rest is for the weak' kind of person. But the fact that he was being so gentle and understanding with her meant that this really had knocked him down when he went through it.

Audra hummed softly. She knew that they had both already gone through this even if it was at a smaller level; he had felt this weak, this...immobilized. Did someone else take care of him like he was taking care of her? She really hoped so. Her heart ached as she envisioned a teenage Eric and a teenage Luc all alone, huddling in on themselves to keep warm and shivering from the high fever.

No, no, that couldn't have happened. She thought. *God, I hope that didn't happen. They had told me they'd been friends and worked together, had each other's backs. Maybe they had each other through this, too.*

It made the ache lessen slightly. But moreover, she was so thankful that she wasn't alone through this.

Eric reached the top of the stairs and used his free hand to push open one of the four doors on this level. All the doors were shut, and Audra assumed that

Luc was in one of the rooms resting.

She caught a cursory glance at the landing with hazy eyes, but the hardwood floor continued from the first level of the old farmhouse. Worn, but well maintained. There was one lone window that took up most of the hallway's back wall and it gave her a clear - or as clear as she could see through the pain - look at the moon and stars shining brightly down on them. The full moon overhead gave an ominous glow that streamed through the glass, lighting up the dark hallway.

Eric walked into the first door on the left, the bedroom that was on its own side of the house. Then he guided her to the bed and helped her climb in. As her back hit the mattress, she groaned loudly in bliss. The comfort of the memory foam mattress felt amazing on her skin, on her sore muscles. That bed felt like a godsend.

"I'm sorry. If either of us had known you were in that much pain on the couch, one of us would've moved you. We just didn't want to cause you more pain. I didn't even think about it if I'm being honest." Eric said, running his hand through his curls.

Audra could feel the exhaustion threatening to pull her back under again.

"Thank you." She said quietly.

"I'll be right across the hall. Luc's in the second room, I'm in the third. The first is a bathroom," Eric explained. "If you need anything, just shout."

Audra nodded, pulling the thick white blanket up to her neck. Everything smelled freshly washed and she was so comfortable.

"Goodnight, Princess." He whispered.

"Goodnight." Audra whispered back.

And when the blackness took over, she didn't fight it.

* * *

"How are you feeling?" Audra knew she was in a dream with the man again, the man she had yet to see.

"It's a bit unnerving to try to talk to someone who only answers me in my dreams and who refuses to show themselves." Audra snapped.

She heard a breathy chuckle and could hear steps against stone. Someone was walking closer. Overhead, there was one lone light casting a beacon around where Audra stood by herself. Then the steps stopped, and she was able to see the body of a man from the waist down. Whoever it was was wearing a pressed black suit and shiny dress shoes.

"That's it?" She asked.

"That not enough for you, sweetheart?" The voice chuckled, the sound sending arousal to her core.

"I would like to know what your face looks like. Not just your shoes." She stood straighter and threw her wavy hair over her shoulder.

"Not yet. But I'm here if you need to talk about anything, if you want to vent about the two buffoons you're hanging out with or the wealth of information you've been told."

"They aren't buffoons. They're my friends."

"Only one of them wants to be. And even that one...he wants to be more than friends with you." The man put his hands in his pockets and shifted his weight to the side. Audra couldn't see much of him, but just that small movement was sexy.

What is wrong with me? She thought.

"You've got it wrong." She said vehemently.

"Do I? A beautiful girl like you, come on. You must know the effect you have on people around you. We're like moths to a flame, sweetheart."

That gave Audra pause. So was he saying that he also found her beautiful, which was sweet, but this person, thing, vision was very possibly just a figment of her imagination. But regardless, she felt a blush rising to her cheeks.

"I don't think that we've properly been introduced. I'm Audra. But I gather you knew that. Am I actually interacting with a figment of my imagination now? I must be hallucinating from the fever or something." She started to ramble. The man just laughed, the deep sound reminding her of the turn-on his voice is.

"I'm not a figment of your imagination. I'm real. I just...have special gifts that I can use to talk to you."

"If you're real, what's your name?"

"I can't tell you that yet. Soon."

"You keep saying soon! Yet you come to me every time I close my eyes!" Audra threw her hands in the air, frustrated and annoyed at the secrecy.

"Please, Audra. Please don't make me lie to you." His voice was soft, full of regret and sadness. *"I haven't lied to you, and I never plan on doing so. But in order to keep you safe, to keep us safe, you can't know some things. At least not yet. But you will. I promise."*

She deflated a bit, her anger turned to understanding.

"Okay."

"I know you can't see my face right now, but I'm smiling."

Audra giggled, *"Me too."*

"Audra…" She heard far off in the distance.

"Do you need something?" The voice asked Audra, and with one last glance at the black pants, was pulled out of her dream. The first thing she realized was that she was hot. Too hot.

She felt like she was smothering in sweat and heat. Her breaths were coming in pants, trying to breathe through the dry, sweltering heat. Had the guys cranked the heat up?

"Hey," she said, opening her eyes to see Luc sitting on the edge of her bed.

"Hi." He smiled down at her. "Do you need anything? It's been more than a couple hours and I'm sure you're hungry." The only place she didn't feel like she was on fire was her hand. Audra glanced down and saw Luc's hand over hers. The coolness felt amazing.

Audra tried to turn over to face him fully, but she still felt so weak, like her muscles and bones couldn't even hold her own body up without outside help. Letting out a groan of pain, she tried to roll over, hoping that the change of position would afford her some cooling relief.

"Can you put your hand on my forehead?" She croaked out.

Luc looked at her with his eyebrow cocked and a confused expression on his face but obliged her. Once his hand touched her skin, she moaned in relief. His cool skin felt wonderful against her. Luc looked a touch uncomfortable but didn't move his hand.

"Thank you. Your hands feel so good." She said.

Realizing how that sounded, she blushed and tried to correct herself.

"I mean, wait. Your skin feels good against mine. Fuck, that sounded worse. I didn't mean it like that. Your hands feel cool against my skin. Oh, god." She rambled. When she put her head in her hands to hide her face, Luc laughed and touched her forearms.

"That's a compliment. Thank you." He smiled.

They both sat silent for a moment. Luc moved his hand from her forehead to the column of her throat. Audra moaned at the touch. The sound was involuntary.

When she opened her eyes and forced herself to make eye contact with him, his eyes were hooded, and he moved his bottom lip between his teeth.

"Do you need anything?" He asked, his voice deep and husky.

"You've asked me that a few times now." She said with a smirk.

"You keep distracting me, I'm sorry."

"Yeah, okay." Audra rolled her eyes. She could feel how tired she still was, how much her body ached. Her body was still fighting this change, and she really wished it would happen faster. She hated not feeling well, feeling in a weakened state which made her not able to fully feel in control of herself and her surroundings.

How long would this take? She thought with an audible groan.

"I'm okay. I'm not too hungry right now. I just want to sleep. Is that okay?" She asked, trying to shift her body again. She could see the sunlight trying to break through the thick blue curtains that hung and were drawn on the two large windows by the bed.

"Yes, of course you can. Eric and I are just hanging out and making sure that the property is guarded. You sleep as much as you want. You're still really warm so the fever might have broken, but you're still going through it."

"Can you turn the fan on?"

"Sure." Luc reached up and pulled the string for the ceiling fan to start circulating. "There."

"Thank you." Audra said, drowsily. Her eyes closed slowly, and she tried to fight it.

"Just sleep, Audra. It's okay." She felt his cool hand trail through her hair, and it pushed her further into sleep. "I'll protect you, baby."

His last words were muffled, soft and whispered like it wasn't meant for anyone else to hear.

Chapter Eight

Audra woke up feeling better than she had in the past week, at least. She actually felt rested; rested, but still weak. She stretched out, reaching her arms up and above her head, arching her back in a delicious stretch to ease her sore muscles. Audra could see the sun streaming brightly in through the edges of the curtains hanging on the two windows on each side of the bed. The fact that she was able to focus on anything other than pain was such a relief to her that she thought she would cry. The sunbeams streaming through seemed like a positive sign for her. Today was going to be a good day. She just knew it.

At some point throughout the time, she had been sleeping, someone had left a fresh set of clothes for her. She could not wait to get changed and out of these shitty clothes that she felt that she'd been in forever.

Audra rolled out of bed slowly and picked up the folded white shirt. She brought it to her nose and sniffed the shirt, taking in the sea air, fresh rain and ocean spray scent that lingered on the neckline. She realized that Luc had left her his clothes. She was grateful. Her jeans and sweater aren't the most comfortable thing to be in any longer and the waistband of her jeans were cutting into her hip painfully with all the laying down she'd been doing.

Audra slipped the shirt and sweatpants on, moaning slightly at the comfort. She crept out of the room, walking on her tiptoes to exit the room, trying not to step on any loose or older floorboards that would groan or squeak as she walked on them.

"Where are you sneaking off to?" Luc's voice said gruffly from behind her, effectively making her jump in fright.

"What the hell, man! You scared me!" Audra smacked his arm in fright with one hand as she gripped the front of the borrowed shirt tightly with the other.

Luc smiled, genuine mirth in his eyes, as he crossed his arms over his broad chest. Luc was a bit taller than Eric and with Audra being taller than the average woman, she was used to looking into everyone's eyes easily. But with Luc, she had to look up to even meet his eyeline. His dirty blonde hair was slicked back, still wet from the shower, his beard was groomed, neat and full. Where Eric was all about showing that he had the biggest and most dominant muscle, Luc was all sleek muscle that was not only visually appealing but made him light on his feet.

"I take it you're feeling better. You're up and about." He said his hand grabbed the wooden railing, and he started to walk down the stairs.

Chasing after him, she fell into step behind him as she took in the rest of the house that she hadn't been able to see. The house was filled with light. Sunlight touched every corner of the house. The worn wooden floors, but the hallway was covered with a soft pale grey rug. She followed Luc quickly through the first floor, where open French doors led them into the fully stocked, fully renovated kitchen. It was beautiful. All stainless-steel appliances, white trim and cabinets, grey walls. Not to mention the back wall was full of wide, tall windows, illuminating the breakfast nook in the corner.

"Wow," Audra whispered. This house was not just a regular old farmhouse she had thought it was that first night.

"I know, right? It's a pretty nice safe house." Luc said, as he started making coffee in a fancy-looking machine.

He seemed to know where everything was stored, the cups, the coffee, the utensils. Not to mention, the cupboards were stocked with canned and dried foods.

"Have you guys been here before? Do you spend a lot of time here?"

Luc turned, crossed his arms again, and rested his hip on the granite counter as he looked at her. The only noise being the coffee pot kicking to life and the birds singing outside.

"We stayed here when we first arrived. The King and Queen have kept it stocked and ready for us once they realized we would need a safe place to bring you once you started the Change. The house is completely warded, guaranteed protection from outsiders. The grounds are too, but it is more difficult to ward the outside, seeing as all of our powers are derived from nature and the elements." Audras eyebrows shot up.

Why the hell would they live in that dump of an apartment when they could be here?

"We didn't spend a lot of time here. We had to start putting protection in place when we located you. You were in the city, so we needed to be." He said plainly, turning to grab the full pot of coffee and pour himself a mug.

"Why would you spend even a night at that nasty apartment when you could be here? Or at least a better, more well-kept apartment somewhere?"

It just boggled her mind. She would not be living in that place if she didn't have to, but they had. They actively had chosen it.

"We were, are, exactly where we need to be."

"Don't be goddamn cryptic or anything." Audra muttered, walking over to the cupboard she watched Luc pull a coffee cup out of and grabbed her own.

"Why did that creature attack me back at the apartment?"

"Your scent bloomed when you started to receive your fire element. You probably realized Eric and I have distinct scents as well, well when you started 'burning' like you said, your scent exploded. We could smell you across the hall."

"What did I smell like?" Audra asked, her curiosity peaked.

"Before, you smelled nice. Human; plain and clean. But once you started the change...God." He groaned and took a deep breath. "You smell like fresh, hot baked cookies, rain and citrus, all in one. It's amazing."

His words seemed innocent, but the way he was looking at her made her blush. She bit her bottom lip and his eyes darted down.

"What do I smell like?" He asked her.

"You smell like fresh sea air, ocean spray when it crashes against the sand and coconut. The perfect day on the beach."

"Do you...Do you like it?" He brought his coffee cup up to his lips and looked to the side. He asked so softly, almost nervously, but with a faux confidence.

"Who doesn't like a day at the beach?" She said, mirroring his movements as she brought her coffee cup to her lips and took a sip.

They both sat quietly, sipping on their coffees, and enjoying the quiet.

"Where's Eric?"

"Sleeping. We took shifts sleeping so that one of us would always be awake in case you needed something." Luc explained. Audra nodded. Eric had already told her they were sleeping in shifts.

"So, when will I begin training?"

"Training?"

"Yeah, Eric said I would need to train to learn how to use my magic. You guys said that there are those Dark Fae that are against the High Royals, and not to mention the creatures that could come after me. After us."

"Eric and I will handle it for a while. You just focus on you and what you're going through. Then when it comes time to awaken your magic, we will get through that as well. One day at a time, Aud." Luc put his hand on her shoulder in a reassuring way.

"But shouldn't I know what I'm up against? Eric said I needed to train, needed to learn about my powers and abilities, but so far I don't feel much different."

"Just wait. Be patient with yourself." He said as he lifted the mug to his lips again.

"Why did you both volunteer to bring me back to your home?"

"Eric is the First General of the Royal Guard. The highest-ranking officer in the guard. He worked for years to climb the ladder with me right alongside him. I am the First Lieutenant, second in command. I remember one day, maybe six months ago, your parents requested our presence and explained the situation. They explained how they had an heir, how they had the blood test had determined their baby's power would be the first Total Elemental and they had to send the child away for their safety. Your mother started to tear up, which is uncharacteristic of her; she is one of the strongest women I've ever met. And she broke down in tears in front of Eric and me. They explained you should be approaching your 19th birthday and they wanted to bring you home after you Changed. We were their picks to retrieve their precious daughter. It was and still is a great honor."

The way he said that made Audra know that he was finished with this conversation. Luc was always willing to talk and discuss but he had a definite tone when he was done being pushed.

A tone he had just used.

Audra thought it over; all the new information she had been bombarded with over the past few days. She had parents, parents who wanted her. She had magic.

She was a Fae.

"Do I look different?" Audra asked Luc, pulling the warm mug of caffeine closer to her face.

Luc looked at her, his eyes never straying from her face.

"There are certain differences that are obvious. You still look like you. But you are...glowing. You've always been stunning, but now it's on another level."

He turned quickly and poured himself another cup of coffee, turning his back to her. Audra didn't know how to react. Luc hadn't ever really shown her that he cared for her any more than a good friend, yet since that night when her apartment was attacked...

"I'm going to head to the bathroom, take a long, hot shower." Audra announced as she set her empty mug down next to the deep farmhouse sink.

"I'll get food started, I bet you're hungry."

"I am hu-" She was cut off by the sound of heavy footsteps, slowly walking overhead and down the stairs.

"Audra, hey. How are you feeling?" Eric asked, rubbing sleep from his eyes.

"Better. I'm going to go shower. Luc said he was going to make food. I'm so excited, pancakes? Please?" She drew out the 'please' and gave Luc her best puppy dog eyes, with her fingers crossed in front of her and a small pout. He'd be powerless to resist.

Luc looked at her with his fresh coffee, his hip resting against the counter.

"Oh, don't give me that look!"

"Please?" She smiled.

"Fine! You win. Pancakes and eggs with lots of vegetables that you have to eat." He said. It must have been a fair compromise in his mind, but Audra knew that she would eat whatever he made. Luc was a great cook, and he took good care of both Eric and Audra. The last time Luc had made them pancakes was after she had aced her midterms that she had spent weeks studying for. He knew how much she relied on sugar and carbs, so when she aced them, he immediately hugged her tightly and promised breakfast-for-dinner. It had been months since he'd made them.

"Yes!" Audra made a little fist pump in the air. "I'm going to go take a shower. I don't know how many days I've been out, but I do know that I feel disgusting."

"Yeah, you smell like it too." Eric jabbed her shoulder with his fist and smiled. "The shower is upstairs, first door on the right."

"Thanks, I'll be back soon."

"Take your time." Eric reassured her that they had nothing else to do that day and she didn't need to rush.

* * *

The warm water under the shower made Audra moan with how good the heavy pressure felt on her sore muscles.

The bathroom was just as impressive as the rest of the house; all white tile, grey accents and a massive shower with a glass door and a rain shower head. Someone had gotten supplies because just like the kitchen, the bathroom was fully stocked, shampoo, conditioner, soap, razors, toothbrushes. Hell, there were even tampons and pads.

She was content here. No need to do anything else today.

Audra grabbed some of the shampoo, lilac scented, and she took comfort in the familiar smell of the shampoo. She took her time lathering, rinsing, shaving, exfoliating and by the time she was ready to step out, her fingers had turned pruney.

Reluctantly, she turned the water off and wrapped herself in a fluffy grey towel and turned to grab one of the unopened toothbrushes in the cabinet she had snooped through.

One thing that Audra kept thinking about was. Why was everything such a big secret? Why hadn't her parents tried to contact her while she was suffering when she was younger - just to let her know that they were there? Why hadn't the guys told them who they were when they first met? Maybe she would have been more prepared for all of this. Yes, they had told her a lot of information, but she had thought that the three of them really knew each other, really truly let her know them and vice versa.

But maybe it was just her who was out of the loop.

The two had known about her all along. They knew where she was from, who her parents were, and they just sat back and let her feel like she had no family to fall back on, to love her.

She was still wrapping her brain around the fact that she had a family. Parents. Parents who had wanted her and only gave her up to protect her.

The two guys had been there through drunken tears dedicated to the family she didn't know, the family she thought hadn't wanted her and simply dropped her on a doorstep. They knew how devastated she was about it.

She towel dried her hair and slipped back into the oversized clothes she had borrowed.

Looking into the mirror, the glass foggy from the shower steam, she looked at her new reflection.

And her jaw dropped.

Her wavy brown hair, which she had always thought was somewhat mousey, gleamed in the light. Suddenly, highlights of spun gold caught the light. Her curls were more pronounced and thicker, and they fell softly down her shoulders.

Her skin looked brighter, healthier and blemish free. Her freckles and the beginning of her laugh lines she had collected vanished. The angles and structures of her face were so much more pronounced, as if she had lost any roundness or soft curves.

She was striking.

She was different.

She was like new.

But she was thankful that she could still see some of the old her within her new face. She wasn't quite ready to believe all of it or leave her whole life behind for some fairy tale where she was a princess. But seeing the physical changes that had occurred after her change...she believed it a little more.

Chapter Nine

"How was your shower?" Eric immediately asked her the second Audra rounded the corner to join the guys in the kitchen. The smell of bacon and pancakes was too tempting to pass up.

"It was heavenly. Just what I needed." She answered with a bright smile.

"Good. Come eat. Luc made a feast."

He didn't need to tell her twice.

She grabbed a plate and loaded it up with all the goodies that Luc had made. She realized then just how truly hungry she was.

A massive scoop of the loaded-up eggs, a pile of bacon and at least 5 pancakes smothered in butter and syrup. She knew she could eat more; she was just that hungry but would go slowly. She didn't usually eat this much. She hadn't exactly had the budget for it before. As she was eating, both guys looked at her surprisingly.

A moan left her lips at the fluffy texture and sugar filling her mouth. Luc could cook, he was usually the one to keep the three of them fed correctly. Eric could survive on protein shakes and could only cook vegetables in the microwave. Audra was a pro at making noodles in a cup or peanut butter and jelly sandwiches.

"So, how are you really feeling?" Eric asked, pushing his own food around on his plate. Normally, Eric could eat three times as much as Audra, no problem at all, but it looked like he had barely touched his minimal serving. Like he had just put some food on a plate in order to be less awkward as she ate.

"I'm okay. I have a lot of questions and I noticed how different I look." She gestured to her face.

"You don't look that different." Luc mumbled under his breath.

"You say that, but there are a lot of differences and I saw them upstairs." Audra rolled her eyes.

"She does look different." Eric said.

Luc looked at her, his eyes raking over her face. Audra felt her cheeks heat up again from his stare and his eyes darkened.

"She looks like she always had. At least to me." He said softly.

"I'll take that as a compliment because the person in the mirror upstairs was much more beautiful than I ever remember being." She tried to chuckle, to pass it off as a joke. Eric chuckled, taking a small bite of his food. Luc, however, had anger in his eyes.

"You have always been and always will be beautiful." Luc said. His voice was vibrating with anger, and it dripped with sincerity. He stood up from the table and stormed into the kitchen.

Their eyes locked over the table and the kitchen island as he looked back at her briefly. Audra wondered if he felt weird about his outburst, but when they locked eyes, she could see resolution in his eyes.

He said what he meant, and he meant what he said. And it took her breath away.

He turned back to the sink and started to clean up the dishes from breakfast. Luc's broad shoulders moving and his muscles rippling with every move. She wished she could tell him just how beautiful he was in turn.

"Luc, man, I'll take care of those. You cooked; I'll clean. Or Audra will. You don't have to do both." Eric said with his mouth full of bacon.

"It's fine. I need something to do." Luc shot him over his shoulder, never looking back at them.

"If, you're sure." Eric said, taking a pancake off Audra's plate and cutting into it.

"Hey! Those are mine!" Audra smacked Eric's wrist with a laugh and then hunched over her plate to protect it from any more food being stolen from her.

"He's right, you know?"

Audra stayed silent and avoided answering by shoving a big bite of pancake in her mouth. She made a non-committed noise and avoided looking at Eric.

"You have always been beautiful." Eric said softly.

Swallowing, Audra started to get annoyed. Here were two drop dead gorgeous guys that had never really shown any interest other than friendship to her, were now calling her beautiful and hitting on her after she's become Fae.

"Yeah, okay, you say that now. After I've transformed into this new being. Before, you saw absolutely nothing in me. And that's fine. I've seen the models that walk out of your house in the morning. Nothing like me, whatsoever." She pushed her plate away and leaned back in her chair, crossing her arms over her chest.

"Maybe I was just waiting for you." Eric looked at her through hooded eyes and smirked. That cocky, panty-dropping grin that she had seen him unleash on poor unsuspecting ladies on the rare occasions the three of them had gone out on the town.

"And why would you say that?"

"Because, Audra, you're a bit intimidating. You're strong and brave, you're selfless to a fault and gorgeous. But now, you're just like us. Fae. Magical." He turned towards her, leaning into her space.

A crash sounded from the kitchen, like a plate breaking and a pan dropping at the same time.

"Sorry." Luc said harshly, through clenched teeth. Even from the dining area, Audra could see Luc's fists clenching over and over. His chest was heaving as he looked like he was trying not to punch the cabinet door.

"So," Audra said after she got over her shock, to try to draw attention away from the awkward tension that was very quickly rising in the room. Luc was upset and Eric was telling her, albeit in a backhanded, complemented kind of way, that he liked her? She couldn't deal with either of their shit right then. "How do I work on my powers? Nothing has happened yet."

"Like we said when this started, everyone is different. Your powers could need a catalyst to come to the surface. You have been living in the human world for a very long time." Luc said, his voice still tight and rough as he dropped a tea towel on the counter and came to sit at the table.

"So, what, I need to touch fire or ice or something like that?"

The two of them shared a look and Audra knew them well enough to know that the look passed between them meant she was not going to like what they said next. But at least it wasn't awkward anymore.

"Not exactly." Luc said slowly.

"Then what? Just tell me for fucks sake."

"Audra," Eric said, drawing her attention to him, "most magic is tied to emotion. So, when you're angry or overwhelmed, your magic has the possibility to flare. Like when we were fighting, and the ground started to shake. For some people, it's calmness that strengthens their magic. Everyone is different. But the easiest way, the simplest way to check what works for you is to cycle through strong emotions."

That was...surprising. She realized that she had been calm, relaxed even since she woke up and there was no sign of her powers. She didn't feel any sort of difference.

"Why do you both look like you're guilty of something?"

Luc's gaze was down on the table as he traced the patterns in the wood and didn't try to meet her eye line. Eric was staring right at her, but his gold eyes were filled with intrigue.

"We are going to have to elicit strong emotions. Good and bad." Luc told her, his voice was almost pained, as if it upset him about her not fully understanding what was going on and making him say the words.

"I know, *we* know, you well enough to know what might cause a reaction. But I'm worried that you might be upset with the methods we are going to have to use to bring your magic out." Eric explained as his grip on his fork tightened to the point that Audra was worried the metal might bend to his will.

"You're not going to hurt me, right?"

"Not willingly."

"Not physically." The guys answered at the same time.

"I can handle it. Let's get started." Audra said, her voice full of confidence. She wasn't sure she had in his type of situation, but she would do whatever she needed to.

She stood from the table, taking her empty plate, and put it in the sink. When she turned to look at the boys, they were still sitting, locked in a silent argument.

"Is this going to be a problem? I'm sure I can figure out some shitty memories and things that have hurt me on my own." Audra snapped. Successfully pulling the two out of their staring contest.

"No, princess. No problem. Let's go." Eric said, rising from the table and setting his plate in the sink on top of hers.

"Eric..." Luc started to say, but Eric cut him off with a severe look.

"I'm doing this." He snapped to his Lieutenant.

"I can help...Let me." Luc started to offer.

"No. I'm going to do this." Eric said. He wasn't smiling at Audra, but his expression was sinister. She started to wonder what exactly this all entailed.

"I'm going to go out on the porch." And she turned around, leaving them alone in the kitchen to keep herself from worrying too much.

* * *

The sun was shining, the pine trees provided the illusion of being secluded, which Audra guessed they were. She was way too out of it with pain when they were driving up here to notice how far they were from the city.

It was like stepping into a picture-perfect oasis built for the purpose of connecting with nature and being with your family. The deck was a wrap-around porch, well-maintained wood, and clean seating. The porch swing hanging from the ceiling was calling her name.

She'd always wanted one as a kid. She thought they were meant for relaxation in the early morning to watch the sunrise and at dusk to watch the sunset. Audra remembered the night she confided that wish for her future with the boys. They had all been discussing what they wanted in life after; after college, after their design job had run its course, after everything that was standing in their way. She wanted stability; a home, a place to finally feel safe and comfortable.

The light breeze made the trees sway and blew the fresh, clean forest smell into her face. She took a deep breath, letting the air free of fog and pollution that is so thick in the city.

Audra was met with an overwhelming calmness that settled within her. She could almost let her guard down and feel that she was finally where she had always dreamed of. Safe, comfortable, completely relaxed and calm.

The porch screen door creaked, but she didn't turn to see which of the men followed her out here.

"I'm sorry about him." Luc said softly as he sat down next to her on the swing.

"There's nothing to be sorry about."

"I think there is." Luc sighed. "He's very invested in helping you reach your full potential with your gifts. Your parents asked us to show you the ropes and so Eric is trying to go full speed ahead." Luc shook his head.

"It's fine. Are...Is it important to them that I can use all my powers?"

"I don't think that's what they meant. But that might have been how Eric took it. I'm not sure, but regardless, if he does anything..." Luc let the sentence drop and took a deep breath.

"It's okay."

"It's not okay, not at all, if it makes you uncomfortable. I saw how you looked at him with apprehension and fear before you walked out here."

"I just had concerns about how he was going to bring my powers out. We all were friends in the city, good friends, now he is telling me he thinks I'm beautiful, like wants me-wants me and then saying he is going to elicit strong negative and positive emotions in some way while looking at me like a predator that just caught its prey. I'm getting whiplash. It's getting weird. But right now, the only situation that he needs to worry about is helping me figure out my powers and bringing me to my kingdom. That's all I'm focusing on."

Luc nodded; his mouth was pressed into a thin line.

"I understand. But realize that I won't let him hurt you, so you will tell me if he does something that makes you feel off." He told her. His tone was dominant and protective but laced with obedience. Something that she had only heard in movies about royals, his tone was indicative of a loyal servant serving his Princess. "But if I may?"

Audra nodded, "Haven't you always?"

He chuckled, and she realized just how much things had changed between them all, and in such a short amount of time.

"Eric tends to be laser focused and will not take no for an answer. If you feel like you need a break or you need to go cool off, do not let him bully you into pushing too hard."

Audra could feel herself clenching her jaw, she could feel her teeth grinding together.

"I can do this." She said resolutely.

"What do you mean?" Luc shifted his body, so it was angled towards her. It showed her just how much he cared about what she was going to say. Luc had a talent of listening while multitasking, but you could always tell if he was really interested or invested in what the discussion was if he turned his full attention towards you.

"I mean, I can do this. I can defend, protect, and make sure I am okay, all by myself. But I also mean that I can learn these powers, I can learn about that other realm, and I can become the best Princess I can be so that I make my parents proud. I just need to get started."

Luc sat completely still.

"You think so, right?" She added softly, her insecurity bleeding through.

"Audra, of course I do. You can do anything and everything you set your mind to. I've seen it before when you were working multiple jobs and going to school just to make a better life for yourself. You never give up. And now it shouldn't be any different. You won't give up and will become the best Princess Vesperitus has ever seen." Luc wrapped his large hand around her small one, resting their entwined hands on her thigh.

"I've always been here for you Audra. Things are going to be difficult, but I am here for you through the thick and the thin."

Audra could feel tears start to line her eyes. Luc didn't make deep, strongly emotional declarations. He was the type to act. He would make her food if she was worried about not having the money to buy groceries or once Audra had walked into her apartment and found Luc fixing her radiator when it was on the fritz during a snowstorm.

Never had she heard him say anything so emotionally. He usually showed her how much she meant to him.

"Thank you." She whispered, but the emotions were so strong, so overwhelming that she couldn't help the tears that fell.

"Oh, don't do that." He groaned. "I didn't mean to make you cry."

Audra let out a watery laugh and wiped her cheeks.

"These are happy tears. But I guess we should get to work, shouldn't we? You guys said that this wasn't going to be a pleasant experience."

"It won't be terrible if we can help it, but we do need to discover your triggers. Eric...well, Eric wants to be the one to help you."

"I'm ready."

Luc chuckled again as he ran a hand through his hair.

"Oh, trust me, we know you are. But can I ask you for a favor before I send him out here?"

Audra nodded and crossed her arms over her chest.

"Don't let him fixate on any one thing for too long. He might push you in one direction but make sure that he doesn't see exactly what it is that makes you emote. Keep some of those trigger's secret. You are the Princess here; we work for you."

Audra let his words sink in. Luc was staring at her intently, waiting for her to say something, but she was confused. Did Luc know something she didn't? Did Luc not trust Eric like she did?

"I understand." She nodded subtly.

Luc stood from the porch swing and stood in front of Audra, staring into her eyes. She wasn't completely sure what he was looking for within her eyes, but he must have found it because he nodded and turned his back on her, striding into the house.

Audra took a deep breath of the fresh air, preparing herself for Eric to come find her so they could get started with this discovery torture.

"Are you sure?" Eric asked as he stepped through the screen door and his eyes seemed to drink her in.

"What choice do I have?"

Chapter Ten

They stood out in the field in front of the farmhouse. It felt good to be outside; the sun beating down on her skin, the breeze lightly blowing in the air, the birds chirping. It was a beautiful day, and she seriously hoped that the weird emotional trigger thing that they said she needed to do wouldn't ruin it. Both Audra and Eric were standing facing each other, stuck in a staring contest, almost as if Eric was searching for any doubt within Audra's eyes.

He isn't going to find any.

"You both have warned me this isn't going to be pleasant, so just get on with it. What, are you going to hurl insults at me? Bring up my parents, abandoning me? Maybe take the different foster family's issues out for a ride? Let's go." Audra snapped.

And in that moment, Audra saw a viable change in Eric's demeanor. Gone was the flirtatious, confident man, and in his place was the dangerous warrior he told her he was. His eyes hardened. The gold seemed to solidify. He stood straight as an arrow, which caused his firm chest to puff out slightly and made his pecs and shoulders seem even more muscular than they already were. But the biggest change was that there was no smile gracing his lips. Eric always walked around with some kind of cocky smirk or even a full smile on his face. Audra always thought that he resembled sunshine personified, always making everyone around himself brighter.

But it was like the sun had set. In the worst way.

"Okay, *Princess.*" He sneered the word, the way he said it was not meant to be a respectful title, but a taunt.

Eric started to circle around her, taking in her body in a learful way before stopping and rolling his eyes.

"Well, we obviously have an enormous amount of work to do to get you ready."

Audra clenched her teeth. She was not used to him looking or talking to her like this. But she followed his directions.

"Good little girl, maybe she can follow simple directions." He taunted her again as he followed her into the yard.

"You think that this male bravado bullshit is going to get a reaction out of me?"

"Oh, my. What a mouthy bitch you are. But let's see how brave."

Before Audra could realize what was happening, Eric lunged for her. His fists were raised, and she felt a booming pain in her arm from a solid punch to her shoulder.

"What the fuck, man?" She yelled to him as she held her throbbing shoulder.

Eric didn't answer, just sneered, and chuckled mockingly at her. That sound seemed to reverberate through her head. Eric had never laughed at her with malice. He had laughed at her, in jest, in agreement, in fun. But never with an evil edge to it.

"Back off." She hissed through clenched teeth.

"It was one punch. You are so weak." He laughed again, the sound making her heartbreak and her temper rise at the same time. Eric lunged again, this time his fist connecting with her chest, causing her to fall back and wheeze as the air was literally knocked from her lungs.

"Motherfucker." She gasped.

Eric stood over her, his eyes alight with humor as he took her in.

"I usually like my women on their backs. But..." He trailed off, leaving her to fill in the rest of his sentence.

"But not you." She imagined he'd say. *"But I don't even want to think of you on your back for me."*

Humiliation and anger flared through her again, and her fists balled. As he laughed that mean, sickening laugh again, she threw a punch at him. He had been leaning over so close to her that her fist connected with his jaw and snapped his head up.

Eric didn't move. He was built like with long, lean muscle after all, but the hit had definitely surprised him. Audra could see surprise in his eyes before the cold, mocking mask slid into place.

"Like I said, you're weak."

Enough was fucking enough. Audra felt a warmth grow in her chest, anger, and need rising. A need to prove him wrong.

Her vision tinged red, and she could feel the warmth turn hot.

"Wanna bet?" She snarled as she stood up and raised her fists, preparing to fight him even if there was no way she would walk away. She had never been in a full-blown fist fight before, let alone with a man who had at least 30 pounds of muscle and 5 inches on her. All that didn't matter, she would win. Her anger and adrenaline were running too hot now.

"Let's fucking go." She snapped.

"Audra..." Eric started, his hands up in surrender.

"Not so much to say now, huh, big man? What's the matter, don't want to fight now? Well too bad."

"Audra... look."

Audra was seething still, the hotness and tight feeling in her chest was only growing. But she looked down at her hands, still balled tightly for a fight, and they were on fire.

She stared and stared.

The flames were blue at her hands, but a beautiful orange and red the higher they went. She felt no pain, no uncomfort which was surprising, off-putting.

"Are you okay?" Eric's voice floated in. She tore her gaze from the dancing flames she had created and nodded.

"I told you, I had to find a trigger."

Audra nodded again.

"Can you make the flames stop?"

Panic set in. She didn't know how to make the fire die down. Would they hurt someone? They didn't seem to hurt her, but maybe that was because the fire came from her.

"I can't. I don't know how. Oh god."

The flames shot up higher from her hands, causing Eric to jump back slightly to keep himself from catching.

"Relax, try to calm down."

"Calm down? Calm down?! You're expecting me to know how to calm the fuck down after this! I don't know how to get them to stop!"

The flames grew from her hands yet again. They had to be close to 7 feet high by now.

At least Eric had them go into the grass, so the house isn't in danger. Audra heard the screen door smack against the wall and suddenly Luc was by her side.

"Audra, listen to me." Luc called to her, "listen to the sound of my voice. Relax, just relax. Let the tension and the fear and the rage go."

"I can't!"

"You can. You got this." She looked over at him, standing as close as he could to her without the flames burning his body. Proving yet again, that he wasn't leaving her alone. That they were in it together. Audra looked to Eric and saw him inch backward another step, but his eyes still held that interested, calculating look.

"That's it, Aud." She heard Luc's calming voice encourage her, and she saw the flames reduce to nothing. The more she listened to him, the more she felt herself come back to a neutral point.

* * *

The sun was beating down on her face. It was too bright, too much.

"Thank you, Luc. That could have been really bad."

"No problem. I could see the flames from the living room windows and needed to check on you." He said to her but was locked eyes with Eric.

"I had it under control." Eric mumbled.

"Did you? Because to me it looked like she was going to burn out and you were backing away from her." Luc's words to Eric were laced with venom.

"She wasn't calming down or listening." Eric said with a shrug.

"And so that makes it okay that you said, 'calm down' and she didn't, so you just leave her to burn? The fuck is wrong with you?" Luc shoved Eric back. He stumbled a bit but righted himself and shoved Luc back.

"You watch your goddamn tone with me, Lieutenant. I am still your First General."

"Then fucking act like it." Luc growled.

"Last warning. Now, leave so the Princess and I can continue our lesson."

"No," Luc said, crossing his arm in his black muscle tee that had Audra staring. The material of the shirt strained around his bulging biceps. "I'll be staying right here, making sure she is okay."

"What, don't trust me?" Eric taunted; the cocky smirk plastered on his face. His chest was buffing out and his hands found purchase on his hips. "Need I remind you that the King and Queen chose me for his assignment. They trusted me enough to ensure her safety and help her through the change."

"Luc, it's okay. I can handle it." Audra put her still warm hand on his arm, squeezing it slightly to pull him back from this stand-off.

Luc looked down at her. She could tell Luc was still very unhappy with the situation, but he was willing to trust her and back off. That's all she needed.

"So, fire. That's fun." Audra said cheerfully, trying to break the tension. The air was filled with masculinity and bravado, and it was killing Audra.

"Now we just have to teach you to control it. But remember what I told you about total elementals? You have all the elements. We now need to bring them all to the surface." Eric explained.

"Okay, let's get to it then."

"You almost exploded with fire, why don't we give it a minute." Luc snapped.

"We don't have time. I need to get this going. What was the fire brought on by? Rage?"

"You felt like you needed to prove that you weren't weak." Eric said.

Flashes of their fight came back to her, the hurtful words that he said, the mocking smiles.

"I said, let's get going." She told them through clenched teeth.

"I will have to antagonize you again."

"I know."

"Luc, go inside."

"I already told you that wasn't happening." He said with a snap.

By the time Audra brought her attention back to Eric, his mocking, sinister mask was back in place.

Fantastic. Audra fought to keep from rolling her eyes.

"So, you feel like you need to prove that you aren't a weakling? Haven't you always felt like that?" Audra felt her fingernails bite into her palms. "That's right Princess, you should feel weak. Weak and alone. Maybe except...when we moved in next door. Then you finally felt like someone cared. Finally,"

"Shut. Up."

"Don't you wish someone had cared about you growing up? It's a little too late now, huh? To have two random guys who have spent the better part of three years lying to you, care even a little? Talk about damaged goods." Eric sneered and said with an awful smile on his face.

Luc shut his eyes and took a deep breath, letting the scene play out but having a very hard time at letting it happen. Audra could feel the tension radiate from him.

"You know I have to do this." Eric snapped at Luc, who was standing on the side clenching his fists over and over. Audra looked over at Luc and saw that his eyes were that bright aqua, like they turned when he was using his magic.

Audra wasn't going to let Luc's protective ass stop her from unlocking another element. No matter how hurtful the method was.

"Why? Because it will elicit some reaction? Pull on some emotion? Why can't we try some fucking positivity instead of you saying things that you know will piss me off? Or should I pull some of the things that I know about you to do the same?" Audra knew Eric wasn't trying to intentionally hurt her, that he felt like this was the only way to pull her magic out.

But she didn't want this to work like that.

"I know how to use my magic. It's a part of me now. I barely need to think of it before I use it. You, newbie, don't know anything." Eric said and pushed her down. Her back hit the grass and the wind was knocked from her. Eric laughed loudly, cruelly, as he leaned over her.

"I'm telling you now, this isn't going to work for me. You said positive *or* negative emotions, but you seem to think that only the negative will wake my magic up. Let's try something better. I'd prefer our friendship to make it out of this intact."

Eric smirked but rolled his eyes. He let out a sigh and dropped his hands to his side.

"We can give it a shot, but if it doesn't work, don't get discouraged. Negative emotions usually get a quicker response. What did you have in mind?"

She couldn't help but smile as she stood up.

"Thank you."

"Can I step in then, if you're not going to bully her into submission?" Luc said from the sidelines with a sneer at Eric.

"You're getting on my last goddamn nerve with all this second guessing your commanding officer. The next fucking time you speak to me like that, I'll be demoting your ass. Understood?" Eric held his hand up towards Audra in a sweeping gesture. "But if you feel that strongly, by all means." Eric walked away, turning his back on them both as he walked into the house, letting the screen slam as he disappeared.

"I'm very close to pummeling his face in." Luc said under his breath, just loud enough that Audra could hear him.

"It's not worth it. It's fine, I'm fine. Let's get started."

"What did you have in mind?"

"Honestly, I don't know. I just wanted him to stop being such an asshole."

Luc laughed and held both her hands in his. His rough thumbs swiping over the backs of her hands.

"I want you to close your eyes." Luc said, asking her to do so softly. She let her eyes slide shut.

"Now imagine a stream, a bubbling stream running through the forest. The water is calm and clear. You can see the smooth rocks under the water, the small fish swimming. You can hear the birds singing in the trees and the crickets chirping. The sun is shining down overhead and warming your skin, but the breeze blows through the trees, cooling you and making the leaves rustle."

His voice is low and soothing, transporting her to the place he was describing.

She relaxed into the picture he was painting and shivered at how sexy he sounded. She could really feel the sun beating down on them and the breeze picking up around her.

"We follow the stream down, walking hand in hand along the grass until the steam opens into a large pond. A pond surrounded by trees and wildflowers. The perfect oasis."

She sighed in contentment and held his hands tighter. She felt so at peace, relaxed and looked after. Within her chest, she felt a tug, a pull that whooshed up and out. She opened her eyes and looked around her, wondering what that feeling could be. That's when she saw it. A faint shimmer around the two of them, like a ripple in the air.

Audra pulled her hands from his and walked closer to the shimmer. It was like looking through a sliding glass door. You could tell something was there but there was a barrier.

Slowly, carefully, she lifted her hand and pushed the shimmer.

All she felt was a force of wind. She could feel it, the air circulating and protecting her, them, in a bubble. Audra knew that nothing would be able to penetrate the wall of wind, but it seemed like an extension of her peacefulness. She had created it subconsciously, to keep them safe, protected, loved.

"I did this." She whispered, barely loud enough to be heard over the low hum of the wind.

"You did. Do you know what you were feeling to make the air element wake up?" Luc came up to stand behind her, close enough that she could feel his body heat, but not too close where she felt trapped. Eric was standing out the barrier, his mouth open like he was talking to them, but she wasn't able to hear anything.

"Peace."

Audra nodded without turning around.

The moment seemed to stretch on, with neither of them speaking.

"I need to tell you something." Luc broke the silence with a rush.

"Yes?" She said, still enamored with the barrier she had created.

"I care for you."

"I care for you too." She said, turning to face her bearded friend with a smile.

"No, Audra. I really care for you. As more than a friend."

"Since when? Since I changed into a prettier version of myself? Since I became powerful?" She was frustrated, annoyed that these declarations hadn't come when she was just herself and not Fae.

"Since the moment we ran into you on the stairwell of our apartment building. You've always been beautiful. You've always been sweet. Becoming Fae...it doesn't change how I felt for you before. I don't care about your power. If you want to skip town and forget about this, I'll go with you. If you want to train to become a warrior, I'll do it with you. I never want to make you feel like you are stuck. And I don't mean to make you feel uncomfortable. But I had to tell you how I feel." Luc said, his words genuine and held a hint of desperation. Audra lost the anger that she had felt brewing before, left with surprise.

"Really?" She asked, her voice barely above a whisper.

"Really."

The barrier slowly dissipated slowly as the two of them stared at each other. Audra was at a loss for words. She hadn't ever really let herself think about engaging in a relationship with their man because they seemed so perfect, so unattainable to her, so she settled on being their goofy friend. But now, here she was suddenly having the option of being with them.

She would be lying if she said she didn't want to grab Luc by the neck and pull their lips together just to see how he'd taste. But she couldn't do that now, not when she didn't know how she truly felt.

"What in the actual fuck was that? Didn't you guys hear me screaming at you! Come on!" Eric was exploding with anger towards them, effectively breaking the bubble between Audra and Luc.

"I don't know." Audra said softly. She wasn't lying. She really didn't know how she had made it happen or if she could do it again.

"Air. When she was at peace, her air element woke." Luc reported to Eric, positioning himself slightly in front of her between her and Eric.

"Good. We only have two more to go then. Are you able to handle a little more pushing, little girl?" Eric taunted Audra, faking a pout as if he thought Audra was hiding behind Luc.

"Fuck off, man." Luc rolled his eyes.

"Do you always have other people fight your battles? Already a High Royal, letting everyone else do your dirty work."

"That's not what's happening." Audra's voice shot out.

"Then please, enlighten me as to why Luc feels the need to talk for you." Audra could hear Luc growl from beside her as she stepped around him to face Eric straight on.

"Don't bring Luc into this. You're being nasty to me. You know you're only doing this to awaken my magic. So, stop getting so into this fucking character."

"Who says it's a character? Maybe I've been this way all along."

"Then I feel sorry for you." Audra crossed her arms over her chest.

Eric tipped his head back and laughed.

"That's rich. Tell me, why does the naive little girl feel sorry for me?"

"Because if this is really how you are on the inside, then no wonder you constantly have a string of lovers that never want a second night with you and sneak out at the break of dawn. I thought you were different; loving, strong, and funny. It's disappointing that you think you're not that way."

"You bitch." Eric snarled, his expression turning dark and evil.

"You were being nasty to me, so I'm just being nasty back! Turnabout is fair play!" Audra shouted.

"Calm down, General." Luc said, low and dangerous from behind her.

"You...you think you're so much better than everyone, simply because of the family you were born into!" Eric crowded Audra and pointed a finger at her accusingly. "But you're going to destroy Vesperitus. Peace isn't always the answer. Sometimes you have to dig deeper, play by a new set of rules and hope for the best. You think you know the first thing about being a Total Elemental, being a High Royal? I've been there for the King and Queen for years, years! I've dedicated my life to protecting the crown, to protecting and fighting for my country. But you are going to get all the power; both magical and political. And you're going to fail." Eric struggled to breathe, his rant turning more and more venomous as he went on.

"Fuck you!" She yelled. Audra knew she couldn't talk to him while he was like that and any other discussion they might have would only end in more screaming, so she tried to storm off.

Only to fall a good three feet from a formation that had randomly formed under her feet. In fact, looking around, Audra could see boulders of dirt formed where there used to be green grass. It looked like there had been a hailstorm but instead of hail, there were large earth boulders.

"Audra, are you okay?"

"Did I do this?"

Luc nodded, "Yeah, you did. Earth magic."

Audra climbed to her feet and noticed one of her ankles was tender from the fall.

"I wonder what brought it on." She started to hobble towards the porch to sit.

"Rage, despair, annoyance, I mean, just pick one." Luc slipped his arm under hers and helped her walk across the field.

"Let me help you." Eric said as he slung his arm around her waist to support her weight for her.

"I can walk by myself, guys."

"We know you can, but you don't need to."

"I'm going to go inside...I need some time. I'm sorry Audra, I know our arguments were the most pleasant thing, and I didn't enjoy acting like that to you. I hope you didn't either." Eric said, showing her that she had hurt his feelings with the things she had said.

They approached the porch just as Eric stepped out, letting the screen door slam behind him.

"What now?" Audra said, crossing her arms over her chest and staring down at her ankle.

"We made sure your ankle is okay. We rest a bit and then we keep going." Luc said softly, taking off her tennis shoe, then poked and prodded her skin and when his thumb hit one particular spot, she winced.

"Not broken, just sprained. We are done for today." Luc said.

"Thank god." Audra said sharply. It had been too much today. Her body felt great, healed, and strong, but the emotional and mental hurdles from everything were weighing on her. She put her remaining energy into getting back into the house so she could lay down on the lumpy couch and try to keep her heart together.

She was done, her energy zapped. Three out of four elements in one day and high emotions.

She needed to sleep.

She needed to keep herself together.

She could do this. She was meant to do this.

* * *

The now familiar feeling of the dream meeting with her mystery man swirled around her.

"Sweetheart." The man was back. Audra breathed a huge sigh of relief. She realized she was quickly forming an attachment to this faceless man. Caring for him.

"You're back." She whispered.

"Of course. I'm always here for you."

"But you still won't show me your face?"

"Not yet, but soon."

"Again, with the 'soon'." Audra rolled her eyes and crossed her arms over her chest.

"I see you are fully through the Change. I can feel your magic and how strong it is."

"I am. I even had my magic awakened today." She said proudly. Even though she intrinsically trusted this person, she didn't know him. Didn't know who or what he was, so she was hesitant to give him all her information, her powers. The guys have said that Total Elementals are hunted and sought after. So, keeping that information close to the chest until she knows who her actual allies are is the smart thing to do.

"Which one?" The clicking of dress shoes against stone echoed throughout the area. She watched as his body was exposed bit by bit. First, she saw his black, shiny

dress shoes and long, lean, muscular legs wrapped in black, pressed suit material. Audra was prepared for the revealing to stop there, but to her surprise, he stepped farther into the light. She was able to see the white dress shirt tucked into his pants and his large hands slid into his pockets.

Just his hands sliding into pockets shouldn't be as fucking sexy as it was.

"Well?" He asked.

"What?"

"Which one?"

"Which one what?"

"Which affinity did you wake?" He asked with a chuckle. Audra's jaw dropped.

"How did you know?"

"I know everything about you, sweetheart. You're the first Total Elemental Vesperitus has had in centuries."

"Oh," she thought about everything, about the warnings Eric and Luc had given her. "How do I know you're not just using me? Somehow infiltrated my subconscious to gain favor and control." Audra stared into the direction that he was standing in. She could hear him take a deep breath and watched as he pulled one hand from his pocket and moved it up into the darkness.

"If that is what I wanted, I would have done it years ago. All I want is for you to be looked after, safe and loved. In fact, that's the only reason I haven't swooped in and taken you from the over-inflated ego, monkey man and the one who cares for you. Have you figured out which is which yet?"

"I have. Why don't you care for Eric? Why don't you trust him either?"

"Either?"

"Luc told me he doesn't trust Eric. And they've been working together for decades. So, I've been trying to keep my distance." She said with a shrug.

"He's a good man, that Luc. As much as I want you for myself, I understand how he could have fallen for you."

"You want me for yourself?"

"Is that not obvious?" The man's tone was low and husky.

"No, I guess it's not. At least not to me. Seeing as I can't see your face." She said with a smirk and a mocking tone.

"Again, sweetheart, I will reveal myself as soon as I can without putting us in danger. Come here." His hands reach out to her, and she quickly walked to take them, hoping that when she got closer, she would be able to see his face in the shadows. But when she reached him, his face was hidden securely behind an opaque wall of shadows and darkness.

His hands were soft, warm, and large, engulfing her hands. She loved how small she felt with him.

"Let there be no mistake. I want you. I want to be with you in every sense. You are beautiful and I adore you as a person, not just a Total Elemental or Princess. When I finally can be with you in person and reveal myself, I doubt I'll be able to control myself. So, you better be ready." His words were dangerous and deep. They sent a flush of arousal to her core. The way he was holding her hands and speaking to her showed her just how true his words were.

"I don't want you to."

The man groaned, the sound making her drip into her underwear, and she was sure she hadn't been so turned on ever.

The man retreated into the darkness, releasing her hands, and taking a deep breath. Audra bit her lip and stepped back as well.

"So which affinity?" His voice was strained.

"Air, fire and earth."

"Just water next."

"Almost done." She added. "What can I call you? It doesn't have to be your real name, but just something so I don't have to keep calling you 'The Man' in my head."

"You can call me... Seb."

"Seb. I like it." She smiled.

"Good." She couldn't see his face or his hands, but when he said that one word, she knew that he was smiling too.

Chapter Eleven

The sound of rain softly woke her from her nap. Audra could see that the sun had set through the large windows of the living room, an orange haze streaking through the sky along with the storm clouds rolling in.

"Good, you're awake. My ass is starting to hurt from sitting in this chair."

Audra's head turned in fright to the side where Eric sat, shrouded in darkness, in a wooden chair that could not have been comfortable at all.

"You didn't need to sit there while I slept."

"I did though. One of us has to be with you at all times."

"Oh great, your overprotective streaks are now in overdrive." Audra said with an eye roll. She looked around and saw Luc on the other side of the room. They really were protecting her on all sides.

"At least you know why we have always been so protective of you now. As the Crown's First General and Lieutenant, we are bound to protect the Princess at any cost." Eric said stoically.

"Protect the princess..." Audra trailed off, surprised at how much that hurt. That they only were protective and cared for her like they did because of their sense of duty. Her face fell.

"We did our best, are still trying to do our best." Eric said quickly, looking to Luc for help.

"You did great, both of you. Above and beyond."

"We tried. We saw you struggling, and we had to intervene. We couldn't take it. I couldn't take it. The winter we first met you, you were so skinny. It killed me to see your hollow cheekbones and hear your stomach growl. But we hadn't built the backstory enough to start giving you things. I'd watched you pass on taking extra tip money that Kalia offered you on shift. So, I knew you were very opposed to any kind of handouts. I had to build a relationship with you. Eric was easy to convince, he needed a way to get closer to you as well in order to protect you better." Luc said from the side, he hadn't made a move to come closer to her. That pull was still there. She felt slightly better knowing that he was in the room.

"Oh."

"Yeah. It was a lot of planning on our part. A lot of building a fake life in order to pass off as two bachelors who just moved to the big city." Eric said.

"I feel a bit blindsided, guys. I really thought we were all friends and being honest. I opened up to you about everything. And here I find out that you two were hiding massive things from me."

"General, may I have a moment with the Princess?" Luc said suddenly. If Eric was surprised by this, he didn't let on. He nodded to Luc and went to Audra, cupping her chin.

"I really am sorry, Princess." He said swiftly. His tone was half like a toddler who was being forced to apologize and half genuine apology. It was confusing to her.

Eric released her and walked straight out of the room, closing the door behind him without looking back.

Audra looked at Luc and he stood up silently, slid out of his chair to the ground and knelt in front of her. He wrapped both of her hands in his and brought them to his chest, placing her palms over his heart. She could feel the heavy *thump, thump, thump* of his heart beating.

"Please know that I have never lied to you about the things that are important. About who I truly am as a person. Yes, I have a water affinity and am from a completely different realm, but I didn't want to keep it from you. It was a direct order until you had started the Change."

"How can I trust you?" She said, her voice wobbling with unshed tears.

"Please, Audra. I will never lie to you again. How can I prove it to you?" He asked. His blue eyes, that reminded her so much of the deep ocean, were eager and hopeful.

"I don't know. I know you care for me. You show me every day. And I care for you, so much." Audra reached down and cupped his cheek, running her hand over his thick, dark beard.

"I have an idea." Luc said, standing up and pulling her up with him. "Come with me."

The two of them walked through the property, which was much larger than Audra had thought it was. Walking out into the thickly wooded areas, Audra could feel the energy from all the different life sources within the elements. The trees seemed to sway and talk to her, just nudging her as if to let her know they saw her. The breeze swirled around her, warming her, and making her hair lift. Electricity sparked invisibility through the air, letting her know that she could bring flames to life if needed.

It was amazing.

It was overwhelming.

"I understand how you're feeling. Well, maybe just a fraction of what you're feeling since I only have one element. But I still remember when water started reaching out to me. It was wonderful and scary, amazing, and awful, all at the same time. It gets better."

Audra nodded and kept following him, all while trying to ignore the energy poking at her.

"Where are we going?" She asked after a bit longer of exploring. It was obvious that Luc had a very specific location in mind. He had led her in all different directions, turning at random forks in the road. She wasn't one to go hiking or trapezing through nature, so she wasn't well-versed in subtle clues or recognizing landmarks.

"We're almost there. It's a small lagoon I found while exploring one day back when we first got here. My water magic seems to echo when I'm there, so I thought maybe..."

"Maybe it would be the same for me." Audra finished his sentence, and he turned to her.

"You're right. We don't need to push you in a negative manner in order to get your magic to awaken. It's hurting all of us. So maybe, just maybe, this area will help you and open you up to the water."

"It's worth a shot."

They continued to walk in an unknown direction in silence until they reached a thick grove of pine trees layered so thickly on top of each other that it looked like a solid wall. The spaces between were so tight that Luc pushed Audra in first so he could stand behind her in protection.

Luc's hand was on her lower back, keeping her calm as they weaved through the trees.

Audra stepped through the trees and was blown away with the view.

"Wow," she whispered, the view taking her breath away. How could such an amazing property be littered with different pockets of beauty?

"No one knows about it. Just me. And now you."

Her jaw opened slightly. The lagoon was pure and blue, the soft wind made ripples in the water. Around the water was a small sandy area, just enough for them to lay down and let the sun dry them off. The grass surrounding the water was thick, bright green, and soft. It was like a picture taken straight from a storybook. A small area forgotten by nature and perfectly preserved.

"Beautiful." Her breath was stolen from her at the sight. She almost didn't want to disrupt the beautiful scene. Like her presence would somehow taint it.

"Let's go for a swim." Luc said softly, pulling his leather jacket that he had thrown over his black t-shirt off and tossing it on a fallen tree.

The water was moving, dancing, and flowing around its area. Drops and orbs of water floating through the air.

Audra was mesmerized at the water, the way it was flowing through the air in controlled measures. The sunlight was reflected, and rainbows were visible.

Luc was standing at the shoreline, staring out into the water. He was showing her his magic, showing her that there was nothing to be afraid or nervous about. It was simply beautiful, peaceful.

Her chest felt lighter, the weight of her nerves lightening.

He turned around and smiled at her, then stripped his shirt over his head. The water continued to dance and float over the water, but her eyes were focused on him. His dark t-shirt fell on the ground and Audra's eyes drank in his toned physique.

He had always been in great shape the whole time she knew him, thanks to early morning runs and body weight workouts daily. Both Eric and Luc had tried to get her to workout with them, but after hearing their insane routine, she quickly declined for fear of embarrassing herself, but seeing Luc shirtless through her new eyes...

Suddenly Audra felt very hot.

His abs flexed as he unbuttoned his dark wash jeans and pushed them down, leaving him in his black briefs that hugged his body.

An audible gulp exited her body as her mouth became dry.

Watching Luc wade into the lagoon, the water pushing and flowing around him as his strong legs led him deeper and deeper into the water. She wanted to be in the water too; she needed to be closer to him.

Luc let the water under his control fall back into the mass, and water splashed down all over him, wetting, and darkening his dark brown curls.

It was secluded. It was quiet. It was oddly romantic.

"Come on!" Luc called over to her. "It's so nice in here!"

Audra didn't let herself think too much about undressing. She knew she wasn't as skinny as she used to be, thanks in a large part to Luc's nutritious meals and Eric's junk food habits. The extra food over the months had given her rounder hips and bigger breasts that spilled out of her too small bra cups. She pulled the borrowed t-shirt over her head and let it fall to the ground while she stepped out of the leggings she'd thrown on this morning.

Audra knew her chest looked amazing in her lace bralette, the one bra that fit her nicely, it was see-through, yet the wine-red color complemented her skin tone. She slipped off her leggings and dropped her clothes right next to Luc's.

Luc had not let his gaze stray from her for a second. He looked like he hadn't even blinked. Like he was scared to miss a moment.

The second Audra's foot touched the water, she felt the water element within her wake up screaming. It was like a toddler being woken up from a nap, reluctant but so happy to see their parents that they weren't mad, just overly excited. The water was overly excited that Audra was there.

She waded in until the water was touching her ribs and she was right in front of Luc.

His eyes had not strayed, drinking the sight of her in.

"You're beautiful. Gorgeous." He said with a sigh. His praise made her cheeks blush bright red.

"You are too."

"No Audra, you are...stunning. I really hope this is okay."

"What?" she asked as he leaned down and captured her lips with his. His hands came to her hips and pushed her up to his chest. Audra is taken aback for a split second, torn between giving into her growing feelings for Luc while recognizing the infatuation she has with the man in her dreams.

But she gives in. He feels too good not to.

There is no resistance from either of them as they fuse their mouths together. Lips, teeth, tongues fighting for dominance and Audra nearly fell from the aggression of their movements. She knew she would have if Luc hadn't leaned over and slid his hands under her, lifting her and holding her by the backs of her thighs.

His hands were so large, so warm, and he was so strong that it just added to her heightened arousal. Audra wrapped her legs around his waist, locking her ankles together.

"Luc..." Her moan was breathy and low as he moved his lips to her neck, lightly nipping at her.

In the back of her mind, Audra noticed that the bright sunlight overhead had started sparkling even more. The light had become fractured. Sending small prisms of color all over.

Audra turned her attention to his neck, grabbing at the wet strands at the nape of his neck and giving him open-mouthed kisses to taste more of the warm skin and sea air that was pure Luc.

She heard his low growl rumbling deep in his chest. She loved it, how he responded to her, and how he obviously enjoyed her touch.

"Baby, baby wait." Luc whispered, but Audra was having none of it. His scent and feel were too much for her, too intoxicating for her to pull away from him.

She felt like a woman possessed. Everything was Luc, his touch, his taste, his smell.

"Audra," His voice dropped even lower, his tone more in control and her body jolted as he gently pulled away. "Wait."

All her movements halted, and she did what he asked. She waited.

The look on Eric's face was a mix of guilt and regret.

"As beautiful as everything is right now, as amazing as you are, I don't want our first time to be here." He gently pushed a lock of her hair out of her face as she felt herself become more in control. "Plus, look around us."

Audra, still clinging to Luc, her core still on fire, looked around them. An encasing of water swirled around them. A wall of shimmering waves, constantly moving, ever changing, but always maintaining the shape of a dome around the two of them.

"So, I take it that your water element has woken up." Luc said with a smirk, his eyes full of pride.

"It looks like it did. I wonder what caused it." Audra said with a teasing tone, and she wrapped her arms around his shoulders and pulled him in tighter.

"I'm just saying, it seems like making out with me caused you to feel something *strongly.*"

"The same could be said for you." She joked, shifting her hips up to feel how he had also gotten excited.

"Touche, Aud." He chuckled, seemingly unembarrassed about her calling him out.

"It's beautiful." Audra whispered, enamored with the walls of water, siphoned from the lagoon to protect them like a chrysalis.

That seemed fitting, Audra thought. A chrysalis, strong and shiny, encasing her to then - when she was ready - break apart to reveal her new, true self. Her past, the hard start to her life, only to have it be broken wide open to let her emerge stronger. Her human form changing and evolving into her Fae form.

"You're beautiful. It makes sense that your magic and all its forms are as well." Luc held her close, staring deeply into her eyes. She could see the truth behind his words.

"Thank you. For everything."

"You don't have to thank me."

"I do though. You have been in my corner since the day I met you, all that time ago. You both have done more for me than I even knew back when we were in the city. And now I find that you've been doing and working to be better for me since before you even knew me. I don't know how I can ever repay you." Audra could feel her heart lurch. He really had done so much for her, and she didn't even know it. He had completely changed his life, just for her.

"Audra, look at me." A strong finger slid under her chin and tipped her face up towards him.

"I wouldn't change a thing."

Audra's heart threatened to beat out of her chest.

"Could we just stay here forever?" Audra hugged him tighter to her chest.

"If that's what you want. I'm sure we could figure something out. But if that is truly what you want, I will make it happen for you."

"But..." Audra could tell that there was more he wasn't saying.

"But" Luc ran his hand through his wet hair. "If you don't, then the kingdom *will* fall into ruin. Anarchy and chaos will erupt and for the first time in millennia, Vesperitus will not have a monarch. But they could form a democracy of some kind."

"Could someone else not become King or Queen?"

"It *has* to be a High Royal. Someone from the original bloodline of the total elemental. You are the first total elemental that has been born in about five generations. But the monarchy falling, that's the best-case scenario."

"What's the worst case?"

"The Dark Fae could gain control and your kingdom, your people, could become slaves to them, trapped in fire and brimstone, forced to do their evil bidding for the rest of their lives."

Chapter Twelve

Audra felt, more than saw, the water crashing down around them. Effectively breaking the dome around them and again sending water all over Luc.

Water forced his dark hair back down from where they had air dried in the sun from earlier. Luc wiped the water from his eyes quickly while shaking his head back and forth to get extra water from his hair and beard. Audra definitely would have been distracted with the view of him, glistening with water and basically naked, if her brain wasn't overloaded with the information, he had just dropped on her.

If she doesn't become Queen of Vesperitus, there is a possibility that the people depending on her will become virtual slaves; examples made and taken by the Dark Fae.

She still doesn't exactly know what it is that the Dark Fae do but based on the tone Eric and Luc take when they talked about them, Audra could tell that they weren't just a benign political group. Making a mental note to ask for more details later, Audra realized that the life that she had planned on, had worked for, was never going to happen. She wouldn't be able to become a teacher, she wouldn't be able to buy her own house or live a ridiculously normal, but happy life. If she chose to run away, even if she did get to bring Luc with her, she would never be free. The guilt and pressure would eat her alive. Knowing that people were suffering because of her, because of her selfishness, was almost enough to bring her to her knees.

"You'll teach me?" Audra asked, her voice was husky with emotion and nerves.

"About your powers? Yes, I told you we would."

"No," she shook her head, meeting his eye. "I mean, you'll teach me how to be a Queen, a Queen they deserve."

Luc's jaw dropped slightly, then closed quickly. It happened again, his mouth opening and closing, and his head tilted to the side. It looked like he wanted to say something but thought differently. She could feel the relief emanating from him.

That was interesting to her. He had just said that he would help her stay here if she said she wanted to leave the royal life behind. But he didn't want to, or he had already come to the same conclusion she just did - that if they ran, there would always be the knowledge that they had condemned people who needed them.

"I don't know how to be a Queen. I barely know how to be an adult! But if this is my destiny, what I was born to be, if people are depending on me, I need to at least try."

Luc kissed her softly on the forehead, and she breathed in his intoxicating scent, letting it calm her.

"No one is expecting you to be perfect right away. There is a lot for you to learn, but everyone's main concern is bringing you home safely. Your parents, they are beside themselves with worry, knowing that you had to go through the change without actually knowing what was happening. Hell, I was worried, and I got to be here taking care of you."

"I have no idea what to do now." She whispered towards his chest.

"I do." Luc said, as he dropped a kiss to the top of her head. "You are going to learn how to control your elements and you are going to let us help. You are also going to let us protect you, however we have to. You went through the change, which means your scent has changed and is now noticeable to Fae and creatures alike. More dangers could come to you if we aren't careful."

Audra nodded. A flash of the dead man with fangs trying to break into her apartment, whispering over and over how he 'needed to get in, needed to get her' ran through her head and caused a shiver to run down her spine.

"I'll be careful."

"Damn right you will. I just got you. Nothing is separating us now, baby." Luc said, as he flashed her a toothy grin that made her insides warm.

She reached up on her tiptoes and planted a sweet kiss on his lips. The water rippled around them, creating soft waves on the surface. It wanted to play with her, but she had no clue on how to talk back.

"How do I learn to control my powers?"

Luc gave her a confident smirk.

"Let's get to work."

* * *

"I'm fairly certain you're just trying to get me to light myself on fire for your own enjoyment." Audra panted. She was trying to keep the fire in front of her going, while also forming a makeshift fire shield in front of her, all while Luc was circling around her, calling out shapes or animals for her to make the flames form into.

"You know I just started training *today*, right?"

"Yes, Aud, I know. But do you know that *you* are prophesied to have more power, more strength, and more control than all of your previous ancestors? You already intrinsically know what to do and how to control the elements. You just need some more practice and for us to build up your stamina. The fact that you are even creating a controlled fire is astonishing for being so new."

"I can think of a few more enjoyable ways to build up my stamina." Audra said under her breath.

"I heard that."

Her face felt very hot. But she was sure it had nothing to do with the flames in front of her.

"It's true!"

"Be that as it may," Luc said, his tone shockingly strict and concise as he came to stand in front of her with his hands clasped behind his back. The stance made his already large chest look so much broader.

Audra tried to contain her thoughts.

"You need to build up your elemental stamina. Using magic will drain you quickly if you just barrel in. If you're in a fight where you need to keep a flame going while also trapping an enemy in stone while keeping a wall of water between you and the rest of the enemy, you will need to have stamina and good control so that you don't just pass out. It takes time and practice, but you can do it."

Damn him and his logic.

"Fine." She said through clenched teeth as she redoubled her efforts into making a horse grow from the fire in front of them. Audra felt a sweat droplet roll down the side of her face. It was physically and mentally taxing trying to hold on to the multiple strains on her power.

"It's important that you know how your magic feels, how your body reacts to you pushing yourself so hard. We don't want you to overdo it. It's vital that you don't overdo it."

Audra fought an eye roll. If it was important that she didn't overdo it, then why is he forcing her to push so hard?

"You need to know the warning signs that you're going too hard."

"Aside from the obvious of knowing my own body, why do I need to go this hard if it will hurt me?" Audra could feel that the time under tension of just the one element taking its toll on her already. A headache was starting to form behind her eyes, but she pushed through. Audra was nothing if not stubborn. She was determined to do more, do better. It had only been maybe fifteen minutes of true power-draining drills of Luc talking her through what he wanted her to do. She didn't have much time, she had to make every moment count.

"Because, baby, I need to know the warning signs before you burn out. You're a stubborn one and if I don't take care of you, you'll go right to the brink. Dolphin and sword."

He wasn't wrong, but she wasn't going to let him know it.

"Baby, huh?" Audra said with a smirk and Luc just shrugged his shoulders. She liked it.

Audra ground her teeth and continued to keep her hold on the fire in front of her while trying to shift the flames into the different shapes he had ordered.

As the crude shield of flames twisted and warped into a long cylinder, tapering at the end into a sharp point. The flames danced in her hand. She could feel the heat, but there was not one lick of a flame that became too hot or burned her.

The headache pounded stronger behind her eyes.

Her nose started to run. Ignoring it, she forced her attention to the fire in front of her, forcing a dolphin to form above the orange blaze. When Luc started talking to her, the dolphin that she had conjured from the fire slowly fell apart. Like embers being blown from coals.

"Audra..." She heard faintly, but her ears were buzzing.

The dolphin was becoming clearer, more defined and Audra was in awe. The flames were flickering and fading yet kept their shape completely. Like the flames were staying inside invisible lines.

"Look at that." She whispered, amazed at what she had done.

"Audra, stop. Let it go!" She could hear Luc cry out from beside her.

"Look,"

"Baby, please." It was the panicked desperation that caused her to pull her attention from the orange flames.

He looked panicked. He was definitely worried and with fear swimming in his blue eyes, his eyes were shining again, and Audra could feel how close he was to drawing on his own magic. Just in case.

"Stop, let everything go." He stepped in closer to her slowly, so that she knew exactly where he was at each moment. No surprises.

Why was he acting so odd? Like she would hurt him. She would never, could never hurt him. But she was hurting; her head still pounded, her muscles were aching, the buzzing in her ears was getting louder and her nose was still running profusely. But still, she could not let the beautiful flickering dolphin disappear.

Audra wiped her nose quickly and a splash of bright color was all over the back of her hand.

"Audra...Please." His voice was drowned out by the loud buzzing.

"I'm bleeding." She whispered.

"I know." Luc brought his hands up and rested them on her shoulders. "Let the fire go."

Audra closed her eyes, breaking the connection. Once the connection was severed, it was like her own internal fire was extinguished as well.

Right before she lost consciousness, she saw Luc lunge to catch her. Her name on his lips as she fell.

* * *

"What the fuck happened?" Seb roared from the darkness.

"What?" Audra said sluggishly, her head still hurting. She reached up to wipe her nose to see if it was still bleeding, which it was.

"Why are you bleeding? Did Eric do something? I'll kill him." The voice snarled. Audra could hear his dress shoes clicking rapidly as he moved closer to her. He walked to her and fell to his knees next to her. Audra's eyes shot open because she thought she would finally be able to see her mystery man. But she was immediately disappointed.

He had somehow shrouded himself from the neck up.

"What?" She repeated, her brain trying to catch up to what he said.

"Eric. What did he do?" Seb's arms came around Audra's waist and propped her up on his thighs, holding her to his chest. She was so tired and weak that she let him move her around like a rag doll.

"Nothing. He didn't do anything."

"What happened to you?" His voice was soft and broken and he cupped her face.

"Magic overdid it. I was practicing with Luc."

"Luc, let you get like this?"

"He tried to stop me; I didn't know how."

"That surprises me." Audra felt him wipe the blood and sweat from her face softly, checking her for any bodily harm. Seb's hand waved over her body like a sensor, his open palm facing her body as he started from her head and moved it slowly down to her feet. She could feel a spark drag over her body in time

with his hand, sparking heat and arousal within her.

"You just need rest," he said with a relieved sigh. *"God, sweetheart, you scared the hell out of me."*

"I thought I was resting." She said with a bloody smile.

"Smartass."

"Just hold me while I sleep. Please. I feel so comfortable with you." She mumbled, her eyes closing, and she didn't have the strength to keep them open.

"Of course, sweetheart. Anytime you want. I just want to keep you protected, loved, and safe. If I can bring you any sort of peace, I will do it." He whispered. She could feel his breath on her hair as he pressed a soft kiss to her head. Audra tried to clutch at his white dress shirt, but she was falling into the deep darkness of the recesses of her mind.

* * *

"Why does this always seem to happen when she is practicing her elements? Will this always happen? It kind of sucks to be a babysitter." She heard Eric say gruffly, like a teenager who'd been asked to watch a baby when really, they just wanted to go out and party. Audra didn't know where she was, but her head was throbbing in pain.

"Shut the hell up, Eric."

"You were meant to be training her, not pushing her past her limit."

"And how are we going to know what her limits are if we don't push her? I tried to bring her back, but she became entranced. Look," Luc took a deep breath and forced it out. "I don't like it. Every part of me is screaming that I need to protect her and keep her hidden. But she wanted to learn. She needed to. I would much rather know her signs of when she is pushing too hard so that I can step in and give her strength because you know, *you know*, she will not ask for help. She is the strongest person I know, and I will do anything to keep her that way."

Audra groaned, being ripped from her dream by the arguing voices behind her. She heard Luc gasp softly and Eric must have walked away from Luc because footsteps rang out on the hardwood floors, walking away from her.

"Why are you guys fighting?" Audra croaked. Her head still felt heavy, but she was able to open her eyes. Slowly.

"Audra. Thank God." The relief in Luc's voice was heartbreaking.

"What happened?"

"I pushed you too hard. I'm so sorry. I can tell you and Eric and myself that I just wanted what was best for you and so that we knew your signs of fatigue, but it's killing me inside. We should've started slower. I mean, what the fuck was I thinking? You had just changed. God, I'm so stupid. I'm sorry, I'm so sorry." Luc rambled on; his large hands enveloped her one small one.

"It was a smart plan. You were right. I'm fine, I promise."

"You passed out! Your nose was bleeding, and you weren't responding."

"Luc, look at me." His gaze had fallen to where their hands were clasped together. She realized that she was once again laying on the lumpy couch in the sunroom they had first brought her into a few days ago.

"You made the right call. That's what you were doing. You were looking at my learning as a warrior would. Find the weaknesses and strengthen them. Honestly, if you had gone easy on me, I might have punched you. You know I don't take well to being treated with kid gloves." Audra pulled herself up to sit on the couch so that he could join her, see for himself that she was fine by closing the distance between them.

"You're a Princess, not a soldier." Eric muttered and rolled his eyes. Luc's head hung down and Audra knew then that Luc agreed with Eric on this one thing concerning her.

"You're right. I'm not your soldier. I'm your Princess. Not only am I determined to be strong with my powers, but also in fighting. I will not be some helpless damsel who can't do anything but call for a man to save her. And I'm telling you now, I am willing to do what needs to be done in order to have full control of my powers and be best prepared for what is lying in wait for us in Vesperitus. If that means I pass out from using too much power, so be it."

Eric nodded slightly, the gesture showing that he had listened and respected her words. It was a small step forward for them. Ever since Eric had tried to awaken her powers by being so cruel to her, the tension between them had dissipated. His declaration about thinking she was attractive, that tension between them had never been talked about or acted on, and if she was honest, she was relieved. She recognized that her attraction to him was very surface level and that her attraction didn't go deeper than that.

"I'm serious." Audra said as she tried to put as much authority in her words as she could.

"Okay, okay. Damn, Aud." Luc muttered under his breath, low enough for only her to hear.

"So there. It's settled. Now, I'm going to go shower, change my clothes and by the time I get back, I'm going to stuff my face with any food I find in the fridge. I'm so hungry." Audra stood up gingerly and stretched. She felt the sweat that had dried to her body, making her skin feel grimy and sticky, especially where it mixed with the blood along her face and neck. When she looked down, she saw blood droplets stained down the front of her borrowed shirt.

"Well, Luc, the Princess has spoken." Eric said with a chuckle, clapping his hand on Luc's shoulder. "Let's get food sorted."

"As you wish." Luc said with a sweeping bow and a wink at her as they both left the sunroom and let her go off to wash the day from her body.

Chapter Thirteen

The next morning Audra took her coffee cup outside to sit on the porch swing and just appreciate the morning. It wasn't something she often got to do in the city, and by not often, she never got to do it in the city. Life there was too hectic, too loud. There was always something that needed to be done; classes, work, studying, etc. As hard as it was, it was what she had been working so tirelessly for. She'd been determined to graduate and help people, but isn't it crazy how life changed for her so fast?

The boys and Audra had stayed up late to discuss their next steps and the timeline. She was meant to be in Vesperitus in no more than two months. Her parents were expecting her fully through the Change and with some understanding of her elements. Enough understanding to help the boys protect herself while they traveled.

It nearly brought tears to her eyes to realize that she would never see Kalia again, never complain about her job at Moe's or how exhausted from classes she was. Her shot at a normal life was well and truly gone.

A Princess. She was a goddamn Princess this whole time.

She still couldn't believe it and she seriously had doubts that it would sink in until she was standing in front of the Queen and her Consort.

Her Mother and Father.

She had parents who wanted her. They didn't just abandon her because they didn't want her or because they didn't want to be parents. If what Eric and Luc had told her was true, they left her because they wanted to protect her.

Most of the night she had spent tossing and turning, trying desperately not to think of the multitude of ways her life would have been different if they had just kept her close.

Taking a sip of her coffee, she stared off onto the property. Relaxing with each sound of the crickets and slight creak of the porch swing as it gently rocked her.

"You're up early." Luc said from the side. He hadn't opened the creaky screen door that would have alerted her to him standing there.

"I have a lot on my mind."

Luc walked out, letting the door slam softly behind him. He was still wearing his sleep clothes; black sweatpants and a white undershirt, his sleeve of intricate tattoos poking through the short sleeve and his hair rumpled with sleep still.

"I would be surprised if you didn't. You've learned a lot of life-changing things in a very short amount of time." He sat next to her, resting his arm behind her on the back of the swing.

"I don't know what to do. Where to go from here."

A dam broke inside her and all the fear, all the sadness, all the doubt, came pouring out of her. Tears started to stream down her cheeks, but she refused to make any noise. There was too much, too many emotions, that she felt like she was drowning.

"Audra, have Eric or I ever left you in a time of need since you met us?"

Unable to meet his eyes, she just kept her gaze on the milky coffee in her mug but shook her head.

And it was true. They hadn't ever left her when she really needed them. Not when she had the flu and couldn't keep anything down. Eric had stayed on her couch for the three days she was out for the count; forcing her to drink broth, wiping her forehead with a cool towel when the fever got too high, making sure she didn't stay slumped over the toilet after it felt like she was going to throw up her organs. They hadn't left her when she thought she was going to lose her apartment and Luc had gone out, found her five different places within walking distance that was hiring. Then he bought her groceries, so there was one less thing for her to worry about.

That was a moment when she broke down like she was trying to not do now. When Luc and Eric were standing in her small kitchenette, putting away at least three weeks' worth of groceries, she fell to her knees and cried. Eric had wrapped his arms around her and helped her stand. He hugged her tightly for a moment and then moved back to the kitchenette to joke with Luc. Luc had caught her eye, winked with a soft smile, and pulled out ingredients to make dinner. They both had stayed the evening with her until she had fallen asleep.

"And this is no different. We will not leave you."

His words broke her resolve, and a sob escaped her lips.

She hated crying in front of people. It made her feel vulnerable and weak. Audra had made it a point to only cry in front of a select few people that she explicitly trusted, like Kalia and the boys.

Luc wrapped his arms around her, letting her cry on his shoulder.

Audra heard the door creak, but she couldn't stop the spiral. There was so much changing, so much that had happened already, but so much more that she couldn't even imagine yet.

"What happened?" Eric's deep timber of voice rumbled in his chest, his voice still rough with sleep. Audra covered her face, pushing deeper into Luc's chest.

"She just has a lot going on, you know that. You can feel her." Luc mumbled, his arm holding her closer.

"I know you're feeling overwhelmed, but you don't have to keep it in. Talk to us." Eric said from the doorway.

Audra looked at him. He had always been the more open of the two. He was there for her to vent to, or for her to vomit her emotions all over. But somehow, this time was different. His eyes weren't open and welcoming. She could see him trying to put on a more caring expression, but it never reached his eyes.

Before, she would have opened up completely, trusting Eric entirely. But she didn't this time. Something felt off.

So, Audra sat up, wiped her eyes, and put on a smile.

"I'm good. Thanks though. Is there food for breakfast?" She said in a fake cheery voice. She didn't need to convince anyone but Eric that she really was fine, and he seemed to fall for it.

A small chuckle rumbled Eric's chest again.

"That's our Audra. Always wanting food. What do you want? I'm cooking this morning." He said.

"Pancakes with whipped cream and sprinkles!" She said excitedly. Eric would actually make her that because she asked, whereas Luc would try to make it healthy somehow. She turned back to see Luc's face, and sure enough, it was in a grimace. His blue eyes shrunk in disgust, but he stayed silent.

"You got it." Eric smirked and walked back inside, letting the screen door shut with a bang.

"You're not fine and I know it." Luc said softly.

"I know." Is all Audra said. The pair sat in silence for a moment, relaxing again into the soft rock of the porch swing and the peacefulness of the morning.

"What do I do now? Where do we go from here?" Audra groaned and tucked herself further into Luc's embrace.

"One step at a time, Aud. First things first; we need to get you used to your magic and trained. After that, we will figure out our next steps." Luc said calmly.

Audra was able to refocus on that, she only needed to focus on one thing at a time. She knew that they didn't have an unlimited amount of time to get things sorted, but she did have time to sort through it all. Bit by bit.

"Then let's start with my elements. I feel more comfortable with fire now, but I still have three to work on."

"We also need to work on not letting you push too far. Promise me, you won't go too far."

Luc was looking at her like he knew that she wouldn't listen to him, which she wasn't planning on doing, but he had to get the words out, anyway.

"I will do my best to recognize the signs of getting too close to my limit."

"Spoken like a true royal." Luc said with a smirk.

* * *

The sunlight reflected off of the lagoon, blinding her slightly as she tried to take in the beautiful oasis.

Luc and Eric had argued about which element to work on next, and water had won. Eric had wanted earth so that they could spend the day training together, but Luc had made some good points. If fire was the element, she was most comfortable with, then water would need to become second nature so that if anything out of control happened, she would be able to keep everyone around her safe by extinguishing the flames with water.

Since her water element had awoken, she was able to feel the energy and life floating through the water, in all water actually.

After Luc had decided, they were going to work on her water control today, he had informed them that they would be heading to the lagoon, and it was going to just be the two of them. He wanted her to focus, but she was fairly sure that all she would be able to focus on was what they did the last time they were there together. Alone. Isolated.

There they were the pair standing in the small hidden pocket of peace.

Audra tipped her head up, soaking in the warm rays of the sun shining through the tree leaves above.

"So, there are a few things that I want to try to work on today. First, manipulating water already present, creating water from water and creating barriers with water." Luc said.

"Oh good, nothing too big then." She said with an eye roll. Those things all seemed incredibly difficult.

"One step at a time, baby." He said, kissing her head softly as he passed her and walked around to the other side of the small lagoon.

As he walked, he kept his hand outstretched over the edge of the water. Small splashes rose abnormally high and floated in the air as he passed. As he walked past, the water floating in the air seemed to freeze.

When he got to the other side, half of the lagoon had a floating barrier. Luc hadn't even looked back to make sure that his magic was working. Audra stared on in awe.

Luc looked right at her, and with a blink of his eyes, the barrier dropped.

"Two birds, one stone." He explained with a shrug and Audra realized that he had both manipulated the existing water and created a wall. "Try to do what I did."

And that was how the rest of the morning went. Luc would demonstrate what he wanted her to try, and she would try to replicate it.

After a few hours, she was dripping with sweat. The baby hairs on her neck completely stuck to her. She was even out of breath, despite not having taken a step.

"Again." Luc ordered, standing next to her with his arms crossed as he waited for her to fill up a makeshift bowl he had fashioned out of a piece of bark.

Audra had been able to create water, pulling moisture from the air around her and condensing it to make water appear. It was by far the hardest thing she had learned today, and it had taken a long time and help for her to do it. Audra could feel the energy within her draining at an alarming rate but refused to wimp out. She could keep going.

As she grit her teeth, she focused even harder on the miniscule drops of moisture floating all around her. She couldn't see them, but she could feel them, feel them floating in the air like dust motes.

Her head was starting to hurt again, but Audra was sure it was just from the repetition and the strain of hard work.

The bowl slowly filled with water and Audra groaned. The relief of completing her task took some of the tension in her shoulders out.

Luc turned over the bowl, letting the water drop to the forest floor.

"Again."

I don't know how many more times I can do this. Audra thought, her headache starting to travel down her neck. She was sure she wasn't overdoing it, no spotty vision, no bleeding nose. But as soon as she focused on the water in the air again, there was a dark haze that came over her.

"Good job, Aud. Rest." Luc praised, and he lightly put his hand under each of her elbows. He must have seen her sway slightly.

I need to sit down. Audra thought, her legs starting to give way.

Her attention went towards finding somewhere to sit, as she steeled her spine to not pass out. Luc would blow a gasket if she passed out, especially after all the drama earlier.

She felt around for the fallen log behind her and rested her weight against it while holding her head, willing the pain to stop and the darkness to recede. Luc followed her, ready to catch her if she fell.

"You pushed too hard." Luc said, his tone equal parts frustrated and soft.

"I'll be okay. It's just a headache."

"You know I know you, right? I can read your body and you have some tells, baby. It was more than a headache and you know it. If I hadn't said stop then, you would have passed out. You would have pushed it too far instead of speaking up. You know what getting close to your limits feels like, yet you ignored it."

He was furious and scared but trying to show her logic. She knew she shouldn't be mad, but she couldn't help the anger that rose within her chest as well.

"I know my own limits. Trust me a little, why don't you."

"So, what, I should just let you pass out repeatedly until you get seriously hurt? Just let you push yourself until you can see straight due to pain? I'm not going to do that, so you might as well just get over it now and tell me when you need a break. We can't keep having this argument every day."

"I didn't lie! I sat down when I needed to!"

"After I had said you could. You most definitely would have kept going if I had asked you to do it again."

"You don't own me!" Audra knew that the anger wasn't fully just about this, but it didn't mean that it wasn't influencing her own feelings.

"You're right, baby, I don't. But I hope that I can be someone that you feel can protect you, care for you, save you if you ever need it. And I will, even if you fight me every step of the way." Luc's voice dropped as he continued talking.

He knew the effect his voice had on her, and he was using it to his advantage.

"Don't confuse love with possession. Our feelings for each other do not mean you get to make decisions for me." Audra tried to keep her tone strong and formal, but she could feel his attraction to her, and it only amplified hers towards him.

"I am going to protect you, as I always have. Even if it is from yourself." Instead of an angry tone, he was almost purring.

"Trust that I know my limits. I might push them sometimes, but how else am I going to grow?" Audra stepped into his chest. The both of them had been standing off like two warriors ready for battle. Luc's chest puffed out and his spine was ramrod straight, Audra had her hands on her hips and was not backing down. Even though Luc had a few inches of height on her, she was still tall and had the fire of an Amazonian.

They had already been standing toe to toe in their argument; defiance, anger and spite hung in the air, but now there was an electric charge between them.

A tension that crackled in the air, the kind that all it took was one look and they would be drawn together like moths to a flame. It was inevitable, and they both knew it.

"I trust you, baby. I hope you trust me too." Luc cupped her face as a panty-dropping smile that she hadn't seen on his face before. He never did use that ridiculously sexy smile on her, but she had seen it a few times when they had first met and had gone out for a drink as a group. Eric and Luc talked to some girls as she grabbed the next round. Eric had gone home with one of the girls, but Luc never did bring anyone home that she knew of.

Of course, Audra had been insanely jealous. Turning to the first attractive guy she saw and tried to flirt, which ended poorly. Her flirting game has never been strong.

"Don't try to flirt your way out of this."

Luc's smile morphed back into the genuine, loving one that she knew was just for her.

"I trust you with my life, with my heart. But Aud, you are not good at taking care of yourself. And you can't even deny it! We've always tried to take care of you in any way that we could and now is no different."

"Luc, I..." Audra started to say, lifting her hands out in front of her, then dropping them to her sides with a sigh. "I understand. I'm scared too, but the only way I won't be is if I keep working. I have to build up my stamina. I have to be able to use magic longer and with more force if we are attacked. I refused to be completely blindsided and helpless like last time. Not to mention, if I am going to take my place on the throne of Vesperitus and prove that I am worthy of being the first Total Elemental in centuries."

Luc was quiet at that. He must have been able to feel the steel resolve wrapped in fear behind her words.

After a few minutes of staring into her eyes so hard Audra was sure he could see each and every thought flowing through her mind, he let out a shaky breath and dropped his head in resignation.

"Fine. But no more nose bleeds. If there are, I step in. As soon as that headache starts, you stop. I told you overdoing it and draining your magic so extremely is deadly."

Audra beamed at the compromise. She knew it was difficult for him to willingly let her put herself in harm's way, even if it was necessary. She could feel the panic and helplessness rolling through him in waves.

Putting a hand on his chest and pressing her body into his, she nestled into his neck and took a deep breath. Audra could feel him do the same. The two of them wrapped themselves in each other.

"Nothing will happen to me." She whispered.

"Damn right. Nothing will happen to you. I just got you, I'm not letting you go without a fight." Luc kissed her forehead.

Chapter Fourteen

The pair decided to head back to the house soon after their reconciliation. Audra was starving from all the use of her power and her head was still killing her. Luc took the initiative and pulled her from the lagoon, walking hand in hand through the trees. The sunlight was peeking through the treetops, the birds sang around them. Audra had never much been one for nature, seeing as she had only ever lived in the city, but the longer, they were out in the open space, the more she found the beauty in everything around her.

Audra thought about their argument and how quickly things were changing. How much had changed and how much more was going to change? She understood that she couldn't go back to her daily routine, to her 'old' life of waitressing, struggling to make ends meet and putting everything into her classes. She didn't miss her apartment or the struggle to make sure she could eat that day and pay her rent while making sure her grades were high. But she knew that she would miss the safe house; this peace that they had found. What would happen when they inevitably went to Vesperitus?

It was a question that had briefly entered her mind, not wanting to think about how they would have to leave this perfect home one day. And every day the deadline to master her powers inched closer.

"What happens to the safe house when we go to Vesperitus?"

Luc was quiet while he walked, his large hand squeezing hers slightly. He could tell she was nervous about making that final step and leaving Terraus.

"We will have to leave it behind."

"But..."

Luc stopped abruptly, causing Audra to walk into his back.

"I know. But we have to. Once you become Queen, it will be expected that you live in the palace. The palace that you will be going to is magnificent; grand and beautiful. There are so many rooms, so many bathing areas, and ballrooms. Grand, beautiful ballrooms."

"But the safehouse...it's peaceful and comfortable."

"I know. Perhaps we can come visit."

"There has to be a way to, I don't know. Move it with us?"

"If there was a way, I would do that for you. But baby, honestly, moving a whole house is pretty low on my priority list right now. The top thing on my list is keeping you safe. Teaching you your powers and keeping you happy. Maybe later, when we get settled in Vesperitus, we can find a place like this. A place that brings you peace and calmness."

"You'd do that?"

"Of course, I would."

Audra was struck again with how amazing this man was, how selfless and devoted he was. Her heart fluttered in her chest, full of adoration and wonder for him.

* * *

The sun was setting when they broke through the tree line and the aged white, two-story house came into view. Audra felt melancholy as they walked towards it, sad with the knowledge that they would have to leave it before actually getting to thrive in it.

"Did you finally figure out the water element?" Eric teased, standing in the open front door, and Luc threw his middle finger up at his friend with an eye roll while Audra just laughed awkwardly.

"I made dinner, come on." Eric disappeared into the house. Audra's mouth started to water.

If Eric made dinner, it had to be some goodness full of butter and salt that tastes like happiness and calories.

"I'm making dessert then." Luc announced, coming to the same realization that Eric's dinner was going to be on the very unhealthy side.

"You'll make it or you'll, be it?" Audra said under her breath, just loud enough for Luc's ears.

Luc moaned softly. His eyes closed and Audra could feel the pure want course through his body, causing her own lust to double.

"You're trying to kill me." Luc muttered under his breath.

"Never." She said teasingly, with a sultry smirk. Luc's eyes darkened with lust again and Audra could feel the want and need to say 'fuck it' to having family dinner, just throwing her over his shoulder and running up the stairs.

"Come on, lovebirds. I'm hungry and I bet you are too!"

Audra laughed at Eric's singsong manner and dragged Luc into the kitchen area where Eric had dinner waiting on the counter for them all to serve their own food, buffet style. Back in the city, they hadn't had the space, or the time, for Luc to play chef and make super fancy meals. All the food that he sent over to Audra when he knew she wasn't eating was simple, but effective, chicken and broccoli over rice, spaghetti with whole grain pasta, taco bowls. All things that were healthy, infused with vegetables and protein. But this dinner was nothing short of exactly what she would have from Eric's cooking.

On the countertop was what Audra could only describe as a 'hungry man's feast'. What looked to be a whole bag of chicken nuggets in the formation of a mountain in the middle of the island, a white porcelain bowl filled to the brim with instant mashed potatoes. Crescent rolls were piled high in a bowl, and the butter dish right next to it. Not to mention, one of the frozen lasagnas steaming in the aluminum dish and what Audra must have guessed was Eric's attempt at keeping Luc happy was a bowl of canned corn.

Audra couldn't help but giggle at Eric's food choices, but it was making her mouth water.

"Wow, Eric. You've outdone yourself." Luc said, trying to be nonchalant, but giving his General actual praise. Even though Audra could tell he was cringing inside.

"Let's eat." Eric clapped his hands together with a smile, a real genuine smile that showed Audra just how much he was happy to push Luc's buttons.

"Yes, let's." Audra said, as her stomach growled loudly.

"I'm going to make a fruit parfait with chia seeds and plenty of fruit for dessert. To counteract all this." Luc announced.

"Live a little, Lieutenant. Let yourself have a night of junk food without worry." Eric said sarcastically. "One meal isn't going to kill you."

The way that Eric spoke, as if his words were carefully chosen, sent a cautious feeling through Audra. She paused over the bowl of mashed potatoes slightly before scooping a bit on her plate.

"Yes, sir." Luc said, his eyes darting around the table.

Eric clapped Luc on the back, picked up his own plate, and started piling food high on it.

Luc and Eric walked around kitchen island talking softly to each other as Audra stepped back, that feeling of caution still filling her chest.

She put her plate down and excused herself, ignoring the questioning looks from both guys as she climbed the stairs and closed her bedroom door quietly.

What was this? Why was she feeling like this, especially after Eric's joke?

She needed to talk to Seb. She felt calm and safe with him, even if he was just a figment of her imagination.

* * *

After a couple minutes to regroup with herself, she went back downstairs to see that the guys had made a plate for her already. The gesture made her smile softly, and she rushed to join them.

They were sitting across from each other at the wooden table, both men hunched over their plates, deep in conversation.

Audra picked up silverware and walked over to the dining room table. The conversation stopped and the silence was deafening. She knew that they were waiting for an explanation as to why she just up and left, but she didn't really feel that it was their business.

"So...what were you guys talking about?" She said, dipping a chicken nugget in her mashed potatoes, thanking her lucky stars that the meal was still warm.

"Just how much the food here differs from in Vesperitus. It's no less delicious, but it was difficult to find things we liked when we first got here." Eric said, putting a large piece of lasagna in his mouth.

"Oh."

"It effects the Fae form a bit differently; you require more food to keep your muscle, the more nutrients within the food, the better for your powers. It's why I like more nutrient dense food and the General feels that he is good enough with his light affinity, so he prefers to partake in the tastier, but trash for your body food. I would prefer to have any added help I can get." Luc smirked as he took a bite of the lasagna, which Audra guessed he had assigned as the healthiest part of the main dishes.

"I didn't know that." She said, looking down at her plate. She was starving, the increased appetite she had most definitely noticed, but she had always been hungry. "Why didn't you tell me that?"

"It's only been a few days."

"That still seems like a vital thing to know." Audra said shortly and gripped her silverware a bit tighter.

"There are a lot of things you don't know, Princess." Eric snapped, putting a nugget in his mouth, and chewing quickly without really looking at either of them.

Anger bubbled up. Of course, there were a lot of things she didn't know, a lot of things that they didn't share, and it bothered her still. She wanted to start the conversation, about all the things that they had hidden from her, but she also knew that if she started talking, the accusations, the anger, was going to come out.

"Baby, are you okay?" Luc asked hesitantly.

Audra took a deep breath. She knew she was being unreasonable, not understanding. They had explained their reasoning, and she said she had understood. But then she finds out things they've kept secret, and she is thrown right back into the fear and isolation.

"Is there anything else you guys have hidden from me?"

The room is silent and stifling, like all the air has been sucked out.

"What do you mean? We already talked about everything." Eric seemed lost.

"You just said it. There are a lot of things about myself, about you guys, about vital information that I need to know about my own body and my own life that you two haven't shared. But let's start with before all this change. Let's start with how you felt you couldn't show me how much Luc liked to cook by spending actual money you two seem to have while we were living in that broken down building and you two were supposed to be 'struggling' to make ends meet. It is just…"

"One more thing that we didn't share with you." Luc finished her thought, dropping his head in resignation.

Audra nodded.

Eric ran his hand over his face.

"I just want to know you as well as you know me. I completely opened up and let you guys in, even when it was hard."

The silence that filled the room it was awkward, and Audra knew it was her fault. Her outburst brought back the uncomfortableness that they had all thought they had discussed already. She reached for her roll and picked it apart silently, refusing to be the one to break the silence. Even though she felt awkward, she didn't feel bad about it. They had used her in a way, used her trust when she had thought that they were being genuine.

"How can we make it right?" Eric asked, his voice barely above a whisper.

"Answer my questions. That's a start."

Luc took a deep breath. Obviously, there were some things they were still trying to shield her from. The boys shared a look that immediately put Audra on edge.

"Within reason." Eric said, his head tilting slightly as if he was preparing for a fight. "Ask away."

"Let's start from the beginning. It's safe to say that you two aren't freelance video game designers?" Audra started, figuring the obvious lie in their occupation would be a safe place.

Both boys laughed slightly, the high tension in the room lessened slightly.

"No, Princess, we don't. We get paid by the Crown to watch over you." Eric said with a smile to her but continued. "We were always watching you. We kept our distance obviously, stayed out of sight, but we were your bodyguards. I followed you to classes and Luc followed you to work."

"You followed me...everywhere?"

"Everywhere. I think I was learning quite a lot in that Justice course you were taking. Professor Lin was very interesting." Eric said, popping a chicken nugget into his mouth and shrugging his shoulders.

Audra's jaw dropped.

"And you," she turned to Luc, "you were at all my shifts? At all my different jobs?"

"Outside or I sat in another waitress' section and paid them off to make sure you didn't know I was there. I even used a disguise from time to time. I found the animal shelter the most difficult to blend into the background of. I was so relieved when you started at the cafe."

Audra was astounded. She had always had them watching her back.

She was well aware that should have creeped her out, but if anything, it made her feel loved.

"I'm so sorry, I'm sure you guys were so bored."

The soldiers both looked at Audra with blank stares upon their faces. It was impossible for her to read what they were thinking just based on their faces, but then Luc broke into a huge grin. His aqua eyes filled with laughter as his deep laugh filled the room. Then Eric joined in, his laugh complementing Luc's in the best way.

"Why are you laughing at me?" Audra crossed her arms over her chest as she felt anger flare within her chest. She was, yet again, opening up and trying to get to know them, and they were sitting there mocking her.

"Because only you, you sweet girl, would feel worried about your bodyguards being bored while they were doing their duty to protect you." Luc cupped her hand, brushing his thumb over her knuckles in a tender caress.

"I just feel like I lived a pretty boring life before all this nonsense started, so I probably wasn't that entertaining to watch." She muttered.

"We protected you because it was our job, our honor." Eric told her, matter-of-factly, as he cut another piece of lasagna from the pan and added a mountain of parmesan cheese.

"Still."

"Don't you worry about us."

"So, you only hung out with me because it was your job?" She asked hesitantly, bracing herself for the answer she knew would be hurtful for her.

"I'm not going to lie to you. It started out that way." Eric said, tearing into a roll and slathering on butter. "But trust me, you wiggled your way into our hearts and lives so fast that we actually started to like having you around."

Audra felt taken aback. She knew that Eric didn't mind spending time with her back then. They were closer than she was with Luc. With Luc, it always seemed like he didn't want to talk much, didn't want to partake in the drinks or games they played. Aside from their educational chats and when he would feed her, then she would catch him looking at her lovingly, when he would take care of her subtly. With Eric, she knew he cared about her like a sister, an annoying kid sister, but she would have assumed that he resented having to watch over her like that.

"Yes, baby, I didn't mind it so much. Stop looking so surprised." Luc said, before he stuffed another bite into his mouth and chewed.

Eric smirked, his mouth full of bread and preparing another bite with the goods on his plate.

"What are my parents like?" Audra asked next. She was dying to know more about them. She couldn't lie and say that she wasn't, but at the same time, it was tricky. They'd left her. Even if they *had* to have done it, they didn't try to keep her. It hurt.

"Well, we are soldiers, so we haven't had a lot of one-on-one connections with them to know them on a personal level. But from what I have seen and heard from our interactions; your father is a passionate man who is not afraid to say what he feels is right. He has a knack for never being disrespectful about it but making sure that he thinks is known and understood." Eric said, picking up his water cup for a drink.

"And my mother?" Audra prodded.

"She's strong and brave. She took on her family legacy with headstrong determination to make Vesperitus the best it can be without sending warriors off to war needlessly. Everyone loves them." Luc supplied from his seat.

They sounded amazing; passion and bravery, headstrong and determined. The Queen and King of a country who were beloved and peaceful.

No pressure.

"Have you been reporting to my parents?" Audra's voice was soft, insecure. Both soldiers stopped suddenly, aware of the energy change in the room. Eric was the one who broke the silence.

"Yes. They are up to date with everything regarding you."

"Everything?" She asked. Audra would be mortified if they knew everything, her upbringing, her abandonment issues, how she struggled and scraped by just how much she leaned on Eric and Luc to make it through the week.

"Everything pertinent to the mission of keeping you safe." Eric cut in, no nonsense.

"Oh god." Audra gasped.

"No, Aud, not everything. Damn it, Eric." Luc muttered under his breath. "They know how you've been living; they know what you're going to school for, how we planned on keeping you safe, the logistical side of things. But I think what you're worried about them knowing the issues from before, they don't need to know that. Unless you tell them."

Audra felt an immense relief. They didn't know about the foster families. They didn't know about her time on the streets, what she had to do to see the next morning.

"Thank you."

"You'll never be alone again. You'll never be cold or hungry again. I will always be here for you." Luc said quietly.

Tears lined her green eyes, blurring her vision.

"Thank you." A tear fell from her eye and Luc quickly ran his thumb over her cheek, wiping the errant tear from her skin.

"Always."

"Any other questions?" Eric cut in with a cough, obviously feeling a bit awkward at their little bubble. Audra sat back in her chair and Luc did the same, pulling his hand from her face and digging back into his plate.

"What else do you like to do for fun? Obviously not just play video games and workout, which is what you told me before."

"I do like to play video games; I also like to cook and experiment with foods. It brings me peace. Working out is great and all, but it's more for protection than it is for pleasure. I started to figure out cooking was my thing when we were at training camp all those years ago. The food they served was literal slop, some mush with a properly calculated protein-carb concoction with added vitamins and minerals to keep the warriors healthy and strong." Luc said.

"It was absolutely vile. Tasteless, the worst texture, and smelled god awful." Eric interrupted as he speared another nugget and ate it in one bite.

"So, after a few weeks of that, I made friends with one of the cooks in the kitchen in my free time and asked him if I could learn a thing or two. This big lug wouldn't stop complaining about how hungry he was and if he had to eat that mess one more time, he was going to throw a punch." Luc rolled his eyes at comrade's antics back when they were both fresh faced soldiers. "So, Pierre and I, that was the cook, showed me the protein packs, the carb packs, and all the required sludge the higher ups made him serve us. After once or twice of messing with some seasonings and some add-ins that I convinced Pierre would help, I had created something palatable."

"And by palatable, he means a small step above vile." Eric teased.

"It was still an improvement. And all the guys that ate it seemed to be in better spirits that day. It was then that I realized the importance of caring for what you eat and liking it. Because all the men were getting the requirements to stay strong, stay fit, stay healthy, keep their magic strong. But they were so unsatisfied because their taste buds weren't happy. So, I kept at it. I kept playing around with anything I could convince Pierre the kitchen needed. And I've never felt so...relaxed."

"That's amazing." Audra told him, her eyes sparkling with awe at what Luc had taken on for himself and their whole squad.

"That's why you're so into home cooked, healthy food."

Luc nodded. "The food you put in your body should taste good, but it needs to keep you strong, able and focused. The fast-food crap that you two partake in only hurts you in the long run and it messes up everything."

Eric and Audra shared a knowing look and a smile.

"That fast food crap is delicious." She taunted Luc. Every time the two of them would bring fast food back to the apartments, they had to hide the evidence of their misdeeds before Luc got home to give them a lecture.

"I am definitely going to miss McDonald's. French fries and greasy burgers in thirty seconds." Eric groaned and Audra laughed at the grimace on Luc's face.

"Don't get me started." Luc grumbled.

He's so easy to rile up. She thought as she chuckled.

"What about you?" She asked Eric.

"I don't really have any secret hobbies that I haven't been able to share with you. I like working out, I like fighting, I like reading, I also like watching movies back-to-back and eating my weight in chocolate. All of these are things that you know." Eric shrugged.

"Look baby, there were things that we had to do to show to the unsuspecting world around us that we belonged where we were. No fancy cars, no designer clothes, no gourmet meals on the daily. We had to keep up appearances that we were freelance graphic designers who were just friends with the girl across the hall." Luc explained.

"I get that."

"It's not like we wanted to, I don't know, deceive you. I promise." He added.

"I understand, I do." She grasped both of their hands on either side of her, so they were all connected.

"I know now what you guys have been doing for me, to protect and care for me, and I'm sorry that I got so hurt. It just sent me right back into that mind space of being forgotten. Thank you for sharing your passion for cooking with me, with us, and sharing your story." Audra gave Luc's hand a squeeze, hoping that he understood just how much she appreciated him opening up to her.

Not his full truth. She was sure there were stories and explanations as to why Eric liked fighting and why he didn't, but enough that it made Audra feel safe again.

Eric quickly dropped her hand but smiled at her. Again, his smile didn't seem to reach his eyes. It was a show, a fake. But why? Why now? Audra wasn't going to bring attention to it yet, but something was wrong. Something had changed with Eric.

"Make sure you eat Princess. It would be a shame if all this amazing food got cold before you could eat it." Eric said with a wink towards Luc, who rolled his eyes.

Audra picked up her fork and dug in.

Chapter Fifteen

"Oh my god." Audra moaned into the first bite of the fruit parfait.

She knew that Luc could cook the simple stuff, but damn, could he also make a good dessert. She didn't think she had ever been so full after Eric's cooking.

"I take that as a good thing." Luc smiled.

"A very good thing, I'm going to need this level of cooking and food for the rest of my life."

Eric laughed and started to pick up the empty plates in front of them.

"It would be my honor, your majesty." Luc mockingly bowed his head and Audra didn't have the energy to smack him for it. She was nursing a food baby and fighting falling asleep right at the table.

Audra just giggled and reached for another spoonful, letting the creamy, sweet but slightly frozen vanilla yogurt melt on her tongue.

"It's so good." She moaned and took another bite. Luc's attention snapped to her, and she could see the fire behind his blue eyes. The lust flared at the sound she made, and Audra wanted nothing more than to keep pushing him to see what would finally make his careful control snap.

They both locked eyes, trapped in their heated looks. Luc looked like he wanted to swallow her whole, and she wanted to let him.

"I don't want to be here for this. Ick. No, thank you. I'm going to go drive into the city, check on our apartment and see if there are any residual magic users sniffing out her scent." Eric announced. "I trust that you are capable of keeping the safe house in check and keeping the Princess' safety your top priority?"

Luc nodded stiffly, lowering his head to Eric in a gesture of respect. No matter how close Audra and Luc had gotten, Eric was still the highest ranking official here. Luc would show him respect as long as Eric served the crown. Eric stood quickly and swiftly left the dining table.

Audra wanted to feel bad about making Eric uncomfortable, in some small part she did, but the main part of her just wanted to have Luc to herself again.

"Don't worry," Luc said quietly. "I asked him to leave. He didn't feel awkward."

"You asked him to leave?"

"I wanted some time alone with you, time in the house. We first started caring deeper for each other, now that we have no secrets between us. I want to make you mine in *every way* and I would rather my superior not be here for it."

Audra's breath caught in her throat, and she felt heat settle in her belly.

"Oh, you like that, do you?" Luc's voice seemed to get lower with every word he spoke, and Audra *loved* it.

Words evaded her, so she just nodded.

Luc moved his chair closer to hers, sliding his hand under the table to rest on her thigh, and Audra was as still as a statue. His hand placement could be innocent, if she wasn't aware of where he - she, they - wanted the night to go.

With his other hand, Luc picked up his spoon and scooped a small bite of yogurt, offering it to her.

She leaned in and took the spoon in her mouth.

His gaze was locked on her mouth, where she had the spoon trapped between her lips, licking off the yogurt.

Slowly, she released the spoon from her mouth and licked her lips, paying special attention to get each and every bit of the cream. Audra loved the way that Luc watched each movement she made like a hawk. Nothing was going to escape his attention.

His hand under the table had been rubbing soft circles around her inner thigh; comforting and sweet. But as soon as she had licked her lips while staring at him, his touches turned rougher, more urgent. The soft circles became tighter, and they moved upward with every rotation.

The intense warmth that always seemed to radiate from him was scorching now. She was barely able to contain her moans as he reached the top of her thighs, barricaded within her jeans, so he wasn't able to get to where she really wanted him.

"Let's go take that bath." He said huskily. The touch of his fingers barely touching the apex of her thighs had her squirming.

She would happily destroy these jeans, her favorites, if it meant his fingers on her, in her.

"Okay."

Luc stood from the table, leaving the ice cream, and pulling her by her hand.

Then they both moved as one; both of them crashing down to kiss the other at one time.

His tongue traced her lips, begging for entrance. When she opened her mouth, his tongue plundered hers, fighting for dominance. But she wasn't going to let him win so easily.

She met him; swipe for swipe, tug for tug, grab for grab. His hands slid down her back, over the curve of her ass, and gripped her thighs as he ripped her towards him. She pressed against him and wrapped her arms around his neck, using his shoulders as leverage to hold herself up and even more tightly to him.

One of his large hands stayed under her bottom and the other wrapped around her back, keeping their centers pressed tightly together. He flipped them around and placed Audra on the table.

Her legs wrapped tightly around him to keep him from leaving her space.

"We aren't going to make it up to the bathtub, are we?" She asked breathlessly as Luc's lips trailed down her neck, leaving large open-mouthed kisses. He reached the pulse point between her shoulder and neck, the spot that made her eyes roll back in her head and sucked. Hard.

Audra let out a low moan. She was barely able to keep the sound somewhat quiet.

"We will...at some point. But for now, lift up your arms." Luc commanded, having pulled back just enough so Audra could stare at him in the eye. His golden eyes, that usually held such heaviness, protective and on guard, were full of want. Full of need for her.

Audra lifted her arms up, as Luc lifted the hem of her shirt and pulled the cotton up. He never broke eye contact, and it made the simple motion seem a million times hotter.

Luc tossed her shirt and Audra could not have cared less about where it landed. The black lace bra she had on, she knew looked amazing on her. It was her favorite for that reason. It never failed to make her feel sexy.

Luc let out a pained sounding groan.

"You've been wearing things like this the whole time?"

Audra nodded and his expression turned almost feral.

"Lacy, see-through, sexy things?"

"As much as I can. I like how I look in them."

Luc's hand came up to cup her breast, feeling the weight of each of them. When his fingertips lightly traced her nipples, Audra arched her back to chase more of the sensation. All she could think of was the heated stare that transferred from her face to her exposed chest.

"Goddamn, you look sexy. More beautiful than I had ever imagined. And trust me, baby, I imagined this a lot." Luc growled as he pinched her nipple hard.

She gasped. "You did?"

"So many times. There was one time when you came home from work and passed me in the stairwell. I watched you walk past after you gave me a breathtaking smile and your pert little ass was swaying right in front of me as you climbed the stairs. It took everything I had in me to not make a sound, not follow you to your door and push you against it as I kissed you senseless."

Audra moaned at the picture he painted. Luc's eyes lit up with her noises and he placed another open-mouthed kiss on her neck.

"Do you like the sound of that? Me pushing you up against the wall and taking you?" He whispered roughly.

"Take your shirt off." She gripped the ends of his t-shirt and pushed it up. Luc chuckled and pulled the back collar of his shirt over his head, revealing his toned, tan chest. Audra took a moment to appreciate his body, drinking him in now that she was able to without fear of getting caught checking him out. But when that moment was done, she simply had to touch him, to feel him pressed skin-to-skin.

They met again in the middle, kissing deeply. She let him devour her, loving every second of it. Audra ran her hands down the broad expanse of his back, savoring the way his muscles rippled with the pass of her hands.

Without warning, Luc gripped one hand in her hair, twisting and locking her in place, while the other went to the button of her jeans. She knew there was no point in keeping the underwear she had on; the lace was no doubt ruined with her arousal.

Just before he popped the button open, he pulled back and stared at Audra. She could see each emotion flow through him. She knew him well enough to know exactly what he was thinking, just based on the looks he was giving her.

He wanted to make sure she was okay with what came next. He wanted her to choose him, for him. He wanted to be inside her as soon as he possibly could. But most of all, she could see how much he wanted to make this good for her, to prove to her that he was there for her.

"Is this, okay?" Luc asked, his voice low and quiet. With an unspoken question in his eyes, his hand hovered over the waistband of her jeans.

The hesitation was killing her. Hadn't they already proven themselves to each other? That gave her pause. Maybe they hadn't, really. With all the changes, all her life altering changes and information, maybe he thinks she is just settling. Eric did say he had wanted her too, that weird ass declaration that never was talked about or thought about again. Audra had tried to show him just how much she cared, just like he cared for her. She would even say that they loved each other, but they hadn't ever discussed crossing this line. Maybe they should.

No, no, she thought. *I love this man. It might be too early to tell him, but I know I do. So, I'll show him.*

With that, Audra wrapped her hand around his neck and pulled him back into as passionate of a kiss as she could muster.

Luc smiled into the kiss and popped the button on her jeans, both hands going to the waistband to slide the denim down her legs, along with her ruined panties.

Pulling away, Luc stood back, her discarded jeans still in one of his hands.

He was gripping the material so tightly that his knuckles were turning white. It didn't even look like he was breathing.

Watching Luc look at each and every part of her naked body both sent her arousal into overdrive, but also, the longer the moment stretched on, the more self-conscious she felt.

"So gorgeous." Luc said softly, his voice full of awe and lust. He tossed the jeans in his hand and knelt on one knee in front of her. He lightly touched her knees and slowly spread her legs apart.

Audra's breath caught in her chest, and she forgot how to breathe.

"I've thought about doing this basically every single day since I found you."

And before she could respond, he started to lick her center. Slowly, sensually.

And Audra thought she might die from pleasure. Her head fell back, and she thanked her lucky stars that there was nothing on the dining table, save for the one fruit parfait that was sitting half eaten.

"Oh, my god, Luc."

"Fuck, baby. You taste..." He went back to alternating between sucking and licking.

"Bad?" Audra asked, head thrown back against the wooden table.

"Fuck no. Like the best thing ever, better than anything I've ever tasted. Fuck me, Audra. This is...everything I've wanted." He groaned against her center, his words causing another gush of slick to pour from her, and he moaned when he felt it.

He redoubled his efforts then, taking in each and every response she gave him, even when she tried to hide it from him. She was trying her best to stay quieter; she didn't want to overwhelm him.

"You better fucking let me hear each and every noise you make. I earned it; I want it. Let go, baby, I've got you." He growled, grabbing both of her thighs, and throwing them over his shoulders. His large hands covering the expanse of her thighs and the visual of him holding her in place, like that...

She let go then. She let herself be as loud as she wanted, not worried about embarrassing herself any longer.

With one particular pull of his mouth, Audra lost it. Her back arched, and she tried her best to not squeeze her thighs together, as to not squash his head, but the scream that left her was guttural, raw and real.

Luc continued working her through her orgasm, and when she was coming down, he kissed her inner thigh once, twice, three times before looking up at her with the biggest smile.

"Goddamn baby. I don't think I'll be able to live the rest of our lives without that every single day. Fucking perfect." He said as he wiped his mouth with the back of his hand and leaned over her.

"Damn you. You're amazing at that."

"Just for you."

Audra rolled her eyes and smiled. She sat up and pulled his pants down, shoving them past his knees with her toes.

"Are you sure?" Luc asked, the tone of his voice having gone from confident and sexy to insecure and worried.

"More than anything. I want you. All of you." Audra confessed and leaned up to kiss him, tasting herself on his tongue.

Luc met her kiss, wrapping his hand in her hair to lock her head against him. Not that she would have broken the kiss for anything, except to feel him.

Audra slid her hand down his chest, feeling his abs flex and twitch under her touch, down to where his cock stood erect and weeping.

"Is this...for me?" She whispered, running her hand back and forth over the velvet texture.

"All for you. Always."

"Always?"

"I only ever get this hard for you, when I'm thinking about you or when you would wear those tiny fucking shorts that showed half your ass."

"Why didn't you say something earlier?"

"I couldn't do that to you, to us."

"Lies." She teased, she knew he wouldn't have made a move when she didn't know about her powers, about her true self. He wouldn't have made a move when he knew the full truth and she didn't. He was too good and honest to take advantage of her. Even if she wouldn't have seen it that way in the end, he would have.

"But I can say something now. And I am. I fucking want you, Audra. I want you more than anything, and I want everything. The hard days, the great days, the love, the sadness, the thick and the thin. I want it all, baby."

"I do too."

She ran her hand back and forth over his cock, paying close attention to the groans and grunts passing his lips.

He pulled back harshly, surprising her.

"Did I do something wrong?"

"No, baby. But I won't last if you keep touching me like that. I need to be inside you. I need to show you that you're mine."

"Yes, yes, please." She begged breathlessly.

Luc yanked her down to the edge of the table and lined himself at her entrance. Audra held her breath, excitement and anticipation singing through her.

He leaned over and kissed her chastely, sweetly, full of love.

As he pulled back just enough for them to rest their foreheads against each other, breathe the same air, he cupped her cheek and whispered, "You're mine now."

All the breath left her lungs at his confession and her heartbeat wildly.

But he didn't give her time to respond before he sheathed himself inside her fully. The sudden pressure making her scream out and her toes curl.

"Fuck, *fuck*." Luc groaned as he hovered over her, trying to control his breathing and movements.

"Oh my god. You feel…"

"I know." He finished.

Audra brought her hips up to meet his, slowly, experimentally, and he let out a moan.

Together, they moved in tandem. Chasing their own release as well as trying to help the other feel as good as possible.

Luc felt perfect, like he was made for her. She also knew that she was not going to last long, a second orgasm building as quickly as the first.

"I'm not going to last long this first time, baby." Luc grunted, his movements becoming more and more aggressive.

"Me neither. I want to feel you cum."

"Fuck, you're perfect."

"No, it's you who's perfect. Perfect for me." She whispered in his ear, kissing the shell of his ear while clutching his ass to try to keep him as close to her as possible.

Luc's hand slid from her waist to her clit, and he started to rub small circles, helping her cross the finish line.

"Luc, Luc, right there, please!" She called out, her peak climbing higher and higher.

"That's it. Cum on me, baby." He grunted, pushing harder against her clit as well as grinding harder into her. His cock hitting a spot inside her that made her gasp each time he hit it. His thrusts were getting more aggressive, harder, and more powerful. Vaguely, she was aware that the wooden table was creaking and moving beneath them, but she was much too occupied to care.

"Good girl, come on." He whispered as he bit down on her neck, and she saw stars.

Her whole being exploded with pleasure. She came harder than she ever had in her life, screaming his name.

"Fuck, *fuck!*" Luc's hips pistoled in and out of her quicker, losing any finesse he had managed to have the moment she clenched around him, squeezing him tightly through her orgasm.

"I've got you, love. Give it to me." She wrapped both of her arms tightly around his back, pressing her chest up into his, and shifted her hips up. When she did, he thrust in once, twice and one last time before he spilled into her.

"Baby," he groaned.

Music to her ears.

Both of them laid on the dining table, breathing heavily, wrapped in each other's arms. Audra ran her fingertips slowly up and down Luc's back, softly assuring him she was there.

"That was…" He started.

"Incredible. Overdue." She answered.

"Worth the wait." He smiled and kissed her deeply.

Chapter Sixteen

"I think a spoon is digging into my back." Audra groaned as she felt around for whatever it was that was sharp and rough under her weight. They were still catching their breath with half their bodies on the sturdy wooden dining table, their sweat slicked chests pressing together.

Luc sat up slightly and moved his hand to her lower back. He pulled out a spoon and tossed it to the side. It clanged on the floor and Luc laid back down.

"So much better." Audra sighed in relief.

"It could be even better if we moved to one of our rooms." Luc pointed out.

"But that would require us to move from this spot."

"Come on," Luc pulled away from her and stood back. "Let's go to your room, sleep in your bed where I can hold you now. As tightly as I want."

Audra smiled, letting him guide her through the house, up the stairs and into the white, airy room that screamed comfort.

"Let's go to bed." Luc whispered as he let his hand roam over her naked form, bending slightly to capture her thighs in his hands and lift her to his body. "Before I take you again."

They both moaned at the feeling of the naked bodies touching. Audra ran her fingers through his hair, pulling at the thick curls at the nape of his neck, angling his head up to capture his mouth in another kiss.

* * *

"Are you tired?" Luc asked after their second round in her not-so-pristine white sheets.

"After you rocked my world for the third time tonight? Yes, I'm tired." She mumbled, her face tucked into his side as they lay next to each other, cuddling and basking in the glow.

Luc chuckled and ran a fingertip down her spine, causing her to shiver.

"Sleep, baby. We can talk in the morning."

"Talk?"

"Yes, talk. It's time you knew everything. Dark Fae, your parents, Vesperitus. I'll answer all your questions. I should have already." He hung his head slightly, like the guilt of keeping things from her was too much.

Audra gasped. She was going to learn about her home, her family.

"You'll teach me?"

"As much as I can and know." He kissed her forehead.

"Sleep."

Her eyes felt heavy, and she let sleep take her.

* * *

Audra knew it was a dream. She could feel the familiar haze that accompanied a dream. But whereas her dreams usually had her looking through the main character of the dream, be it her or someone made up, she was aware that she was a spectator in this.

"You will work with us. Wouldn't it be such a shame for your lovely fiancé to suddenly turn up missing?" A short, stout man sat beside a beautiful, breathtaking woman with gorgeous chestnut curls and an angular face that Audra now knew meant that she was Fae.

"I will not betray my country, my people. You are just going to have to find someone else." She said with a tone that ensured finality, but the short man kept pressuring.

"There is no one with your level of power."

"Surely you haven't checked Vesperitus in its entirety?"

"We have. You are the only one with power great enough to overthrow the monarchy."

"I am the monarchy." She snapped.

"Not yet. Aodhan and Fiona are still in control. They are causing unrest within the lower circles and if we don't do something, they will run this country into the ground."

"Yonas, I will not betray my country and the institution that it was built upon. The Crown Queen, my mother, is doing the best she can."

"And it's not enough!" Yonas, the man, yelled at the woman as he slapped his hand down on the plain wooden table they sat at. *"It's not enough! People are dying and they show no signs of acknowledgement, of change."*

"And my power would do something to help that?"

"Maeve, don't be dense. Your power could change the world. With your power and the Fullmas influence... you would be unstoppable."

So, the woman's name was Maeve, and she was a Royal in Vesperitus. She had to be a relative of Audra's. Audra thought. She didn't know what this was, a memory, a vision? But she knew that she needed to remember this.

"I don't want to be unstoppable. I want to be a righteous and fair Queen when it comes to be my turn." Maeve crossed her arms over her chest, her opulent gown of silk and jewels sparkling in the light.

"This is the last time I ask you. The next..."

"There will be no next time, Yonas. I am telling you once and for all, I will not give my powers over. I will not let my gifts be tainted or manipulated."

A storm cloud covered his features and his sharp eyes turned even sharper, harsher. His mouth shifted into a snarl; his teeth elongated into fangs. Yonas' plump face turned evil before Audra's eyes, and she gasped.

"You think this now, Maeve. But I have warned you."

And with that, the man vanished in a poof of grey mist.

Audra turned to Maeve, her silk dress covered in the grey mist, which Audra could see was actually ash, and her eyes looked wild. Hectic as they darted around, trying to take in whatever was around her. All Audra could see was her.

Was she taken? Was she hurt? Audra wouldn't know.

"I have to get to Callum." Maeve whispered in fear, as she clutched her hand to her chest and darted away from Audra.

"Wait!" Audra called out, but it was no use. Maeve was already gone, and the tendrils of awareness were starting to pull her into consciousness.

The darkness threaded through the picture, giving her pause but also had her relax. She was going into a dream with Seb.

The darkness surrounded her and enveloped her like a comfort blanket as she closed her eyes and let the shadows take her wherever they wanted. The one light shone overhead like normal, keeping Seb out of sight, but she knew he was there.

"So. Which one of them won you over?" His deep voice rumbled.

"Hello to you too."

"I'm guessing it was Lucien. He always was the better of the two. If it had to be one of them."

"What are you talking about?" Audra asked. She knew what he was trying to get her to admit and wanted to play dumb for just a few seconds longer.

"You're naked sweetheart, and fully satisfied by the looks of it."

"Jealous?" Audra asked, fighting the urge to cover herself.

"Extremely." Audra could see his hands fist and clench at his sides like they wanted to grab her, but he was showing restraint.

"Let me see you. Please." Audra begged.

"Not yet. Please, don't make this harder than it is."

"Seb..." Audra tried to step closer to him and was struck with a guilty feeling. Like she had cheated on Seb.

"You aren't mine, as much as I want you to be. But you will be soon. I promise." He said, his voice full of confidence.

"Who says?"

"History, the stars, my heart, take your pick. But we will be together, regardless of what I have to do." Seb vowed.

"I care for him." Her voice was small, but she refused to be ashamed of her feelings towards Luc.

"I know. He cares for you, too. But you and me? Sweetheart, you, and I have

been intertwined since you were born. You were always mine, but I'm willing to share. If I have to." He stepped closer and closer, his dress shoes clicking on the ground as her breath became more rapid.

"*Are you even real?*"

"*I guess we will find out.*" His hand cupped her chin and trailed down her neck, causing her to shiver as the light above her turned brighter and brighter. The white blankness started to dissipate, and her eyes opened.

"Baby?" Luc asked from her side, his heavy arm over her waist as he held her from behind. "Everything okay?"

Audra pushed his arm off her and went in search of paper and a pen. She knew that the first part of the dream wasn't just a dream. Wasn't just a figment of her imagination. It had been real.

Pulling open the closet door, she began searching through the shelves of clothes for a piece of paper, a receipt, anything that she could write on.

Nothing.

She pulled on one of Luc's big shirts from the floor, any kind of pants she could find, which happened to be her sleep shorts, and ran out of the room. There was paper in the kitchen on the fridge. They always kept a magnetic pad on the fridge so they could write down groceries that they needed.

"Audra, wait." Luc called from behind her, but she was already out of the room.

"I need to write it down." She muttered back, not caring if he could hear her.

Her feet thundered down the stairs as she ran.

"What happened?" Luc was right on her tail. He must have forgone putting clothes on in favor of keeping up with her.

Audra made it to the kitchen and ripped the notepad off, pulling open the drawer right next to the fridge where everything seemed to be kept; pens, string, rubber bands, stamps, all the odds and ends.

She found a pen and started scribbling down everything she could remember from the dream.

"Baby, what is wrong?" Luc stood beside her, his warm hand covering her upper back.

"Shhh." She shushed him.

"Dude! Way too much for me to see first thing in the morning!" Eric came walking in the kitchen. He must have heard the yelling and running.

Audra paused her scribbling when she felt the abrupt and intense change within Luc.

He had gone from worried about her, scared even, to aggressive and possessive. He shifted from behind Audra, to shield her from Eric's eyes.

From behind him, Audra could hear the low growling and even his teeth clenching.

Eric stopped. Frozen in place.

Luc's skin ran hotter than normal. She wanted to check on him, wanted to run her hand down his arm, but a look from Eric gave her pause. Audra brought her hand back to her side, choosing to let the two of them sort out whatever was happening.

"Stay back." Luc growled.

Luc held his hands up and dipped his head down.

"She's mine." Luc snarled.

"She is. I'm not challenging you, Lieutenant." Eric said, each word stiff and carefully chosen.

"Mine."

"It's okay, Luc." Audra stepped closer to him, and Eric's eyes shot to her. A look of terror crossed his face as she spoke, and she realized then that she had stepped into some kind of possessive Fae thing.

"Mine!" Luc roared, pushing Audra closer to him to hide her.

Audra ran her hand up his back, hoping to prove to him just how much she was there, how much she was his.

"Yours." She said quietly.

Luc's eyes stayed locked on the perceived threat, watching his each and every move. Eric still had his head dipped. His eyes were on the floor. The perfect picture of submission.

Luc breathed heavily through his nose. His chest heaved with the movement of each breath.

"I promise." Audra whispered and kissed his shoulder, as close to his face as she could reach with how he was guarding her.

With the touch of her lips to his skin, he turned around as fast as a stroke of lightning. He bent his head down and nuzzled in her neck, breathing deeply through his nose. The air from his exhale tickled her skin and caused goosebumps to erupt all over her.

"Audra, baby…" He groaned and left a long, wet, open-mouthed kiss on the spot in the crook of her neck. "Mine."

And he bit down.

Not hard enough to break skin, but definitely hard enough to leave a mark.

She didn't cry out; she didn't moan or move. This wasn't a sexual thing that Luc was doing, she realized. He was marking her, showing his claim.

Not that he needed to. She was completely his, in every way.

As soon as he bit down, she could feel the tension leave him. The possessive, aggressive need to protect and keep her toned down to a manageable level and Audra sighed.

"Better?" She whispered.

He nodded. His face still tucked into her neck.

"I'm sorry. I'm sorry." Luc said.

She hugged him tightly and turned back to her paper to get back to writing about her dream; the specifics were already starting to fade.

"We good?" Eric asked.

"Yeah, sorry. First time and all that." Eric nodded, keeping his distance still. Audra made a mental note to ask what Luc meant by first time.

"Didn't think I'd be walking into a fight for being within talking distance of your girl."

Audra could hear the two of them bickering, but she was too focused on writing down the dream. Yonas, Maeve, how his features changed, how he wanted her to change sides, how she wouldn't betray her kingdom, everything she could remember.

"Look, she ran out of the bed like a bat out of hell after tossing and turning for hours. I wasn't going to take the time to put on clothes!" Luc snapped at Eric.

"I'm just saying, seeing your ass and your dick is a little much before I've even had my coffee. Not to mention, you trying to bite my head off."

"Then fucking make your coffee because I'm not leaving her until I figure out if everything is okay."

"I'm okay. It's okay." Audra sat up, satisfied with what she had remembered and written down.

"Audra, what the fuck happened earlier?" Luc turned her to him, "You scared the hell out of me."

She stepped into his arms and kissed his bare chest in apology.

"I'm sorry. I had a dream, but it wasn't really a dream. I think...I think it was a memory. Do you need some clothes?" She asked randomly, suddenly aware that he was stark naked still.

"I will go get dressed in a minute." He said quickly and walked over to the connecting living room area, never taking his eyes off of Audra, to grab a blanket and wrapped it around his waist.

"Thank god." Eric said.

"Shut the hell up. Like you never walked around the apartment buck ass nude after boning your latest conquest." Luc snapped. Audra rolled her eyes and continued to scribble.

"But Audra, you said you thought it was a memory?" Eric asked her from the other side of the kitchen island. "What kind of memory?"

"Not one of mine. It had two people I've never even heard of before. But it felt important, like I was meant to know it, like it was given to me somehow. And I didn't want to forget any of the information, so I had to write it down." She held up the notepad full of scribbles. "I'm sorry, I should've stopped and told you, but I didn't want to forget anything."

"Who was in the dream and what was it about?" Eric asked her as he made his way over to the coffeemaker.

"It was about a woman named Maeve and a guy named Yonas."

Both men stopped in their tracks, their shoulders rose as if they were preparing to shield themselves. Eric turned to her slowly and more gravely than he had ever said, "Tell us everything."

Chapter Seventeen

The three of them stood around the kitchen island as Audra recanted her dream as well as she could. She made sure not to mention Seb or how he seemed to know everything, but it amazed her how quickly the memory she was shown was fading. That was what she was scared of. Why she had darted from their bedroom to make sure all the details were written down before they completely left her.

"So, you weren't able to interact with them at all?" Eric asked again.

Audra took a drink of her coffee, letting the warmth of the bitter liquid ground her.

"No, I was just there to spectate. That's why I think I was shown this. Did you guys know about Yonas or Maeve?"

Luc was pacing back and forth, a dark blue fuzzy blanket wrapped haphazardly around his tapered waist and still standing between her and Eric, even though they had already had their little Alpha-Fae territorial standoff. Apparently, after the first time, two higher-level Fae mate, if one of them bites the other, a temporary bond is formed. It caused Luc's instincts to go haywire. Eric insisted that it was a normal reaction, but Audra was still so surprised at it. She didn't want to do anything that would cause him to feel that distressed again, so she stayed exactly where she was, letting Luc pace in front of her.

"I know about Maeve...at least we know what they taught us in school growing up and in basic training, all those years ago." He said, one hand still gripping the dark, fuzzy throw blanket he had hastily wrapped around his waist, while the other raked through his tousled dark hair, still messed up from their night together.

"What do you guys know about her?" Eric took his mug from the counter and backed up to move towards the dining table.

His distance seemed to calm Luc just slightly as his pacing slowed.

"Baby, could you go get me some clothes please?" Luc turned to Audra, too many different emotions swirling within her chest. She nodded and left the room quickly.

To be honest, she was very happy for the break.

Why did this memory come to her? Who sent it? Was it Maeve reaching out or Yonas? What was she supposed to do about it? What did Seb mean by their histories had been intertwined since she was born? Why did she feel like she had cheated on a man she had never met?

At least she knew that there was another Total Elemental within her family tree. The boys had alluded to it, but to know for sure... It was comforting. If someone else had gone through this, had been gifted with this enormous power, then there had to be records of it and advice somewhere. Someone had gone through this, all of it, not just one piece.

She walked into his room and grabbed some shorts and a shirt for Luc.

Audra thought back to the image of Maeve, searching and looking in the face she remembered for any resemblance. Their hair did have the same color, Maeve's curls being tighter than Audras. The shape of their jaw was similar, but that was really where the resemblances stopped from what she could remember.

She had a family. Somewhere. Even though they were in another realm, they were real. It wasn't new information to her, but it was just once again proven.

She felt a small smile start to slide into place as she walked into the kitchen area and saw the two men sitting at the table, deep in discussion.

"Here you go." She handed the clothes to Luc, who slid the shirt over his head with practiced grace.

"Are you guys, okay?" Audra asked. The two seemed lost in their thoughts after whatever they had talked about.

"Why don't you sit down?"

Audra slid into the chair at the head of the table, in between the two of them.

Luc pulled the black basketball shorts up and reached for her hand.

"Is something bad happening?"

"No, no, we just have a lot to talk about."

"Where do you want to start?" Luc asked Eric.

"Let's talk about Maeve."

Good, Audra thought. That's what she really wanted to know about, anyway. Her relative.

"Our high school in Dragomahara is called Overah and in school, we were taught the history of the monarchs. Maeve was the daughter of Aodhan, a fire wielder, and Fiohna. Queen Fiohna had a very, very slight elemental ability to ripple water. Her family had been losing their elemental abilities more and more with each generation born. That's why when their daughter, Maeve, was born, everyone assumed she would have a smaller affinity for some kind of fire or light. When she turned 18, she started to go through the change, like everyone in Vesperitus does, only she went through the change for each element. Sound familiar?" Eric said. Audra nodded and gestured for him to keep going.

"Through much trial and error, the royal family discovered that she had exceptional strength for each element. Raw, pure strength unseen by anyone in millennia. There wasn't any information on what she was, what her powers were. So, King Aodhan and Queen Fiohna decided to reach out throughout the country to see if anyone had any information, any folktales, legends, anything, to help their precious daughter through it. Unfortunately, as they spread the word about her gifts, it also alerted their enemies to what they were going through and what power they had on their side." Eric said, stopping to take a sip.

"All throughout history, there has been civil unrest with the monarchy. Most people agree and love the monarchy, what it stands for, their King and Queen. But as with any government system, people don't agree one hundred percent on anything. There will always be nay-sayers, people who think they can do better than the people already in power. Thus, a group rose to power silently, right under the High Royals nose. They called themselves the Sparlings. Underlings that wanted to overthrow the High Royals, thought that they had been in power long enough, that the original bloodline was weakening and would soon be extinguished of magic. Then Maeve came along, stronger, and more powerful than any of her ancestors. They wanted that power for themselves." Luc jumped in to continue telling the story. When he paused to take a breath, Eric started up again.

"It all started with Helenina and Jefferat Fullma. The Borgmayors, leaders of the city of Fullmaster, on the far west coast of Vesperitus. They were convinced that because they were leaders of the second largest city in the whole country, they should have a shot at becoming a monarch. But all throughout history, the bloodline of the first Helios has always sat on the throne. But the Fullma family disagreed. Over time, they built a cult following. Preying on people who needed financial guidance, people who were on the fence about certain policies in place, people who felt that their voices weren't being heard. They fed their discontent and pushed for change. When the High Royals; Aiodhan and Fiohna Helios didn't pass one of the bills presented by the Fullma spouses. Everything went to hell."

Audra's eyes widened in surprise.

"But that was years ago, right? There is still the Sparling unrest?" She asked.

"Unfortunately, Mr. and Mrs. Fullma had sparked enough doubt that a bigger group formed. A more radical group. Willing to use dark magic." Luc answered, both hands wrapped around his coffee mug. He didn't bring his head up to make eye contact, and that made a ball of dread form in Audra's belly.

"Dark magic?"

"The radical group took the Fullma's goals and statements and thought that they needed more magical power. They were convinced that if Helenina and Jefferat had more magic, stronger magic, they would be able to overthrow the Helios line. But... it backfired." Eric explained.

"How did it backfire?"

"All magic has an equal and opposite reaction. So, our magic, your magic, comes from your life essence. We were born with these powers; they stem from our very souls. Dark magic must be created. And the easiest way is to draw power from evil, corrupt things. Murder, torture, and more. The worst things you can think of can bring dark magic if one knows how to harness and wield it. The Dark Fae, what we now call them, have the Book of the Dark. It is an ancient magic book that is full of dark magical spells. It's given them power to build an army and ever since then, they've been pushing back their territory lines. The Dark Fae versus the Elemental Magic."

"So, what does this have to do with Maeve? If she was a Total Elemental, she should've had the power to, I don't know, push them back?" Audra asked.

"There was an attack on one of the safe houses that the Helios family was rotating, keeping Maeve in. Because of the search for information, new legends, new lore had been uncovered. Prophecies. The main prophecy that sparked what is known as 'the hunt' was that a Total Elemental would overpower each and every other magical being in Vesperitus. They were gifted their raw power from the God Helios himself and if their intentions were pure, there wasn't a limit to what they could do."

Audra gasped.

"They hunted her?" She whispered, afraid to hear the answer.

Luc and Eric shared a look, full of worry, apprehension, and nerves.

"Tell me." She demanded.

Eric looked down at the table and Audra could feel the anxiety radiating from him.

Luc took a deep breath and clenched his jaw. The muscle ticking as he ground his teeth.

"Tell her, Luc." He leaned back in his chair and crossed his arms over his chest.

"Audra, baby," Luc looked her in the eye as he took her hand and held it tightly. "Maeve was hunted down after she went into hiding. Aiodhan and Fiohna had a disagreement with Helenina and Jefferat over territory. History classes tell us that Aiodhan Helios had tried to reason with Jefferat, tried to get him to see that being united would be best for Vesperitus. But legend had it that Jefferat denied his offer at peace and told him that he would have the power of the Gods at whatever cost."

"Aiodhan took that as a threat on his daughter and sent her deep into hiding."

Eric interrupted, adding more to the story. "But they found her, after many years. She had married and had a baby, a daughter. The Sparling group had officially become the Dark Fae; with each spell they used, another part of their bodies was disfigured or darkened. Darkened fingertips, snarled teeth, grey iris', hunchbacks. Dark magic had become a tool each person used in their army. When they found Maeve, she fought as best she could, but after years of hiding her magic instead of strengthening it, she didn't know how to use it effectively. She was killed."

"The baby?" Audra asked quietly, eyes closed.

"Callum, the King, Maeve's husband, was taking their daughter on a trip to his family, under the radar. He hadn't heard about the attack until much later because no one could find him."

"They killed her for her power..." Audra felt like she was going to cry. How could people be so cruel? "Were they able to get her power? Use it for their agenda?"

"No, no, they weren't. The lackeys that they had been sent to bring her to the Fullma's so they could siphoen her power into one of them, killed her. She was murdered, but at least her power wasn't abused."

"That's good. Right?"

Eric sighed.

"Civil unrest continued for centuries. Wars were fought, *so* many lives lost on both sides. After Maeve was killed, Aiodhan and Fiohna had Callum and their granddaughter live deep within the castle. They weren't heard from until Aiodhan died and Callum ascended the throne. The Fullma's were desperate to gain more power and swore that the next Total Elemental born would be theirs, no matter what."

"Okay..." Audra knew there was another bomb that was going to drop. She could feel it.

"You, Audra, are the next Total Elemental born. The next chance for the Dark Fae to gain the power of Helios by draining you of your power. And they will stop at nothing to get it."

Chapter Eighteen

The hits just keep coming.

Audra moved to the dining room that was connected to the kitchen and sat at the head of the table with her head in her hands. She was doing her best to keep her breathing steady, to keep focused on the matter at hand. There was too much going on, too many moving parts, too many changes happening all at once.

"Baby," Luc said softly, putting his hand on her back and scooting his chair closer to hers. As he got closer, his presence calmed her slightly. Not enough that she wasn't on the verge of tears anymore, but enough that she could take a deep breath.

"It's going to be okay." He finished.

"How Luc? How is this going to be okay?" She whispered; head still hidden in her hands. She could feel the tears starting to form, but she did not want them to fall.

"We will figure it out. Nothing, and I mean nothing, is going to happen to you."

She wanted to believe him, she could feel the determination and protective-ness coming from him, but how were they supposed to go up against an army of magical beings that are willing to use dark magic by performing disgusting, awful, truly terrible acts and have had centuries to plan her take down? She couldn't see any scenario where they would win. Where she would live.

"Hey." Eric's tone was hard and fierce. He gripped her bicep and forced her to turn to him.

"Eric!" Luc snapped as he jumped up to grab Audra back from his grip, but

Eric snarled at him and said, "Know your place, Lieutenant."

His grip was strong, Audra knew that if he pressed any harder, she would have bruises from his fingertips. "The Dark Fae are strong. They are powerful, but you have the power to wipe them all out. Not only do you have the power of the Gods running through your soul, but you are also the Princess, a leader. Not everyone was born so lucky. So, stop your bitching and get to work." He snapped at her, his golden eyes aflame with anger. Misplaced anger, but all of it directed at her, nonetheless.

She felt the tears pour over her lashes but didn't let the heaving sob that she could feel building inside her leave her lips.

"General," Luc stood at attention, trying to draw Eric's attention from Audra to him. "How was the apartment? Any break-ins or people sniffing around?" Luc asked, without taking his eyes off of Audra. Eric's eyebrow twitched slightly, but he released her arm.

"Unfortunately, there were signs of more Wincts and other creatures sniffing around. Her scent was strong on her bed from where she started the change, and the mattress was ripped apart. I picked up at least three different tracks in the hallways and within her apartment. We need to be more careful. Redo the scent-shielding wards around the house more frequently. Her scent has increased tenfold since she has changed, and we don't need any loners scenting her up here."

Luc's posture changed. His protective instincts were flaring up again.

"You think they would be able to? I think we shouldn't take any fucking chances." Luc asked.

"At least we can agree on that. We need to move forward with the plan, we need to contact the Queen and King Consort. Now." Eric had transitioned into his rightful role of the First General to the Crown. He stood, his chest broadened, and shoulders squared.

"Let's do it." Luc said strongly. Audra didn't know what they were talking about, but she trusted Luc to do the right thing by her. If he thought going along with Eric's plan was the best way, then she trusted him.

"I'll go get the conduit ready. You two wait here." Eric said. He slowly stood and walked out the door with his shoulders slumped.

That struck Audra as odd. Why was he disappointed to be contacting her parents? What wasn't she aware of?

"It's going to be okay." Luc said, not even to her, but more to himself. He was the picture of determination, not a crack or edge of insecurity in his decision anywhere, except for deep within his eyes. Audra could see the doubt and fear lurking.

"Luc," Audra stood and joined him where he was standing, wrapping her hands around his one to be completely encircled. "What aren't you guys telling me?"

He took a deep breath, holding it for a moment and then releasing it loudly before bringing his other hand up to rest on top of their joined hands.

"If we go back, you and I will have to change how we act in public. How we communicate together and all that."

"Why?"

"You are a Princess. The future Queen."

"So?" Audra replied.

"So, I might be the First Lieutenant, but I am not of noble blood. I'm lower in the nobility chain than Eric. Some people might see our relationship as something to...dissolve or forget in hopes of creating a better alliance with a surrounding kingdom. There is a chance that your, or my, hand will be forced or manipulated. I don't want that to happen. I don't want there to be even a moment of doubt for either of us."

Audra was taken aback. She could feel the hurt, the festering disappointment, the hesitation that she might also feel that way.

"I would never, ever, do that to you. I won't let other people, who I don't even know, voice their stupid, unasked for opinions get in our way. You're mine, Luc Antonov." She said passionately, her eyes flaring with determination and resolve.

"As you are mine." He leaned down and kissed her soundly.

Nothing was going to stand in their way now. She was sure of it.

* * *

Eric walked into the sitting room, the room that was warded more deeply that they brought her into first, as Luc reached for the bowl of dark water that Eric brought in.

"What's that?" Audra whispered to Eric, not wanting to pull Luc's focus from whatever he was doing.

Luc slid down to the hardwood floor and sat cross-legged, hands over the bowl of dark liquid. His eyes were closed, seemingly completely still, except for the whispered mutterings of his barely moving lips.

"It's the conduit. We brought a few vials of it when we came through the Gate but have tried our best to not use it. Think of it as an 'only in emergencies' cell phone straight to the Queen and King Consort. The King Consort, your father, is a very skilled water element user."

"I'm in." Luc said, his hands still extended over the bowl, except now the water was rippling.

"Your Highness." Eric greeted, his voice firm and full of respect.

"Is my daughter, okay?" A deep voice that sounded like it was far, far away, and underwater. It was a struggle to hear what was said, but it blew Audra away, nonetheless. It was her father's voice on the other end of that connection. *Her father.*

And the first thing he wanted to know was if she was okay.

"She is safe. I have her protected. Lucien and I both do." Eric assured him, crossing his arms in front of him.

"Good. You keep her safe, whatever you need to do to keep her safe."

That was her father. Her father was worried about her.

Her eyes lined with tears. The feeling of belonging was astounding. She had always wanted to belong. Wanted to know where she came from, but never had anyone to ask or even start the search for.

"I will. On my life."

"Good."

"Sir, we have some things that we need to discuss."

"Go on."

"Audra has gone through the change. She is indeed a Total Elemental, as predicted. Her powers are immensely strong. We are working on controlling and growing them."

"Good, good."

"The problem is; when she began the Change her scent shifted strongly enough that a Winct was able to find her. We got her out in time, and she has been at the safe house with us through the rest of the time it took her to continue through the Change. But when I went back to make sure there were no followers, I was able to scent her from much farther away than normal. We are concerned about others being able to hunt her down."

There was a pause before her father answered.

"What would you suggest, General?"

"I believe that Audra needs a bit longer to fully hone her powers to an acceptable level where I would feel comfortable for her making the trip across the Gate."

Audra wondered what was this mysterious Gate they continued to talk about and why it was such a big deal if she went through it before she was fully ready to use her powers.

"That's...disappointing, but understandable. Her mother and I were hoping that you would be able to bring her to us sooner than later. How has she taken the news?" Her father's watery voice replied.

"As well as could be expected. Your daughter is exceptionally strong. In both mind and spirit. She is already inquiring about what is expected of the Princess of Vesperitus and how she can best serve her people. However, we believe it would be best for another guard to be sent to us for us to begin a guard rotation as well as keep the Princess working on her magic and learning about her nobility status. A teacher for her as well as another guard to help with security."

"Agreed. Her safety is our number one priority. We shall send our personal aid and guardian, Tomais. He is a skilled warrior and would also be capable of teaching her the inner workings of the court. Would that bring her some peace?"

Audra released a breath she wasn't aware that she had been holding. Relief flushed her body. There would be someone to teach her specific things that would be expected of her when they arrived. She wouldn't have to worry about embarrassing herself in front of her parents anymore.

"I believe it would." Eric answered, looking at her with an amused smile.

"Good. Expect Tomais in two to three days. It will take us some time to prepare him and send him through the Gate. Are you or Lucien in need of anything? Is Audra?"

"No, thank you, Your Majesty. Simply the manpower to help protect her as she deserves to be."

"Very well. Anything else to report?"

Before Eric could say anything, Audra jumped into the conversation.

"Dad?" Her voice was shaky and meek, but she had to meet him, had to tell him she was there. There was a pause that seemed to stretch on forever. Silence filled her ears, aside from the ripples of the conduit splashing into the bowl.

Eric and Luc shared a look one of worry. Audra could tell.

"Audra, darling?" His voice sounded just as taken aback, no louder than a whisper.

"Yeah," she said, her eyes lined with tears. "It's me."

"My darling girl. I'm so sorry. So sorry."

The heartbreak in his voice broke her. The tears ran freely down her cheeks, and she faintly felt her nails bite into her palm. She was clenching her fists so tightly, but her focus was elsewhere.

"Dad…"

"I'm so sorry Audra, I can't hold it much longer." Luc grit out. Her attention went to him, and she could now see the perspiration dripping along his brow, down his neck and absorbing into his shirt. He was breathing heavily; his muscles were taunt and straining. However, this connection worked, it must take an obscene amount of power.

"My darling daughter, we will have so much time to catch up and discuss anything and everything when you get here. Work as hard as you can and come see us. We've been waiting for you. We're so proud of you." Her father told her, his voice was strong and proud. She could almost picture what he looked like in her mind's eye.

"Your mother and I, we love you so much. More than you know. I promise you; we did what we had to do to keep you safe. To protect you. We would do -" The connection cut out as Luc's eyes rolled to the back of his head and he fell down, passing out on the floor.

"Luc!" Audra and Eric yelled, and they darted to him.

Eric reached him first, and he got to work, positioning Luc's body so he would be comfortable.

"What do I need to do? How can I help him?" Audra asked, terror lacing her words.

"He needs rest. Rest and water. Lots of it. Can you go get him some?"

Audra nodded and dashed through the room, back into the kitchen. She ripped open cupboards to find the biggest container she could find. Once she had procured a tall blue plastic cup, she turned to the stainless-steel faucet and pushed it all the way on.

It felt as if time was moving in slow motion. The water wasn't filling the cup fast enough.

Audra put her hand over the faucet, focusing on the water. The cold, clear liquid that could help bring Luc some relief or at least wake him up.

Time slowed down further.

Her focus funnelled down into a point.

It was just her and the molecules that were vibrating, dancing, and pulsing through the flow of the faucet.

Faster. She commanded, feeling the magic flow through her fingers, her mind, her skin, as she poured herself into the command. Forcing the water to behave how she wanted.

Audra could feel the strain, a headache forming once again behind her eyes. But she would get the water for Luc.

Within a moment, the cup was full, and water was running down the sides.

It was amazing. She could feel each part of the water moving and forming together, flowing apart and back together.

Follow. She commanded. She didn't know how much water Luc would need, if he needed a cup, a bathtub full, if he needed to feel its energy or anything like that. So, she made a decision and thought of it as an experiment.

As she picked up the overly full glass, she walked as quickly as she could back into the front room. A single ribbon of the water flowed behind her. She did her best to not be distracted, but it was beautiful. It was a life source all on its own, flowing and changing, following her through the house, floating in the air like a single string from the faucet.

The energy from the water was refreshing, innocent, and hopeful.

"Here," Audra shoved the cup into Eric's hands and knelt at Luc's other side.

Eric lifted Luc's torso so that it was resting against him and brought the cup to Luc's mouth, forcing him to drink.

"When he uses the conduit, it uses the strongest source water magic to keep the connection open." Eric explained as he forced another mouthful of water down Luc's throat. "Typically, when we are in Vesperitus, it's not a difficult feat. The magic is so much stronger there, but here, there aren't any organic magical properties. He had to forge his magic, along with your fathers on the other side, to maintain the connection."

"What can I do?"

Luc's eyes were still closed, but the color of his face was coming back to his normal tan shade. Less pale than it was while they were talking to her father.

"Can you have that water mist on him?"

Audra nodded even though this was something completely new, something completely out of her comfort zone, even more than normal.

She focused in on the energy surrounding her, that dancing ribbon of moisture swirling through the air, waiting to be called on. It was simply following her.

Audra raised her hands up, calling the water to wrap around her hands in tight tendrils. The water was cool to the touch, and it had almost a joyful exuberance as it forward through the air.

As it all came to form around her hands, she closed her eyes to concentrate on making the liquid form turn into a mist.

"You can do this, Audra. He is depending on you. Focus." Eric whispered, his words being the push she needed.

The moisture around her fingers hardened. It became a malleable object that she was able to move and fold within her hand. All while it kept its shape.

Mist. She commanded, and the gloves of water vaporized, sending mist throughout the air. Beads of water decorated the air around them, glinting in the light.

Audra's jaw dropped.

She had done it.

"Send it to him." Eric said, his tone equal part awe and patience, like a teacher would have with a student.

Audra pulled her attention back towards Luc, laying there with his eyes still closed. Resting on Eric's thighs, all because he was trying to help her. She thought back to how she had commanded the water to follow and pushed one hand out in front.

To Luc. She told the mist and watched as the miniscule droplets swirled through the space above them, much like snow in a blizzard as it looped through the wind, then dropped down over him.

Instead of remaining as droplets and drenching Luc as Audra was expecting to happen, his skin instantly absorbed the water like a sponge.

"Good job." Eric smiled at her.

"I hope it works."

"It will."

"You don't know that."

"But I know him." He emphasized. "And his magic will be able to recognize yours and accept it the fastest. Think of it as mouth-to-mouth resuscitation. This is no different. Luc will be fine."

"Damn right I will." Luc said weakly.

"Luc!" Audra gasped, clutching his hand in hers.

"How are you feeling?"

"I'm fine baby, I've definitely got a headache though." He sat up on his own, tossing a grateful pat on Eric's arm.

"I'll go get you some pain meds. Don't pass out again. Dumbass." Eric smirked as he walked out of the room in search of the promised pain relief.

"I'm so sorry. I'm so sorry. I didn't mean to make you keep the connection open."

"You didn't do anything wrong. And based on how I'm feeling, like I'm hydrated, and my magic is replenished. I take it you used your magic to refill my tank. So, to say."

She nodded and looked down at her hands intertwined with his.

"I did my best."

"Thank you."

"Thank *you*." She whispered and leaned in to hug him. He had held out as long as he physically could so that she could say a few words to her father. He had endured what she knew was a painful, stinging headache (and a killer one later) so that she could meet the man she so badly wanted to know. He had pushed himself too far for her.

Because he wanted to give that to her.

He wrapped his arms around her, tucking his face into her neck.

She was grateful for many things, but she would never be able to show just how grateful for the man in her arms she was.

* * *

"We need to talk." Luc said later that night as she was climbing into bed. They had all decided that Audra would share with luc while he was still recovering from overdoing it to keep the connection open with her father.

Dread filled her with those dreaded four words.

"Okay...what would you like to talk about?" Audra asked, hesitantly.

"Seb."

"Seb?" She asked, genuinely confused as to how he knew that name. Audra was certain she had never uttered it outside of her thoughts.

"He came to me when I passed out. Threatened me within an inch of my life to care for you until he can help. I couldn't see his face, but I heard his voice." Luc said, reclining against a soft, white pillow with a sigh.

"I don't know who he is." She whispered, laying down next to Luc on her side.

"I don't either, is he real?"

"Seeing as both of us have met him in a dream, I'm guessing yes."

"Do you trust him?" Luc asked. She looked into his eyes, expecting to see jealousy or anger, but instead saw genuine curiosity.

"I do." Audra said softly. Luc took a deep breath and looked up at the ceiling.

"Okay." Luc said suddenly.

"Okay what?"

"We trust him. He obviously takes your safety seriously and I can't fault him for that. He and I had a little chat and even though every bone in my body is telling me that you're mine and only mine," He took a deep breath and sighed. "I know how he cares for you. He made it very clear that he would do anything to keep you happy and protected. And I can't fault him for that."

Audra felt a small smile grace her face, and she put her hand on Luc's bare chest.

"I've never met the man out in reality. Yes, we have been somehow linked throughout my whole life, but up until recently I just thought it was a dream. He was a figment of my imagination born out of trauma. We've grown close throughout the years. But that doesn't mean that my feelings for you are any less. I care for you, more than I have ever cared for anyone." She confessed; her eyes locked on where her hand traced small circles over his heart.

"I care for you too. More than you know." Luc said softly and moved his hand around her waist, drawing her body closer to his so there wasn't any space between them.

"It doesn't mean I'm not going to be jealous."

"I understand." She said with a smile and kissed him soundly, effectively ending the conversation for the night.

Chapter Nineteen

The next few days brought lots of focused, quick draw magic tricks that the two soldiers would yell out at random intervals like Audra was some circus monkey. There to perform for their entertainment.

"Fire ball!" Eric yelled as she was running through the forest on a trail, they had discovered the day before. Audra concentrated on calling her magic to the surface and bringing out the fierce heat within her that would form into balls of fire about the size and weight of a baseball in her hand.

All while running, of course.

Eric and Luc had woken her up the morning after they talked to the King with a more concrete training and workout plan in order to get her prepared for any sort of fight. Initially Audra had fought against the idea, not seeing why she needed to take time away from learning and experimenting with her magic. Plus, she was already quick on her feet, so running three to five miles a day - depending on the mood the boys were in - didn't seem like a good use of her time.

Eric had won her over by compromising the ideas. They would work on her magic ability and control interwoven with the endurance and weight training.

The swish of her ponytail against her shoulders brought her back into the present as she tried to dodge a pop of exploding light that Eric sent her way.

"You're getting a little close there, General." Audra called out, ducking just in time to avoid the hot flash.

"You're not focusing."

Audra came to a stop, bending over and bracing herself on her spandex-clad knees.

"I am! How is this supposed to help me? You and Luc are having me run circles while throwing different elements at you. I get the weapons training, I get the hand-to-hand fighting, but this?"

"When we go through the Gate, you will be more vulnerable. There is more evil than just the Dark Fae in Vesperitus, Audra. And being a Total Elemental on top of a High Royal? Your scent will be so distinctive that as soon as you are within six feet, everyone will know who and what you are. You need to be prepared in any situation. Hopefully, to simply throw an element and run."

Eric stood in front of her, seemingly unaffected by the two miles they had already run. Not a hair was out of place amongst his golden head, barely a glisten of sweat over his tanned skin.

Audra was jealous and annoyed. It wasn't fair that he looked that good when she was gasping for breath, bent over in exhaustion, her hair sticking to her shoulders and sweat pouring out of every one of her pores.

She felt gross, hot, and frustrated.

"I can take care of myself. Plus, I have these two guardians: The First General to the Crown and his First Lieutenant. Apparently, they are the best warriors in the land, you know." She added cheekily.

"We aren't taking any chances." Luc came to a stop behind her.

She wanted to roll her eyes, play off their utter need to teach her to defend herself as something unnecessary. Something blown way out of proportion. But she knew that it was something that frightened both of them.

The thought that soon she could possibly be in a situation that they both couldn't help her, couldn't protect her with their lives.

Not that she ever wanted them to lay down their lives for hers. It made her sick to her stomach to think that they felt that way, that they would toss their lives aside so easily. And for what? Hers?

Not worth it.

So, she ran. She learned how to fight more effectively with Luc. She let Eric stand on the sidelines and critique her form or technique. She let Eric teach her about swords, daggers, small guns. Anything that she could use to injure someone and get away.

Audra did all of that so that should the situation ever arise where Luc would be forced to throw himself in front of her, she could hold her own and maybe protect him as best as she could.

"Now, make some boulders. Big enough to make someone that is chasing you pause." Luc demanded, stepping back out of her space.

With his command, she knew that he meant for her to start running again.

So, she did.

"Boulder!" His voice boomed behind her.

With a flick of her wrist, a grand mass of soil shot through the grass and stiffened at jagged peaks. The smell of freshly turned earth filled her nostrils, but she kept running. She had stopped for a slight moment to get the boulder formed where she wanted and took off again.

But that moment had cost her.

Audra couldn't see Eric any longer. He was running behind her a dozen meters or so back, but he was not within her eyeline.

She could still feel someone watching her. She could only tell they were both close by but staying hidden.

Looking back and forth, she strained her eyes, trying to see either of them between the trees. But they weren't there.

This had to be a test. She was sure of it. Intentionally trying to catch her even more off guard.

Audra closed her eyes and reached out with her Fae senses.

She sniffed the air and tried to isolate the notes that were distinctly Luc. Her feet moved on their own, hunting down her partner to make sure he was okay.

She stopped.

She listened.

There were the subtle noises of the wildlife, of nature flowing through the forest. Insects buzzing, the wind rustling the leaves in the treetops above, a songbird flying overhead.

And a twig snapping.

She turned in the direction of the noise, seeing him right before he lunged for her. The twig snap had been the only warning she got before he tackled her to the ground, causing Audra to hit the ground with a thud and the air being knocked out of her chest.

Her adrenaline spiked in her blood, and she forced a gush of air towards him, throwing Eric off her. It disoriented him enough that Audra was able to grapple to her feet and take a defensive stance.

"What the fuck was that?!" She yelled at him. Her head had hit the ground hard, not having had enough time to brace herself, and it hurt like hell.

"I wanted to see what you would do." He said nonchalantly. As if tackling and hunting her down in the forest was a normal thing for them.

"You wanted to see what I would do. You prick."

Audra felt the back of her head, feeling a raised knot at the base of her skull. Luc came up next to the pair and started dusting her off.

"You did well, if it's any consolation." Luc said, trying to show her the positive.

"It's not. Now my head hurts."

Eric crossed his arms over his chest, looking broad and indifferent. Like he didn't care that he had hurt her. But before Audra chided him for his lack of remorse, she realized that maybe his reaction was genuine. Was he actually trying to hurt her?

"Let's get back to the house. There are painkillers there, your highness." Eric said, turning on a dime and leading the way back to the house.

"What, you're not going to make me run more?" Audra asked.

"Not right now."

"Wow. Mr. Warrior is cutting me some slack on my training. Are you okay? Did you hit your head?"

He didn't respond, and she lost track of him through the trees.

"Nothing? Nothing from you either? Man, you two must be sleepy or something if a 21-year-old girl can keep running when you're stopping. It's that old age catching up to you, huh?" She smarted off to Luc, trying to press his buttons.

"Keep it up, baby. See what happens." Luc taunted. His voice deepened and his grip on her hand tightened.

"I'm just saying you have been so strict about my training. Are you sure you are going to be able to let another two-mile run slide? What would the rest of your squadron say?" She mockingly gasped.

"First off, I am the First Lieutenant. I train the warriors. I myself am a fully honed weapon. Second, you're my girl. My love. And I am not going to make you keep pushing yourself when you are already injured. But you know what. You're right." He dropped her hand and his pupils dilated as he looked her over.

"Run along, baby. If I catch you, you are in for it."

"And if you don't?" Audra's voice was barely above a whisper. She could feel the beginnings of that sensual heat building in her belly, the pain in her skull subsiding in favor of the excitement from the new game he was starting.

"I will."

"We'll see." She taunted and took off running again. This time, she would ignore the panic of not seeing him behind her. She knew what was going to happen now.

She kept her attention on the trail ahead of her. Feeling how the leaves crunched under her feet as she flew through the forest. She felt free, free, and utterly alive.

"Run, run, run, baby! I'm going to get you!" Luc yelled behind her, his voice booming through the trees.

Audra was torn between wanting to beat him, to keep her pace ahead of him so that she would win, but also wanting to let him catch her to see what he was going to do.

She ran.

Flying past fallen trees and greenery all around her, she slowed her pace down just a bit. With her mind made up, she slowed down, wanting to see what he would do.

She also didn't want to make it too easy on him.

The joy, lust, and determination were pulsing through the both of them, feeding off of each other and growing in need of one another.

Audra felt her breaths come shorter as she willed her legs to run faster. She turned her head quickly back to make sure she had run enough that she had a buffer between the two of them.

And in that split second, she turned, her foot landed on a slippery pile of leaves. It was just wet enough that when she put her weight on it, the whole pile moved and brought her down with it.

"Fuck." She muttered as she caught herself on her knee.

There wasn't any other damage. Her ankle felt fine, but the slip had cost her time.

"Well, well, well. I caught you."

"I tripped. You didn't catch me." Audra knew she should stop smarting off, but she couldn't help it.

Luc gripped her bicep and lifted her to her feet, never once breaking eye contact. The heat and desire he felt for her burned into her, making her own heat build even higher. It threatened to combust.

And once it did, all bets were off.

"I got you, baby. You know what happens now." His voice was husky as he tugged her back up to his chest.

"What?" She whispered, her breaths coming in pants. She loved this side of him; dominant, assertive, and not afraid to take what he wanted.

They hadn't been together but a handful of times since they formally become whatever it was that they were. But when he let this side of himself free, Audra couldn't help but shiver in pleasure.

"I claim my prize."

Luc's hands started to roam her body. His touch was harsh, unforgiving, but she loved it.

His hands, easily twice as big as hers, groped her chest, teasing her nipples through her sports bra. She already could tell that they were hardening against the fabric.

Audra moved her hands behind her to touch him, but it was like a shock current through him as her palms met his thighs. Luc's hands dropped from her body and wrapped around her wrists. She was injured, and she knew it, but she was so turned on that nothing else mattered except for his hands on her.

"You don't get to touch me right now. *I'm* claiming *my* prize. Hands behind your back and keep them there." His tone changed into that deep vibration that made her powerless to do anything but obey him.

"Good job, baby." He whispered in her ear when her wrists locked behind her bum.

Luc moved slowly around her, circling her like a predator that had caught his prey.

"You're so beautiful. I'm so fucking lucky that you're mine." He asked her, cupping her jaw, and bringing their faces closer together. The smile he gave her was radiant. It took her breath away. Then he leaned down and kissed her.

It started sweet, loving, but quickly turned deeper, hotter. His tongue swiped across her lips demandingly, insistently. She opened her mouth slightly, and he plundered. Audra couldn't help it and a moan escaped her.

"We're just getting started, baby." Luc said. One of his hands slid up her arm, leaving goosebumps in its wake, until it reached the nape of her neck where he ran his fingers into the hair there.

It stung because her hair was tied up in a ponytail, but he gripped her hair and yanked, tipping her head up to get better access.

Luc's other hand ripped her hair tie out, letting her wavy brown lock fall.

"So, fucking beautiful." He smirked and started to place hot, wet, open-mouthed kisses on her neck.

She knew she'd have marks on her neck after they were done, deep purple marks across her throat. A claim on her.

"Luc..."

"I know, baby." He shushed her.

His hands slid down over her tits, over her waist, down the front of her leggings. He touched her slit lightly over her clothes and Audra felt her arousal drip out of her.

"Is this what you want? Do you need me to touch you?"

"Yes, yes, please." Her pleas were breathy.

He pressed his warm chest against her back, reassuring and strong, so she let all her weight rest against him. Her head tipped up, resting on his shoulder as she closed her eyes. Focusing solely on his touch.

"Let me unwrap my prize." Luc's voice rumbled in her ear as his hands drifted to the waistband of her leggings, slowly pulling them down until her front and her rear were exposed.

The cool air on her overheated skin made her gasp, and Luc just chuckled.

One of his fingers slid up and down her slit, testing her as he played with her clit.

"You're so wet, baby. Is this all for me?"

Audra was so close, so on edge from all of his teasing that she didn't think she could answer.

"It is, isn't it?"

His finger dipped lower, sliding just the tip inside her. Audra's eyes rolled back.

"You want this, don't you? For me to take you out in the open."

Audra nodded, too far gone to do anything else.

"Say it, baby. Say you want this."

He slid his finger into her heat deeper and deeper until she couldn't anymore, then slid out achingly slowly, only to push back in.

The slow pace was torture for Audra. She needed more but at the same time, relished the feeling of her walls clenching around his finger, trying to keep him inside.

"Say it or I'll stop."

His other hand that was holding her hips slid up her body, never breaking contact, and gripped her throat lightly.

"Say it." He whispered.

"I want it! I want you! Please!" She cried out, so close she wanted to cry.

Luc groaned and withdrew his hand from her legs, causing her to whimper from the loss.

"Please Luc, please, I'm so close." She was aware she was blabbering, but he did this to her, caused her to lose her cool.

"Hush baby, I know." He murmured in her ear.

Audra heard the rustling of clothes and was yanked around to face him.

"I'm going to give you a choice now. Do you want me to fuck you against a tree or on the forest floor? Make your decision quickly because if you don't answer by the time it takes me to get us both naked, I'm deciding."

He was already shirtless, but she only had on her sports bra, leggings that were wrapped around her knees, and he had his basketball shorts.

"Is this what you want?" He asked her huskily, his voice lowering with his want for her.

Audra nodded.

"No, baby, I need your words." He said roughly and ripped the tight spandex from her body, handling her like a doll to take her clothes from her body as quickly and as efficiently as possible.

"Tell me." He demanded.

He wrapped his thumbs in the waistband of his shorts as she said, "Yes! Yes, the tree," quickly.

Smiling, sexy and confident, he took the last piece of clothing standing between them and stepped out of his shorts.

"Good choice."

He wrapped his hands around her thighs and lifted her to him, carrying her to the nearest tree. Luc slammed her against it with so much ferocity, she let out a cry. He swallowed her cry as he kissed her deeply.

"Please…" Audra asked.

"I could never deny you, baby." He whispered. He reached down between them and rubbed his cock against her slickness, coating himself in her. Luc groaned. He notched himself at her entrance and his hand went to tweak one of her rosy nipples.

He whispered as he thrust up into her. Audra gasped as much at his confession as she did at the sudden fullness, the union of the two. "I love you."

"I love you too." She gasped, finding her grip in his hair and on his shoulder.

"Hold on."

He set a brutal pace, one that had her scrambling to match with each drag of his cock through her tight walls.

"Fuck, Audra. Fuck, baby. You're so tight."

"Luc, Luc."

"I'm not going to last long."

"Me neither." She confessed and yanked his head to hers, meeting him in a clash of teeth and tongues. As they kissed, their mouths were fighting for dominance, rough and hard.

Audra could feel how hard Luc was, how deep he was hitting from this angle, and every time he bottomed out, she swore she could see stars.

"Come for me baby, please, please come for me." He grunted against her neck.

Audra could feel the familiar tightening happening, but when Luc slid his hand to rub her clit as he was slamming inside her, she lost it.

"Fuck, that's it. That's it, baby." He groaned. Her walls clenched down on him as her orgasm ripped through her violently.

Audra's head tipped back, and her eyes screwed shut as Luc continued to thrust hard through her orgasm, chasing his own.

"Yes, yes, fuck, yes." He groaned in her ear as his pace increased even more.

Audra didn't even have time to come down from her peak before he bit her shoulder and hit a spot inside her that had her seeing stars. She could very quickly feel a second peak forming, but she was still reeling from the first.

"I'm going to come, baby. I can feel you tightening again, come with me." He demanded in a husky tone, his shallow breaths fanning her neck. One of his hands snuck around to her front and rubbed her clit with fast, concise, borderline too harsh circles.

Audra cried out; it was too much for her. The deep thrusts, the hard circles on her clit, the sound of their coupling ringing through the forest, her back digging into the bark of the tree he held her against. Too much, it was all too much.

"Let go, I've got you." He whispered right before she clenched down around him, crying out his name.

"Yes," Luc groaned, his thrusts turned sloppy as he continued to fuck her through the waves of pleasure. Audra felt a pull. A pull outside the two of them, but it didn't feel dangerous. At least not to them.

It was a darkening of shadows surrounding the trees, as if the shadows cast from the trees were growing darker. It was so steady that Audra had to focus as the darkness grew. She wasn't afraid, not worried enough to stop Luc, but it was interesting. She knew someone was watching them. Was it a friend or a foe?

Audra knew Luc couldn't see what was happening, he was far too busy bringing them both mind numbing pleasure. Whatever was happening with the shadows was familiar. The energy that was shifting through the trees, through the ground beneath them, it all felt so familiar to her.

Luc grunted, and he stilled, buried deep inside as she felt his release fill her.

The two of them were breathing deeply, faces tucked into each other as they came down from their mutual highs.

"What is that?" She asked, out of breath.

"Fucking awesome is what it is." Luc replied with a laugh, pulling back to look at her face. She unlocked her legs that had clung to his hips and slid down him.

"As much as I agree with you, that wasn't what I was talking about."

She stepped out of his arms and gestured around them.

Luc's attention left her as he took in what she was showing him. The shock was very visible on his face. His eyebrows were so high they almost touched his hairline.

"It looks like..."

"Like what?"

"Like darkness spreading through the forest. We need to go." Luc withdrew from her and grabbed their clothes, handing her outfit at her and redressing quickly.

Chapter Twenty

"Is that a thing?" She asked, standing in the middle of the forest, scrambling to put on her sports bra.

"How? Why does it feel familiar?"

Luc lifted his head and watched as Audra moved closer to the darkness which had grown from just shadows to full-blown cover. In between two thick tree trunks was a darkness so opaque Audra was sure if she stepped through it, she would fall into nothingness. It wasn't scary to her but calming.

She put her hand into the darkness, and she felt another grab hers. She startled but didn't cry out at the large, warm hand that enveloped hers in the darkness. Audra wasn't able to see anything, and she tried to move forward to see what was on the other side, but she ran into a force. It felt similar to the wall of wind she had constructed around her when she was awakening her powers.

"Why can't I go through?" She said, quietly. The hand on the other side was caressing her skin, stroking her knuckles, and grasping her palm. It felt nice, sweet, and loving. Audra was about to pull her hand back when the pair of hands on the other side grasped her hand tightly and moved it up. Under her palm was a warm chest, muscled pectorals, and a heavy heartbeat. She was touching someone's chest, or rather, someone was having her touch their chest.

Her heartbeat moved faster in time with the movement.

"Audra?" Luc called out, walking over to her from where he had been tying his sneaker.

"Coming!" She hollered back and tried to pull her hand away. The hands on the other side lifted her hand, and she felt a soft pair of lips press a gentle kiss on her knuckles.

Audra's breath hitched and before she could do anything else, the darkness was dissipating like fog. The opaqueness had lessened, becoming see-through and translucent before disappearing altogether.

"That was really odd." Luc said, dropping his hand to her lower back.

"Yeah, yeah it was." She agreed, staring down at her hand. The hand that had been so lovingly looked after through the void.

"Let's get back." Luc said, taking her other hand and leading her through the forest, back towards the safe house. Audra let him pull her along, but the whole time, her mind was focused on other things. Especially, who was on the other side of the darkness?

$$* * *$$

"Finally!" Eric's voice boomed across the expanse of space between the two of them as they stepped out of the tree line opposite the front of the house, where Eric was leaning against the column.

The white of the house was a stark contrast to Eric's dark shirt, pant combo and his grim expression.

"We have a visitor." Eric said when Audra and Luc had crossed the yard.

Luc had kept himself slightly in front of Audra throughout the entire walk home and she was not surprised that he was keeping it up even as they entered their home. Luc was on edge, willing to throw himself at this newcomer to protect Audra. She could feel his nerves, his doubts at bringing in someone else.

"This is for the best, love." She murmured softly to him, giving his hand a quick squeeze.

"I know," he nodded and hung his head slightly. "Remember how we said we would have to act differently around others? Unfortunately, that has to start now, baby."

Luc gently unhooked their fingers and extracted his hand from hers.

"Already? But we aren't even in Vesperitus." She gasped.

"He is the most trusted advisor to your parents, to my Queen and King. If they discovered I am not being... respectful of your position, I could lose my job, my title, and then how would I be worthy of you?" Luc said as his head fell, his eyes dropping from hers. His whole demeanor had changed and the air surrounding them was tense but mixed with sadness.

"Hey," she cupped his chin, feeling the dark stubble scratch her palm. A reassuring and soothing feeling. Audra gently moved his chin up so his eyes had to meet hers.

In his eyes, she could see his fear; the fear that he might not be worthy of her. The fear that maybe he isn't because of how their relationship progressed. But also, shining right beside his fear, was adoration. She could tell that he would never regret how their relationship was, how they interact, or how it came to be. She was his and, in turn, he was wholeheartedly hers.

"I am the one not worthy of you, Luc. I love you." Audra reached up on her toes to close the distance between their lips and gave him a light, chaste kiss. She knew how nervous the soldiers were at suddenly having a chaperone, especially with one with a direct link to the High Royals. So, she wouldn't push it, but she would not let people who she hadn't even met yet dictate how she interacted with the family she *knows*.

"How do you want to proceed?" She asked quietly.

"I am your guardian, first and foremost. Eric and I will enter the room before you conclude that it is safe for you to enter and then escort you inside. I will wait here while Eric does the sweep and meets Tomais."

She nodded.

"You know that wasn't what I was asking."

"I know. We can't touch, no nicknames, only formal titles. I'll call you Princess, but you can continue to call us by our first names."

"But above all," Eric cut in, his arms crossed over his chest as he leaned against the column and watched the two of them. "You two need to be appropriate and professional. If they or any of the Court discover that you've been together intimately, it could be bad."

"Bad like we've already talked about." Luc reminded her.

"I get it! I get it. Will you please go inside and meet the guy so we can get this over with?" Audra snapped, dropping her hands to her hips, and tossing her hair over her shoulder.

"I'll give you two a minute."

Eric turned his back and stepped just inside the screen door.

Audra turned to Luc and as she opened her mouth to tell him how regardless of how much things would change soon, her feelings for him never would. His mouth devoured hers. It was a rough, heated kiss that took her breath away. She wasted no time in returning it.

Through their bond, there were so many emotions swirling and twining together, love, adoration, fear, nerves, wonder, lust.

Luc broke the kiss as swiftly as he started it. His hand wrapped the column of her throat, and he leaned his forehead against Audra's.

"I would do anything for you." He whispered.

"I know. And I would do anything for you."

Luc smiled brightly, the light in his eyes brightening his whole face. Audra hoped she had reassured him but made a mental note to show him just how much she loved him later that night. She assumed they would still share a room. She hoped they would.

* * *

Luc walked into the house after Eric had come out to guard her, the screen door snapping against the frame.

"How's he doing?" Eric asked her, coming to stand right beside her as they both stared at the house from the grass.

"He was worried. Nervous that something between us would change. The big oaf." She rolled her eyes.

"He just got you. Now he has to pretend that he is just your appointed guard. Luc's always worn his heart on his sleeve with those he cares about."

Audra nodded absent-mindedly crossing her arms loosely across her middle.

"I still don't get it. Why would it matter if we are together? But I'm not going to push the subject. Not when it could cost you both your positions within the Guard."

Before Eric could say anything, Luc walked out. His stance and demeanor remained aloof and confident; his soldier face was on.

"Princess, General. If you would please join me."

Audra walked forward, Eric right on her heels.

"I'll keep you protected." Luc whispered as Audra walked past him, squeezing past him through the door frame.

Eric led the trio into the front room.

"This is Princess Audra Leah of Vesperitus." Eric announced, as he stepped to the side to reveal Audra to the advisor.

"Princess." Said the unknown man, staring right at her with wide eyes. Like he couldn't believe she was real.

Chapter Twenty-One

Standing in the middle of the room, a tall man with shaggy white hair, kind eyes filled with light and dark skin that looked so soft Audra wanted to run her hands down his forearms, stood with his hands clasped behind his back as he dipped his head. A small bow, but a monumental show of respect.

"My name is Tomais Sarcantov Anton the Third. I am the Royal Advisor to the Crown, but I am also a skilled warrior. I've led many men into battle and made it my mission to keep them alive. It is an honor to help protect the long-hidden Princess." He bowed lower in front of her. Audra looked to Eric, unsure how to handle this. Her first instinct was to shake his hand and thank him, but is that what was proper in the court?

Luc surely was able to feel her nerves about the situation as he stepped to stand closer to her. Still behind her, but close enough, she could feel him like a phantom.

"Please stand. Thank you, Tomais, for coming so quickly to help us. I hope there won't be much need for your military experience, but I appreciate it. I know Eric wanted to discuss protection details and training with you." She said, keeping her head high and shoulders back. Fake it until you make it, right?

"Of course." Tomais stood from his bow with a small smile. He dipped his head again towards Audra and then turned to Eric and Luc.

"General, Lieutenant."

"If you want to follow me, we can head to the kitchen and let Lucien help the Princess with her water element." Eric stepped around Audra, keeping his arm out to guide Tomais through the house. Both Tomais and Eric stopped at the door, turned to her, and bowed.

Shock must have been visible in her expression because Eric looked like he wanted to burst into laughter but controlled himself before turning and leading Tomias out of the room.

"Well Princess," Luc said, his voice full of mirth, like he was talking with a smile on his face. "You did good. Very professional, very regal."

"I'm so glad I was able to fool you all." She rolled her eyes.

"Or you just stepped into your role that has been ingrained within you. Trust yourself more, Audra. You're going to be wonderful." Luc said. She felt his comforting hand on her shoulder.

"Thank you."

"Anytime. Come on, let's go play with some water." He said with a smile, taking her hand and leading them out of the house.

* * *

Audra stood at the top of the porch steps, watching on as Luc summoned water. For a few moments he stood there, eyes glowing blue, with his hands raised overhead and his palms facing in front of him.

Nothing was happening.

"Just going to stand there?" He called out, his focus never breaking from his magic. He never turned his head back to look at her.

"What exactly do you expect me to do? There isn't any water around. Aside from the water in the hose. Want me to get that for you?" Audra said with a smirk, her arms crossed over her chest.

She truly did love sassing off to Luc, especially because of what it would lead to.

"Nice." Luc said with an eye roll, the blue of his eyes never dimming. "Really embracing that smart ass, Princess cliche aren't you?"

"Hey! Not nice."

"Wasn't trying to be. Just stating a fact."

"Fuck you."

Luc was smiling so brightly that Audra couldn't help but return the smile. He wasn't changing how they interacted yet, but she was aware that both of them would have to become colder, more professional, and less like lovers out of respect to her position and their gained honor, gained favor with the royal family.

"Come on, Princess. Help me call the water from the pond."

"All of it?" She asked in awe. That was...That was a lot of water to try to transport, a lot of water to hold control over and a lot of distance to cover.

"As much as you can."

Audra nodded and closed her eyes. She pulled on the thread of magic that was tied within her to the water in the air, the ground, the energy surrounding them. She could feel Luc's magic through the scarce water in her immediate area. It felt cold and strong. Like ice. Reinforced over time; dense and steadfast.

She could feel that he was calling on an enormous amount of power. Was that what he felt like each time he used his magic? Or was it just related to how much water he truly was wielding at the time?

"I can feel you." He said, his eyes never leaving the area in front of them, never dimming. "Your magic, I mean. It's loud."

"Loud?"

"Like a firework going off in a library."

"Is that bad?"

"No baby, it's just different from mine. But try to focus on the water signature I'm holding onto. I've started collecting and holding water from the pond. Can you help?" Luc said.

Audra's magic seemed to follow parallel to his. Her 'firecracker' magic crackling alongside his ice.

In her mind's eye she followed his trail left behind, watching it twine and turn throughout the forest until it made its way to what she felt was their safe haven, their little oasis.

As her magic approached the large body of water, she could feel just how heavy and dense the whole pond would really be. She pushed her hands up, palms together, before she cupped them and made a circular motion through the air. As her hands moved together, she started to feel the weight of the water she was lifting into the air.

"There you go." Luc said quietly beside her.

"The whole pond?" She asked him, the strain was very evident in her voice.

"As much as you can."

"As much as I can?"

"You can do it. Consider this a test."

Audra was too distracted within her own head trying to figure out how to lift the ton of water, how to communicate with the water effectively and quickly. She didn't exactly want to show how little she knew, or was able to do, to these guys. It felt easier to be weak and vulnerable with Eric...they had had one too many drunken confession nights for her to not be comfortable. But with Luc... he had always seen her as a strong individual, given her independence, but never made her feel as if she was a burden. As she looked back at their times together before...everything, she saw that he had always treated her like a Queen, his Queen. And under his gaze, she felt strong.

With a muffled grunt, she forced more water to flow from the pond up into the air. She could tell that Luc was standing by, ready to jump in. His nervous jumpiness was impossible to ignore, but to his credit, he never said a word.

She commanded the water to lift higher. In her mind's eye, she was able to see the water float up slowly, forming an amorphous blob hovering over the reduced waterline.

Audra could feel the sweat break through her hair line and start to bead, dripping down her temples and to her neck.

"Maybe you should..." Luc started, but Audra cut him off.

"Shh."

She dug deep, keeping a firm grip on the other teathers of her magic, as she reached within her and pushed all her energy into the task.

"Audra...please..."

"I can do this."

"I know you can. That's not even a question. But" Audra cut him off again.

"No, please, let me try." Her voice has started to waver from the exertion. It was a lot, borderline too much.

If Luc could do it, I could too. Audra continued to repeat in her head.

She brought her hands together and pulled the threads connecting her to the water. The water started to travel down the invisible line, making its way towards them.

Audra could feel that Luc had withdrawn his magic. This feat was all her own.

"Princess." She heard the deep voice of the General call out for her, but she was unable to lose any of her control. Any of the hold she had on her magic and the pressure of the pond she carried.

"General, let her focus." Luc stuck his hand out to halt Eric's onslaught.

"She's pushing too hard. Her magic is going to burn out." Eric snapped under his breath at Luc. They must have been far enough away from Tomais for Eric to speak that way about her.

"Baby, don't push it." Luc whispered towards her, but not moving any closer.

"I can do this." She said, strong and true.

The sound of bubbling water creeped into the clearing, announcing the arrival of the water and the end of the impromptu test Luc had set out for her.

"Slow down." Eric whispered; his arms crossed over his chest as he displayed on his face just how upset he was at her pushing her limits too far.

They weren't wrong. Her vision was starting to dim, the sunlight becoming too much for her to handle. The telltale sign that a migraine was beginning.

Just a little longer, just a little farther. She wanted to bring the pound to Luc, right in front of him, and have the water crash around his feet. He could send it back. She brought it here.

"Princess." Luc's tone was sharper, deeper. His disapproval at her obvious pain was very evident in the one word. Audra absentmindedly wondered how far Tomais was and what he would make of their relationship if she snapped at him.

"Relax Lieutenant." Eric said.

"Do not tell me to relax."

Audra brought her hands together, feeling the magic ripple from her, through her magic and out into the blob of water settling in front of them.

"What now?" She said through her clenched teeth.

"Let it go, I'll take it from here." Luc said softly.

"Can you send it back?" Eric asked.

"Um," she hesitated.

On one hand, she wanted to prove that she could do anything. But on the other, she promised them both she wouldn't push too hard and burn out. Audra could feel the signs coming on. But she wasn't a quitter.

"I can." She decided with a grit to her teeth.

She knew that Tomais was watching her somewhere. She knew that he would be reporting to her parents. The last thing she wanted was to look weak, to not even try. So, what if she failed? At least she had *tried*.

Luc let a growl rumble in his chest, barely audible to anyone but Audra.

"This is a bad idea."

Audra looked at Luc, her partner, her protector, her love. He was, without a doubt, pissed off now. His jaw was set in a hard line, his fists clenched under his arms where they were tightly crossed over his chest still, and his breaths were coming in huffs.

"I can do it."

"I know you can, Princess. But you're pushing it too hard." Luc snarled.

"I can determine that."

"Can you? You're not the best at stopping when something is bad for you."

"Lieutenant!" Eric snapped. The words sounded harsh and cruel coming out of his mouth. "Know your place."

Audra turned and gave him a sharp look, wanting to defend Luc but knowing that they were trying to keep respectful appearances. This shit was getting old already.

"Right, apologies to Your Highness." Luc dipped his head towards Audra in a small bow. He stepped closer to her and got on one knee.

"You're going to be the death of me one day. Please don't hurt yourself." Luc said in a whisper, but she rolled her eyes at her stubbornness. But at least it seemed like he wasn't going to try to stop her anymore.

Standing up, Luc clasped his hands behind his back and stepped back.

"Just think about how you brought the water here, but then let it flow back to where it is meant to be. It should be slightly easier to take it back, it wants to go home." Luc explained from beside her.

Audra took a deep breath and approached the water floating in front of them. She could hear the water ripple and splash; she could feel its energy flowing. It wanted to go home. It wanted to be back in its cradle. Audra reached up and felt the cool water lap at her hand. It recognized her and was caressing her.

"It's okay." She whispered.

Her headache was increasing by the second, but she put the pain to the back of her mind.

Closing her eyes, she reached back on the thread that connected them and held it close. The faint line of Luc's magic that she had followed to get the water had faded.

"How do I know where to send it?" She asked.

"How did you find it the first time?" Luc said.

"I followed the trail your magic left. It was easy to latch on and follow it."

"The water holds memory. It knows where it wants to go, where its home is. When you're working with your water element, the best thing is to connect with it. Let it talk to you, let it tell you what it wants or what it heard. If the water holds some kind of connection to you, it becomes like an old friend. Which is how I was able to call out to this pond so quickly. I tend to out to the pond frequently. It knows me, my magic, so it was more willing to follow."

Audra nodded.

She returned her focus to the water in front of her.

"Do you want to go back?" She asked it quietly, still not totally understanding how to communicate with it other than speaking. But then the water answered her. The energy she had felt earlier spiked in a happy way.

"I take that as a yes." She chuckled. "But the problem is, I don't know where back is for you. You're going to have to show me."

She pushed her magic into the water, letting the water guide her. The blob moved across the clearing and disappeared behind the tree line.

But Audra could still feel it, could still see it.

At each bend or fork in the trail, the water would give her that same happy energy spike to show her which way to go.

Her breathing was becoming shorter, the strain was feeling like she had been running sprints. Each muscle in her was becoming more fatigued. Luc had stepped closer to her again, close enough that she knew it was not appropriate for the vision they wanted to portray to Tomais.

She was so close, so close to passing this self-inflicted test.

When the water broke through the treeline of their little oasis, the happiness and joy was unmistakable. The water longed to be back there.

So, Audra gathered her last remaining strength and shoved her magic into the water to give it one last push so it could fly into the empty, drying cavern in the ground, missing something very vital.

"You did it." Luc's voice said, calming her and praising her at the same time.

The water clashed down into its holding spot like a tidal wave. The relief she felt from releasing her hold on such a large amount of element was almost enough to bring her to her knees.

Audra turned to Luc. The exhaustion was most likely very clear on her face, but also the pride. She smiled, wide and genuine.

"I did it."

"I knew you could." He said quietly.

"Thank you for letting me push myself. Even when I know you didn't want me to."

The headache she had tried to ignore came back in full force, the pain nearly causing her vision to black out and her stomach rolled.

"Aud?" Luc asked. She cupped her stomach and her forehead, pushing some pressure to her eyebrows to try and slow the torment.

"Luc." She groaned. He put his hand on her back, and Audra's skin tingled where he touched her. "I need to lay down."

"I told you. I knew that this would happen." Eric's voice cut through, sharp, and mean.

"At least I tried." Audra said softly, too ill to fight him or try to get him to change his mind and be proud of her.

"But now look at you. It wasn't worth it. Why do you even try? God." Eric rolled his eyes and crossed his arms over his chest. All of the confidence and pride that she had felt with such gusto not a moment ago drained from her, leaving her with embarrassment and feeling thoroughly mocked.

"Eric, she has to learn how to push her limits in order to learn. She didn't faint, didn't pass out. She's still standing after performing that monstrous feat for someone who has only had their magic for a few days now. Fucking back off and be better." Luc snapped quietly under his breath, and he helped lead Audra back towards the house. One hand on her waist and one cupping her elbow. Audra could tell that he was trying to keep a respectful distance for her, for Eric, for Tomais. But it didn't stop her from focusing on his hands and the heat rippling from him. Her chest filled with pride at his words to Eric, how he had defended her and praised her at the same time.

"Thank you." She whispered once they were out of earshot.

"He's being a dick. You're one of the strongest people I've ever met, and you can do this and everything you set out to do. You are going to be such an amazing Queen. But he thinks he can keep you in a fucking bubble to ensure that nothing happens to you." Luc rolled his eyes.

Audra had no idea that Luc felt that way, felt so strongly about how Eric had been so hesitant at her learning anything. It felt...comforting to know that she wasn't alone. That she wasn't crazy in feeling that way like Eric had made her believe.

"Thank you, Luc." She turned to face him and cupped his chin. His deep blue eyes looked like a tidal wave of emotion.

Luc's hand held her forearm, keeping her close to him for a moment. Then, as if he was burned by her touch, he ripped his hand away and stepped back.

"Do you need anything, Princess?" His words were utterly polite and distant. She looked over his shoulder to see Eric's fuming face and Tomais staring at them with such curiosity. Audra knew there was no way he wasn't aware something was going on between them now.

"No. Thank you. Can you let Eric and Tomais know that I am going to be resting and not to disturb me? I just need a little bit of time." Audra rested her hand on the banister, staring down into Luc's eyes. They were deep and full of emotion that she knew he was trying to tell her how he felt without needing words.

"Of course. Get some rest."

Audra opened the door to walk into the room but made sure to look back at Luc as he turned to walk back down the stairs. He stalled at the top stair, looking back at her.

An electric charge filled the space between them, buzzing and alive. She could not turn away from him, and it seemed he had the same problem.

"Please rest, my Princess." Luc said quietly and closed his eyes, leaving her alone at her door full of conflicting, confusing emotions.

Chapter Twenty-One

"Excuse me, Princess." Tomais's soft voice pulled Audra from her dreamless, exhausted sleep. Her head was only lightly throbbing. The soft, feather white pillows certainly helped ease the pain.

"I don't want to." Audra mumbled into the pillow. Why did she have to get up? She knew she was already in a bad mood because Seb hadn't been in her dreams at all.

"Dinner's ready." Tomais said very formally, standing at her doorway with his hands behind his back.

Audra couldn't help but laugh. Even Tomais found out she would do anything for good food.

"Okay, but I want hot chocolate and a whiskey on the rocks."

Tomais coughed as if he was uncomfortable. The silence stretched, and it made Audra smile into her pillow.

"I'm sure that can be arranged, Your Highness." His clipped, awkward words made her laugh out loud before she threw the comforter off and let Tomais out of his misery.

"I'll be right down. And don't worry about my spiked hot choco, I'll handle it." She called, running her fingers through her tangled curls, and swiping under her eyes for any sleep stuck there. Her clothes were still rumpled from sleep, but she just couldn't find it in herself to care. She haphazardly threw the white duvet back in place and left her room.

"Luc! It smells amazing!" Audra exclaimed excitedly as she bound into the kitchen, barefoot and feeling completely better. She walked right into his space and hugged his back as he stood at the stove.

"Princess." He said, his tone clipped and short. She felt his hard muscles tense at the contact.

Audra's body tensed at his dismissal of her and was getting ready to give him some choice words before she stepped back and saw Tomais sitting at the breakfast nook writing notes in a leather journal.

"Princess." Tomais said, closing the book. He stood and bowed his head slightly.

'Nope, don't feel comfortable with that yet.' She thought.

She turned to Luc and watched as he did the same.

'Oh god, not you too.'

"Please, you do not need to bow in any way, shape, or form to me. Not yet."

"Tradition. Respect." Luc mumbled under his breath, letting her know exactly why they would continue to do so.

"Princess, may I have a moment to go over the lessons I hope to have with you in the next few days?" Tomais held his hand out towards the table, gesturing for her to sit and join him.

"Of course. I am going to get my drink first if that's alright? Would you like one? Either of you?" Audra asked the room.

"Of course, Princess. And no, thank you." Tomais answered and returned to his writing.

"Lucien? Would you like a drink? Hot chocolate and whiskey?" Audra asked.

He had turned back towards the stove, stirring a large pot full of different vegetables and liquid. She wasn't lying when she had said that it smelled amazing.

"No, thank you Princess. I should get my own beverage. Or even go and get you yours." He said. Audra could see the flashing in his eyes as he must have realized his mistake, and he dropped the spoon to go get her drink.

"No, no! It is fine, I can get my own. In fact," she said with her hands raised in front of her. "I am going to go get you one. And you can't say no. Because I'm the Princess."

Luc laughed quietly, shooting her a wink, and picking up his spoon and stirring once again.

"Found a loophole, did you?"

She just smiled as she walked out of the kitchen and into the sunroom where, among the many bookshelves, there laid an alcohol cart. Eric was already at it, pouring her a generous helping of whiskey and himself a gin and tonic.

"Thank you." She said quietly. She was still hurt and pissed off at his words earlier, his belittlement and humiliation.

"I apologize for earlier. It was uncalled for."

"Yet you still said it." She took a sip of the whiskey he poured her.

"My plans, our plans, rest on you knowing your powers. And you aren't making as much progress as I had hoped. I was frustrated." Eric said offhandedly.

"Your plans? I'm not making enough progress? Fuck you, Eric." She turned and started to storm out of the room.

"Wait! I can't have you jeopardizing my position or the mission."

"Do you even hear the things coming out of your mouth, or are you that fucking arrogant to think that everything revolves around you? From here on out, you are not to talk to me. It's like I don't even know you anymore." Audra snapped.

Audra didn't know why he was doing this, treating her this way, but she was sick of it. It had gone from tolerable to worse. She turned away from him and grabbed the clear crystal bottle of whiskey to make Luc the drink she had promised him.

"Don't be like that, Princess." Eric said, his tone surprisingly nasally and pouty for someone so concerned about his image as First General.

"I'm not being like anything. Stay away from me." She snapped, filling a glass for Luc.

"Not an option, sweetheart." Eric snarled.

"Do not call me that." She snapped, her eyes blazing with rage, and she knew that the drinks in her hands had gone from cool to hot due to her anger.

"Dinner!" Luc called out, his voice cutting through the dangerous tension in the room.

Audra picked up the two glasses of whiskey, and with her head held high, she walked back into the kitchen ready to face what was coming.

* * *

"I understand that you are worried about not knowing the history of Vesperitus, of Dragmahara and the crown." Tomais said.

Audra brought a spoonful of the stew Luc had made to her lips and savored the meaty thick soup. Eric had rolled his eyes as Luc discussed all the different vegetables he'd used, all the nutritional facts and how it would fuel her body instead of hindering her progress to be stronger. As much as Luc loved to cook, he also loved to explain why his cooking was superior. Much to Eric's dismay.

"Dragmahara?" She asked, confusion coloring her tone.

"It is where the Royal family resides." Tomais said as he opened the notebook, she saw him writing in earlier to reveal a hand-drawn map.

Vesperitus wasn't a world or a city, but a country itself. Filled with a mountain range that separated the country into West and East.

"These are the Helios mountains," Tomais said as he ran his finger across the page. "They are named that in dedication to the commander of the light, Helios. Dragmahara sits right in the middle of the valley where the mountains meet the sea. They have freshwater from the Synuki River that runs wide and true directly to the south of the city. And they trade for anything they need that is not readily available by merchants who port at Port Honor, to the north or Port Marlevoski to the Southeast."

"What is this land? There does not seem to be much information written down about it." Audra pointed to the southwest corner of the country. A vacant emptiness that was cut off by a forking river, the mountain range, and a dark area.

"That is the territory still governed by the Dark Fae. The lead city is called Fullmaster. It is where the original rebels came from and where their supporters have decided to stay."

"Why would the King and Queen give them their own territory?"

"They did so, your Grandparents, in an attempt at peace. To keep the Dark Fae from terrorizing cities and trade towns. They could rule their own little piece but leave the rest under their rule and in peace."

"Smart." Audra couldn't help but admire the non-violent way her ancestors had tried to handle things. It was something she could see herself doing and wished she would be able to do the same.

"Or stupid." Eric mumbled low under his breath. Just loud enough for her to hear. Luc's eyes flashed in anger and Audra could see how his jaw clenched. He may not have agreed with how her ancestors handled things, but he was respectful about it.

"So Dragmahara is like the capital?" Audra asked, ignoring the mumbled insult, and moving on.

"Exactly, Princess." Tomais said with a small smile on his face.

"There is so much I don't know and am expected to know before I can lead. Before I can truly call myself, a Princess or embrace my role as a Total Elemental and protect the country."

"That is why I am here. Your father, King Anders, wanted to make sure you were taught the history of our land. Of your land. He had utmost faith that the General and the Lieutenant would be able to train you in magic and in physical combat, but he wanted to make sure that your knowledge of the Crown and of the country was similarly sound. I have made a plan that incorporates the three of us," Tomais gestured to the three men, "taking shifts with the Princess, doing guard duty, and also seeking out the potential threat."

Tomais flipped to another page in his journal, filled with charts and messy but concise handwriting.

"Tomorrow, I will work with the Princess, and we shall learn the Royal Family back two generations, Royal customs and mannerisms. The General will be going to the city to search for any possible signs of the intruder. The Lieutenant will be here on guard duty around the homestead. Then in the next two days, our roles will shift; I will head to the city or wherever it may be to search for the threat. The Lieutenant will work with the Princess on her magic and the General will be on guard. The last day, we will shift again."

"Very clever, Tomias. Thank you for taking care of this." Audra said with a smile, her nerves dissipating with the knowledge that she would be working, training, and learning every day from here on out.

Tomais blushed slightly and nodded. "You're very welcome."

"Sounds good to me. I am to focus on her physical combat training?" Eric asked, shoveling a large spoonful of stew into his mouth.

"That seemed to make the most sense to me, seeing as you trained warriors back in your early days as a Knight for the Crown."

"Perfect." Eric agreed.

Luc stayed quiet, contemplative as he read over Tomais' notes and his schedule.

"I will require more time with the Princess to help her with her magic. She does not just have one element to master, but all of them." Luc said.

"I can always spend a few hours with you after I train with Eric or am done with lessons with Tomias." Audra volunteered a solution.

Eric's eyes narrowed at his right-hand man and his nose flared, but he didn't say anything.

"That would be the best solution, Princess. Can we plan on that, Lieutenant?"

Luc nodded and took another bite of his dinner.

"Let's begin the schedule tomorrow. The General has alerted me to the evidence the lieutenant found at your home in the city, and we have discussed the next steps."

"What evidence? You didn't tell me about anything." Audra's gaze shot to the two guys who she had counted on for years. Who she had learned to trust and be honest with.

Suddenly, she was a Princess and they had resorted to secrets to 'protect her'.

"There was–" Luc began, and Eric cut him off with a sharp look.

"We discovered evidence that there had been a Dark Fae that night, not just the few creatures you knew about previously. And we thought it best to keep it quiet while you were training and unpacking all the new, raw information we gave you."

What a diplomatic fucking answer.

"Was that your choice to make?" Audra lowered her voice, but the anger was very clear.

"It was. I am your guardian. Your protector here. I chose to keep sensitive information quiet until needed for your mental health and wellbeing." Eric said, keeping eye contact with her the entire time.

He truly believed that what he was saying was true. And that he had done nothing wrong.

"Lucien?"

Audra turned her attention to Luc. His shoulders were slumped, and his head dipped lower. It was clear the decision had not been his, but he had gone along with it, anyway.

"My apologies, Princess."

"I cannot believe you kept this from me. More evidence than just my apartment being trashed? Evidence that there was someone there that night, trying to hunt me down? Not just a random creature like the one that I had known about, but a Dark Fae. Someone that is actively trying to kill me in order to gain my power. And you two just thought I didn't need to know that information. How *fucking dare* you?" She was seething.

Luc took her outburst, as he continued to look more and more guilty with each word she spoke. Eric was staring straight at her with absolutely no remorse in his eyes.

"It was a Dark Fae, Princess." His tone was mocking and harsh. Gone was her best friend and confidante. In his place was the man that had teased her, had ridiculed her in order to awaken her magic; the course, mean General. "Would you prefer to know he had left his mark on your pillow, had taken your things that we had to leave behind and that his shadows were lingering, trapped there in case you had returned? No doubt to try and incapacitate you or worse, kill you."

Audra paled. It was worse than she had thought.

Knowing that someone had done all that, had known where she was and was meant to capture her while she was so vulnerable, was enough to knock the breath from her lungs.

But the fact remained that they had kept it from her.

Audra stood from the table, deathly quiet.

"The fact is that it still wasn't your choice. It was mine. Don't do it again." She ordered and walked out of the room.

Chapter Twenty-Two

Audra stormed back up the stairs and slammed the door shut.

At least she wouldn't have to worry about Eric coming in to talk to her with his desperation to keep his good standing. She restrained herself from throwing herself on the bed like a dramatic Disney princess and instead walked over to one of the windows that framed either side of the large fluffy bed. The window overlooked the back of the house that lined the trees. They truly were secluded out there, far enough away from everything that it had probably given her a false sense of security. Now that she knew a Dark Fae was hunting her, she'd be more alert. More on guard when alone.

Not that she would be alone anymore with her three protective warriors.

Audra was still seething. She was upset because she had thought they finally, finally, understood each other and how she had felt tricked by their deception. Even if it was to keep her safe. They had discussed it, had sat at the table, and hashed everything out. Only to find them doing it, yet again. It was frustrating, condescending, and offensive.

Not only was she their future Queen, the person who would know absolutely everything and be the one protecting others, but she thought they were her family.

Her found family. But lately, that sense of familiarity had been fading more and more around Eric while her bond with Luc was growing stronger than ever.

Audra stood at the window, looking out into the thick wall of pine trees, their branches slightly swaying in the breeze. The sun was setting, but it was still light enough to be able to see the trunks of the trees. Rooted strongly into the soil.

A fog of black smoke swirling around two tree trunks directly within her eyesight. It was as if blackness rippled out around the strong trunks, completely encasing them. The opaque shadows brushed outwards from the treeline, making them visible to anyone not already looking.

But she couldn't take her eyes off it.

There was something beautiful about the dance of the shadows that kept her gaze. It looked exactly like what happened in the forest earlier.

The shadows retreated back from where they had slithered outward, back into the safety and darkness of the treeline. Audra watched them pull back, not dissipate like she thought they would. They pulled back like a slow-moving bungee cord.

They pulled back more and more until the shadows weren't abnormal. But just as Audra turned to look elsewhere for a figure, dressed in a fine pressed black suit with matching jet-black hair, leaned against the tree trunk to their side, crossing their legs at the ankles and relaxing into the position.

Audra couldn't believe her eyes. Someone had appeared out of the shadows.

This person, a male by the build of him, wasn't attacking them, wasn't sleuthing around, he was simply standing out of sight and watching the house.

She took a step closer to the window and the stranger's head snapped up to her.

He was breathtaking. And so familiar.

She knew she had some exceptionally attractive men in her life, but this man was handsome in a mysterious, smoldering way. His eyes were boring into the window at her, and even from that distance, she was able to see how shocked he was at her as well. His mouth dropped open slightly and seemed to drink in the sight of her. This man personified darkness; black hair, black eyes, black ink swirling around his neck and up to his ears. His smooth, pale skin only seemed highlighted with his apparent favorite color. Audra was gob smacked. He was beautiful and stared openly at her as if he thought the same of her.

A knock interrupted her ogling as she turned to face the door, but when she looked back at the mystery man - who she knew she had seen somewhere else before - was gone. Vanished.

Like the shadows.

"Come in." Audra called out. Her prior anger and rage had died down, as her curiosity about who the mystery man was increased.

"Baby?" Luc said hesitantly before opening the door.

At least it is Luc. I don't know what I would say if it was Eric. Audra thought. Her anger at his last words to her still simmering.

"Can I help you or are there more secrets you wish to keep from me?" She snapped, walking around the bed to aggressively pull the sheets back.

"Audra, baby, please. I know it seems like we were keeping more things from you but," Luc walked towards her, his hands reaching for hers as if to plead with her to believe him with touch.

"There is no 'but' about it, Luc. You did keep more things from me. Things that I should have known about before. I could have been more careful. I could have helped you look. I could have helped. Period. But you and Eric seem to think that I'm still some fragile little girl that you need to foster and fix. Well, let me tell you something, I can take care of myself just fine. I did it fine before I met you two and I will do it just fine when you two are gone." Audra poked him in the chest to emphasize each point.

"You're still learning your powers and it's our job-"

"I've said this already once to Eric and I'm not going to say it again, so listen up. Your lives are not more expendable than mine. We are family. I want to protect you two as much as you want to protect me. So, get over the whole 'she's our future Queen' thing and let me help. If I am the Princess, then you guys need to start acting like it and believing in me when I tell you something."

During her rant, she had gotten up on her knees on the bed and stood taller than Luc at his full height, so he was looking up at her slightly. She was angry, hurt, and tired of feeling one step behind. Luc nodded. A smirk crossed his lips, and he offered his hand out to her for her to get down.

"My apologies. But in my defense, you know how hard it is to change Eric's mind once it's set. Especially when it is your safety."

Audra had figured that was how it had gone down. Eric made choices for the both of them and then refused to hear any other option. She sighed. The longer that the three of them were here, outside of her reality in the city, the less she felt connected to Eric. It felt like he was changing along with her, but where she felt she was changing for the better, for a noble purpose, he was changing for the worse.

The Eric she knew back in New York was becoming like a flickering candle she could only catch glimpses of. Was who he was back home a facade as well? A mask he put on to get close to her and learn her secrets? To get close and learn how she ticked? She felt betrayed.

"Luc, was anything real? Between Eric and me? Was our friendship real at all? He... Since we've gotten here, you and I have gotten closer, continued on like before and then some. But Eric's changed and not for the better." She asked him softly, keeping her eyes trained on the floor.

He didn't answer right away, and the silence sent Audra into all the negative thoughts she was feeling and thinking, all the things she had tried to keep out. She heard him sigh and felt him plop on the bed right by where she was standing.

"Aud, I know. I don't know what is going on with him either. We've worked together for over a decade now and we've lived together for three years, but I've never seen him be this awful. Maybe he's just trying to distance himself from you."

Audra snorted. "Yeah, okay."

"I don't know, baby. I'm sorry. That's all I can say, I'm sorry."

"I know, love. I know. I just wish I could be both. Still the strong and independent Audra Jackson, not Princess Audra Heliander of Vesperitus. Heir to the Crown Royals and the throne. The future Queen that needs to be protected and hidden. The first Total Elemental in generations. I used to just be me. Now I feel like he thinks I need to be in a bubble directly under his thumb."

"Is that really so bad? We just want you to be safe." Luc asked, taking one of her hands in his and kissing her knuckles.

"Not necessarily, but I have to be able to grow. To learn. To push my boundaries and limits. But mostly, to be respected. Respected enough that others believe in my choices. Eric has continually taken that from me and humiliated me. Not only that, but I keep getting this feeling around him."

"What feeling?"

Audra paused. She knew that she could trust Luc. She has for years, but she was reminded tonight of how he decided to choose Eric and follow his directions, even if it went against what Audra thought. Maybe she couldn't trust him with everything quite yet.

"Nothing. It's nothing."

"Audra," Luc said, as he took both of her hands in his and brought them to his chest. His warm, calloused fingers wrapped around her slender wrist. "You can trust me, I promise."

He was so sincere, so genuine that it made Audra want to confess everything. All her doubts and fears. All her worries and thoughts. Luc sighed and gave her wrist a gentle squeeze.

"I'm here for you if you need anything. Even if you just want to vent about Eric. He is my General, but you're my best friend, my...love. All I want is for you to be happy." He cupped her cheek and dropped a soft, meaningful kiss to her lips.

Audra looked him in the eye and nodded. A small, barely there nod that let him know she understood him and was grateful that he wasn't pushing for more.

"What is wrong this time?" Eric's voice boomed from the doorway. Audra could hear the eye roll in his voice.

Lucs grip on Audra's wrist tightened, but he moved back slightly.

"Nothing, I was just checking on her. I came to apologize." Luc said quickly, standing and stepping in front of Audra.

It did not go unnoticed by her that Luc had put himself in between Eric and herself.

"There's no reason to apologize. I told you that downstairs. We did what we had to do to keep her safe."

Audra fought to contain her eye roll.

"Eric, do you really not even understand why I'm mad?"

"Do you really not understand that I'm trying to protect you? Stop being so fucking naive." He shot back. Audra could tell that he was getting more and more agitated, but what she couldn't fathom was that he was so closed off to anything she said regarding her own life.

She took a deep breath and let it go slowly, feeling the tension between her shoulder blades.

"Eric, I appreciate all that you are doing and all that you've done for me. But this, this way of going about it now that we are actually with other and around the formalities of the court and all the bullshit...it's not working! It needs to change. How we are treating and acting around each other needs to change. Now."

Luc looked as if he wanted to grab Audra and put her behind him while Eric's golden eyes lit ablaze with anger.

"I think I would know a little more about the royal court." His tone made Audra's jaw drop. "You're just a little girl trying to make it through with her independence still intact."

"What the fuck is wrong with you?" Audra could feel her own anger reigniting. All calmness from before Eric walked in had vanished.

"You don't understand what is happening. You don't understand how to defend yourself with your magic, yet you want to be involved in keeping everyone safe. You don't know how brutal and nasty the Dark Fae can be. I do. I know first-hand how barbaric they are. They will taunt and manipulate you until you don't know which way is up. They will use their powers to burn you, suffocate you in darkness, torture you with air, drown you alive and so, so much more. So, excuse the fuck out of me for wanting to keep you out of this."

With each word he spoke, he puffed his chest out and clenched his fists more and more. He looked deadly, every inch the First General who had led his troops into victory each time they were sent in.

"I understand. Really, I do. I understand why you want to protect me. I'm starting to see why even more that it isn't about me. It's about your own track record as the reigning best, most respected First General. Must protect your legacy at all costs. Fuck what I want, what I feel and our relationship." Audra fought to keep her voice down. As angry as she was at Eric, as belittled as she felt, she still wanted to protect his image and reputation.

He was still family.

"Stop being such a brat. It's done and over. Get over it." He snapped at her and slammed the door to her room with her and Luc still inside.

Before she had changed, back when they were still living in the city, he rarely spoke to her like that. Eric had always had a dominant streak, an unwavering sense that he was right above anyone else. There were times where Audra wouldn't wear her heavier coat when it was cold out and Eric would snap at her and lecture about how she couldn't take care of herself properly. Then there was the time, early in the beginning that she had commented on his... endeavors with the ladies, and he had slammed the door in her face and called her a 'nosey, idiotic little girl' (which he clearly hadn't meant for her to hear).

Since they had grown closer as friends all those years ago, she thought he had changed how he saw her.

But she knew now that she thought wrong.

* * *

"What the hell was that?" Luc hissed.

"I don't know. But I need some air." Audra ripped the door open and practically ran down the stairs. She could hear Luc following right after her.

"Audra, baby, wait a minute."

"I just need a minute. Please, Luc." She turned to face him before she walked out the front door.

"Princess," His switch to her title made her realize that there were people listening. His next move would be judged and reported.

"Lucien."

He took a deep breath and let it go slowly. Audra was aware that she was also holding her breath, waiting on edge to hear what he would say. Would he let her go? Or would he force her to stay with them inside the house?

He looked at her, and she felt like he was washing away her thoughts, wave by wave. But he must have found what he was looking for because he nodded.

"You remember how to summon the water? How to send a message?" He asked.

"Yes."

"If you need anything, feel for close water sources, or if you really need to, pull water from the ground. It's tough and difficult, but you could do it if you really needed to. Send a message to me and I will be able to find you. And please, please, stay close. Within yelling distance."

She was happy she would have kissed him. If not for the audience.

So instead, she smiled at him and let him see the pure joy and gratefulness that she was feeling as she walked outside into the night.

Chapter Twenty-Three

Most people Audra knew were afraid of the dark. They feared the unknown, the possibility of something stalking them in the darkness without being able to see what it was that was watching them. It was the complete absence of a sense. Audra had seen it plenty when she was living in foster homes. Most every home would have a nightlight stuck in the outlet to bring some light into the darkness. Most of the girls she shared rooms with were petrified of the dark. Of nighttime where they had to be vulnerable. But not Audra.

She loved the dark. The shadows swirled around, making her feel comforted. Because even though she couldn't see, it was always a constant. There would always be darkness. There would always be shadows.

As she walked out of the house, being very aware of how far she was going, she felt the same calmness overcome her that she had almost every night since she was a young child. She did not fear the dark. Most people were their most authentic selves in the cover of darkness.

"I saw you." She called out softly into the trees, where shadows danced around her.

The silence was deafening.

"Show yourself. I am not afraid of you."

"Are you sure about that, sweetheart?" A deep, melodic voice breathed in her ear from behind her.

A shock went through her body. It was him. Seb. Right behind her.

"I am. Seb?"

A light chuckle breezed through the air as if it was riding a gust of wind.

"Is that you?" Audra asked, hoping.

No answer came, and she was getting impatient.

"Answer me! I only know one person who calls me sweetheart. Now tell me, who are you?" She asked.

"I think you know who I am." He said, his voice making her shiver just like in her dreams.

"So, it is you, Seb. From my dreams."

"Why didn't you tell your guard dogs about me?" He asked, his voice genuinely curious.

"Why don't you show yourself and I might tell you." She taunted. She crossed her arms over her chest and stood tall.

Suddenly, yet slowly, a speck of darkness seemed to pull all the shadows that had danced around her into a single spot in front of her. The shadows all condensed to create a human shape and out walked the gorgeous man she had seen from her window. Up close, he almost took her breath away.

"Sweetheart." He nodded; a smirk that should've been illegal graced his lips. He was tall and broad, like had appeared in her dreams, but his face. She breath caught. It was like his features were carved from marble, the symmetry, and the smoothness. Seb had a sharp jaw with angular features that screamed power. His eyes were such a dark brown that they almost seemed black, which was fitting with how he was always shrouded in shadows. His black hair was long and pushed back on top with short cut sides.

"Seb. It's you." She said breathlessly.

"Yes, it's me." He smiled, and she felt as if a weight lifted off her shoulders.

"Who are you? Really?"

"My full name is Sebastien Fullmas. I've been waiting to meet you in person for a very long time." He said, cryptic and arrogant, taking her hands in his.

"I'm sorry to have kept you waiting. Why didn't you meet me earlier? Why only come to me in my dreams? No, wait, first answer me this, how do you know me? Are you real? Or have I finally cracked?" She said.

"I've always known you."

"Informative. But I'm going to need more than that."

Sebastien chuckled. His laughter made her heart race. His dark eyes roaming over her body, and it was like he was caressing her with each swipe of his eyes on her skin. Audra realized then that she was still wearing her sleeping shorts and a thin tank top.

"I'm from Vesperitus. I'm aware of who you are, but I've always known who you are. We are...tied by history." Sebastien said, a smirk that crossed his face like he was telling an inside joke. One that she was not in on.

"Yeah, okay." Audra rolled her eyes. "Come on, please. I finally have you. I finally am able to see your face and know that you're real. Tell me. Tell me more, please." She poked at his chest before laying her palm flat over his heart.

"I will. But not yet. Just...Can we enjoy this moment together?"

She wanted to know everything, being so tired of the secrets and information bombs dropped left and right around her again. But she could see the pleading within his dark eyes and her heart leapt for him.

"Okay. But we will have the conversation later." She said in her most stern voice.

"Yes, of course, Your Majesty." He said with a smirk.

"I should probably head back before they come looking for me." She said, watching his face as his sharp jaw clenched tightly and his eyes turn hard. "I take it you don't want them to know about you just yet."

Seb shook his head, the frustration evident as his muscles tensed and his grip on her tightened slightly as if he wasn't able to let her go. If Audra was being honest, she didn't want him to let her go. She finally had him, the mysterious man that she felt at home with.

"Now that we've cleared that up, I'm going to go." She started to turn from him, hoping that she was making the right choice; that she would see him again and that he wasn't a threat to them. She felt no fear, no ill intent from Sebastien Fullma. But as she turned, his hand shot out and wrapped around her bicep.

A jolt rang through her body at the contact, but there still was no fear.

"Audra, do you remember me?" His voice sounded broken. The whispered fragmented sound made her heart ache.

"Just from my dreams where we've talked. I've never seen your face." She said quietly. Her eyes locked onto his, searching for something. Anything.

"I had hoped that you would." He looked at where they were touching and slowly trailed his hand down to hers.

It felt right. His hand in hers. Right in a way that she hadn't realized she was missing. But having this stranger hold her hand, it was soft and gentle, comforting in a way that shocked her.

"Who are you?" She whispered.

"Call me when you remember." He said with a full smile as he squeezed her hand and let it go.

"How do I call you?"

"Just whisper into the shadows, like you used to."

"How did–"

"Also, don't be fooled by that big buffoon in there. He cares for you, but not in the way that you need, and he will always put himself first. Always has, always will."

"What–"

"The other one, he's okay. Trustworthy. We've come to an understanding, he and I. Lean on him sweetheart, until you can trust to lean on me."

"Will you stop–" Audra snapped, but the shadows twined around him and before her eyes, he vanished into them. It looked as if his whole body turned to smoke.

What the hell was that?

Her mind was reeling, but the main thing that she realized as she was walking back to the farmhouse was that the sense of calm she always had from the shadows was even stronger when she was talking to Sebastien.

* * *

"You thought it was a good idea to let her go? Let her out of your sight? Do you not realize exactly who she is? What she is? What the fuck, Lucien!" Eric's thundering voice was audible through the wooden door.

Audra wasn't able to hear Luc's reply, but whatever it was must have been sarcastic because Eric roared. A crash was heard, and she knew he had toppled a table.

Who was this man? She didn't recognize this Eric at all.

"I'm right here, relax." Audra said, walking quickly into the room and to Luc's defense.

"Your Highness." Tomais bowed. He was standing off to the side, letting the two warriors have their fight.

"Princess." Eric said through gnashed teeth, his nostrils flaring.

"I gave Luc an order. He followed it. Back the fuck off."

"I gave Luc and Tomais orders that were to keep you safe. Your orders do not supersede my orders. Not yet at least. No one here has a higher authority than I do, and you all are going to have to accept that." He said and Audra noticed that he was clenching his fists.

Was she really being that difficult? Was what she was asking too much, too outlandish?

"May I speak with you privately, General?" Audra asked, her voice calm and confident.

Eric must have understood the shift in her, must have known what was about to happen because his entire body rippled with tension.

"Excuse us, gentlemen." Eric spat out, as a clear dismissal.

Tomais nodded, bowing once again towards Audra, then scurried out of the room. Luc watched the two of them, noticing their posturing and the energy around them. How it was full of venom.

"We will be in the next room if you need anything." Luc said, putting a glass of water next to Audra and standing to leave the room.

"Thank you, Luc." Eric said, but Audra knew the words were meant for her. He would be right outside the door in case things got out of hand. He would protect her, even if it meant going against his General.

Before he left, he turned around to close the French doors. Luc made eye contact with Audra over Eric's shoulder. His eyes dipped down to the water and back up at her. A message that she could use. Then closed the doors, sealing the two of them inside.

CHAPTER TWENTY-THREE

"Eric…" she started, but he put his hand up to silence her.

"I know what you're going to say. But you're just a little girl, Audra." He said slowly, as if she didn't understand what he was really saying. "A little girl with power and influence she doesn't understand. But with help, you could. You could be the best, most ruthless Queen Vesperitus has ever seen. With guidance, the Dark Fae could finally be eradicated."

Audra took a step back. The look in Eric's eyes, the expression on his face was that of a man possessed, a man drunk of power, a man willing to do whatever necessary to achieve his goal.

"And who would offer this guidance to me?" Audra asked.

"Why me, of course. There isn't a better option for you. I'm in good high standing within the court. I know all about Vesperitus and its history. Meaning I know the best way to attack Fullmaster and destroy the Dark Fae once and for all. I simply lack the elemental power to do so on my own. You've had your fun with Lucien, but now…we could be the most powerful, the most ruthless and most advantageous couple Vesperitus has ever seen."

"That's all your friendship to me was, wasn't it?" Audra could feel the hurt blossom in her chest.

"It would be a great political match, Audra. Come on, you're hot, I'm hot, together we would be so good. I know you're inexperienced, but we can change that." His hand rested low on her hip, almost touching her ass.

"I won't be doing that, thank you. And as far as I'm concerned, you will from now on only be a guard to me. Try not to let the power go to your inflated head. Now if you excuse me." Audra turned to leave, but Eric's hand shot out and grabbed her forearm. His large fingers biting down into her skin.

"I don't think so. I've worked too hard, sacrificed too much to fall now."

Audra was shocked. She had never seen this side of Eric directed at her before. His teeth bared, fists clenching.

A man possessed and watching the power he thought he had well within his grasp slip away.

"Let me go."

"What did you think, Audra? That I was just going to let you walk away from me without any proof? I mean, don't be so naive."

"Proof? What proof? For what?" She asked, trying to wiggle away from him and his grip.

"That you have had relations not fitting for a princess." He said with an evil grin. Her jaw dropped.

"It's not like I was some virginal princess locked in a tower until marriage, so fuck off." Audra snapped, and she tried to rip her wrist free from him.

"But what do you think dear Mommy and Daddy will say when they hear you scream for Lucien? A lowly guard that was meant to protect you." He whispered harshly in her ear.

"He did protect me. He has always protected me. Do you think I care what other people think?" Audra didn't really, she knew it wouldn't be a great look to present the first time meeting her parents, but she sure as hell wasn't going to be bullied or blackmailed by a big-headed asshole.

"I really think you do. You don't want to come across to your kingdom as a used up tramp who lets anyone defile her. Now, wouldn't it be tragic if suddenly all the supporters of the High Royalty pulled their backing? After all, Vesperitus may be advanced, but they still tend to follow Terraus' Middle Ages customs."

She hadn't thought of that. About how it would look to political allies and what that meant. But her brain wasn't trained to think like that yet.

"You wouldn't do that to me. You wouldn't betray me or your precious Crown like that."

"I think you'll find that people will do truly heinous things to secure a better, more profitable future for themselves."

"And what do you get? You're already the First General. I'm sure that makes a decent salary. What more do you want?"

"I get to be King. I get to be the one that wipes out the Dark Fae for good. I get wealth and power beyond understanding."

"You get that, but at the cost of my free will."

Audra hoped by explicitly stating it that way that he would see reason, he would see her as his friend again. Not some political move.

With the glint of madness in his eye, Audra closed her eyes and summoned the water from the cup Luc had left. She knew she wasn't getting out of this without help, without assistance from him. In a magical fight, her raw power might overpower his, but with his knowledge and control over his magic, there was a very real possibility that he could take her. In a physical match, she knew some, but all the tricks she had learned from him. She wouldn't be able to catch him off guard enough to take him down.

Over his shoulder, she saw the water slither across the floor and pass under the door. If Luc was standing outside like he promised, he would be able to see it.

"I have my reasons. And let's be real, shall we? Being married to me wouldn't be the worst thing in your life. We could have some real fun." Eric's arrogance stance returned, but his possessive yet painful hold on her was still present.

He'd lost his damn mind if he thought all Audra wanted in life was decent sex.

"It wouldn't be that fun, Eric. You shouldn't think so highly of yourself. Those girls always looked so unsatisfied when they left your apartment in the morning."

His eyes narrowed, and he clenched his jaw.

"You little bitch." He said through his clenched teeth and gripped her shoulders tighter. Audra didn't know what he was going to do, but she wasn't going to go down without a fight.

"You listen here," Eric started to say before the door broke open. Luc stood in the doorway, fists clenched at his sides, ready for a fight.

"Let her go." He said, his voice calm but full of promise for a fight if Eric chose to keep holding Audra.

"It's just a discussion, Luc. No need to get protective. She's fine with me." Eric said, turning to Luc but still keeping a tight grip on Audra's shoulders.

"She doesn't seem fine with you. Let her go."

"Audra, honey, are you unsafe with me?" Eric's voice had turned mocking, cruel. Audra could see the slight glow in Eric's golden eyes, signaling that he had called his magic to the front and was ready to use it.

"Luc, it's okay." Her voice sounded shaky, even to her own ears. She knew that she had called for help, but now, seeing how Eric was acting, she didn't want to hurt Luc.

"Like hell. Eric, I'm not going to ask again."

"I order you to stand down, Lieutenant. The Princess is safe with me. In fact, we are going to go for a little walk outside."

"Then you won't mind if I join you." Luc's calm tone was helping Audra stay calm. She would feel much better knowing that Luc was there wherever it was that Eric wanted to take her to do God knows what.

"That won't be necessary." Eric's grip on Audra tightened once more, causing her to groan. Luc's eyes dropped to hers, and she pleaded with him to let this go.

"I insist." Luc was not backing down. Audra knew that he would follow them regardless of if Eric let him or not.

"Very well. You can watch, I guess." Eric's smile turned dark, and Audra knew whatever happened next would change her life forever.

* * *

The trio walked outside, back into the darkness of the shadows of the forest. Eric made sure to walk with Audra trapped firmly to his side as he stomped through the silent forest with Luc trailing along silently. Audra could feel his anger and rage radiating from him and she hoped he didn't do anything stupid. If he got hurt because of her, she would lose it. The way Eric was pulling her reminded Audra of a toddler throwing a tantrum.

"You don't have to do this. We can work this out, Eric." She tried to barter with him. The way he made them leave the house suggested a sinister plan he had.

"I think I do. Someone has to remind you of your place. You know nothing, you come from nothing, but because of your blood, they are willing to put a complete novice on the throne and hope she can lead a whole continent? Fucking stupid." Eric ranted, pulling on her bicep harder, making her cry out.

"If you make her hurt one more time, Eric, I swear to god I will end you." Luc snapped from behind her.

"And if you interfere one more time, I will strip you of all your titles. Not to mention, I can leave your ass here in Terraus. I'll make up a story about how you forced yourself on the poor princess and tried to kill her. Of course, Audra, if you keep trying to get away, I might just tell them that story, regardless. Seniority and all that, your parents would definitely believe me over you." He said with a sneer. His grip on her bicep was hurting her, but what hurt more was when she looked over at Luc and saw the horror on his face.

"You are such a son of a bitch." Luc snapped at him, his chest rising and falling rapidly with his rage. Audra could see the glow of his aqua eyes, signaling that his magic had flared to life with his emotions.

Eric ignored him and kept trekking through the forest. The moon overhead provided enough light for them to see where they were walking, but shadows overran everything.

Out of the corner of her eye, Audra saw movement. She wasn't sure exactly what moved, but something had.

Probably an animal, she rationalized. *One problem at a time.*

"Where are you taking me? Us?"

"Shut up." Eric snapped.

"No, tell me. Where are you taking us?" She tried to pull her arm from his grip. She felt the give from his fingers and wretched herself back.

"Get over here."

"Fuck no. Do you really think I'm that stupid?"

"Eric, come on. Nothing has happened yet. Let's go back to the house and I will get a conduit and we can have the King reassign you to another mission. Please, let her go." Luc tried to rationalize with Eric, circling to stand closer to her, but Audra could see that Eric was too far gone for that.

Eric and Audra stood facing each other, both in defensive positions.

"No, I don't think I will." He said slowly before he lunged at Audra. She braced for impact, ready to feel the heavy weight of Eric on her and the pain from the rough forest floor.

But none came.

She opened her eyes to see Luc and Eric locked in combat, the two of them fighting fist to fist. Audra watched Luc send a punch into Eric's jaw hard enough that she was sure he cracked a few teeth. When Eric recovered, he stared at Luc with enough fury to burn him alive.

"How dare you? Disobeying a direct order from your supervising officer?" Eric said, his tone deep and full of hatred.

"I made a promise when I joined the High Royal Guards to protect my country, my crown, and my monarchs. She is my monarch. She's your monarch too." Luc said, never taking his eyes from Eric. His fists raised to protect his face, and he shifted his stance so that Luc was directly in Eric's line of sight and obscuring Audra from him.

"Your monarch? I think you want her to be a little more than that." Eric sneered.

"I do want her more than that. She's mine as much as I'm hers. But our relationship is none of your fucking business."

Audra didn't like where this was going.

"Enough! Eric, you will end this now. You will stop this bullshit and come with us back to the house where Tomais and I can discuss what is to be done." Audra yelled. She was out of patience.

"Oh yeah? You think that's what is going to happen? You poor, naive girl." Eric brought two orbs of light into his hands and threw them at Luc and Audra. Audra was taken by surprise and was hit. The light was fire like but white. It was hot and burned right through her shirt, burning her abdomen. She cried out as Luc started to meet Eric - attack for attack. Light and water. Audra tried to get back to her feet, but the hole in her stomach was black, aching and she was in enough pain that she thought she might pass out. In fact, her vision was starting to blur with the pain, and she felt the fight drain from her with the wound.

She could hear them trading grunts and insults, but she was entirely focused on not passing out. The shadows swirled around her again, reminding her of when she met her mystery man earlier. The shadows were beautiful, dark smoke and specks glinting in the moonlight. They were swirling like a storm cloud above her when her mystery man stepped out and ran right to her. He dropped to his knees, placing one hand on her arm and one on her forehead, brushing away her waves from her face.

"Seb...Help."

"You're going to be okay. I promise, sweetheart." He whispered to her.

"How?" She grunted, talking hurts. Breathing hurts. Moving hurts.

"I've been having my shadows watch you, I got here as fast as I could." Sebastien said and put his hand over her wound. From the look on his face, Audra could guess that it didn't look good for her. She can feel her body getting more and more tired, her senses draining slowly from her. His eyes were frantic, the dark irises darting from her face to her stomach over the wound. She could see sweat bead on his forehead and he bit his lip as he continued to focus. Audra could feel her get closer to the peaceful darkness, so she focused on his handsome face.

"This is going to hurt, sweetheart. But I'm sure you can take it." He whispered and winked at her. If Audra had any energy left, she would have rolled her eyes.

She's about to give him a piece of her mind when whatever Sebastien was planning on doing hit her. The white-hot searing pain invaded her body, filling every part of her. It was worse than getting hit with the light ball. Worse than breaking her forearm in the fourth grade. Worse than falling down the stairs at her foster house in high school. She started screaming and screaming.

"Sleep." Sebastien said, and his index finger touched her forehead.

Immediately, her world turned black.

Chapter Twenty-Four

"Wake." She heard through the darkness.

Audra didn't want to wake up, though. The darkness didn't hurt. It didn't attack her. She could float and relax. It was peaceful.

"Sweetheart…" The voice said, stronger this time.

Her eyes opened to see the darkest eyes she'd ever seen and was immediately comforted by who was holding her hand.

He, Seb, had somehow saved her. Appeared when she needed him most and kept her from dying. She was certain that if he hadn't helped her, she would be dead on the forest floor.

Forest. Eric. Luc.

"Luc?" Audra asked Sebastien, her voice hoarse and anxious.

"I'm right here." Audra turned her head and saw Luc standing at the entrance of the living room, arms crossed and leaning on the doorframe. She was on the same couch that the boys had set her on when they first brought her here.

Audra was beginning to hate this couch. She was always waking up from an injury, pain, and aches on this couch.

"Are you okay? What happened?"

"I should ask the same of you. I finally incapacitated Eric, only to see you passed out with an intense injury, thinking you had died. Seriously Aud, your stomach looked like it had been bombed. And Seb kneeling over you, doing something to you, and your stomach was piecing itself back together. He was healing you." Luc ran his fingers through his hair. He obviously hadn't showered or changed clothes yet, he was covered in mud, sweat and small burns from the fight.

"When I tried to fight Seb, he explained that I could trust him. He was healing you, so I didn't have much choice. I couldn't let you die."

Audra looked at Sebastien, wondering how much more they talked about while she was out and why he came for her. Again.

"Where's Eric?"

"I have him tied up and enchanted to sleep, your highness." Tomais said from behind Luc. "He will be dealt with as soon as we reach Dragomahara. I have already sent word to the King who is sending a team to retrieve him as we speak."

"How?" Audra whispered weakly.

"I have an air affinity that can be manipulated to cause the Fae to fall into a slumber. It can come in handy sometimes. Especially in times like this." Tomais explained gently.

Audra's stomach rolled. She didn't know how the King or Queen would handle his punishment. On one hand, he had almost succeeded in killing her because he wanted more power. But on the other, she had all these memories of the three of them. Just living in the city, before all this shit.

She landed on a simple nod and tried to sit up, but her head had other plans and she had to lie back down.

"Easy. We used a lot of magic to heal you. I had to drain your reserves in order to fully heal you. You'll be exhausted and sluggish for a while." Sebastien explained, patting her leg affectionately.

Her eyes flew to Luc, who was watching his hand move with hawklike precision.

"You had to drain my reserves?" She asked.

"When I heal someone, I need to use their own kind of magic to double down on their injury. Almost like double-sided tape. It works to stitch injuries to the body back together. But the more severe an injury, the more magic required. I'm sorry, but I had to."

"Thank you." She said and reached for his hand. Sebastien's eyes lit up and she could see this dark, mysterious man blush from her touch.

"I think we need to talk." She said, looking at Luc and Tomias. She hoped they would get the hint and leave them for some privacy.

Luc's eyes were filled with rage, his arms were crossed and bunched under his biceps, making them look bigger and more intimidating. His jaw was clenched, and Audra could feel the disapproval radiating from him.

But he nodded.

"I'm going to go change and bathe. Tomais, would you go check on Eric and stand the first rotation of guard? I don't want him alone for a moment."

"Yes, understood." The two turned to leave, but Luc walked over to her and kissed her thoroughly. Effectively staking his claim.

It made her heart race and worry at the same time. She didn't want word to get back to her parents and have him demoted or something because of her.

Once the door had shut, Audra turned to Sebastien who had kicked back on the couch with his arms crossed behind his head and feet propped up on the coffee table.

"Talk. The truth this time." She said.

She was done accepting his half-truths and cryptic messages.

* * *

"Go ahead and ask your questions. I'm not going to just volunteer information." Sebastien said, looking like the picture of relaxation with his arms crossed behind his head and feet propped up on the table. He had a smirk on his face that told Audra he wouldn't be telling her the whole story tonight. If at all.

"How do you know me?"

"I've known you and watched over you since you were young. I've tried to keep you out of harm's way, keep interested parties away from you. It's been a full-time job with as much as you moved around and as much as you went looking for trouble."

"How? I've never seen you before tonight?"

"I have eyes and ears everywhere."

"That's not creepy at all." Audra rolled her eyes. "Why me?"

"Let's just say I have a vested interest in you. Always have."

"Why?"

"I can't tell you yet."

Audra groaned. She wanted to scream at him, curse him out, even shake him for being so intentionally obtuse.

"How did you watch me?"

"I have my ways."

"You're just being a smug asshole now." Audra crossed her arms over her chest.

"I can't give it all away yet, sweetheart." Sebastien stood up and grabbed his dark leather jacket from the back of the couch.

"Haven't you any sense of adventure? Don't you love a good mystery? I know I do. And I know you do too." He said with a smirk, and he walked towards the door.

"Where do you think you're going?" Audra followed right behind him, stomping her way through the room.

"I have to get back. I've already been away too long, but I had to check on you and I am very glad I did." Sebastien turned and cupped her cheek in a loving, sweet gesture. As Audra looked at him, she saw the truth in his words.

"Try to stay out of trouble. Keep leaning on Luc. That guy has a thing for you." Sebastien said with a wink over her shoulder, and he gave her hand a quick peck on the lips.

"If you need me, whisper to the shadows and I'll be there." He whispered softly, so softly that Audra wasn't sure she had heard him correctly.

"Thank you." She whispered back, her hand reaching up to touch where his lips had kissed her.

"Keep an eye on her." Sebastien said roughly, his words aimed over her shoulder.

"With my life." Luc responded with a single nod.

"Till next time, sweetheart." Sebastien said with a smirk and walked out the door into the night.

Audra went to walk out with him but tripped slightly over the threshold. When she turned her attention back to the night air, he was gone.

* * *

Audra stalked past Luc's watching eyes and went straight for the stocked bar in the living room. She pulled a glass out and poured a generous amount of whiskey in.

"What was that? Who is he really and why does he seem so comfortable with you? Huh, 'sweetheart'?" Luc sneered.

Audra tipped the glass back and felt the burn of the whiskey as it went down her throat. She poured another splash into her glass.

"Look, I'm working with limited information as well. His name is Sebastien, and he just appeared out of thin air earlier today. I saw him from my window, and he looked like he was standing guard, so I went to find out who he was and…"

"You went out of this house, unprotected, without telling me anything about this to go find out who this stranger was? Don't you realize how dangerous that is?" Luc ran his hands through his hair, frustration, and anger seeping into his tone with every word.

"I was safe! I promise, he didn't feel dangerous. I never felt unsafe with him."

"So, you've been around him before? And we could also have said that about Eric but look what happened."

Audra sighed and filled another glass with whiskey for Luc. It had been a crazy, awful, enlightening day. She walked over and plopped on the couch, needing to rest her body. Too much had happened in too short of a time.

She felt the couch dip next to her, with Luc also falling into the cushions. He looked exhausted and weary. His dark hair was sticking up in every which way, a sign that he had been pulling at it and running his hands through it over and over again. Obviously, when he had told them he was going to take a shower, he stood guard for her. He smelled strongly of smoke, so Audra knew that Eric had gotten a bit close to burning him as well. The fact that Luc had been able to fight him off and come out relatively okay physically was a blessing. One that she would continue to be extremely grateful for.

"How are you doing, baby? Really." Luc asked her, slinging one arm across the back of the couch behind her and pulling her body to rest against his as he took a long drink of the whiskey in his other hand.

"Confused. Tired. Scared." She sighed, resting her head back against his shoulder.

"I get feeling tired and confused. There's been a lot that has happened. You almost died, for fuck's sake. Then some strange man comes out of nowhere and claims to know you. Our friend, who I looked at like a brother, tries to force you to marry him and I'm sure was going to do some dark shit to you, tries to kill us. I'm angry. I'm angry that I couldn't see who he really was. I'm angry that I followed him for so long. I'm angry that he almost killed you!" Luc stood up from the couch aggressively, his glass empty and forgotten on the table. He started to pace; his chest was heaving with each breath.

Audra stood gingerly from the couch. She knew that she needed to diffuse Luc's temper. He was starting to spiral into his rage and guilt.

"Luc, it's okay. I'm okay."

"How is any of this okay, Audra? He knows about us. He could use that against you!" He yelled. Audra flinched at that.

"Love," she said, standing up and cupping his face to force his gaze to hers. His beard was scruffy against her palms, and she loved it. "I don't care that he knows about us. I will proudly say that we are...whatever we are. You're mine and I'm yours. If you still want me."

His eyes bored into hers and the look on his face said that she was crazy for suggesting otherwise.

"I'm sadder about the fact that the family I thought I had found was all a lie."

"Maybe with him. But it wasn't fake with me. We are friends, family. I kicked myself for feeling that way knowing that you didn't actually know who we were, and it killed me to watch you every day, knowing that I couldn't tell you how I felt because I didn't want you to feel like I'd lied to you. I didn't want you to get hurt. That's why I kept my distance. The only reason I did." Luc explained, he gripped her small hands in his larger ones.

"I'm so sorry that I didn't see what he was planning sooner. I never wanted us, him, our mission, to hurt you. Please believe me." Luc said quietly, an edge of desperation in his voice.

When Audra looked into his eyes, she could see the truth in his words. He truly had no idea what Eric was planning. He wanted her. He wanted them to still be part of a little family.

"I know that. I know." She pulled him into her arms for a hug. They needed each other right now. They were both feeling betrayed by someone they had looked at as a dear friend, a confidante, a person in their corner.

Audra could feel his quick, shuddering breaths on her neck as he held onto her.

"It's going to be okay, Luc. I know it." She whispered to him, her arms coming around his narrow waist and pulling him closer.

"I know, it's been a very long day." He pulled back slightly, enough to look at her.

"I think it's almost the next day." She said with a chuckle. "We should go get some sleep. Everything seems more manageable with sleep."

Just as Audra thought of sleeping alone in the big bed with Eric still in the house made her panic. Her chest squeezed tighter, and she could feel the terror set in. What if he got free from wherever Tomais had him and he came for her? What if he finished what he started? He obviously had some sinister plans for her if he had tried to pull her into the woods and told Luc he could 'watch'. She would be sleeping, vulnerable. Unable to fight him off.

"Audra, what is it?" Luc's hand came up to cup her cheek, forcing her to stare at him instead of getting lost in the panic. "Tell me, baby."

"Eric...what if...Oh, god." Her breathing started to come less and less than her fear increased, and her gasping echoed in the room. She was having a panic attack now; it was very rapidly becoming completely full blown.

"Eric is secured and knocked out cold. I checked on him myself while you were talking to Sebastien. He will not escape us. If I have anything to say about it, you will never see him again. I promise you. Baby, can you hear me?" She could feel both of his hands cradling her face and she tugged on his forearms, keeping her close to him.

"He will not get past Tomias, and I will stand guard over him myself in a few hours. But you're right, we need sleep."

At him mentioning sleep, her gasps increased as she tried to get air for her lungs. It was too much. Eric would find her. He would ruin her. He would finish the job. He was too strong for her, and he wasn't afraid of killing. He'd proven that much. The fear of another fight that she felt so unprepared for, so ill-equipped for, nearly crippled her. She didn't fight. She hadn't even had the chance to before he took her out and, in this state, with this anxiety, was too much.

"No...no, please, no." She mumbled.

"I will stand guard outside your door. He is not getting to you, baby. I promise."

"Please."

"Let's go." Luc dropped his hands and picked up hers, leading her out of the room.

Audra let Luc softly and slowly guide her up to her room. "I can't sleep here. This would be the first place he would look." She whispered brokenly.

Luc nodded, understanding where her mind had gone.

"You can sleep in my room." He said softly and walked her across the hall to where his door was. Audra didn't think that he had slept in his room except for the first few days. Once they'd slept together, it just made sense to sleep in her bed. It was so late, and they were both exhausted, so Audra climbed in his bed and snuggled into the thick, warm covers. Comfort coming from Luc's scent, knowing that he was there. She opened her eyes long enough to see that Luc tucked her into his bed and then walked away, going to the door.

"Where are you going?" Audra sat up, alarmed.

"I'm going to sleep out here, guarding the door." He said with his hand on the doorknob.

"No, please. Come, lay in here with me. I just...I can't be alone." She murmured and patted the space on his bed next to her.

"Are you sure?"

"Absolutely."

Luc walked back to the bed slowly, then he took off his shoes and pulled his shirt over his head. Audra had seen him shirtless before, but with the early morning sun filtering in through his window, all eight of his abs were on display. She shouldn't have been surprised. He ate extremely well; he worked out with precision and dedication and treated his body like a temple.

But still, seeing the proof of his hard work up close again and again made her mouth water.

She turned on her side, facing him as he slid under the covers.

"Goodnight, Luc."

"Goodnight, baby." He whispered back.

Chapter Twenty-Five

Audra woke up alone in a room that was definitely not the oasis of white sheets that she was used to. Confused for just a moment before last night's events slammed into her. She sat up and looked down at herself. She was still fully clothed, but the cookbooks tucked into the corner of the bookshelf reminded her that she had slept in Luc's room last night. Too panicked and afraid to try to sleep in her room, afraid that he would come find her and kill her for good this time.

She didn't know where Sebastien ran off too, and she didn't even know about contacting him if she needed him. He had said to 'whisper to the shadows' but she didn't know how much she believed that would get a message to him. But hell, if she was able to send Luc messages in the water, then maybe the shadows did the same.

Speaking of Luc, Audra climbed out of his bed and went in search of him. Remembering their conversation last night as she was having a panic attack, she knew he was probably guarding Eric like he promised he would, and she really didn't want to see that man ever again. Audra went off in search of some food and coffee, then to see what Tomais thought she should learn or work on today.

She had to keep busy. If she didn't, she'd never be strong enough to not only defend and protect herself, but a whole country. A whole country that would look to her.

Yes, she needed to learn. To train. She wouldn't be blindsided again.

Walking into the kitchen, she noticed that coffee was already made. The sweet, bitter aroma of coffee beans hitting her nostrils and caused her to relax.

"Good morning, Princess." Tomais said, bowing his head slightly. He scrambled from the table to make her a cup of coffee, but Audra just smiled and put her hand up.

"Please, sit. Relax. I'm not a Princess here, you can call me Audra. In fact, I'd prefer it." She chuckled and reached up for a coffee mug out of the cabinet.

"Oh no, I couldn't." Tomais said, sitting back down at the table where his notebook was laying open.

"Why? I don't feel like much of a Princess yet. And besides, Luc and Eric do." She stumbled over Eric's name. It wasn't that she was scared *of* him, she wasn't. But it was the look in his eye, the way that he had been willing to hurt her, kill her even, to do what he had set out to do. How long had this plan been in the making?

"I didn't spend years working with you as they did, Princess." Tomais said quietly.

"You're not going to give up this whole calling me Princess, are you?" She smirked and brought the coffee cup to her lips. A long drink of the warm, comforting caffeine grounded her. Made her feel like today was just another day. If she closed her eyes, she could pretend that she was still in her little shoebox apartment, standing in front of the tiny window next to her bed, nursing a cup of coffee in her favorite chipped mug and was watching the sun rise over the sleeping city.

But she wasn't.

She was standing in the beautiful safe house that her parents had secured for them. Standing with an advisor they had sent to protect her, while the two warriors they had sent were more than likely exchanging insults right now.

"I would like to get started on learning about Vesperitus today, if that works for you." Audra walked over to the table where Tomais pulled out a chair for her to join him.

"Are you sure? Wouldn't you like to take today to rest, what with everything that happened..." Tomais sat down next to her and closed his notebook.

"No, I need to keep busy, and I need to get started on learning its history."

"I understand, Princess."

"Speaking of what happened, have you told my parents what happened?"

Tomais nodded but twisted uncomfortably in his seat.

"What did they say?" Audra pressed on. She could tell he was uncomfortable, but she wasn't going to back down. She had to know.

"They apologized profusely for his betrayal. They knew nothing of his plans or his want to hurt you. They were also angry and feeling betrayed. Eric was their First General, their most respected warrior."

"What is...What is going to happen to him?" Audra was almost scared to ask. They way that all their customs and behaviors were screamed Middle Ages and from all the movies she had seen, the punishment for attempted murder of a monarch was death. Usually, a gruesome one.

"I understand you still care for him, but there are procedures and punishments for things that happen, especially to royals. His punishment will fit his crime. Are you sure you want to know?"

She nodded. She had to know.

"The King and Queen are sending four of their Royal Elite guards to escort Eric through the Gate and to Dragomahara where he will be thrown into the dungeons until his trial can take place. Eric will be tried by the King and Queen, along with the testimony from myself and Lucien. If he is found guilty, which he will, he will be sentenced to death by fire. The very element he wields and tried to kill you with. The fire will blaze strong and high until the last of his bones turn to ash."

The tone in which Tomais explained everything; calm, factual and as if it was absolutely normal to be discussing death, surprised Audra. She felt sick to her stomach at the thought of Eric going through that, even though he had tried to kill her, Luc and who knows what else he would have done if he would have succeeded.

Tomais must have seen how her mood soured even more because he rested his hand on her forearm, albeit very hesitantly. As if he was scared to touch her at all.

"I understand. It is a lot, and you have two versions of Eric in your head. The kind, best friend, and the mean, cruel, General. But what he did, what he was trying to do, he would have hurt more people. Trust me when I say his murdering tendencies would not stop at just you, or Lucien or myself. He was going for complete control over the monarchy. So, don't feel as if you are sending him to his death. This is out of your hands."

Audra felt tears slide down her cheeks, the guilt and the fear mixing together.

"I am going to go take a walk for a few minutes and then I'll be ready to start our lesson." Audra stood up quickly, abandoning her coffee. She walked swiftly out the front door and ran into the treeline where she had seen Sebastien last night.

Audra was almost certain she was having a panic attack. Her breath was coming faster, and she wasn't able to think of anything except for how she was responsible for having someone killed. Eric was going to die, and it was because he had attacked her. She ran towards the small cove of trees grouped together, where there was a shadowed area.

Whisper to the shadows, he had said. Well, Audra needed him. She needed him now and she needed that calm, comfort that her mysterious man provided her.

"Sebastien. Sebastien, please." She whispered. She was barely able to draw a full breath as she stumbled back and sat down in the shade of a tree. She fell back against the closest tree trunk and put her hands over her face, letting her sobs be contained by them. It was too much; everything was too much, and Audra felt like she was breaking.

"Audra, sweetheart, what is it?"

Audra turned her head towards his voice. Sebastien was crouched over her, alarm and shock written clearly across his beautiful face.

"You came." She whispered.

"Of course, I did. I told you I would." Sebastien's low timbre of voice was soothing and like a dark, cool spot in her otherwise flaming hot soul.

"I...I don't know what to do. I don't know how to recover from this."

Sebastien sat down next to her and wrapped his arm over her shoulders. As soon as she was cocooned within his side, she rested her head on his chest and listened to the steady beat of his heart.

"Who are you?" She whispered. "Why do I feel this way with you? Comfortable and safe. Like nothing could happen to me when we are together."

"Because I've always been there for you. I've always watched over you. There was a reason you always feel safe in the dark, why the shadows are comforting. Sweetheart, I *am* the shadows." Sebastien brought his hand up and an elegant swirl of darkness followed his hand, like smoke but sleeker, smoother.

Suddenly it is as if a movie reel started to play in her head of all the times growing up where the darkness or shadows felt comfortable; like when she was scared or hurt and the darkness seemed to crowd around her, when she begged for the room with only one light emphatically explaining to her foster parent that it didn't bother her, how no matter how late it was she never felt unsafe walking in the dark because no one dared to come up to her.

It made sense. How Sebastien knew her, understood her, and why she felt so at ease with him, despite not knowing him.

"How long?"

"Since you came to Terraus. I've been watching over you since you were an infant." Sebastien ran his hand over her face lovingly. Audra couldn't help but nuzzle into his touch. It was like her body craved his touch.

"Since I was an infant? How old are you?"

"You know that Fae age differently..."

"Ha! So, you're Fae, like me." She smiled at him as he rolled his eyes with a smirk.

"You're adorable. Yes, I'm Fae, like you." He poked her nose lovingly and held her closer. "I'm a little over 80 years old."

"You cradle robber!" She mockingly gasped and hit his chest lightly. Seb laughed loudly, the deep sound made her mood lift, and she smiled brightly.

"I suppose." He chuckled.

"Why?" She asked softly.

"I can't tell you. I promise. You'll find out in time. But for now, just know that I will always protect you, even if it doesn't seem like it."

Audra didn't really know what that meant because so far, all he had done was take care of her and protect her. Hell, he had even warned her against Eric. She just hadn't caught it.

"I know it seems like a lot. And you're probably feeling like everything is your fault right now. What happened, what's going to happen. But I promise you, it isn't. This has been brewing for so long, sweetheart. I've been watching Eric from a distance, and he has been planning on how to gain more access to the Royals for years. Decades even. So, the fact that he will have to face the punishment for his crimes, crimes that almost killed you I might add, is just what has to happen."

"But I could-"

"No, Audra. No. This is out of your hands now. Look at me," he said as he forced her to meet his eyeline. "You are not responsible for his actions. He is."

Audra let the sob that was building in her chest free, tears started to track down her face as she cried loudly and messily into his chest.

And he just held her. He held her in the darkness, his shadows swirling around them both forming a small cocoon around the two of them.

* * *

"I need to go. I told Tomais I would just be a few minutes and I'm sure it's been a few hours." She said, head still nuzzled into Sebastien's strong chest as he trailed a finger up and down her spine. Audra had somehow shifted over him, so she was sitting on his lap as he laid back against the tree trunk.

"I also should go. I need to get back to my court."

"Where is your court?"

Sebastien stilled, his body underneath her tensed. Audra just took a deep breath. She knew he wasn't going to tell her.

"Let me guess, you can't tell me. This shit is getting old, Seb."

"Soon, sweetheart. Soon."

"Thank you, for coming for me."

"Always." He whispered and brought her hand up to his lips. When he gave her hand a kiss, Audra swore her heart skipped a beat. She tried her best to cover her shy smile, but there was no doubt that he saw it. His dark eyes were practically sparkling like stars in a black night sky. Sebastien moved his hand from her lap and Audra stood up.

"If you need me, you know how to find me." Sebastien said as he dusted his black suit pants off.

"Thank you."

"Trust Lucien, trust Tomais, but don't let your guard down."

"Will you be watching me?"

"Whenever there are shadows." He said with a smile.

"So, you'll see me soon then."

"Cheeky. But yes." He winked and pulled his hands together, making a sweeping motion with them. The shadows all around them from the forest suddenly felt alive, Audra was able to denote them as she hadn't before.

A large circle of darkness appeared in front of Sebastien. He turned back to Audra and leaned down to kiss her cheek.

"Be safe, please."

"I'll do my best." She smirked, to which he groaned.

"You better, sweetheart." He said before he walked into the darkness. As soon as both of his feet were within the strange dark doorway, it swallowed him up and vanished. Like he was never there.

"Audra!" She could hear her name being faintly called. Luc called out for her with a frantic tone, which she knew would mean that she was gone far too long.

Audra pulled up a few drops of water from the earth, infused her message and sent the water towards Luc as fast as she could before making her way back to the safe house. Back to Luc.

Chapter Twenty-Six

Audra walked back towards the front door of the farmhouse, fully prepared for the brunt of Luc's anger. She had done it again, run off into the forest without protection, without telling Luc specifically that she was meeting Seb. But if she was being honest, she hadn't planned on calling him. She needed calm, the comfort and security she had felt with him.

She felt safe with Luc as well, especially after all they had been through, but he wasn't available right then, and she didn't want to pull him away from his job. There wasn't time.

Breaking through the treeline, she saw Luc pacing back and forth on the porch. Obviously, he had gotten her message, aware that she was coming back and unharmed, but that didn't mean that he was happy with her.

"Where the fuck have you been?" He growled as he advanced on her, storming to meet her halfway.

"I needed a break."

"You couldn't have taken Tomais with you? Come and got me? Have you forgotten that there are people after you? It's not just Eric who is sick in the head and wants you gone, Audra!" He shouted. Audra could see how stressed and anxious he was, just from her being gone and her heart softened. She knew he wasn't yelling at her out of anger, he was yelling at her out of fear.

Audra reached up and cupped his jaw. She wanted to show him how she truly was fine and how sorry she was.

"I'm sorry. I just needed a moment. And I called Sebastien, so I wasn't completely alone out in the forest."

Luc's body tensed as if he had been shot.

"You called Sebastien? Over me?"

"No, no, Luc. Not over you. You were busy, and I didn't want to inconvenience you. I already am asking too much of you and you didn't sleep last night and-" She started rambling, desperate to have Luc see that she didn't think or care less for him at all.

"You are never, ever an inconvenience to me. I'm always here for you, baby." Luc said with so much emotion it caused Audra to reel back.

Audra reached up and brought her mouth to his.

She loved how he tasted. Luc deepened the kiss, his tongue swiping along her lips, begging for entrance, which she gave. His arms wrapped around her waist, pulling him closer to him, and she wound her arms around his strong shoulders. One of her hands lifted up to grab at the nape of his neck, pulling him in even closer.

"That was..." Luc pulled away with a gasp. Both of their breathing was haggard, but when she looked into Luc's eyes, she could see the adoration he had for her and the lust as well. His pupils were dilated, and his cheeks were flushed. Audra was sure she looked similar, like her world was just rocked. Because it was. He had wanted to prove that he cared for her and release some of that fear he had, and he did. She could feel his anger at her doubt and was trying to show her to not do it again.

"Amazing." She finished.

"I'm serious. Anytime you need me, I'm here. Never doubt that." He said softly.

"What do we do now?"

"We go about business as usual. We keep training, you keep learning about Vesperitus before we have to go, and we take each day one at a time." He smiled down at her as he brushed a lock of hair behind her ear.

"Do we still need to be careful around Tomais because I'm getting really tired of it."

"You are allowed to be with who you want. I'm not going to throw our feelings in his face or be inappropriate, but I don't want us to pretend anymore like we are platonic. Unless..."

"Unless what?"

"Unless you do." Luc looked like he was pained to say that, but she appreciated his willingness to put her first. Regardless of how he felt.

"What are you proposing?"

"I would like to be with you Audra, your boyfriend or whatever label you wish. I want to care for you, fall in love and protect you every day from here on out. And I will do whatever it takes to make sure you're in my life. We've been together, we've proven that we are good partners and I want us to give this a shot. A real shot. However, you'll have me."

Audra felt like her heart might combust. Luc was giving her his heart, his future, and she was hesitating. She knew how she felt about him, but she also had to reconcile with how she felt about Sebastien, even if she didn't truly know him like she knew Luc.

"I care about you, Luc. I always have. I want to try, but..."

"But what?"

"I have feelings for...him...too." Her heart was beating so hard she thought she might have a heart attack if it beat any faster. Audra didn't want to hurt Luc, the opposite actually. She wanted everything he offered, but she couldn't lie to him either.

Luc stepped back, dropping her face but keeping ahold of one of her hands.

"Sebastien?" He asked, his voice rough and hoarse.

"Yes." She whispered, dropping her head. Audra couldn't help but feel bad, guilty. She didn't know what feelings she had exactly, but she knew that she had more than friendship for Seb. And based on how he was acting with her, he also felt a certain way. She couldn't ignore it. The comfort, the calm, the longing.

"I understand. I thought that there was something between you two, I just... I had to tell you how I felt. I couldn't just sit back and wait again."

"Luc, you're mine and I'm yours. I want you."

"You do?"

"Yes." The word breathed out of her. She should have felt guilty, selfish for wanting two men when she knew she didn't deserve it. But she couldn't ignore her feelings. She couldn't ignore the pull towards them. "So, so much."

"I want you, Audra. And I told you I would be in your life however you want me. If I have to share your affection, I will try. I promise." Luc sauntered over to her and slid his hands under her thighs and hoisted her up to him. She let out a small cry but quickly held onto the strong, selfless man in her arms.

"Kiss me again." She whispered as his lips were a breath away from hers.

He wasted no time at all in devouring her lips again.

"Princess, I'm sorry to interrupt!" Luc and Audra broke away, and he set her back on her feet. Albeit her knees were a little weak.

Tomais walked out of the house, letting the screen door slam behind him.

"Of course, no problem, Tomais. What is it?"

"There has been a change of plans."

"What do you mean?" Luc asked as he stepped up close to her, putting his hand on her lower back, and she leaned into his touch.

"There has been a royal decree that Princess Audra is to return home to Vesperitus."

"But I'm not ready! I haven't learned the history, I don't know how to act in court, I barely know how to control my magic, I–" Audra started to ramble, her panic and stress picked up again. She thought they had time. She thought she had time to learn everything that she needed not to embarrass herself when she finally met her parents.

"It's not up to us anymore." Luc said softly behind her.

* * *

Luc and Audra walked through the front door, following Tomais as he led them towards the front room. Sitting front and center was Eric, his blonde curls matted and greasy from being kept in isolation. Audra wondered if they had some kind of dungeon on the property. The safe house must have some kind of place to hold prisoners. Luc and Tomais had kept Eric away and were both seemingly comfortable with where he was being kept, not at all seeming worried about him getting out.

Eric's wrists and ankles were bound with iron cuffs, connected to chains which a burly-looking man held onto.

Once Audra walked fully into the space, each of the soldiers standing guard dropped to their knees and bowed their heads to her.

"Princess." All four guards said in unison.

"Please, stand."

Following the chain of hierarchy, three of the guards looked to the man holding Eric's chain. He obviously was the warrior in charge.

"Princess, my name is Holt. My team and I will be escorting you, Lieutenant Lucien, Advisor Tomais and the prisoner through the Gate and back to Drogmahara. It is a great honor and I guarantee your safety." Holt said, his fist coming to his chest and resting over his heart as he dipped his head to her.

He was easily six feet tall and simply stacked with muscle. He rivaled Eric in his physique, but obviously his muscles weren't just for show. He was a warrior through and through.

"I appreciate you and your men coming to help. Truly."

"Holt, may I have a word?" Luc said from beside Audra, slipping right into his lieutenant role. His face was unreadable, his eyes were hard and determined. A man on a mission.

"Of course. Princess." Holt acknowledged her and handed the chain to the man next to him, dressed in heavy armor and a red sash around his waist, same as Holt.

"You do not let him out of your sight." He told his men behind him, and the three other guards shifted their posture to a more intimidating (at least to Audra it was intimidating) stance.

"Audra, do you think you might want to go shower and get ready to leave?" Luc looked at her, his eyes begging her to leave the room. He must not have liked her around Eric any more than she did.

"Yes, that sounds lovely. I'll be back shortly."

All the males in the room dipped their heads in a small bow towards her as she left the room. Audra made it to the stairs before she felt a warm hand wrap around her wrist, scaring the daylights out of her. Literally.

Her magic flared and lights shot out of her hands, illuminating the dark hallway, and showing her the warm face of the man holding her wrist.

"Call Sebastien. Have him guard you from a distance while they are here. I don't trust anyone here except for Tomais. And I won't have anyone, or anything endanger your well-being again." Luc said, his voice hushed. Audra could tell he was nervous and on edge. He was constantly looking over his shoulder and keeping an eye on their surroundings as if something or someone was going to pop out of the shadows.

"Are you sure?" Audra cupped his jaw, needing to see that he truly meant what he was asking. Especially after their discussion earlier.

"Yes, I'm sure. We already discussed this, didn't we? I can tell he will keep you safe. He feels the same way I do about you. He came to you when you were in trouble and helped me subdue Eric, so I guess I need to try and..." He stopped speaking suddenly.

"And what?"

"Trust him. I should try and trust him. I trust him a whole hell of a lot more than these guys that have come from Dragomahara. I don't know who is on Eric's side, if any of them, and I won't put your safety in jeopardy again." He said, taking both of her hands in his and looking into her eyes.

"Did you guys have some kind of discussion about this while I was passed out or something?" Audra joked.

"We did, actually. He made his feelings for you clear, as did I."

"You what?" Audra yelled, before Luc shushed her and pushed her up the stairs away from listening ears. When they were on the landing, Luc did another look around to make sure they were alone and then shoved her into the bathroom, locking the door behind them.

"Is that why you are so okay with my feelings towards him and you both? Because you two already had this weird little agreement between you two? Oh my god."

"I prefer to think of it as having you in my life, getting to be with you and giving you everything you want."

"I haven't even talked to Seb in person yet about this. All I know is these subconscious feelings I have when I'm with him and you are telling me that you two already have come to an agreement about me."

"Audra, baby," Luc wrapped her in his arms, and she breathed in the warm, fresh scent that she associated with Luc. His strength and understanding mixed with never ending patience. "I think you're looking at this the wrong way. We never tried to trick you. You can ask him. We simply can't live without you, and this is the way to ensure that we both get you. We both get to watch over you, we both get to love you, we both get to care for you."

"I just...How do...I feel..."

"There is no reason for you to feel guilty, baby. You say you care for me and want me, yes?"

Audra nodded against his chest.

"Then just focus on the fact that I care just as much for you and want you just as badly." Audra could hear the smile in his voice as he kissed the top of her head. "I need to coordinate with the soldier's downstairs. I have some demands for us traveling through the Gate and security measures I want implemented. You trust me, right?"

"With my life." She looked up at him, amazed at how selfless and loving this man was. And he wanted her, he wanted to give her all of himself, only wanting her in return. Audra felt wholly inadequate.

Luc cradled her face between his hands and kissed her soundly. His lips wrapping around hers and leaving no room for any doubt about his feelings for her. He wanted her. She could feel it.

Unfortunately, he pulled back before Audra could deepen the kiss.

"I have to go. Before I take you right here in the bathroom."

"I couldn't mind that." Audra said with a roll of her hips against his, which caused Luc to roll his eyes and groan.

"You're a siren. And you deserve more than a rushed fuck in a bathroom while soldiers are right downstairs."

"What a gentleman." She gave him a peck on the lips.

"I try to be. You make it hard sometimes. Besides, next time I take you, I want you to be able to scream my name."

Audra groaned and pulled him into a deep kiss that she desperately wanted to turn into more. She didn't feel like she deserved him. This strong, loving, giving man who was doing everything in his power to provide her with everything he could.

"I need to go now." He groaned, pulling away from her but keeping his grip tightly on her waist. "Call Sebastien. I still don't know him fully, don't trust him, but I know he will protect you. I've seen it." He stepped out of her embrace and left the bathroom before she could say anything more, leaving Audra with more to think about.

"Fuck." She whispered.

* * *

Audra turned the lights off in the bathroom so that the white tile was bathed in darkness. She took a deep breath, readying herself to see him again so soon.

"Seb, please." She whispered into the shadows. She fought the urge to pace within the small space, but still wrapped her arms around her middle. So much had happened and so fast, Audra was grasping onto any and all lifelines to keep her afloat. Her wish to be enough for her parents so they won't leave her again, enough for Luc to continue loving and caring for her, enough to not be fearful of whatever this was between her and Seb, enough to be a good leader.

"Two times in one day, aren't I the lucky guy?" Sebastien was leaning against the countertop, looking the perfect picture of a confident, sexy businessman. He was wearing a crisp black suit with a black button down underneath and his black hair was tousled in the way that was meant to look effortless, but really must have taken a lot of effort. He smirked at Audra and crossed his arms, making his biceps strain against the suit jacket.

"I'm so sorry to bother you. Were you at work?"

"I was...busy. But I will always come for you. You called, and I promised I would always answer. What do you need, sweetheart?"

"You were busy? That's all I'm going to get? Were you busy with your girlfriend or wife, maybe?"

Sebastien laughed and again, it was one of the most beautiful sounds Audra had heard. She wanted to make him laugh all the time.

"No girlfriend or wife, sweetheart. Just you."

"Then what were you busy with? I hate to disrupt your busy schedule." She teased.

"Work stuff. I was working, but I'm here now and I want to help you, so what do you need?"

In the darkness of the bathroom, Audra could feel her breathing pick up as she felt him move closer to her. He was invading her space, and she loved it.

"Or did you just call because you missed me?"

Audra felt her breath escape her lungs as Seb grazed her cheek with his. The smooth skin and masculine scent made her eyes roll back in her head.

"I...uh...oh, god." She struggled to find words as his arms wrapped around her waist and she catapulted into his strong body. He knew what he was doing. He knew that she had such a strong reaction to him, and he used it to his advantage.

"Tell me, sweetheart. You just missed me, didn't you?"

"Oh, god, yes." She moaned as his hand slid up her shirt and tweaked her nipple.

"I missed you too." He whispered seductively in her ear, nipping on her earlobe. "But I have a feeling that you called me for something a bit more serious. Didn't you?"

Audra could barely think. His hands were everywhere, his mouth leaving marks across her throat. With each movement, he caused her to become wetter and wetter. If she wasn't careful, these two men were going to make her drip through her leggings.

"What is it, darling?" He asked, his voice low and husky.

"Help. Luc and I need your help." She groaned. Her words pulled his attention from where he was covering her neck with kisses, sucking, and nipping at her neck.

"What's happened?"

"Luc wanted to know if you could watch over me a little more closely. There are more soldiers here from Vesperitus and with Eric -"

"Being the next General, he doesn't know who exactly to trust. I get it. It's a smart move. Even if it means having to call on me. That must have been hard for him." Seb smirked, the shadows in the room receding slightly so the light from the window was filtered in.

"He said my safety was his priority. And speaking of Luc, I hear that you two had a very...eye-opening discussion about me."

"Oh, we did, sweetheart. It seems the Lieutenant's feelings for you run deeper and more vast than I was expecting. He won't let you go, and neither will I." Sebastien said. She was still trapped against him and the sink with both of his hands on either side of her.

"So, what does that mean? For us, for me, for you?"

"It means as much as I don't like it, I can't keep you from him. And if I'm being honest, it makes me feel better knowing you have someone to keep you safe, even when I'm not there. I will warn you Audra, I'm not known for my sharing skills, and I don't know how this all will work. But I have to have you. I stayed away; tried to fight against the vision I'd had of us together when I was younger, and I tried to stay away as I kept you safe as you grew up. But now that I can have you, can be with you..." He trailed a finger down the front of her chest, down the valley of her breasts. "I have to keep you. You're too good for me, but I will do everything I can to make sure I keep you happy. If Lucien makes you happy, if I make you happy, then that's a no brainer. You will be my only one, my sole love and that I can promise you."

Audra's eyes filled with tears, unsure as to how she deserved both of these men. It seemed too good to be true.

"It's me who doesn't deserve you."

"I can assure you that that is not the case, sweetheart." Sebastien chuckled and ran a hand down her back. "I want you to know, everything I do, everything I've done in the past 20 years and before that, is all for you."

"Why? Why me?"

"When I was a boy, I was told over and over again that the magic I had was special. Yes, I can control shadows and the darkness, but it's more than that. I'm able to see through time as well. I can't change anything, I can't interfere, I can only observe. But that was enough for me to see you. You in your foster homes, you in college, you with Eric and Luc, you all throughout your life. But mainly, I could see us, see us together. So when I came to monitor you the other day, it was time for our paths to cross. I've never been able to show myself in person to you before."

Audra's mouth dropped.

"So, you really have literally been watching over me all this time." She whispered.

"Yes, I found a loophole. I couldn't appear to you, couldn't talk to you, but I could send my shadows to you. The shadows were able to intervene, wrap around you, comfort you. I did my best. I did what I could. It wasn't until recently when I could come to you in a dream, I wish I could have sooner."

Audra pulled his hand into hers. His eyes were downcast as if he was disappointed in himself for not being able to do more for her. And that wouldn't do.

"Seb, I don't know how to thank you. For always being there. For choosing me. Until I met Luc and Eric, no one had ever chosen to stay with me before, never made much of an effort to stay in my life. Now I learn that you've been there, you've been doing everything you can to stay with me. I...it's...you're..." Audra grasped for words that would show him just how much she meant her words. How taken back she was with his actions.

"My whole life I have felt like I've had to put on a mask, a front, in order to be who everyone in my life wants me to be. But with you, you're the light to my dark, Audra." Sebastien said softly as he rested his forehead to hers.

Audra took the final step and reached behind his neck, holding him to her as she devoured his lips. He groaned, and she took the opportunity to deepen their kiss. Sebastien wrapped his arms around her waist tight enough that she felt each inch of his body pressed deliciously against hers.

"You kind of like me then, huh?" She teased him as he attached his lips to her neck, sucking on her skin hard enough that she knew she would have marks. But Audra couldn't find it in her to care at that moment. She just wanted him to keep kissing her like that.

"Oh sweetheart, you have no idea." He whispered into her skin, making her shiver.

Right as one of his large hands was sliding towards her backside, a loud, heavy, urgent knocking sounded on the bathroom door.

"Princess, the Lieutenant asked me to inform you that we have very little time before we embark for the Gate and to please hurry if possible. My apologies for the interruption of your bathing time." A younger sounding man squeaked through the bathroom door, his voice breaking as if he was nervous. Which he probably was.

"Thank you, I will be right out." She called out in response.

The moment between her and Seb was broken, but they didn't step out of each other's arms. The shadows receded and Audra noticed how the steam from the shower was fogging up the room.

"Of course, I will guard you while you're in the company of new people. Continue to trust no one but Lucien and I, okay?" Sebastien murmured as he cupped her chin.

"Did I hear that you are going through the Gate? So soon?" He asked her.

"The King and Queen have decreed it. I am to return to Dragomahara quickly. I take it we are leaving sooner rather than later." Audra said.

Sebastien looked as if she had struck him, his chest rising and falling quickly. He dropped his arms and stepped away from Audra until his back hit the wall.

"What is it?" She asked.

"It's happening then." He mumbled, not talking to her, but more towards himself.

"What's happening?"

"I have to go." He jumped out of his stupor and hugged Audra tightly. His face tucked into her neck as he breathed her in. "Things are going to happen now, even faster than before. But through it all, believe in me, please. Believe that the words I say to you in private are the truth. Believe that whatever I do, I do for us. For all of us. Lucien included. Promise me, sweetheart."

He was talking quickly, almost frantically, as his grip on her tightened as if he was afraid she wouldn't believe him. In the back of her mind, she realized she probably shouldn't give her trust away quite so easily, given how Eric turned out. But she had to follow these feelings she had. The lifelong comfort and support she felt, which she now knew was from him. He had always been there. He was still right here.

"I believe you. I promise, Seb." She whispered, tucking into his embrace. She felt the tension leave his shoulders with her words.

"I won't be able to come see you while you're surrounded by the court, okay?

But if you need me, whisper to the shadows and I will do my best to somehow communicate with you. It might take me a little while."

Audra immediately felt on edge. Something on his side was changing massively because she was going to Vesperitus.

"Okay."

"Be safe and be careful. I trust that Lucien will keep you as safe as I would. As I wish I could. As I will soon." Sebastien kissed her soundly, his lips moving against hers so passionately that she was forgetting that they had to leave this space, that they had to do anything except keep kissing.

"I'll see you soon, sweetheart." Sebastien said, breaking away from her, and his shadows making the portal that she had seen before.

"Bye." She whispered to the empty space.

As Audra touched her lips, she could feel how swollen they were, how well used and loved they were. But she couldn't deny that the last kiss Seb had given her seemed like he was apologizing.

Chapter Twenty-Seven

Audra stepped out of the bathroom with her hair wet and in the same clothes as she had been wearing before. She hadn't actually used the shower but didn't want to tip off any of the soldiers that she had called Sebastien.

Audra walked into the front room where Eric was still being forced to kneel in the middle of the soldiers. He was being tightly guarded and restrained. A fact Audra appreciated very much.

Out of the corner of her eye, Audra was able to see the shadows of the room darken slightly, and she let out a sigh of relief. Seb was watching, guarding her like he promised. Tomais stood from the chair he was sitting in, writing in his notebook, to turn another lamp on.

"You needed to see me?" She announced to the room but directed her question to Luc.

All the heads in the room turned towards her, but her eyes were only on Luc. He stood shoulder to shoulder with Holt, but his serious, stressed expression melted when his eyes fell on her.

"I did, I do." He said with a smile and beckoned her over to where they were standing. "Tomais, could we see you as well, please?"

"Did you ask?" Luc whispered to Audra, and she nodded once, subtlety. A flash of relief filled his features, but then went right back to business.

"Yes, Lieutenant?" Tomais asked as they all crowded around a table with a map of what Audra assumed was Vesperitus.

"Holt and I were discussing the best ways to go through the Gate. Which portal would be the closest to us here but also set us out on the best side of

Vesperitus, the best spot to make our way to Dragomahara, and the best route to take? Tomais, do you have any recommendations? You both have taken different portals to arrive here." Luc said.

"Wait, wait, wait. Portals? The Gate? Can someone explain to the prior faux human what all these things mean and why we can't just walk through it?" Audra interjected.

"Forgive us, Princess." Tomais said. "Let me explain. The Gate is a spot between the realms which is weakened, and it makes for easy travel. When you approach the Gate, you can see the almost shimmering static of the energy and magic created to bring the worlds together. It's...out of this world. A truly magical sight to see. In Vesperitus, it looks a bit different than here in Terraus. Basically, it brings the folds of the worlds closer together so we can walk through. Now, on Terraus or other realms, we call these gateways portals. You can think of portals as terminals, like in an airport."

"Each portal is like a door to the area before The Gate. But once you are in the area, you're able to walk through safely and peacefully to reach Vesperitus, Terraus, Hel, Plutyain, or anywhere else you want to go. The area between the portal and The Gate is like a no-man'- land, but it's a safe space. Protected and all magic is null there."

Audra wondered briefly about how Sebastien's magic was able to transcend the different realms when it seemed that everyone had to go through these different hoops in order to have any connection to different worlds.

He must be more powerful than I thought he was, then maybe even more than I am. Audra thought. She brought her thumbnail up to her teeth and chewed on it to keep her nerves together.

Luc stepped closer to her and rested his hand on her lower back, lending some of his strength to her. She felt complete relief as she focused on the warmth of his touch, bringing her back to the moment.

One problem at a time. One question at a time. She repeated, and she took a deep breath, leaning back into Luc's touch.

"And how many of these portals are there around here?" Audra asked.

"Within New York, there are three. Around the United States? Maybe a hundred." Tomais answered.

"And you each used a different portal to come here?"

"I used the Westchester portal." Tomais said.

"My soldiers and I came through the South Hampton portal; it is the closest to here." Holt explained.

"Eric and I came through the Westchester portal when we first arrived because it was closer to the city." Luc told her.

"And which would be the best way to go through to get back?" Audra asked the men, and they all looked at each other. The look they shared was one that made Audra worry.

"What?" She asked, almost demanding.

"The one that would be the easiest and closest to the Gate, the one that would get us home the quickest but that would also have the highest chance for an attack, would be the one in New York City. Right outside of the Navitus church." Luc said.

"Navitus, like where I was left as a baby?"

"Yes, the same one." Audra could feel her eyes bug out of her head. What a coincidence if she believed in such things.

"They just left me right on the first doorstep of wherever they stepped out of, didn't they?" She whispered, her heart fracturing a little. Audra had thought maybe her parents chose that church for a specific reason. But no. They had simply stepped out of a portal and dropped her.

"I'm sorry, Princess, but that is not true. The King and Queen had sent me through the portal a week before you were born. There was a prophecy, one that said you would be born a Total Elemental. And with everything going on with the Dark Fae, with the civil unrest and the wars, they were terrified for you. For your safety. Your parents did not want you to grow up behind palace walls, fearful for your life each and every moment, isolated and alone, but they knew that that would be your life if you were to stay. So they had me go and search the city for the best place to leave you. Somewhere where you would be cared for, given to good people and safe. After a few days of non-stop searching, I went to Navitus." Tomais got lost in his story, pausing only to take a breath.

"I met with a nun, Sister Leah. She was kind, loving, nurturing. I asked about adoption and what they do with infants if they are left with them. She was sensitive to my questions, and under the guise of trying to adopt a child myself, she pointed me to the appropriate channels in order for me to do research. And then after doing the legwork on the social workers, the adoption agency, and the state, I presented the choices to your parents. The three of us thought that Navitus was the way to give you your best chance."

* * *

Audra sat on the couch, her head in her hands as she went through all the information Tomais had dropped on her.

Why don't we just throw some more overwhelming, life-changing things at Audra and see how long it takes to get her to break? She thought sarcastically.

"Oh, poor little princess. Finally, finding out someone cares about her. Don't get used to it." Eric sneered, quietly enough that Audra could hear his mean words but not loud enough that Luc or Tomais could hear him.

"Shut the fuck up, Eric."

"Does Luc know how much of a slut you are? No, I bet he's still being a whipped pussy, giving into each and every whim of yours. Tell me, can he even make you cum? I doubt it."

"Awfully confident for a man on his knees." She stands, her anger overtaking her. How dare he talk to her like that, how dare he snide Luc and make her out to be a whore? Audra could feel the ground under her feet start to vibrate, just around the soles of her feet. If she didn't get her emotions under control soon, everyone would be in danger.

"Can't control your emotions yet, you naive little girl. I can't believe I ever thought of touching you. I would have had to close my eyes and pretend you were someone else just to get it up. No one would ever touch you willingly or will ever want you, can't you see? Your parents didn't want you, the fosters didn't, no other guys came close. And now you are stupid enough to believe that Lucien would? But maybe you're holding out hope that the mystery man will care for you too. A Darkling no less. News flash, sweetheart, no one will. Have you seen yourself? Pathetic." Eric spat at her. His words and demeanor sent her straight back to when he had been awful to her, simply to get her magic to activate. She had thought that it was hard for him to say those things, but she was naive then. He didn't care. Obviously, he never did.

Maybe she was being optimistic in believing that both Luc and Seb wanted her and would figure out this relationship in order to be with her. But she never felt that calmness and belonging anywhere else in her life. With Luc, she felt utterly protected and safe, like he was a safe place for her to be vulnerable and open. He'd never judged her or belittled her, just accepted, and supported her. His love was steady and strong. They had built a foundation that would last, she just knew it. With Seb, it was just something that she knew she had to follow. There wasn't a doubt that he was there for her, and she wanted to know him more. The way he looked at her, the way he had held her, spoke to her. They were shadows and light.

Audra knew that if they left her, she would be completely gutted, but she would feel blessed to have known them, to have loved them as she does and to be loved and cared for by them in return.

She couldn't say the same for Eric.

The rumbling under her feet stopped. The anger vanished once she realized that once she stepped foot in Vesperitus and he was taken away, she wouldn't think about him again. Audra walked over to Eric, standing tall over him. The smug, arrogant smirk stayed firmly on his face as she placed her hand on his shoulder. She could feel Luc's eyes on her but leaned down to speak in Eric's ear.

"I feel bad for you. Oh, how you've fallen. Thank you for teaching me a valuable lesson, but I didn't need you back then and I don't need you now. In fact, once we pass you off in Dragomahara I doubt Luc, or I think of you ever again. The mighty General, completely forgotten." She whispered. Under her palm, she could feel the muscles in Eric's shoulder tighten and tense with each word she spoke.

"You fucking bitch!" He sneered at her, teeth bared and fire in his eyes.

"Don't you fucking talk to her like that, you piece of shit." Luc appeared beside her. He never stood in front of Audra, portraying her as a damsel. She was a Queen, and he was treating her like one. A strong, capable woman that didn't need him to take over just yet.

"Yeah, go ahead and defend the whore now. You know she's probably fucking the other guy too. You're not special. So why risk getting beat up for a quick fuck?"

Before Audra could say anything, Luc's fist shot out and hit Eric just once, incredibly hard in the temple. Eric's limp body hit the floor, completely knocked out.

"Oh my god, are you okay?" Audra turned to Luc, grabbing at his hand to make sure he hadn't broken anything.

"I'm fine, baby. Just needed to shut that bastard up. Are you okay? What did he say to you before?"

"Over here." Audra pulled Luc into the kitchen, away from the soldiers who had let the whole encounter happen and looked like they were drinking in all the drama.

"He was just taunting me. Telling me how no one would ever want me and how naive I was for thinking you would. How repulsive I am, and no one would be able to touch me without thinking of someone better." She chuckled, trying to laugh through the insecurity and pain. "But I put him in his place. Don't worry." She smiled softly at Luc as she grabbed some ice for his hand from the freezer.

"You know that I don't feel that way, right?" Luc said as she set the ice on his knuckles. His voice was leveled and controlled, but when Audra looked up at him, she could see the rage burning in his eyes. Luc's muscles were tight and tense. She knew he must want to go beat Eric to a pulp for saying those things to her. Audra didn't want to think about how much Luc also might want to beat up Seb for their odd...relationship? Whatever the three of them were. But he was trying to be civil for her. A thought that made her heart warm with affection for him.

"What?"

"I don't think you're repulsive. It's not hard for me to touch you. In fact, it's the opposite. Now that I finally have you, it's hard for me to stop touching you."

Audra watched silently as Luc moved the ice away from his reddening hand and placed it on her cheek. The coolness of the ice had chilled his skin, and it made her shiver. Luc never once looked away from her.

"You're beautiful and everything to me." He whispered.

She was powerless against him when he pulled her to his body and took her mouth in a passionate, yet demanding, kiss. He wanted to show her how much she was wanted, how much he cared for her, how much he desired her. Luc moved his hands down her waist and under her thighs to pull her up against him, and he set her on the counter.

Audra opened her thighs and Luc wasted no time stepping between them.

"You're not a quick fuck. You're my future. I could care less if I ever get a title or any kind of acknowledgement in court. I just want you. All of you." He groaned as he flexed his hips forward, letting Audra know how much he wanted her. His hard length pressing into the flesh of her thighs. She moaned at the feel of him.

"God, I want you. I want to take you right here, so everyone knows you're mine. Fuck. Please let me." Luc muttered. Each word sent a thrill through her and made her core heat hotter.

"I want you. I want you, Luc. But not here, not where they could walk in." She whispered.

Luc groaned and rested his head on her chest. She shared the sentiment. Stopping was the last thing she wanted to do, especially since both of her men had been riling her up all evening. But she really didn't want any of their times together to be a proverbial 'fuck you' to Eric. She wanted it to be about them. Their feelings for each other.

"Thank you. For sticking up for me." Audra ran her fingers through his thick waves, cuddling his head close to her chest.

"Always."

* * *

"What is a Darkling?" Audra asked Luc after they had calmed down. Luc was holding her tightly to him and playing with a lock of her waves. It was relaxing, peaceful, and almost sensual. She wanted to ask him before Tomais, or Holt came to get them. She knew they wanted to leave sooner rather than later.

"A Darkling is a being that has the power to move throughout the darkness. Historically, they've had unmeasurable powers. The darkness and shadows transform into energy and magic that they can yield to do many other things that are atypical for normal Fae in Vesperitus. Why?" Luc asked, climbing up next to her on the counter.

"Eric said something about how I was stupid if I thought two men would want me, and then he said, 'a Darkling no less'."

"Oh my god." Luc whispered. "It makes so much sense now."

He jumped off the counter and put his hands on her thighs, staring at her with a nervous, amazed expression.

"Sebastien is a Darkling. That's how he was able to heal you. That's how he can talk to you without a phone or anything like that. Especially across realms. Oh my god, first you, a Total Elemental, now a Darkling. What the fuck is happening?"

Audra doesn't really understand why it is such a big deal, but the shock and nerves that radiated through Luc alerted her to just how much it was.

"Princess, Lieutenant?" Holt knocked on the doorway into the kitchen and the two of them stepped apart.

"Yes, we are here. What is it?" Luc asked.

"Tomais and I were discussing the need for us to go through the Navitus portal as soon as possible. We would like, with your approval Princess, to go tonight."

"Tonight?" Audra was surprised and her throat caught.

"It will take us at least a day and a half to get from the Gate to Dragomahara. So, I would like to have my men go get all the supplies and when we are ready, leave Terraus."

"What will you do with Eric?" Audra had to know. She had taunted him enough and pissed him off that he might just try something when he wakes up.

"We are restraining him with magic dampening chains. He is now collared with a muzzle which restricts his jaw so he will not be speaking any more. I also took the liberty of injecting him with a strong sedative while he was already unconscious in order to bolt his chains to the wall so he will not be awake or able to move should he wake before we leave. You are perfectly safe, Princess." Holt bowed to her, and she couldn't help but let out a sigh of relief.

"Thank you for your help and support. I think having everyone go get supplies for a camping trip and hike sounds like a good plan. Luc?" Audra deferred to Luc to make the final call.

Both Luc and Holt turned to her with their jaws dropped.

"What?"

"It is your decision, Princess. Whatever you decide, we will keep you safe and guarded." Holt explained, and she realized why they were so shocked. She had given power to Luc when she was meant to be giving orders.

But she didn't work that way.

"Thank you, I know you will. I would still like to know what Lucien thinks. Ultimately, you have more experience and knowledge of what we are walking into. I will follow your lead, Lieutenant." She smiled sweetly at him, and he closed his mouth with a snap.

His eyes still held shock, but his chest puffed up a bit. Confident and praised by his girl, Luc wanted to show how well he could take care and lead.

"I will stay behind with Audra and Tomais. The four of you will take our car and get all the supplies needed. Tents, food, sleeping bags. Pick up hiking shoes for Audra and hiking bags for us to carry everything. Be back within two hours."

Orders given, Holt nodded, bowed towards Audra, and left the room.

"God, you're so sexy." She reached up and wrapped her arms around Luc's neck, kissing him with a smile on her face.

Chapter Twenty-Eight

"I can carry a bag, Luc." Audra said with a smirk. She could tell that he was still trying to decide how to be chivalrous while still letting her be the badass she was and wanted to be recognized as. She didn't want to trip the bag from his hands, but she was starting to get worried about how much he was carrying on this trek.

"Please, let me carry something." She tried to reach for the backpack he had picked up that had been at her feet.

"I've got you." He said.

"Don't be stupid. You're already carrying everything else we would need for camping overnight and carrying my duffel bag. I can carry my backpack. It's not a big deal."

Luc sighed and dramatically handed the bag back to her.

"I just want you to know," he said softly, yanking her closer to him when she grabbed the strap of the bag. "You are staying in my tent tonight."

"Was there ever another option?" She whispered to him, trying to put what she hoped was a seductive smile on her face.

"No, no, there wasn't." He brought her in closer to steal a kiss from her.

Audra felt her cheeks heat up and her belly light with fire. Suddenly, she was eager to go through the portal so they could rest and set up camp for the night.

"How much longer until we get to the church?" Audra asked. The group of them were walking through the city, having left the safe house behind, and taken two separate SUVs to get back to the city. Holt had explained to Audra after her alarm at dragging Eric through the crowded city center with a muzzle and in chains, that they had glamoured him and they explained to her as they walked that that meant they had hidden them from the human eye.

Audra was surprised and didn't trust it, but then when they had abandoned the cars and started walking, every single person they passed on the street looked right past them. Almost through them. They were invisible. Ghosts walking through the crowd.

But what a sight we all must be, Audra thought. *Four guards dressed in battle armor, a chained-up prisoner, and three average joes walking through the city looking like we are going camping in the concrete jungle.*

"Not much farther now, Princess." Tomais said from in front of them. He was making sure that there was at least one more person between the traitor and her and for that Audra could have hugged him.

Each of them was carrying a thick and stocked hiking backpack with everything they might need. Holt had brought three pairs of boots back for Tomais, Luc and Audra and she was very thankful. They had already walked farther than her beat up chucks could've handled.

The group of them turned a corner and standing before them was a beautiful, monstrous gothic church that looked like it belonged on the tourist route in Paris, not within the hubbub of New York City. It was so tall, its one spire seemed to touch the sky. Perched on the top was a cross that stood tall and proud against the clear blue sky. The sky bled through the iron cross.

Tomais sighed and nodded towards the church.

"This is it. Navitus Church of the Brave."

Audra was gob smacked. This was where her human story began, and this is where her new Fae life will begin. Where she will finally be united with her family.

"Well, what are we waiting for?" She said, striding towards the front steps that led to two ornate wooden doors.

"Audra, wait." Luc grabbed her wrist and halted her in her stride.

"Why? Let's go."

Eric chuckled through the muzzle, drawing her attention from the dark blue of Luc's eyes.

"I would shut the fuck up if I were you." She sneered at him through clenched teeth. Turning to Luc, "Why do we need to wait?"

"We need to get in formation. That way you are most protected, and Eric is completely secured." Luc said, pointing over her shoulder to Holt, who nodded and started barking orders to the rest of the group. "You will be by my side the entire time. If I had it my way, you'd be tethered to me, so wherever you go, I go. But I assumed that'd be too much." He smiled at her, a soft, sweet smile that was filled with teasing.

"Don't worry, I'll stay as close to you as appropriate with an audience." She smirked and held onto his bicep.

"Ready, sir." Holt called through. Eric was now standing, and his chains were connected to two separate soldiers. They looked like they were en-shrouded in chain mail, a shirt made from it with thick, sturdy, solid circles of silver where the chains were connected, tethering Eric to both men beside him. Somehow two additional chains were attached to his hands and ankles.

Audra looked at him with pity. All that weight from the chains must be heavy. It was going to make all the traveling difficult. But then she was reminded of his cruel words. He'd tried to break her confidence in her men, in herself, and all sympathy left her heart.

"Tomais, you're with us." Luc barked, pointing to the spot by Audra.

"Where is this portal?" Audra asked Luc, looking around for anything that stuck out as odd.

"I have to activate it. I will be right back." Tomais said as he walked over to the side of the church, just off to the corner where there was a small dark alleyway between buildings.

"What does he have to do?" Audra asked Luc quietly, straining her neck to try and see what Tomais was going.

"He has to activate the portal by making a blood offering to the space. Four drops of blood; four directions, four elemental traits. Being from Vesperitus, anyone that travels through the portals usually travels with small vials of blood that have a strong, pure affinity for one of the elements. A pure fire user, a pure air wielder, a water user, like myself, and an earth yielder."

"Do you have these blood vials on your person, too?" She asked incredu-lously.

"I do. They aren't like the thick ones that the doctors use when they have blood drawn. The vials only hold four or five drops total. Don't look so scandalized." He chuckled.

"How do you get the blood?"

"Element users donate it. Plus, portal traveling isn't something widely known. It is on a need to know basis only with special permission given by the King and Queen."

Audra was shocked at how the portals were opened. It was a blood rite. But on the other hand, it made sense. Doing things so specifically and through blood made sure that the person trying to walk through the worlds didn't do so by accident.

"We're ready." Tomais said, his head popping around the corner, the rest of his body shrouded in the shadows.

"Are you ready to go home?" Luc asked Audra quietly, sliding his hand in hers.

He gently pulled her towards the alley where Tomais stood next to what Audra thought was a silent black hole. Just a completely opaque cavern where the stone of the church should have been. Audra watched as the two guards connected to Eric pulled him through and, as soon as they walked through, they vanished. Like they had dropped off the side of the world. Holt and the other two guards walked through, vanishing as well. Tomais nodded to Luc, silently asking if he would be okay taking Audra through on his own, to which Luc nodded back. A reassuring gesture which Luc respected the advisor for.

Audra was too enthralled with the phenomenon she was watching to catch the two men having a silent discussion around her.

Tomais walked through, leaving the two alone.

"Will it hurt?" She asked quietly.

"It's just like walking into another room. There is a brief moment of darkness, but then you will arrive out on the other side. A brief moment of darkness where the portal will take us to the Gate, and we walk out in Vesperitus."

"Total darkness?"

"You won't even notice. It'll be like you're blinking. And I'll be right by your side the entire time."

"Promise?" Audra clutched his hand a little tighter.

"I promise, baby." Luc brought their entwined hands up to his mouth to kiss the back of her hand softly.

Audra nodded and let Luc lead her into the darkness.

Maybe Seb can walk with me too, in the darkness. She thought before she closed her eyes and walked through.

* * *

The darkness was alarming, but she never let go of Luc's hand. She gripped it so tightly she was sure that he was in pain, but he never said a word.

By the time her other foot hit the ground, she felt as if she was being pushed forward into a speck of light. The more the force made her go forward, her body felt as if it was being pressurized. The closer her body got to the dot of light, the more intense the pressure became.

"Almost there." Audra heard Luc say from in front of her. A hand slipped into her free one and she realized that Seb had managed to walk through with her. The shadows and darkness allowed for him to be there with her.

"I'm right here." He whispered in her ear and squeezed her hand twice. Regardless of the pressure, she felt like she could breathe again. She squeezed his hand back before he vanished.

Just when Audra felt like her ears were going to pop from the pressure, they stepped out onto a platform. Audra gasped, the fresh air distinctively smelled of pine and soil. The brisk chill in the air could only be felt when a gust of wind swirled around them, lifting her hair, and taking her breath away.

"Welcome home, Princess." Luc said, tugging her to his side and smiling out into the valley.

The platform they stood on was an old, weathered white stone surrounded by gigantic pine trees that formed a semi-circle around the platform. It felt as if this place had been abandoned, forgotten in the generations it had stood.

"This is the Gate you guys keep talking about?" Audra asked, gesturing to the platform and surrounding trees.

"It is. We are in the south area of Vesperitus. It's mostly forest here. But only a day, day, and a half from Dragomahara, mostly through the woods, but the closer we get to the castle the more mountains you will be able to see." Luc said.

The rest of their group was already waiting at the bottom of the platform, waiting for their Princess and lieutenant to continue on. A few of the men were looking through their supplies, checking over things, while Tomais stood staring right at the pair, a nervous expression on his face.

"Is everything okay?" Luc asked him, noting his nerves as well. Tomais' eyes darted back and forth between the dense forest and the group of soldiers.

"Yes, sir. We are trying to get everything sorted so that we can hustle. I'm hoping that we are able to reach Dragohmara by tomorrow morning if possible." Holt cut in as he strapped his bag tighter on his back.

Luc looked at Tomais, then down at Audra. It was obvious something was bothering Tomais, but with a subtle shake of his head, Luc let it go.

"Then let's go." Luc barked, threading Audra's fingers through his and pulling her with him.

As Audra walked into the woods, she was hit with all the energy in every living thing surrounding her. She had felt it back at the safe house, but it was absolutely nothing compared to the surge of power she felt then.

She gasped loudly, letting the lightning bolt of energy flow through her.

"Baby?"

"I'm okay. I'm okay." Her fingers clenched his tighter. It wasn't painful, but very shocking. It was as if her body was getting a reboot. All her powers had been so difficult to hold on to once she started using them. It was a struggle. But here, with this energy that seemed to overflow through her, Audra knew that if she had to move a lake, it would be like lifting a pebble.

"Wow." She breathed out, the word sounding like an exhale.

"What is it?"

"The energy here...it's so powerful. So strong. I feel like I'd be able to do anything."

"Sir!" Tomais called out, rushing forward to catch up with Luc and Audra.

"Her scent is so much more noticeable now. As soon as she passed the treeline, it was as if a giant arrow was over her head and screaming that she was a Total Elemental. We need to do something to cover her scent as much as possible or we are going to be fighting a lot of creatures to keep her safe."

"Agreed." Luc said, sniffing the air.

"What can we do?" She asked, sniffing herself subtly. She didn't smell anything but their detergent; floral and clean.

"It's not you or your clothes. It's your powers, your energy, your blood." Luc said, running a hand down his face. "Tomais, would covering her pressure points with another scent work?"

"It might, we would need to reapply it frequently."

Luc nodded. He took a breath and looked at Audra. When their eyes met, she saw resolve.

"What does that...Luc!" She cried out as Luc pulled out his pocketknife and slit his palm.

"What are you doing?!" Audra tried to grab his hand back, but Luc moved out of her reach so he could continue slicing his hand and gathering his blood.

"Stop!" She yelled at him.

"This is how we mask your scent, baby. If we apply blood to your pulse points, where the skin is the thinnest, we can mask your energy with my own. It's a slim chance it works, but it's better than just walking around with you basically being advertised as a Total Elemental and a free for all with any other predators." Luc looked at her, pleading with her to let him do this.

"How do you even know about that?" She asked him, her eyes wide as she thought about it.

"I read about it in a book back in high school. Never really thought masking a scent would be as big of a deal, but the knowledge comes in handy right about now." He said with a small smirk.

Audra looked at his hand, the pool of blood starting to drip down his wrist and stain the edge of his shirt.

"Okay." She whispered and bared her neck for Luc to cover her with his life source.

"I know it's kind of gross, but it will keep you safe. That's the biggest thing to remember." He whispered. Luc stepped closer to her and kissed the column of her throat softly, intimately, before dipping his fingers into the pool of blood and started to cover spots on her.

It was an intimate thing, a very vulnerable act that Audra was forced to partake with an audience. When it got to where Luc had to cover her thighs and chest, he left a bloody handprint over her clothes.

"It looks like I've been grabbed all over." Audra said, looking over all the handprints that covered her body. The marks on her skin were drying and felt tacky.

"You have. By me." Luc smirked at her, winking quickly. Audra rolled her eyes and smiled.

"Let's get going. I already want to wash this off my skin."

"As you wish, baby." Luc wrapped his hand with a spare rag and turned back to the group. "Let's go!" He yelled.

* * *

The group walked. And walked. And walked.

Audra did her best to keep up but was definitely not used to hiking for hours on end. Their surroundings were breathtaking; the sky was clear and serene. The trees looked like a mix between great tall pines but with the coverage of jungle trees. Every now and then Audra could look up and see the birds soaring through the air, but mostly shadows were cast through the leaves and needles.

The ground was soft; the soil never being compacted from overuse but constantly watered and within the shade. Audra was thankful, her feet were already killing her within her new boots.

The sky started to darken, signaling that night was approaching, but instead of the sunset coloring that she was used to, the sky turned green.

Then the green turned to purple.

The darkness of night wasn't simply black night like what she was used to, but a deep purple color that caused everything around her to take on a plum tint.

"This is new." Audra said softly to Luc while he was reapplying his scent over hers.

"Yeah," he smiled, "it'll take a little while to get used to."

"Was it weird when you came to New York?"

Luc nodded. "The sky here never gets as dark as it does in Terraus. It was abrupt and off-putting for a long time, but then when the stars came out and we could see them as we hiked towards the city, it was breathtaking."

"You don't have stars here?"

"No. No stars like you are used to. More like tinsel that streams through the sky."

"What?" Audra asked with a laugh. "I cannot imagine what that looks like."

"You won't have to. They will dance across the sky soon." He wrapped his arm over her shoulders, and she cuddled into his side.

"This is a good spot for camp. We are close enough now that we will reach Dragomahara in the morning. But we should rest." Holt advised, to which Luc agreed.

"Very well, set up camp."

* * *

Camp was set up very quickly after Luc had confirmed the order. They erected tents and a fire pit quickly and without issue, bringing together their small space for the evening.

They chained Eric to a tree nearby, far enough away that Audra could relax but not far enough that he was completely out of sight. The two soldiers that had been chained to him removed their links and joined the rest of the group around the fire.

Luc set up the small tent for the two of them. It was so small that she didn't know how they both were going to fit in it without sleeping right on top of each other. Not that she thought Luc minded, but she wanted to be respectful of the people around them as well.

"Want to go for a walk?" She asked Luc, bumping his shoulder with hers.

"We probably shouldn't. Besides, aren't you tired from all the walking we've already done today?" Luc chuckled. His reluctance to tell her no straight out was so obvious Audra wanted to groan in frustration.

"Look, you just reapplied the gross blood mask, so I'm safe from whatever the hell you guys are worried about. I can go by myself if you want, but I'm trying to be responsible and tell you what I'm going to do. What I need. And right now, I need a break from everything."

Luc sighed, and she knew she had won.

"How can I say no to you?" He smiled at her.

Audra stood up and dusted off her pants, being mindful not to smear any of the blood on her. It was an odd sensation, and she was trying very hard not to think about how much Luc had probably lost by doing this. He wouldn't even consider anyone else doing that for her and Audra secretly thought it was because he didn't want anyone else's hands on her.

Audra and Luc walked past the tree where Eric was chained, and his eyes never left Audra's. His golden eyes were staring her down, but without any evil or anger in them. All Audra could see was a sparkle, as if he was laughing under the muzzle.

"Don't worry about him. We've taken all the necessary steps in order to keep him secure and to keep you safe." Luc entwined their fingers between them.

"I know."

The pair walked for a few minutes, when they were far enough outside of the camp where they knew no one could hear them. The darkness lurking through the trees would have caused others to cower in fear or made them start to be anxious about the things in the trees that they couldn't see. But not Audra. The darkness was soothing, comforting, just like old times.

The shadows seemed to graze her skin in a loving caress and Audra knew that Seb was watching over her. No matter what, he was still protecting her.

"Want to tell me what is going through that pretty head of yours?" Luc murmured, leisurely continuing on the path they were on.

"I just...it's been a lot. I just wanted to be with you if that's okay. I didn't want people around us that we didn't trust, I didn't want us to be worried about traitors or attempted murders, I just wanted to be able to hold you, to kiss you, to talk freely like we used to, about nothing and everything."

"I understand. Is there anything I can do to help you?" Luc said as he put both hands on her hips, bringing her body into his. Audra smiled and bit her lip. She knew what she wanted. She wanted Luc. She wanted all that he would give her, and she wanted it now.

"I can think of a few things." She whispered against his lips, leaning up to take a kiss before he could pull away.

But, of course, her strong, sensitive, understanding man didn't pull away. He understood what she needed. What she wanted. And he was willing to give it to her.

The smell of pine and earth intensified around them, the darkness preventing them from double checking their surroundings.

Audra slid her hand up under his shirt, reveling in the feeling of his hard muscles flexing and tensing under touch. Luc groaned and threaded his fingers through her hair, deepening the kiss.

"Here? Are you sure?" Luc whispered. Audra could feel his breath on her lips, and she bit back a moan.

"I'm sure." She leaned forward and stole his mouth once again, nipping at his lower lip, and drew a growl from her usually sweet man.

"You're driving me crazy. You've been driving me crazy all day. Come here." Luc demanded, gripping her ass, and lifting her against him. Audra's hands gripped his broad shoulders and one of her hands threaded into his thick hair, keeping his head to hers.

Audra felt Luc down her back, her legs firmly wrapped around his waist, and she felt her core drip with arousal. Luc forced them back into a tree, using his hips to keep Audra pinned. She ground down on his hips, feeling just how excited he was. He thrust up against her, his length sliding over her clit with delicious friction.

Audra threw her head back with a small cry and Luc's lips never left her skin. He mouthed at her neck, then down to the swell of her breast and sucked hard enough that Audra knew that she was going to have more marks. In the back of her mind, she was aware that when they walked back into camp, everyone would know what they were up to because of the multiple marks she would no doubt have on her cleavage. And she had no makeup to try to cover them. But she couldn't bring herself to care. Not when he kept moving his hips against hers, hitting her bundle of nerves every single time.

"Oh my god," She moaned as his mouth moved down to her chest and bit the thin skin of her chest. Audra had never thought that she would care being marked, but she found that the slight sting of pain was bringing her higher.

"My name is Luc, baby." He said with a smirk, obviously very happy with himself for her reaction. His hand snaked up her shirt, lifting the material over her breasts, and he pulled her bra cups down. The cool air made Audra gasp, immediately making her nipples harden.

The sight of her, wrecked, open and writhing against him, was proving to be too much for Luc. He growled; a low, guttural noise that sent a wave of arousal straight to Audra's core. He dipped down, keeping her hips pinned tightly, and took her nipple in his wet, hot mouth while he pulled on the other.

"Oh, please. Please." She begged.

"Here? I need you." He groaned.

"What a nice moment. Sorry for interrupting...or am I?" Sebastien's voice called through the air, scaring Luc and Audra. They both jumped slightly, having been so wrapped up in each other that they forgot to take in their surroundings. Luc let Audra slide down his body and she quickly pulled her shirt down.

It wasn't that she didn't want Seb to see her breasts, but she didn't want him to see her bare for the first time like this. Not when she couldn't get his honest reaction to her.

"Sebastien." Luc said shortly in greeting. Discreetly, without turning around, Luc adjusted himself so his hard on wasn't quite as noticeable. Audra smiled because even when he tried to hide his hard-for-her cock, it still was quite a noticeable bulge.

"Hey," She smiled at Seb, unsure as to how to proceed with this conversation. They both had agreed to be with her, had agreed for her to be with both of them, but she hadn't had enough one-on-one time with either to really discuss what this meant.

"Sweetheart, you look positively...wrecked. In the best possible way."

Audra ran her hands through her hair, trying to get her waves somewhat manageable and less like she had just been caught dry humping her boyfriend.

"Don't pull yourself together, sweetheart. You look ravishing." Seb said, his voice raspy and low. His words sent another shock of arousal to her core, and she was sure that her underwear was ruined.

"Thank you." She whispered, feeling like he was pulling her under his spell.

"I think our girl needs a nice release to help her relax. Don't you think, Lucien?" Seb said, never turning his attention from Audra. His eye contact pinning her in place and making her pussy clench.

"I do." Luc said, stepping behind Audra, pulling her back to be flushed to his front. He was still hard, and he rutted his cock against her ass.

"Luc, Seb." She groaned. She wanted this. She was surprised just how much she wanted it. She felt Luc wrap his arms around her waist and caressing her skin, lighting it on fire. Her eyes never left Seb and she could see just how much the sight of her, turned on and aroused, was affecting him. His hands were tucked into his black pants, but she could see his jaw muscles tick and move with each clench. His eyes were pools of darkness, but with one lone speck of light.

Sebastien smiled, his face turning sharp and dominant, like a predator that had caught his prey.

"We are going to wreck you, sweetheart. Aren't we, Luc?"

"Fuck yeah, we are." He muttered against her neck before sucking another mark onto the back of her neck.

Sebastien pulled off his suit jacket, folded it nicely, and draped it over a branch nearby. He turned back to her, unbuttoning his black dress shirt sleeves, and rolling them up his forearms. The sight made Audra clench around nothing and groan. She wanted something, anything, to fill her. They had been teasing her all day, and she was about ready to explode.

"If one of you doesn't touch me to get me off soon, I will do it myself." She threatened, her frustration coloring her tone.

"Soon, sweetheart. Don't you like Lucien's hands all over you, caressing your skin and opening you up?" He asked, slipping a black satin tie from his neck, and laying it over his suit jacket. "Answer me, sweetheart."

Audra moaned and nodded. His use of the term of endearment he had used with her all along sent a shiver down her spine, combined with Luc's hands, pinching her breast through her shirt.

"Lucien, why don't you take her shirt off?" Seb suggested, walking close to the pair, taking in the sight of Audra becoming more and more needy.

"Great idea." Luc said, wasting no time at all as he whipped her shirt off her body. The night chill didn't register like it did before, she was too stimulated by the two men who looked like they wanted to climb between her legs and never leave.

"You're so fucking gorgeous." Seb's eyes traced over her body, and she felt his gaze as if they were his hands touching her skin. His hands on her felt different from Luc's, but no less amazing. Where Luc's touch was easy and his hands were calloused from years of working with weapons and fighting, Sebs were smooth and polished but had an edge to it. Like he wanted her to know that it was his hand on her and she couldn't mistake his touch for anyone else's. The shadows twirled around them, becoming thicker and opaquer like fog. Dense enough that no one would be able to see them, should one of the soldiers wander this way.

"No one else will see you like this, but us." Seb said. The look in his eyes said that he would cut down anyone who did.

Audra nodded. Whatever he wanted, whatever Luc wanted, as long as they kept touching her.

"I think it's time to get you more comfortable, baby." Luc said in her ear. He and Seb shared a look, and Seb brought his hands to the waistband of her leggings and slid them down her thighs, just past her knees.

Audra was gasping, her chest heaving with each breath, just waiting for them to touch her where she really wanted.

"What do you want, sweetheart?" Seb asked with a hushed tone. He was sliding his fingertip softly over her upper thigh, dragging it up to her toned stomach and down to her other thigh, completing the circle of torture.

"Please." She whispered.

"Please, what?" Luc asked from behind her.

"Touch me. Please touch me. Seb, Luc, both of you. Please." She begged. They had teased her for too long. She felt like she was going to snap.

"You don't have to beg, Princess." Seb smirked, cupping her face with his hand, and kissing her deeply.

"But I like it when you do." He said seductively in her ear, never taking his eyes off of Audra. Seb's hand was grazing her nipples while Luc was palming her bare ass. She bent over slightly, forcing their hands closer to her breasts and ass.

"Fuck, baby." Luc swore, his grip going to the front of her thighs and forcing her to open her knees as far as they could go with her leggings restricting her movement. "Touch her, make her feel good."

"With pleasure." Seb bent down and put his face between her spread thighs.

Audra groaned with relief and her body sagged against Luc, who kept her upright and reached a hand up to twist a nipple. Seb pried her thighs apart more before ripping her leggings down the rest of the way and throwing her leg over his shoulder, diving into her heat farther.

"Oh my god, fuck. Fuck." She moaned. "It's too much, please, it's too much."

Seb was fucking her with his tongue so well, that she was almost scared to find out how he would fuck her with his cock. She could hear just how wet she was, how wet her men were making her with each breath, each touch, and each thrust.

Luc was holding her from behind, still, both hands caressing her breasts, holding her throat, pulling her closer. He never stopped moving, always knowing where she needed his hands or his mouth next. Audra gasped, throwing her head back to rest on his shoulder.

"Kiss me." She begged Luc, twisting her neck to give him access to her mouth. Which he took very willingly.

"Come on sweetheart, I know you can give me more." Seb said against her mound and thrust one of his thick fingers into her channel. Audra cried out loud enough that she was sure the others at the campsite could hear her. She just hoped they didn't come looking. She might incinerate them on the spot if they interrupted.

"Seb, Seb, please." She begged him. She didn't know what for, but she threaded her fingers into his inky hair and pulled him closer. He chuckled and curled his finger against her front wall, sending her into a spasm of pleasure. Audra cried out, feeling her peak coming closer and closer with each swipe of his fingers, each lick of his tongue against her clit, each squeeze of her throat, each bite of her skin. Luc groaned behind her, and his hand slid up her body, between the valley of her breasts and to the hollow of her neck.

"Cum for us, baby." Luc growled in her ear as he tightened his hand on her throat just a bit more.

"Let go, sweetheart. We'll catch you." Seb said roughly, adding another finger in his assault.

And light exploded behind her eyes as she reached her peak. Seb's fingers continued to piston in and out of her, riding her through her climax.

"That was so fucking sexy." Luc said in her ear as he kissed her neck and reached down between her thighs, where she was wet and slick. He dragged two fingers between her thighs, gathering some of her slick and bringing it to his lips.

"Fuck." He groaned.

Sebastien didn't say anything. He just cupped her face, staring into her eyes. He must have been searching for how she was feeling, if she was okay with what just happened, because he saw her happiness, how loved she felt, and he kissed her with passion.

It wasn't a kiss that was meant to lead to more, but a kiss that showed her how much Seb loved her. He was telling her he was okay with what happened, okay with this new relationship, and that they were okay. That he still wanted to be with her.

"Thank you." She whispered, tasting herself on his lips.

"Anytime." He smirked.

Luc slid his arm around her waist and kissed her cheek.

"Everything good?" He asked.

"Perfect. Thank you." She leaned into him and kissed his lips sweetly.

"No, I think I can speak for both of us when I say thank you. That was... beautiful." He said with awe.

Both men adjusted themselves, no doubt trying to relieve the ache of their hard cocks trapped beneath the denim and polyester.

"Can I...Can I return the favor?" Audra asked shyly. Why she was feeling bashful talking about sucking them off after what had just happened, she wasn't sure, but she was.

"Fuck. Just the thought of you on your knees has me harder than ever. But it wasn't about us tonight. We did that because we wanted to show you, we care, we wanted to take care of you. Right?" Seb asked Luc, looking to him to back him up.

"Right. As much as I would like to feel your hot mouth around my cock, swallowing me down, right now was about you. You don't need to return the favor...yet." He said with a smirk. Luc bent down and pulled on her leggings as Seb found the shirt that someone had ripped off her earlier.

Audra hadn't felt so loved and cared for before. It was enough to bring tears to her eyes.

"What are you doing here?" Audra asked Seb.

"I wanted to check on you, see how the trek was. I could feel as soon as you came through the Gate and needed to make sure you were okay. In person." He kissed her forehead.

"Anything to report?" Seb asked Luc.

"Not yet. I should reapply her 'gross blood mask' to keep her scent concealed." Luc pulled out his knife and slit the half-healed wound. Audra felt so bad, guilty even, that he was having to repeatedly injure himself for her.

"There has to be another way." She said.

"We are almost to Dragomahara, don't worry." Luc said, shrugging his shoulders as if it wasn't a big deal to continually cut himself to provide her safety.

"Of course, I worry. You have to cut yourself open every few hours to smear your blood over me, never letting your wound heal. What if it gets infected?"

"It won't. I'm fine, I promise. Let me." He pleaded, his hand filling with his blood.

Audra closed her eyes tightly and nodded. As Luc pressed his hand to the same spots as before, Seb was asking about what the plan was when they finally reached the castle.

"Meet my parents. Figure out why they royally decreed I had to return before I have fully mastered my powers. Live my life. With you two, hopefully."

"Sounds perfect." Luc said, finished with covering her in handprints.

"Let me heal your hand."

"You can do that?" Luc asked, shock coloring his tone.

"I can do a lot of things." Seb muttered, reaching for Luc's hand, and having his shadows wrap around their joined hands. After a moment, the cyclone of shadows dissipated, and Seb let go of Luc's palm. Where there had been a deep, fresh gash across his palm, there was nothing. Not even a scar.

"Wow." Luc said in surprise.

"Thank you, Seb."

"Yes, thank you. This is just so interesting. When we have a moment, we should figure out what else your Darkling powers can do." Luc offered his hand for Seb to shake.

"You take care of our girl. I have a feeling I will be seeing you both again very soon. Our paths will finally cross in a more permanent fashion." Seb said, full of mystery. "Come here, sweetheart." He pulled on her hand, and she rushed to hold him. His broad, strong back under her hands moved with his breath as he breathed in her scent, now mingled with Luc's blood. Sebastien pulled her hair slightly, tipping her face up to his so he could capture her lips once again. His eyes were full of trepidation and was it fear? Why was he afraid? What was he afraid of?

"I will see you soon, sweetheart." He whispered to her, reverently.

"I'll be waiting."

"If you need me..."

"Whisper to the shadows." She smiled.

"Good girl." Sebastien said and kissed her again.

And her mysterious shadow man picked up his jacket and tie and walked into a group of his shadows, vanishing into the night.

Chapter Twenty-Nine

"Well...that happened." Luc said softly. Audra and Luc walked back to camp, hand in hand, in comfortable silence. They had been gone for quite some time and Luc wanted to get them back in order to catch a few hours of sleep before waking at dawn to start the trek to Dragomahara.

"It did." She smirked, seeing him smile back at her.

The night air was crisp and cool now that Audra's skin had cooled down from the heat of the moment, from the two pairs of heated, urgent hands roaming over her body. Audra shivered, the sweat had dried on her skin and the wind caused her skin to chill even further.

"Are you cold, baby?" Luc asked, pulling her closer to his side. She let him take the lead back to camp as she let herself fall back into the sharp memories of being worshipped by the two men that she knew she was falling hard for, quickly.

"Thank you." She whispered.

"Of course. Anytime."

They walk through the forest for a few more moments in silence. Their breathing, footsteps and the crickets were the only sounds surrounding them.

"Are you," Luc paused as he took a deep breath, "okay? We weren't too rough or did anything that made you feel uncomfortable?"

"I'm fine, I promise." She smiled, touched that he was obviously worried about her. "Thank you for taking care of me."

"It's my job. Or I hope it's my job to take care of you." He said with a quick kiss to her temple. Audra could see the glow from the campfire through the trees in front of them.

Audra stopped Luc before they got too close, tugging him down and holding him close. Luc wrapped his arms around her, clutching Audra as tightly as he could. She wanted to hold him sweetly, giving him all the emotion, the love and adoration she had for him before they had to go back to the group of men that they weren't completely sure they could trust. Back to their ex-best friend, who had betrayed them both and was hell bent on getting under their skin.

"Are you sure everything is okay?" Luc asked in her ear. "Are we okay?"

Audra pulled away to look into his eyes. Cupping his face with her soft hands, she said, "I'm fine. You and I are good. Better than good. I promise. I'm a bit worried about Seb, how he feels, why he came to see me after he said he wouldn't. But I'm flying high on our connections, our love. Thank you for being you, for caring for me. I hope you know how much I care for you."

Luc's eyes were trained on her, scanning her face for any signs of fear or fakeness. When he saw none, his face broke out into a grin that spanned his face. Audra didn't think that she had seen him smile so bright, his joy contagious. She returned his smile, her chest feeling like it might combust because of how happy she was with him in this moment.

"I care about you, too. You have to know how much." He said before taking her lips in a passionate kiss.

When they reluctantly pulled back for air, the pair rested their foreheads together, standing and holding each other close.

They broke apart when they heard shouting from the camp, angry voices overlapping and escalating.

Luc grabbed Audra's hand, and they hustled through the tree line, right into the middle of two soldiers standing toe to toe in anger, about to throw a few punches.

"What's going on here?" He bellowed, gaining the attention of the group, who were obviously not expecting their lieutenant, and their Princess to be there. Their arrival, thankfully, diffused the situation, but it was still plain to see that one of the soldiers, Mattuis - Audra thought she had heard Luc call him, was clenching his fists repeatedly. The other, one of the men that had been chained to Eric, was leaning against a tall tree, arms and ankles crossed, with a malicious smirk on his face.

"Do not make me ask you again. Mattius, Haltion, what is the cause of this argument?" Luc demanded, hands on his hips, looking 100 percent the highest-ranking male in attendance that he was. Audra couldn't help but admire him as he demanded the attention and obedience of his men; his strong hands that had just been caressing her curves were resting on his hips, his back tight with tension that she wanted to help release, his broad, drool-worthy chest puffed out slightly in order to show how much he truly was the one in charge. God, she wanted to feel his whole body against hers again.

Seb and Luc had created a monster. Now that she had had a taste of them, she wanted it every single moment.

"Haltion had a very inappropriate and curious notion." Mattius said through his clenched teeth. Audra looked at the other men in the group, all of them with a varying degree of agreement on their faces. Tomais wouldn't even meet her eye.

"What was this notion then, Haltion?" Luc asked with a clipped tone, the fire crackling and popping in the background.

The mysterious smirking Haltion pushed off of the tree trunk. His armor that they had all worn that covered his upper body and shoulders was discarded. His chest and arms were encased in a tight, wet-wicking type shirt that Audra would've thought was for athletes in New York if she didn't know he wasn't from back home. He sauntered up to Luc and Audra, then stood tall and proud in front of Luc with his hands clasped behind his back.

"I'm waiting. And I'm running out of patience, so I would suggest that you hurry the fuck up." Luc snapped.

"I shared with the others that I thought that the Princess' pussy must be made of gold if she was able to whip you so much. Not to mention how the First General shared that she was a pretty lousy fuck, but you're following her around like a lost puppy. Maybe he had a point, that the High Royals need to be taken down a peg or two." Haltion said.

Audra jolted back as if she had been slapped by him. The fact that he was able to spew insults and lies at both of them so nonchalantly, so factually, as if he was reciting a passage from a textbook. The other men around them had jumped up to defend her – or protect him from Luc's wrath – but she wasn't paying much attention. She was too lost in the thought of how she was ruining Luc's reputation, his hard work, his career, by openly being with him. How Eric was lying to people already about how she had slept with him.

Luc, however, wasted no time at all. His fist flew out, snapping at Haltion's nose, and blood rained down. Haltion's head snapped back, and he fell down to the dirt without making a single sound. Luc stepped over him, all fury and protectiveness flaring within his chest at the venom that insignificant asshole spewed about his girl. About his Crown. And all of it from one who swore to protect it.

"Stand down." He snapped at the others, all stepping closer to the three of them. Tomais pushed through the soldiers and stood beside Audra, silently giving his support.

"Who the *fuck* do you think you are, speaking to a royal like that, nevermind your lieutenant? If you don't get that type of fucking ignorance out of your head *and soon* you will be in chains right alongside Mr. Tayorkoven. Now, that would make me very happy with how you just addressed Princess Audra, but for now, I think the whole night on watch will do nicely. Maybe an entire evening without rest will clear your fucking head." Luc snarled at the man on the ground.

Haltion wasn't cowering, wasn't fearful. He just took the punishment that Luc had given him and nodded. Audra was surprisingly satisfied with the way Haltion's nose and eyes were bruising already.

Luc kicked some dirt on him and turned to Audra, walking towards her in a storm of fury, barely being restrained. Audra couldn't do anything. She was stuck in her own mind in shock. She could only watch. Haltion climbed to his knees, spitting out blood and giving Luc a nasty look. Audra was surprised that his man, this guard who seemed to have respected Luc and respected the crown, suddenly decided to speak out against them and in such a cruel way.

"Thank you, Tomais." He said, gratefulness and dismissal very evident in those three words. Audra could tell he was still furious, raging, that punch and the words hadn't done anything to help calm him.

Tomais nodded calmly, his eyes never leaving the scene in front of him as he tried to determine what the best course of action was. He was eyeing Luc as if he didn't trust him with Audra, so she decided to help ease his fears. She looked at Tomais and kissed his cheek.

"Thank you, I appreciate you supporting me. Us. Luc will be fine. I will be fine."

Tomaid nodded, stepping back from the pair. Holt stood up from his spot in front of the fire, his raised fist up and clenched, a signal to the rest of his soldiers to stay back. Audra nodded to Holt, a sign that she was okay, that they didn't need to intervene.

"Thank you, all of you. For being willing to help." She said while she met the eye of each of the other soldiers, trying to show them how thankful she was. When her eyes made it back to Holt, all of the soldiers crossed their arms over their chests so that their fists covered their hearts, and they all went down on one knee.

"Princess." They all said in unison.

"Holt." Luc called out and Holt stood quickly, bowing to Audra, then turning to Luc with his hands behind his back.

"Lieutenant."

"See to it that Haltion stands guard for one of the two guards on patrol tonight. I will be taking the Princess so that she gets a few hours of rest."

"Yes, sir." Holt said strongly, staring his subordinate down.

Haltion stood, chest puffed out and his face tilted upward so that he was standing at attention, but not meeting anyone's eye line.

"Get to the post. I will be sending Ereman out soon." Holt ordered, to which Haltion nodded and walked off.

"Ereman, make sure he gets to his post."

"Yes, sir."

The two guards walked off, a sizable distance between them. Audra couldn't help but feel that the fact of Haltion being the only guard who had a problem with her and Luc and was also the one of two guards that was Eric was literally chained to, was not insignificant. It could be a coincidence, but it also could mean big trouble for them.

"Princess." Luc said, his tone short and strained as he gestured for Audra to follow him to the tent, he set up earlier.

Audra looked over at the tree where Eric was chained to, meeting his eye over the flames of the campfire. His golden eyes were staring her down, a hard, calculating look in his eyes as his gaze forced her to stay where she was. He bent his head to the side as if he was inspecting her, looking for a chink in her armor where he might stab her to finally take her down. Audra didn't want to give him anything, any emotion that he might play off of.

She was done being jerked around and manipulated.

She was a future Queen.

Standing up straighter, she narrowed her eyes at the prisoner and turned her back on him. The tent that Luc had built for them was small, small enough that she had to crawl to get in. When she crawled through the opening, she turned and zipped up the flap to give them some semblance of privacy, even though they both knew nothing more was going to happen between them tonight with the tarp being the only privacy they had, she simply wanted to give Luc a place to be vulnerable.

He was sitting cross-legged, facing the back of the tent with his arms crossed over his chest. Audra could see the gears turning in his head, but his eyes showed her just how furious he still was. The usually clear blue was dangerous, dark, and deep, a tidal wave threatening to crash over and drown the city close by.

"Luc…" Audra started, she tried to keep her tone light and supportive, but she knew that it wasn't going to do anything to squelch the fury within him.

"Don't Audra. Just don't."

"It's okay." She said softly, taking one of his hands in her two small ones.

"How can you say that? Did you not hear the same words spew from his mouth that I did? Did you not hear the disrespectful fucking trash? I will not let anyone talk about you like that. Talk about us like that. I could have killed him. He's fucking lucky I didn't."

"You broke his nose."

"I wanted to break his face in!" Luc snapped.

Over the years, Audra had seen him mad, annoyed, frustrated, the whole spectrum of negative emotions. But she had never seen him quite like this.

Protective, furious, defensive, with a hint of possessiveness.

"It's just words, honey. I've been through worse." Audra wrapped her arms around his neck, hugging her chest to his back.

"But you're my girl now. You're mine to care for and protect. Especially against immature, arrogant, buffoons who think they are more important than they are. I will not let anyone talk about you like that. Lie about you like that." He leaned into her touch, holding her forearms.

She felt her heart skip a beat at his words and pressed a kiss to his neck. The comforting scent of sea air, fresh sun, and something distinctly Luc filled her nostrils as she cuddled him tighter.

"Thank you." She whispered.

"Always."

* * *

"I need you to get some rest, baby. It's been a big day." Luc said. They had moved to their sides, Luc holding her firmly to his front. Audra loved being held like this. It wasn't something that had happened to her a lot in her life, being cuddled just because. Typically, it was after sex only and even then it was only for a few moments before they left. But here Luc was, cuddling her. Without her having to do anything. Without her having to 'earn' it.

"I just...If I fall asleep, are you going to stop holding me?" She asked quietly.

"Never." He whispered in her ear, kissing the spot right behind it.

"Promise?" She was half asleep, and she knew it was a losing battle to try to stay awake.

"I just want to hold you in my arms and keep you safe. I promise you, baby, you will still be firmly in my arms when you wake up."

"Thank you," she whispered before she relented to the fight against the darkness.

* * *

Audra and Luc were jolted from sleep very abruptly with shouts from around the tent; yelling and orders being barked. Luc was up and at attention before Audra even gathered her thoughts enough to understand the urgency. He was out of the tent before Audra could scramble to her feet to follow.

"Holt! What is the meaning of this?" Luc stormed through the campsite with Audra trying to catch up to him.

"Sir," Holt turned, looking more frazzled than Audra had seen him. He was in the same thin material undershirt that Haltion had been in under his armor with the thick utilitarian pants and boots with the laces undone. He had just been awoken as well.

"It seems as if the prisoner has escaped."

"What?" Luc's voice boomed through the area, his eyes flashing blue, which signaled to everyone that he was not in complete control of his magic.

"What do you mean, he escaped? I saw him last night, double chained and muzzled to a thick tree. He couldn't have just picked those locks." Audra said quickly, trying to make sense of what she was being told.

"He didn't. He...had help." Holt said, looking to Luc with nervous eyes, but Luc wasn't paying any attention to him any longer. Luc's full attention was on Audra.

It was as if the ground had fallen out from under her. Eric had tried to kill her; he would have succeeded if it wasn't for Luc and Sebastien. Now he was free, on the run but free, and who is to say that he wouldn't come after her again? This time she might not get so lucky. Audra knew she was spiraling, her thoughts turning more and more dark and anxious the longer she stood there listening to Holt apologize and explain.

"Thank you, Holt. Please get the camp torn down and the men ready. We need to reach Dragomahara as soon as possible." Luc ordered.

"Yes, sir. Princess." Holt bowed to her, but Audra felt frozen.

"Baby, it's okay. I'm here." Luc said softly, his hand going to her waist to try to ground her. "I promise you; he will not hurt you again. I will do everything in my power to keep you safe. Speaking of," Luc turned and looked at the tree line. The morning sun was peeking through the trees, but the dense woods were still darkened from the night.

"I think we should tell Sebastian. We need his help." Audra said quietly.

"I agree. Do you know how to get a hold of him?"

"I do." Luc looked deep into her eyes, cupping her cheek. He let out a big sigh and nodded.

"Let's go."

Luc pulled them towards the tree line, away from the soldiers and Tomais breaking down their campsite and softly discussing amongst themselves.

"You have to whisper to the shadows; they are like his conduit." Audra explained.

"Seb, we have a situation." Audra whispered once they were cloaked in the shadows of the trees.

"He told me he might not be able to come to me when I call, something about his work." Audra told Luc after a few moments.

"What are we going to do? Haltion freed Eric. Eric wants to kill me, you, and the royals. He wants to become the new High Royals. How...What do...Should we..." Audra could feel herself start to get choked up with tears.

"Regardless of what happens, I will be here with you."

"What if you aren't able to stay with me when we get to Dragomahara? You surely have family you want to visit and your own place. I couldn't ask you to give that up." Tears started to fall down her face.

"I do have a family; one I want you to meet. My parents and brother live there and have been taking care of my things. But I will be staying at the castle with you. I am the First Lieutenant, so I am able to sleep in the barracks."

"But–"

"That gives me an in to stay on castle grounds, but I will be guarding your chambers. It would be difficult for Eric to get past the guards, but like Haltion, he may have some sympathizers."

"This is going to end ugly, isn't it?" Audra clutched the soft material of his shirt in her fingers, trying to simultaneously calm herself and calm Luc at the same time.

"Not if I can help it."

"Sir! We're ready!" Ereman called out to them.

"Damn." Luc whispered quietly, harshly.

CHAPTER TWENTY-NINE

"I told you, he warned me that he wouldn't be able to come."

"Still. This is...this is serious."

"It'll be okay. He also said last night that we would see him soon."

"Then we better get started on this hike. I'm hopeful it will only be a few hours."

"And then I get to meet my parents?" She asked hopefully.

"And then you get to meet your parents." He said with a smile. Luc kissed her forehead and took her hand, leading her back towards the group, where they could begin the final leg of their journey.

"Princess, how are you?" Tomais asked, lifting her pack up to help her strap it on her back. She slid her arms through the loops and let him rest the weight on her back.

"I'm as well as could be expected. Thank you. How are you? Did you sleep well?"

"I did. Thank you for asking. I'm excited to be home." He smiled at her.

"Thank you Tomais, for all that you've done to help me, to help us. You're a good man." She put her hand on his shoulder.

"The pleasure has been mine. It has been lovely to see what a strong, caring young woman you've grown to be. I think you will do very nicely as a High Royal." Tomais smiled and bowed his head.

Audra could feel a blush heat her cheeks, his words bringing to attention that soon, in a matter of hours even, she would technically be a leader to people here. And she had absolutely no idea what she was going to do.

"Thank you."

"Let's go!" Holt barked through the area and Audra watched as the rest of the soldiers got into formation. Holt and Ereman walked side by side in front, then Luc stood behind them, waiting for Audra to join his side. There was a space behind where Luc stood for Tomais and Mattius.

Audra found Luc's eye, and he smiled, his brown curls unruly and shining in the sun overhead.

"Let's go." She said quietly, ready to get to her rightful place.

Chapter Thirty

The group of six walked through the heavily wooded area for what Audra felt was minutes compared to the day before. She was so focused on finally getting to meet the people she had been imagining, dreading, and hoping for her whole life.

The walk was quiet, no one volunteering to start conversation. Exhaustion and worry overtaking them all. Audra focused on one step at a time. One crunch of leaves and sticks at a time. One breath at a time. One squeeze of her hand from Luc at a time.

Audra gathered from the little bits of hushed discussion she overheard between Luc and Holt before they left that Luc was the highest-ranking soldier. Therefore, any blame would be put on him for doling out the punishment to Haltion, who then freed Eric. Audra was appalled that that was how the hierarchy of their military worked, that he was going to have to face some kind of punishment for something that was out of his hands. It seemed to her that Haltion freeing Eric had been their plan all along. Or they had discussed it before Eric was muzzled and he won Haltion over.

"We're here." Tomais spoke from behind her with wonder in his voice. "This view never gets old."

The sight in front of her took her breath away.

A tall, grand castle, nestled into a hillside made of white-grey stone with three spires along the side she could see. The view was magnificent, a hill full of trees with a hidden gem perched at the top. Audra couldn't count how many windows there were from the distance, but it looked as if there were two for every few feet along the side.

It must have dozens of rooms, Audra thought. She could feel that her jaw had dropped, and she was just staring in amazement.

If the pale grey stone with a black roof and golden glittering accents around the trims of the windows and roof weren't enough, the background the castle set against was unlike anything she had ever seen. Mountains surrounded the castle all around, except for the direction that they were coming from. Beautiful, dark mountains surrounding the one hill covered in dense forest with the one spot of lightness being the magnificent, picturesque castle in the middle.

"Oh wow." She breathed the words out, too shocked to say anything else.

"It's pretty amazing, isn't it?" Luc said to her with a smile on his face, and he wrapped his arms around her waist. "Welcome home."

"That's where I will live?"

Luc laughed, and Tomais chuckled softly. She even saw Ereman and Holt crack a smile. She knew it must have seemed like a no brainer to them. She was the princess, Therefore, she would live in the castle. But Audra was still struggling to accept that part of her new life. That she would be taken care of more than she would be expected to provide for herself. She assumed that she would from now on have enough food that she wouldn't have to worry. She would have warm enough clothing that she wouldn't have to dread the cold months. Just the thought that she wouldn't have to struggle even a fraction as hard as she did back home brought tears to her eyes.

"Baby..." Luc said softly and brought her hand to his lips, giving it a chase kiss. She was thankful that he didn't draw attention to her tears, just quietly letting her know that he understood.

"You won't be alone, ever again." He whispered.

Audra chuckled wetly, her sobs threatening to escape.

"Let's go." The soldier behind Ereman spoke up finally, his deep voice rough with disuse. Ereman chuckled and slapped him on the shoulder.

"Yes, as Mattius said, let's go."

* * *

The group probably looked exhausted, weary, and dirty from their two days of traveling by foot through the woods, but as they walked closer to the front gate of the castle, Audra was astounded by how massive it was. From the distance when they first saw Dragomahara, it seemed big, overwhelming even. But as they got closer, Audra was blown away by its size.

The small village surrounding the castle walls was thriving; small children felt safe enough to run through the valleys throwing blooms of flowers and water spraying from their hands, merchants talking and showing off merchandise to customers in the small market, workers building a cabin, one of them using their air power to lift wooden beams. The small pen of livestock that were being tended were braying loudly next to a cabin and as they walked by, Audra watched the man feeding them stop and stare at them walking through.

"Why is he looking at us?" She whispered to Luc.

"It's not every day that the Royal Elite Guard, the First Lieutenant and the Royal Advisor are seen strolling through the market."

"So, you guys are pretty well known?"

"I wouldn't say well known, but the armor that they are wearing, the colors, are a symbol here of the Royal Guard. So, I'm sure they recognize that. And Tomais, well, Tomais is probably well known, he is always at the King and Queen's side during announcements or functions."

"Oh." She said, looking around at all the people who had stopped to watch them walk through the street. Mouths open, whispers passed between people as they stared at her.

"Yes, it will take some getting used to. Especially for you. But I'll be right here, supporting you from the sidelines, as long as you want me." Luc said, gripping her hand and threading their fingers together. He brought the back of her hand to his lips and kissed it sweetly.

"Good, then you'll always be here with me because I'll always want you."

The front gate to the castle was open, the heavy wooden doors propped open and two guards in similar armor to her soldiers, but instead of red, the armor color was a dull brown, were standing at attention. The guns in their hands were intimidating and nerve-wracking to Audra, but Luc squeezed her hand to let her know they were there to protect her, not to harm her.

Passing through the gate, the sun reflected on the sparkling on the large fountain of a woman holding both of her hands in the air with water spraying from his palms.

"Who is that?" Audra asked.

"The first Total Elemental, your ancestor, Maeve." Tomais said.

"Wow." She whispered.

The group entered the doors that Audra assumed wasn't the main entrance because it wasn't grand, it wasn't overtly spacious and open. It seemed to be the soldier's entrance because the men in her group knew exactly where to go and seemed so comfortable entering that way. The darkened doorways were set inlay small windows overlooking the courtyard, and they opened to a narrow, dark hallway which the men quickly ushered her through.

"Where are we going?" Audra asked. Luc wasn't explaining anything, neither was Tomais, and she was starting to get worried. They all escorted her deeper inside the castle, through the quiet hallways with realistic portraits of regal looking people that took up the entire wall, large crystal chandeliers that hung interspersed throughout the long open hallway, a vibrant red rug that spanned as far as Audra could see.

"We are taking you to the study. Your parents will be there and that way you can reunite without an audience." Luc said quietly as they arrived at an ornate wooden door that was slightly cracked open to allow some light to enter the hallway from within.

"What if..." Audra started, and Luc put his hands on her shoulders.

"Holt, Ereman, and Mattius, thank you for your assistance with our completed mission of escorting the Princess back to Dragomahara from Terraus. You all have the next few hours to rest and recuperate. Please be back at 1800 hours to receive our next assignment." Luc dismissed them with a grateful, yet authoritative way.

"Yes, sir." They all answered in unison and crossed their arms over their chest in the same respectful gesture she had seen when they first met. The men dispersed, all of them walking in the opposite direction they came in.

"Tomais, we will be in in just a moment." Luc said over Audra's shoulder to address him, dismissing him as well so that the two of them were alone.

Audra's heart felt like it was going to explode out of her chest. Her parents were right inside that room. She just had to open the door.

"Aud," Luc moved his hands to hers, threading their fingers together. "What are you thinking?"

"What if they don't like me? What if I am not what they thought I would be? What if I-"

"You can't live in what if's, baby. You may not be exactly what they were thinking, but you are you. You are a strong, independent, loving, caring woman who has been handed an impossible hand, but instead of letting it crush you, you've risen to the challenge. I am so proud of you, Audra. I've seen how you've grown in the past few years...I'm astounded by you. Amazed. So even if they have reservations, just know that I'm here. I know you're amazing and you are going to shine as a leader." He brought one of their joined hands together and kissed her hand. "I love you."

Audra gasped. They had alluded to deep feelings, but he was the first to say those big words.

"Are you sure? I'm...this...with everything going on, it could get messy."

"I'm sure." He smiled, his blue eyes glinting with reserved joy.

"I love you too." Audra smiled, reaching up to kiss him deeply. He wrapped his arms around her waist, drawing her closer, as she wrapped her arms tightly around his neck. Their kiss was electric. The feelings they'd expressed added another layer of tension to their touches. Audra could've easily let the kiss deepen. The touches become more desperate. But Luc didn't let it. After a few moments, he pulled away, keeping their heads close together.

"They're going to love you. Just like I do." He said softly.

"Well, hopefully, not like you do." She whispered, grinding her front to his, feeling how excited he was.

"No, baby, not like I do." He chuckled, reaching down to adjust himself.

Audra took a deep breath, grounding and calming herself down as her anxiety threatened to overpower her again.

"Are you ready?" She asked him and saw him nod. Luc squared his shoulders and adjusted his shirt, smoothing it out to look more presentable. He let her walk in first, taking the back seat and letting her be the Princess she was. Audra took another deep breath, pushing her hair back out of her face.

Audra pressed the door open, letting the wood door swing open to reveal the individuals in the room.

And there they were.

Her parents.

The people she had always wondered about, always wanted to know, always wished that they had kept her.

From behind a sturdy wooden desk, a man with long, wavy greying brown hair shot out of his chair, causing it to stumble.

"Audra." He said with awe. He was shocked, his eyes wide and filled with tears. The woman next to him gripped his shoulder, her long fingers digging into his shirt.

"Is it really you?" She whispered, her voice breaking with a sob.

Audra took a shaky breath. She could see her features reflected in them. Her wavy hair from the man, her eyes from the woman, her body type was similar to the woman. They were her parents. They were her *parents*.

"Hi." She said, her composure breaking, and tears started to run down her face.

"Honey..." The woman, her mother, walked around the desk and pulled Audra into her arms. Audra looked into her green eyes, eyes so much like her own, and she fell into her arms.

"It's okay. You're here. We're here. We're together." Her mother held onto her. Both of them fell to their knees, still holding onto one another when her father came to them and wrapped them both in his embrace.

"Together. My two girls. I'm so sorry we had to leave you, honey." He said gruffly, his voice hoarse from unshed tears.

* * *

After a few moments of tears, apologies, and unbridled joy of being reunited,

Tomais stepped in and murmured to the Queen, "Ma'am, we need to debrief."

"Yes, yes, of course." She waved him off, cupping Audra's face. "My sweet girl. I am so sorry about all that you've had to endure in your life. I am so sorry that we weren't able to bring you home sooner. I'm sorry that you had to leave at all. It just about killed me to leave you. Let's sit down and you can tell us all about your journey."

Audra looked back at Luc, who was smiling at her fondly. He was standing close to the door, his hands clasped behind his back and his stance very formal. She realized that this was his guard demeanor, his official stance as lieutenant.

"You must have so many questions. Please, feel free to ask." Her father said, sitting down in the chair next to hers as her mother walked around to sit behind the desk.

"What are your names?" Both her mother and her father chuckled slightly, but it was laced with pain.

"My name is Anders, and this is Audrena."

"Anders, Audrena and Audra. Really went for the 'A' names." She said under her breath.

"We thought it flowed nicely." Her mother, Audrena, looked at Anders with a reminiscent smile.

"Lucien, can you tell us about your journey? Also, what happened with Eric and why is the traitor who threatened my daughter not in our custody?" Anders turned to Luc, who came forward and bowed his head towards them both in respect.

"Our journey through the Gate was fairly smooth. We arrived at the Navitus church and walked through the portal there. Once we were within the portal Tomais activated, Princess Audra and I were transported to the Gate and when we exited, my men, Tomais and the prisoner were accounted for. We set up camp. Later that evening, Haltion had an altercation with Holt. Haltion shared some...less than appropriate...opinions about the Princess and me. He started to speak out about his thoughts on politics and the High Royals before I detained him and doled out a punishment, I thought was appropriate. I decided a night without sleep, standing guard along with another soldier watching him as well, would be sufficient. So, I went to bed. Then I was awoken by yelling and distress over Eric having escaped. Soon after we discovered that Haltion was also gone, making it clear that he had been the one to free Mr. Tayorkoven from his chains, restraints and muzzle."

"And what of the other guard? Did he not notice them leaving?" Anders asked, his voice full of anger.

"I discussed it with the guard, Mattius. He was injected with some kind of sedative. He said he felt a prick at the back of his neck. He thought it was a sucker bug biting him but then he lost consciousness. Normally, I would question further, but the needle left a mark on his neck. I inspected it myself. He was also feeling the effects still this morning. The hike here was difficult for him."

Audra felt her stomach drop. She had been so wrapped up in her own thoughts that she didn't even consider the other guard. She hadn't even known his name until just before they entered the room. Her eyes dropped to the floor.

"Very well. Does he need anything? A healer?" Audrena asked, her spine straightening and her grey, red curls rested over her shoulders.

"I advised Holt to take him there during their rest period. I will find out more and let you know."

"Thank you." She wrote something down on a notepad she had in front of her.

"And what do we know of Eric?" Anders asked.

"Just that he thinks he knows how to run Vesperitus better, that the High Royals have been in power too long and he 'knows what needs to be done in order to rid the country of the Dark Fae."

"A traitor grew right under our noses, and he rose through the ranks so quickly, so selflessly, that we thought he would be a natural choice to retrieve our daughter. Instead, he tries to kill her. Overpower. Over greed." Anders said, throwing his hands out with, the end of each sentence.

"He didn't just want any power. He wanted my power. My Total Elemental power." Audra spoke up.

All of the heads turned to her so quickly, it was surprising that they didn't complain of their necks hurting.

"He wanted what?" Audrena said slowly.

"He wanted control of my Total Elemental power. He was willing to blackmail me into marrying him for power, and he was very close to trying to take me by force. He was threatening me, had hurt me and thankfully, Luc came with us when Eric tried to take me...wherever it was that he was going to hurt me into submission, because he saved my life."

Audra was very specific about not revealing Sebastien yet. Or her intimate relationship with Luc. She didn't know who she could trust here besides the two of them yet.

"And for that, we are eternally grateful. Thank you, Lucien." Anders stood and shook Luc's hand as Audrena hugged him.

Luc looked shocked and his hands stuck out awkwardly, as if he didn't know what to do with them. Audra had to cover her mouth with her hand to not laugh out loud at the surprise written all over his face. They both released her love, and he had a blush heating his cheeks and he looked as if he was lost for words.

"And Tomais," Audrena turned to her advisor, who stood stoically beside the desk with his hands neatly folded in front of him. "Thank you for making the journey and protecting Audra as well."

She put her hand on his arm, a subtle gesture of appreciation and thanks. Anders held his hand out to Tomais to shake as well.

"It was an honor." Tomais said.

"I would like to discuss the Fae hunting Audra down and what you noticed after they had fled the city, Tomais. Lucien, could you please escort Audra to her chambers and then you are free to rest yourself. Thank you." Audrena stated her orders clearly, slipping into a natural leader mode. Audra was able to see how her mother ruled, how she led her people with confidence.

"Before you go," Audrena said, hesitantly. The words caught in her throat like she wasn't sure if she wanted to say anything or not. "There is one thing that we need to discuss, and I wanted to discuss it with you all here."

"Do you really want to do this now?" Anders shot a hard look at his wife, only to be met with a steel wall of composure.

"She needs time, time to think about what she wants to do."

Her father sighs loudly, running a hand through his long waves. "Fine."

"The reason we needed you to come back so soon after we had talked and decided on you staying in Terraus until you had the chance to learn about everything you wanted to is that we have been communicating with the Dark Fae leaders. The Fullma's. With you coming into your powers, your father and I thought it would be best to try to make peace with them. If we were able to come to some kind of compromise, maybe they would join our forces and we would be able to protect you better. After weeks of discussion and secret correspondence, they have agreed to a peace treaty with one major condition."

Luc stepped forward, coming to a stop behind Audra. She was able to feel his body heat on her back, his steady presence and support for whatever was coming.

"They want a union between the groups. You and their highest-ranking officer."

Audra felt as if she was going to pass out. She was brought back, finally reunited with her family and then married off as a bargaining chip? She had gone completely still, shocked into a state of being frozen at the news. She had finally found love, real love with Luc, and she knew she was falling more and more in love with Seb, but what would her men say about her being married to someone in the Dark Fae camp? They'd leave her. And she wouldn't blame them.

"I don't...No...I...That...is a lot to process." Audra rasped out. She could feel Luc against her back, his chest vibrating with anger or sadness. She couldn't tell.

"My darling girl, we will have all the time in the world to reconnect and to talk more about this, but I'm sure you are exhausted, in wanting a bath and a comfortable bed. Not to mention, time to think this through." Audrena smiled at her again. She rounded the desk once more to clasp both of Audra's hands in hers.

"You're here now. We can protect you here and this is...the best way we know to do so. Striking a deal, forming a union will ensure that our kingdom and all its citizens are able to rest easy from the onslaught of Dark Fae attacks for power. But it will also ensure your protection. So go, rest, relax and think it over. We will call you for the meeting later."

"What meeting?" Luc said through clenched teeth. Audra wanted nothing more than to hold his hand, rest her head over his heart and reassure him that she didn't want to do this. That she loved him.

"The Fullma's have made the journey from Fullmaster to discuss this in person, to meet Audra and best go about how to form an alliance."

"And her safety? Have you thought about how to best guard her?" Luc stepped closer to the desk.

"Of course, we have. She will have a member of the Royal Guard with her at all times and-" Anders was cut off with a grunt from Luc.

"No, I will be her personal bodyguard. I trust no one else to keep her safe. No one would be better suited for this detail." He said firmly, leaving no room for discussion. It was a risky move on his part. The High Royalty in front of him could throw him out for his disrespect of their choices. But instead, Anders' mouth ticked up subtly. A small smile.

"Very well Lieutenant. Her safety will be in your hands."

"Thank you, sir. My apologies for the interruption." Luc stepped back, clasping his hands behind his back again to take up the demeanor of the official he was.

"Go rest and we will send someone to call for you. I will have a bath drawn for you and a plate of food sent to your chambers." Audrena dismissed them and Audra couldn't wait to get out. She needed a moment, time to think.

"Princes." Luc said gruffly, gesturing for her to go first out of the room.

"See you later, then." Audra said with a weak smile and an awkward half wave, to which her parents smiled brightly and nodded at her.

When Audra and Luc had closed the door behind them, Audra could see just how angry Luc was. How furious.

"Luc..."

"Don't. Not here." He said roughly and wrapped his arm around her waist, taking her weight and escorted her to her chambers.

Chapter Thirty-One

It came off him in waves, Luc's anger, as he marched them down the hallway and through the castle. His hand never left her waist, if anything, his grip only tightened with each passing moment. It felt as if he thought she would leave if he let her go.

Workers were buzzing throughout the castle, passing them every few moments and they would always dip their head in respect towards Audra. It was definitely going to take some getting used to. She wasn't sure how she liked it, being bowed to, and so very overly respected to the point of being feared. Most of the workers they passed wouldn't even look her in the eye, casting their gaze downward when she would smile.

Luc ushered her towards another wooden door with a wrought iron handle and pushed it open.

"Your chambers, Princess." He said stiffly, sweeping his hand out to display her room. Room was the wrong word. As Audra walked through the door, it was as if she was stepping into an entire upscale apartment.

"This is all for me?" She asked, walking through the room, and trying to take in every detail. The front room of her 'chambers' was a sitting room, with an ornate, large and opulent crystal chandelier that hung from the 18-foot-tall ceilings. The walls were bare, and pale save for a mirror lined with gold and a benign painting of a seascape. The furniture, though, Audra couldn't wait to plop down on the plush, oversized couch. All the decorations for the room were light and airy, golds and metallics with soft accents were everywhere, giving off the elegant, but definitely rich vibe.

"This way through here is the bathroom." Luc walked through the room and Audra was able to see the grand bathroom with a small pool in the center. The water circulating from the jets and wide mouthed faucets. The room was humid from the hot water and smelled of lavender and citrus, a surprising, comforting scent. Audra could've moaned out loud at the thought of soaking in such a beautiful bathtub. If that was even what they called the mini in-ground pool in the middle of the room.

"Wow."

"And through here is the bedroom." Luc continued the tour, leading her quickly through the bathroom to the white French doors that opened out to reveal the room.

It was beautiful. Windows filled one wall and, they were framed with thick white curtains that gave the room an airy feel. All of the furniture was beige and grey, like driftwood.

But the bed, oh goodness, the bed.

It was at least a California King bed topped with at least eight pillows that looked fluffed to perfection. The bedcovers were a pure white, crisp, and clean, with a heather grey blanket lined along the bottom. It painted the picture of comfort and luxury.

Audra couldn't wait to jump in. As soon as she had seen the bed, she felt just how exhausted she was. The tiredness from the past few days was seeping into her bones.

"It's much different from back in the city, huh?" Luc said in a soft tone. He must have seen how her eyes drooped with the view of the bed.

"Umhm." She nodded and toed off her boots, that were still covered in mud from their journey.

"We should talk about what your parents just told us."

"Yes, we should." She sighed. As much as Audra just wanted to jump in the tub, rinse the past two days of grime off her body and then fall into the cloud that was the bed, she knew they needed to discuss the whole marriage thing.

"You go." She nodded to Luc. He was pacing back and forth. Clearly, he had something he wanted to say.

He sighed, shaking his head, and running a hand through his hair. He was agitated, that much was obvious to see.

"What are we going to do?" His words broke with emotion.

"I don't know. But it seems like-"

"Don't say it!" He said roughly.

"What choice do I have? I have to keep everyone safe."

"I can't believe you're thinking of going through with this. A stranger that you have yet to meet, getting married. For life. Without me. Without Sebastien." He tried to reason with her.

"I'm just thinking of all the options, Luc. I can't just ignore the peace it might bring."

"But you haven't even met the citizens of the kingdom. You're just blindly throwing away your life, and mine, for them."

"You are willing to give up your life for them every day, being lieutenant of the Guard. Why can't I?" She shot back at him.

"Because it will take you from me! And I just got you. I can't...I can't lose you."

"You won't lose me, I promise. I love you." She rushed to him, needing to feel him firmly in her arms.

"But if you marry this man, you won't be mine. I...it's...what..." He started to stutter.

"No matter what, I will be yours. I promise. Just like you are mine." She cupped his face and kissed him soundly.

"I love you." He professed strongly. His mouth captured hers again, trying to tell her just how much he loved her with the kiss.

"I love you too."

"You know I have to do this." She whispered, and he nodded, keeping his eyes scrunched closed. He wrapped his arms around her waist, drawing her body into his. She fit perfectly in his arms, and that made it harder for her to step back.

Luc walked backwards, never taking his eyes off of her, and stepped behind the door, where the light was casting a shadow.

"What are you doing?" Audra asked in alarm.

"Sebastien, you need to get here now. Audra's in trouble." Luc whispered.

"Why would you do that?!" She yelled at Luc.

"He deserves to know. If he is as serious about you as I am, he deserves to know."

"That wasn't your call."

"We don't have time for you to hemm and haww over this! There is a meeting being called tonight for your answer. So, stop being so stubborn and be honest with us!"

The shadows surrounding the room grew darker and wider, the whole room darkening. A swirl of shadows appeared next to Luc and as the black hole grew, Sebastien stepped through.

"Are you okay? What's going on?" He rushed through, taking Audra in his arms, and looking her over for any injuries.

"I'm fine, I'm fine. Don't worry."

"Lucien said you were in trouble. What's going on?"

Audra's heart warmed at his nervous expression. He was truly worried about her wellbeing, and she smiled softly.

"Did you hear about Eric?" She asked. She took her hand in his, threaded their fingers together and led him to sit on the bed. Luc walked around and stood next to Audra with his eyes glued to the ground.

"I heard, yes. I've been keeping an eye on things on my end. I trust you are keeping her safe, Lucien."

"I am. She is safe. But right now, her safety isn't exactly being called into question." He stated with his arms crossed in front of his chest.

"What do you mean? Audra?" Sebastien's gaze went to her, his puzzled expression telling her that he hadn't been able to see this development coming with his powers.

"My parents told us that they are able to come to a peace treaty with the Dark Fae, therefore keeping Vesperitus safe from their terror and additionally able to keep me safe as well. If we have a treaty, they will be forced to call off the hunt for their lackeys to try and hurt me to gain my Total Elemental powers."

"Okay, this is sounding like a good thing." Seb said, and he stood up, also crossing his arms over his chest. Audra momentarily lost her train of thought as her memories of that night in the forest overtook her; how his mouth felt on her as Luc's hands roamed over her body as they brought her to orgasm.

"Audra?" Seb's questioning voice brought her back.

"Yes, sorry." She coughed and felt a blush creep up her neck.

"Naughty girl." Seb smirked.

"Not now. Audra, tell him." Luc ordered, his patience waning.

"So, this is serious." Seb said quietly.

"Very."

"Audra, just tell me, sweetheart." Seb said, linking their hands together.

"My parents said that the Fullma's have declared their condition for the treaty. A marriage union between me and one of their own. Their highest-ranking officer."

There, she said it.

"Who is it?" Sebastien said, his voice was deep and deadly.

"I don't know. We don't know." She said, gesturing between her and Luc. "Just that he is in the Dark Fae camp. Luc and I were discussing the options, but really there isn't one."

"Lucien?" Sebastien said slowly, looking to the man in question.

"Either she marries into the Dark Fae, or she is hunted by them. I don't know what else to do. Unless one of us marries her and then goes public to prevent it, but that still leaves her open to their attacks." Luc said, shrugging.

Sebastien stayed quiet for a long time, his eyes staring off into the distance, but when Audra tried to make eye contact with him, it was as if his eyes were unseeing. They were open but glassed over, as if he was sleeping with his eyes open.

"Seb?" Audra asked after a few moments of very loud silence. Luc had started to pace back and forth across the room, keeping a close eye on Audra and Sebastien.

Audra could see how exhausted and on-edge Luc was. He had been dealing with constant attacks and betrayals all around him. He had been taking on the brunt of the guarding; foregoing sleep in order to ensure she had sleep, and now, this impending marriage of his girlfriend to another unknown man... She could see he needed a moment.

"Luc, darling, why don't you go take a bath and relax for just a moment?

We've been on the go for a long time. Seb is here, I'm safe, so go take a minute and breathe." She cupped his tired, dirty face and kissed his lips chastely. She wanted to take care of him as much as he had been taking care of her.

"Are you sure?" He asked softly, wrapping his hands around her forearms.

"I'm sure. I will come find you after. I promise."

Luc sighed and nodded, releasing her arms, and stepping back to look at Seb and his unseeing eyes.

"Keep her safe." Luc said gruffly to Sebastien. He didn't wait for an answer, just walked out of the room in the direction of Audra's bathroom.

Audra breathed a sigh of relief.

"Are you...can you hear me?" Audra walked up to Seb slowly, holding onto his biceps to try to bring him back from wherever he was stuck.

"Are you looking to the future?" She whispered. Audra tried to walk his body back towards the edge of the bed, situating him so that he was sitting comfortably. His arms were crossed over his chest, and he had a slight scowl on his face from being told about the union and the unknown groom before he was whisked away by his powers.

Audra didn't even know if it was his powers that were causing him to act this way, if his ability to see the future and see through the realms was what this was.

"Audra." He gasped, his eyes snapping back and searching for her. His expression turned fearful and anxious right before he schooled them back into a controlled look. His dark eyes gave nothing away as she rushed to comfort him.

"Seb, it's okay, I'm here." She grabbed both of his hands and held them tightly. "What did you see?"

He shook his head and hugged her close to him. She tugged him closer still and kissed his neck.

"Is it bad?"

"No, it's not bad. Not bad at all. I just need to talk to Lucien. There is one thing I can do." Seb kissed her forehead, then kissed her lips sweetly. His words seemed sad, melancholy, and resigned.

"I'm sorry." She said softly, relishing the feeling of him firmly in her arms.

The first two buttons of his black dress shirt were unbuttoned, the cuffs of his sleeves rolled up to his elbows. He was dressed more casually than she had seen him before and she suddenly felt so guilty about interrupting what small down time he seemed to have.

"Don't be sorry, sweetheart. What I have to do...it's not a bad thing. It won't be a hardship for me in the slightest, but it has the possibility of going sour for me. I'm just worried about what it means for my, *our*, future." He cupped her cheek in his large palm, and she leaned into the touch.

"I need you to know something. And I want you to remember it always."

Audra nodded.

"Never doubt my feelings for you. I told you last night that our paths were close to crossing, it is coming very soon. And I want you to know that every single decision I've made, every path I've taken, was made with you in mind. You're mine, Audra, but I am irrevocably yours. I don't know the depth of your feelings, but I need you to know how I feel. How deeply I feel for you because I'm falling in love with you."

She gasped quietly, her heart thudding in her chest.

"I'm falling in love with you too."

Sebastien smiled softly, fear and resolve still present in his dark eyes, but love was overpowering. She could see how truthful his words were. And besides his words, she could see how much he cared for her, loved her even through his actions. Through how he came for her again and again; to protect her, to care for her, to be there for her.

Audra reached up and pulled him to her, their lips meeting in a spectacular kiss that shocked Audra to her core. His lips were persistent and seeking, trying to explore as much of her as possible before they had to pull away for air. She cursed her need for oxygen because all too soon she had to leave the kiss for air, but Sebastien moved his kisses down the column of her throat and sucked a mark into the middle of it. Claiming her against this new, unwanted future husband of hers.

"Oh, god, Sebastien. Please." She moaned and threaded her fingers through his thick black hair, pulling at the strands slightly.

He growled at her words and actions. One of his hands slid up under her shirt and her eyes rolled back in pleasure. But then, just as he was about to brush against her breast, Sebastien pulled away. His actions were slowed, as if he was arguing within himself.

"Don't stop. Please, don't stop." She whispered through deep breaths clutching at his back in an attempt to keep him from moving away from her.

"I need to go. I need to go get things sorted before your meeting. Most importantly, I need to talk to Lucien."

Audra groaned; a low whining groan that showed Sebastien just how displeased she was at his decision.

"Fine. What do I need to do then, in regard to the meeting?" She said, taking a deep breath.

"Say you'll do it. If anything changes, I will let Lucien know and he will tell you. But if you don't hear otherwise, tell them you'll do it."

Audra was shocked and a bit upset that he was okay with marrying her off to a stranger, but she trusted him. Sebastien and Luc hadn't let her down yet, so if he says that he has a plan, she was choosing to trust him. Them.

"Understood." She nodded.

"And remember, no matter what happens, I love you. Luc loves you. We will get through this. I promise." Seb cupped her face with his palm again, his black eyes staring into her green eyes.

His words were confident, assured, but also held a hint of desperation to them.

"Is something bad coming?" She asked.

"Like I said before, it's not bad. I will make sure that everything is okay. That you're safe. Please, trust me."

"I do."

"Good. I love you." He brought her hand up and kissed the back of it.

"I love you too." She smiled.

"I'm going to go talk to Luc. Please take a nap and rest. One of us will wake you up with time to get ready for the meeting."

Audra nodded. Now that the big talk and confrontation with her men was over, she was feeling her exhaustion seep into her bones once again. She walked around him, letting her body sink into the bed. The pillows were just as amazingly soft as they looked, and she was fighting to keep her eyes open.

She could feel her feet being moved and assumed that Sebastien was taking her shoes off for her.

"Thank you, love." She whispered, eyes closed, and hair fanned out over the pillows.

"Anytime, sweetheart." He whispered back. Audra felt her legs being slid on the mattress and a heavy duvet covering her body.

Her last thought before sleep completely overcame her was that she was incredibly grateful for these two men that, against all odds, decided she was worth all of it. She knew that she didn't deserve them but would do everything she could to prove that she would cherish them.

Chapter Thirty-Two

"Sweetheart, I have to go." Sebastien whispered over Audra's sleeping form.

"I'm up, I'm up." She groaned, trying to sit up to say goodbye to him. She could hear him chuckle and kiss her forehead. Her eyes felt like they weighed a hundred pounds, but she pried them open and wiped the sleep away.

"You've only been asleep an hour or so, but they set the time for the meeting, and I have things to take care of on my end. I didn't want to leave without telling you."

"Thank you." She offered her lips for a kiss, which he took. Their lips met in a sweet kiss, one full of love and care.

"Where is Luc?" She whispered, desperately trying not to pry into whatever talk her two men had without her.

"He went to go get a change of clothes and a plate of food for you both."

"Did you guys talk about what you needed to?"

"We did. We came to a conclusion, and we have a plan in place." Sebastien said, his tone suggesting that he would not be talking any more about it.

"And am I going to be included in this plan?" She asked with as much sass as she could, crossing her arms over her chest. Once again, she was out of the loop and was not happy about it. And she would make sure they knew it.

"Not right now."

"This is my life, you know. I have the right to know what your plan is if it involves me blindly agreeing to this."

"I understand you hate feeling this way, out of control. But this has to play out this way." He said stoically. Sebastien swirled his fingers in the air and the room darkened with shadows.

"Don't you dare just vanish right now!"

"I'm sorry, sweetheart. I promise I will see you soon and this will be resolved. Remember what I said before. I love you." He said and then walked into his shadows, leaving her alone in the room.

"What the fuck." She sneered under her breath. Looking around the bedroom, she vaulted out of the bed and started charging towards the bathroom. Maybe she could get some information out of Luc.

"Luc! Where are you?" She yelled out into the far too big and empty chamber.

"In here!" He called back from what Audra thought might be the living room area.

She marched in there and saw Luc in fresh, new clothes. He was sitting nervously on the couch with his hands resting in his lap. When he stood up, her gaze swept over him and she drank the sight of him in.

His hair was brushed over like he had tried to control his curls, but they were springing up from whatever he had used to hold them down. His beard looked trimmed and neat. Luc looked at her and her heart skipped a beat at the nervousness she saw in his eyes, and could tell in his demeanor. He had put on a military type outfit that she hadn't seen. It was like a mixture of the old clothes she saw him wear in New York and the armor that the guard had worn. His cargo pants were black and loose, sturdy enough to withstand a fight, but light enough he could still be incredibly quick on his feet. The shirt was tight, a deliciously tight fit that showed off his chest, abs and biceps under the sweat wicking fabric, the material wrapping around him all the way from his waist to his wrists to the base of his neck so none of his tattoos were visible. Like Audra was used to seeing in movies, he wore black, shiny combat boots that were tied tightly all the way up and around the end of his pants.

"You look really good." Audra bit her bottom lip.

"Thanks," Luc said with a chuckle, and held out a bundle of clothes for her. "These are for you. A dress fit for a Princess."

She let the bundle unroll and the deep purple fabric fell in gorgeous swoops to the floor. Audra's jaw dropped at the beauty of the gown. It wasn't a dress; it was a gown. The purple fabric was layered with tulle and shiny chiffon for the skirt, the top layer reflecting the light and making it look like stars shining in the night sky. The skirt was belted at the waist with a belt of braided gold strands. The top of the gown had a sweetheart neckline that Audra knew would show off her curves beautifully, and chiffon sleeves that cuffed her shoulders and flowed out all the way to her wrists. The neckline had the same golden braid as the waist.

"It's beautiful." She whispered.

"It's going to be once it's on you." Luc nodded and put his hands in his pockets. He looked sad but determined and it brought Audra back to her plan to get information out of him. She folded the dress over her arm and put her hands on her hips.

"What are you and Seb planning?"

"I can't tell you."

"What did you two talk about while I was sleeping?"

"You. How much we both love you and will do whatever it takes to keep you safe."

"Even at the expense of your own happiness? You have the same sad look in your eyes that Seb did. What is going on? I'm tired of the secrets, Luc. I'm so tired of it." She put both hands to her face, rubbing her temples to try and decrease her anxiety about the secrets.

"I learned some things about Sebastien. He opened up and told me about his job and while I was angry, I understand why he is keeping it a secret. If anyone can help you in this situation, it's him." Luc said, wrapping his arms around her waist, but keeping some space between them.

"So, you trust him then?" She asked, her voice soft and small as she brought her hands up to his chest and laid them over his beating, loving, big heart.

"I do."

"Good. So, I should...tell my parents I agree?"

"Yes. As much as it kills me, yes."

"Nothing with us will change though, right?" She had to know. She had to know that he wouldn't leave her once this was all said and done. She may have to marry someone, but her heart would always belong to him. Audra feared that if Luc left her, refused to be in her life in any way, she would break down.

Luc pushed a lock of hair behind her ear and ran his thumb over her cheek.

CHAPTER THIRTY-TWO

He looked pained, but hopeful, and that fed Audra's hope.

"Things will be different, will look different. But you'll always have my heart and I'll have yours."

Audra didn't know what that meant, and her heart dropped slightly. What did he mean that it would be different?

"Let's get you ready. You need to bathe and get changed. I have a plate of food in the bathroom next to the tub so you can eat while relaxing. Don't take too very long because the meeting is in a few hours and Sabina is going to be here to do your hair."

"Sabina?"

"She is the handmaid your parents have assigned to you. I've asked her to wait outside while we talk, and I'll be here waiting for you."

"You've really taken care of everything, haven't you?" She smiled at him, and he smirked at her in return.

"Always, I have to take care of my girl." He leaned down and kissed her quickly, but the small kiss was enough to ignite her lust for him.

"You can take care of me in another way, you know? Or..." She ran a finger down his hard chest and stopped when her finger hit the waistband of his pants. "I can take care of you."

Luc groaned, low and long, his eyes closing slightly.

"Baby,"

"Please, I want to."

"You're killing me. We can't. We don't have time."

"Yes, we do." She countered, slipping her fingertips under the fabric.

"Baby..." He growled in warning and wrapped his fingers around her wrist, halting her movements. "We can't be late to this meeting, and you have to look the part."

"You don't want to?" She suddenly was flooded with insecurity. He had been talking about how different things would have to be, and maybe this was what he meant. She tried to keep herself from spiraling, but it was hard when she was finally feeling comfortable and safe enough to initiate sex between them.

"Of course, I do. Of course, I want you baby, I want you in every way. It's really, honestly, and truly the fact that this meeting is really important. For you, for us, for everyone." He lifts her chin up to force her to look into his deep blue eyes. "If we had the time, I would be bending you over this couch right now and plunging deep inside you. I've been thinking of all the different ways I could take you, all the different ways I could make you scream my name."

His words made Audra's core clench and flood with arousal.

"Go get in the bath and eat something." He ordered her, turning her around and giving her bum a slap.

"Such a tease." Audra smirked.

"Only for you, baby. Only for you."

It wasn't until Audra got to the bathroom that she realized that he never did tell her anything about what they were planning.

* * *

"Excuse me, Princess." A petite brunette walked into the bathroom, keeping her eyes cast downward and she dropped into a curtsy in front of Audra as she wrapped one of the plush white towels around her body. "My name is Sabina, I'm your handmaid here to help you get ready."

"Hi! Yes, come on in. I washed my hair. I hope that is alright. I needed to get all the camping gunk out of my hair." She laughed.

"Of course, your highness. Whatever works best for you." Sabina met her eye and dipped her head in a small bowing gesture. She was a sweet looking woman who must have only been a few years older than Audra, maybe late twenties, early thirties. But with everyone here being Fae, Sabina could have been 130 years old, and Audra wouldn't have been able to tell. Her long brown hair was pulled up into a sensible ponytail and it swished her shoulders as she walked towards Audra.

It was awkwardly silent for a moment as Audra looked around, unsure as to what she was meant to do. Sabina must have picked up on her change in emotion and walked over to a cabinet, opening it, and pulling out a few different products.

"What would you like me to do?" Audra asked, playing with her robe's sleeves.

"Please, come sit here. I can get started on your hair and makeup." Sabina gestured for her to sit at the inset vanity across from the tub. The mirror was grand, taking up most of the wall and the edges shadowed like mercury glass.

Audra walked to the plush seat next to where Sabina was setting up the different oils, brushes, and dryers. It looked as if she had five to six different tools and at least double that amount of pots and vials.

"Please, relax. I am going to start on your hair." Sabina pulled a brush through Audra's waves, gently but persistently combing through the tangles.

"How long have you worked here?" Audra asked.

"All my life. I was actually five or six when you were born, and the King and Queen took you to Terraus. I remember watching them bundle you up from behind my mother's skirts."

"You knew me?" Audra said softly.

"No, you were a newborn, not a day old yet when your parents had to pass through The Gate."

Audra could feel herself slump. Disappointment flowed through her. It would have been nice to know at least one person who had known her before everything.

"Oh."

"But I am very excited to get to know you now, Princess." Sabina smiled at her through the mirror, running her hand over a clump of wet hair. Audra watched as her hand passed and the wet strands turned dry.

Audra smiled back at her. "Air element user?"

"Heat actually. I am able to manipulate temperature throughout the air, so if I concentrate, I am able to take objects and raise or lower their temperature."

"That must come in handy."

"I'm sure you could learn to with your range of powers, Princess."

"Please, call me Audra. My friends call me by my first name."

Sabina smiled. "Very well...Audra."

"So...what are you doing to my hair?" Audra asked, happy that she seemed to have another person in her corner.

* * *

Audra had to admit, she didn't think that she ever looked better in her life. Sabina had completely transformed her from the woman she knew before she entered the safe house into...this vision reflecting from the mirror.

Sabina had lightly curled her hair, braiding pieces around her ears and twisting them back to meet in a complicated half up do. She had stuck some sparkle accessories sporadically throughout the style, and they looked like starbursts throughout her hair. The makeup she had applied with a steady hand made all of Audra's natural features pop without looking like she had caked on layer after layer of makeup. Her eyes looked bigger, her lashes darker, her lips more pink, her skin glowing. Sabina helped Audra step into the gown, bringing it to rest across her shoulders as Sabina laced her into the dress.

Finally, Sabina held out a small box encased in velvet to Audra.

"What is this?"

"Open it."

Audra lifted the lid and a thin gold necklace with diamonds studded through the delicate chain every few inches. Laying above the necklace was a set of earrings; studs that were at least the size of her thumbnail. They matched the hair accessories and glinted in the overhead light. They were shining like stars in the velvet box.

"These are for me?" Audra asked, her hand reaching out to gently touch the necklace.

"Yes. The Queen requested that you wear them when I told her what gown you were wearing."

"Can you help me?" Audra asked. Sabina smiled and pulled the delicate gold chain from the box and draped it around her throat. It was small, a choker that rested at the base of her throat. While Sabina closed the clasp, Audra put the earrings in.

Her look was complete.

"You look beautiful, Audra." Sabina said, putting her hands on Audra's exposed shoulders.

"Thank you so much for helping me."

"Anytime. I'll go let the Lieutenant know you're ready. I believe the meeting is due to begin very shortly." Sabina left the room and Audra stared at herself again.

Is this who I am now? A princess draped in diamonds, or am I still the girl who hid food because she was scared, she wouldn't have another meal? Audra thought, absentmindedly smoothing the skirt of her gown out over her knees.

"Wow." Luc's voice cut through her inner monologue, and she turned to see him leaning against the door frame.

"You look...stunning. I'm at a loss for words." He walked through the room to kneel in front of her.

"Thank you, love."

"What's wrong?" He asked, noticing her melancholy energy. She wasn't surprised she couldn't hide her emotions from him, he always knew. He always cared enough to look past her walls.

"I just don't recognize myself anymore." She looked down at her hands. Soon she would be engaged to a man she doesn't know, forced to not be with the men she loves and that love her too. She must learn more about her powers and how to be a true leader. It's a far cry from the girl who wanted to be a teacher to make the world a little better, who had to scrimp and save in order to afford both rent and food. "Who am I?" She could feel tears starting to form but refused to let them fall. Sabina had worked too hard on making her look like the Princess she was supposed to be.

"You're still Audra Jackson. You have the biggest heart and love freely. You care about everyone, even people who don't deserve it. You're strong, brave and the best woman I know. So even if you don't know who you are right now, I do. I know you and I will make sure you remember it too." He reached up and cupped her face, grounding her in the moment.

"I love you." She whispered, her voice breaking.

"I love you too. I mean it, baby, you look beautiful, but you are even more beautiful on the inside."

Audra leaned over and kissed him, showing him just how much she cared for him, how much she loved him, how much she appreciated him.

"Wow," he whispered, resting his head against hers, "that was one hell of a kiss."

"Let's get this show on the road." She took his hands and started towards the door.

* * *

"My darling girl, are you feeling rested?" Anders, her father, wrapped his large arms around her and hugged her tightly.

"Yes, thank you. That bed is amazingly soft."

"And the rest of the chamber is to your liking?"

"Oh, yes! Thank you, it's beautiful." She tried reassuring him, his hazel eyes filled with worry that she wouldn't like it in their home.

"It's fitting for you, a Princess." He said with a big smile.

"Audra!" Her mother called as she entered the room, "You look so beautiful. I'm so glad the dress fits." Audra watched her mother stride with grace through the room, arms out in a welcoming gesture. Her brown curls shining as they bounced with each step. Audra was amazed at how young her mother looked.

"Yes, thank you. I appreciate everything."

Audra could see Luc standing on guard against the back of the room, taking in everything as it was unfolding. He was in lieutenant mode, keeping an eye on her like a hawk.

The room he had brought them to reminded Audra of a stuffy boardroom she had seen in college except instead of glass walls encasing the room, it was stone and bronze. In the middle, there was a long, oval wooden table with sturdy wooden chairs all around it.

Like a perfect mix of medieval times and the corporate world.

"The Fullmas' clan should be here soon. Why don't we have a seat? Tomais, you have the paperwork prepared?" Audrena asked, commanding the attention of the room with the command of her voice.

Tomais stepped up. He looked as if he had gotten a chance to shower and change as well. His suit was freshly pressed and his dark hair combed over harshly like it had been when she first met him.

"Here is it, you Highness."

"Thank you."

Audra pulled a chair out and sat down just after her mother had sat, then gestured to her and Anders to sit as well.

"Have you thought about what you want to do?" Her mother asked, sliding on a pair of glasses, and resting them low on the bridge of her nose.

Audra took a deep breath and glanced at Luc. Once she agreed, it didn't seem like she would be able to change her mind.

Her teeth found her bottom lip, and she bit down, wanting to be in a different situation. One where she would be able to be free to love whom she loved and be open about their unconventional relationship.

Her eyes met his, and he nodded.

"Yes. I will marry into the Dark Fae if it means that the kingdom will be safe from any more unnecessary violence and attacks." She spoke strong and clear, straightening her spine while she did.

"I understand that this is not something that you would wish for, being betrothed before you even get to experience this world, but you truly are acting like a High Royal. Your great-great-grandmother, the first Total Elemental, would be proud. I'm proud. And I thank you." Audrena said, kissing her on both cheeks and then on her forehead. Audra had no idea what to do or say. Even though this woman was her mother, the mother she always wished for, it felt weird to her to have her show affection like that.

Before anyone else could say anything, there was a resounding slam of a heavy wooden door against a stone wall, drawing the attention of everyone in the room. Luc had his hand on a sword at his side, ready to defend the royals in the room, as did the three other guards.

In walked a man and a woman, both with jet black hair and sickly pale skin. Their features were almost spooky, gaunt, and tall. Each step they took into the room, their limbs flowed effortlessly like they were strutting down a runway and Audra thought that they were quite glamorous. The woman had pin straight black hair that fell like a curtain down her back, stopping right above her buttocks.

She was wearing a skintight black dress with a jacket that to Audra looked like a sea urchin, sharp, long black spike sticking out in each direction. It was amazing that she wasn't getting stuck with each movement she made. She was already much taller than Audra's 5'10" but add on the six-inch black stilettos and she was an amazon. The man to her side was striking in a similar way; he stood at least four inches taller than the woman and wore a fitted black suit, pressed to perfection, and sharp pointed, shiny black shoes. His hair was slicked back, and he had used so much gel that his hair was reflecting the light from the chandelier above. They looked elegant, in the most haunted way.

"Regious, Siobhan. Welcome to Dragomahara. I trust your journey was pleasant." Audrena said and stood to greet their guests, offering them her hand, which neither made any movement to take.

"It was satisfactory. But let's get down to business." The man, Regious, her mother had called him, said in a bored tone.

"Very well."

"I believe you know our terms of peace. Do you accept?" Siobhan said, her voice as elegant and bored as Regious'.

"We would like to know who she would marry first." Her father interjected before Audrena could say anything.

Audra was thankful he had spoken up. She was just as curious. She hoped that whatever Sebastien and Luc's plan was that they hurried it up. She was about to be engaged.

"Of course. Enter!" Regious ordered, yelling over his shoulder towards the open door.

Audra's gaze went behind them, eyes peeled to the doorway.

In walked Sebastien and Eric, side by side.